Corrupt Promises

TWISTED ARRANGEMENTS

BOOK FOUR

CASSIA QUINN

Wednesday Ink

Corrupt Promises

Wednesday Ink, LLC

Cover Designer: Covers by Aura

Editing by Sinful Aloha

Proofreading by Geissa Cecilia with GP Author Services

Amor vincit omnia.
Love conquers all.

Pronunciations & Meanings

broc meala - bruk my-uh-luh (*honey badger*)
mo stoirín - muh store-een (*my little darling*)
amore mio - ah-MOH-ray MEE-oh (*my love*)
cazzo bastardo - KA-tzo bah-STAR-doh (*fucking bastard*)
testa di cazzo - TES-tah dee KA-tzo (*dickhead*)
mi famiglia - mee fah-MEE-lyah (*my family*)
bastardo testardo - bah-STAR-doh tess-TAR-doh (*stubborn bastard*)
Irlandese - eye-luhn-DAY-zay (*Irishman*)
stronzo - STRON-zoh (*asshole*)
uscite - ooh-SHEE-teh (*get out*)
mo stór - muh stor (*my treasure*)

Content Information

Dear reader, before you turn the page, please know that this is a romance with dark themes and potentially difficult situations.

Please read the entire content list here: http://cassiaquinn.com/twisted-arrangements/

XX
Cassia

Author's Note

Dear Reader, if you've read any other books in this series, I'd like you to know this one's a bit different. The events in this story span a number of years, so you will find some significant time jumps between chapters.

Also, since this story begins prior to *Stolen Vows*, and spans the timelines of *Forced Union* and *Forever Fake*, there may be spoilers of those books in this one.

Enjoy,
Cassia

Corrupt Promises Playlist

Lies In The Dark - Tove Lo
No Mercy - Austin Giorgio
Wildest Dreams - Taylor Swift
Natural - Imagine Dragons
Someone You Loved - Lewis Capaldi
Lose Control - Teddy Swims
Ordinary - Alex Warren
Power Over Me - Dermot Kennedy
Unsteady - X Ambassadors
Just Give Me a Reason - P!nk
Mercy - Shawn Mendes
Dresses - Taylor Swift
Moon - Austin Giorgio
What About Us - P!nk
Don't Give Up On Me - Andy Grammer
Infinity - Jaymes Young

Listen on Spotify

Contents

CHAPTER 1

Ravenna

"Where is your sister?" Mother paces the church's small, dank bridal preparation room. Her long black mourning dress sweeps the floor. "I knew I shouldn't have let her run that last minute errand this afternoon. She's made a run for it. I can't believe she'd do something like that to us. Your father will be furious." She nervously wrings her hands.

I sit on the sofa, dressed in black to mourn my dead brother. Today I'm also prepared to lose my twin sister when she marries Cian O'Rourke, brutal leader of the Irish mob—the Gaelic Devils—and the man who murdered our brother Matteo.

Can I blame her for running? Not at all.

Do her actions totally screw us over? Yep.

Without Elena here to fulfill the terms of this arranged marriage, we'll once again be at war with O'Rourke and his clan of cutthroat Irishmen. This wedding is our one chance at lasting peace. A deal sealed in marriage.

"Are you listening to me, Ravenna?" Mother scowls in my direction. "Call your sister again and tell her if she doesn't show up I'll toss her in a convent and throw away the key."

I do as I'm told, not bothering to tell Mama that Elena would prefer a convent to marrying the man everyone calls *The Beast*. I don't want to even think about how he came by that nickname.

Elena's phone goes straight to voicemail, again. I relay the message, then pocket my phone. The clock on the wall shows a quarter to three. We have fifteen minutes before a Pontrelli woman has to walk down that aisle and seal this deal—or else we all face the consequences.

I am, quite literally, the only option. Is it a crazy idea? Hell yes it is. Not to mention dangerous. But I should have been the one chosen for this arranged marriage in the first place. I'm not sure why my parents insisted they put this on Elena's shoulders, other than she's technically the older twin.

Even so, she's always been the soft spoken one, who hates conflict. While I'm...the opposite. I might just survive being thrown to the Irish wolves. She wouldn't.

I stand up and turn toward Mother. "We have no other choice, it has to be me who walks down that aisle. Father will be in a rage if this peace deal falls through." I inwardly shudder at how he'd react. His wrath could very well be worse than anything the Irish might dish out.

Mother frowns. "You're right, but we can't tell O'Rourke he'll be taking a different bride. This is the man who postponed the wedding when we had to switch venues because the church flooded. He suspected a trap. He's a very suspicious man. How do you think he'll react when we promised him Elena and he gets you instead?"

"Then we don't tell him. They never met face-to-face, so he won't know the difference." Plus, we're identical twins, a lot of people find it challenging to tell us apart until they get to know us.

The more I think about it, the more sense it makes. "We don't tell anyone. I'll walk down that aisle and marry him as Elena Pontrelli. Once he figures out who I really am, it'll be too late. Not that it matters which sister he gets, all he's looking for is the turf, and peace, he'll gain by joining with our family."

"That's true." Mother mulls over my idea. "Your father can't tell you girls apart anyway, so until, and if, your sister resurfaces, our secret will be safe. However, this can't be temporary. A man like O'Rourke will kill you if he finds out we did a bait and switch. He can never learn your true identity."

I swallow thickly. "Then from this day forth, I am Elena Pontrelli." Will it be easy? No. I'll have to act more like Elena around my friends and family to pull this off. Ugh, this is a mess, but we'll figure it out. I'll worry about the future later. My sister has to resurface, because I can't imagine life without her.

Mother glances toward the door. "Are you sure about this? We don't have much time."

"Then we have to hurry." I slip off my black dress and don the wedding gown that was designed for Elena. Luckily our measurements are close enough that it fits well. I slip into her shoes, put on her veil, and then I'm finally transformed... into my sister. And a bride—the wrong bride.

The clock strikes three. It's time.

I release a slow exhale, my hands shake. I have no idea who I'm going to find standing at the altar, but whoever he is, he's some version of liberation from my family. For a chance at freedom, I'll marry an old man, an ugly man, just please, dear God, may he not be cruel to his wife. That is my single wish.

Give me a kind husband.

My father appears and I draw myself up, standing tall, then remember how Elena would act, and round my shoulders. I shrink into myself and avert my gaze, acting shy and compliant.

"Where's Ravenna?" he demands, glancing around the small room.

"She wasn't feeling well, so I sent her home in the car," Mother lies to him. A bold act, coming from her. But she lost her only son because of this war, I know how badly she wants to see the violence end.

My stomach flips. This is the beginning of a life-long charade. Am I really going through with this?

"It doesn't matter. We don't really need her here." He turns to me. "Pull down your veil, he doesn't get to see you until you belong to him."

I lower the veil over my face, obscuring my features from view.

Until I belong to him... *It has to be better than belonging to you, Papa.*

"Good. Come, Elena." He tows me along by my arm, the sensation of spiders crawling up my spine at his touch.

Mother follows behind as we step into the aisle. A solo pianist plays a wedding march. The only other people in the church are the priest, the groom, and his best man. Everyone is wearing black except for me, sticking out like a sore thumb in brilliant white, which is a harsh color against my warm skin tone.

I'm a virginal sacrifice to finalize a contract between two powerful men. I've never felt more like an object, to be traded, bought, or sold, in my entire life.

My gaze flicks between the men at the altar, and I immediately know which one is the groom, because only he could be called *The Beast*.

Huge, built like a Celtic warrior, he has shoulder-length blond hair with a hint of auburn, and pale blue eyes. A scar runs from his forehead straight down to his chin, crossing one eye—the largest blemish among several smaller ones that crisscross his face.

Not only does he have massive shoulders, he's also tall. I'm not short at five foot seven, yet as I climb the stairs to where he stands, I realize he must be at least ten inches taller than me. At nearly six foot six, his presence commands the entire space.

My pulse stutters. What have I gotten myself into?

Father takes my hand and puts it in this stranger's enormous palm. Rough calluses and dry heat engulf my fingers. His touch makes my heart race. The back of my neck breaks out in a sweat.

Suddenly all of this is real, too real.

It's not too late, I can reveal my identity and watch months of peace negotiations fall apart. It will be all my fault when the streets run red with blood, again. Father will take out his rage on me, and then on Elena if we ever find her.

None of that can happen.

So I don't say anything. I remain mute as the priest speaks his words.

At one point, I realize I'm supposed to repeat after him.

My voice emerges strong but soft, "I, R-*Elena* Pontrelli, take thee, Cian O'Rourke, to be my wedded husband, to have and to hold from this day forward, for better, for worse, for richer, for poorer, in sickness and in health, to love and to cherish, till death do us part. I pledge thee my loyalty and honesty." I cringe on that last vow–*honesty*–the one I've already broken. How many more will I have to break in my lifetime?

The huge stranger mumbles his own version of our vows, we slide plain gold bands onto each other's fingers, then the priest is suddenly pronouncing us husband and wife.

There are no cheers. My parents, and Cian's best man, remain quiet as this ceremony comes to its conclusion. My heartbeat pounds in my ears, and I feel slightly dizzy, realizing what I've just done.

I'm married. To a stranger. To the enemy.

The Irishman reaches out and slowly lifts my veil. I can only imagine he's terrified of what he'll find beneath this semi-sheer fabric. When his gaze falls upon my face, he frowns, and I'm hit with a sense of outrage.

What? Am I not *pretty* enough for him?

Who the hell does he think he is to look at me like that? It's not like he's especially handsome with all those scars. *What a jerk.*

Usually, this is where the groom kisses the bride. Instead, he lets my veil fall back into place, adding insult to my injured pride. Then he takes my arm and marches me out of the church. My mother hands me my purse and waves goodbye, while Father is already on his phone and onto the next order of business for the day. He's a don after all, a very busy man.

I'm taken outside and shoved into a waiting car. The behemoth slides in after me and the vehicle pulls away from the curb.

Facing forward, he speaks. "There, your father has gotten his wish to saddle me with his daughter and try to govern me through you. Or perhaps you're meant to be a spy. But listen carefully, you'll stay out of my business. If I catch you poking around, I'll kill you. Are we clear?"

What a charmer. Apparently God isn't listening to my prayers today.

"Yes. Crystal clear."

"Good. Now after this ridiculous honeymoon we have to go on, you'll get your own room. We won't need to bother each other at all. You stay out of my way and I'll stay away from you." The asshole finally angles his head to look in my direction. Pale blue eyes assessing me. "You won't take any lovers. You'll do as you're told. And above all else, if I ask you a question, you'll tell me the truth. I don't tolerate *liars.*"

My stomach swims with nausea. God what have I done?

The Irish brute studies me for several thundering heartbeats. I'm not sure why, because he can't see me clearly through my veil. Even so, his gaze seems to sink beneath my skin and I do my best not to squirm.

"Did you want to marry me?" he asks, his deep, gravelly voice the only sound in the quiet limo.

How, exactly, am I supposed to answer a question like that?

Truthfully. All he wants is an honest answer. Or so he says. Though men often say that, then dish out punishment when the answer is not what they wanted to hear.

"No," I say, swallowing down my fear.

"Then why'd you do it?"

"I had no other choice." It's the truth.

His lips firm and he grimaces. "Those are the answers I expected. Thank you for your honesty."

He's thanking me? Instead of using it as a trick to lure me into telling him the truth only to punish me for it? For one fleeting, insane moment I wonder how honest I can be with him. Can I tell him that my father's a monster? Or the things my brother said to me?

I crush the temptation as soon as it rises. Men like him delight in patting each other on the backs, they don't want to hear about the uglier side most of them reserve for their home life. Daughters are nothing but property and pawns to be passed on to the next generation of *made men*. They're all ruthless killers.

I'll find no sympathy from my new husband. It's best to keep my secrets buried. Just like my true identity.

CHAPTER 2
Cian

Ignoring my new bride, we ride in silence to my waiting jet that will take us to Florida for our honeymoon, escaping the cold New York winter for a while. Don Lorenzo Pontrelli wouldn't budge on this point in our negotiations. I have to take his daughter on a honeymoon, he even paid for it. I can only assume he thinks that if I spend enough time with her, I'll be pussy whipped, and more malleable when I return.

Fuck that. No cunt is sweet enough that I'll lose my wits. Never again. Been there, done that, and have the scars to prove it.

Worse, maybe she's a spy. Not that she'll get any important information to take back to her daddy. If I catch her trying, or snooping around my house, I'll kill her. I don't make idle threats.

I sneak a glance at her, at my wife—*Jesus, Mary and Joseph.* Fuck, I'm *married.* Never thought that would happen. I'm not the marrying type.

It's really too bad that she's so pretty. Beautiful, in

fact. I hate that. Her beauty taunts me. I'd have preferred a plain wife, one that doesn't draw my eye. I knew I should have demanded to see the girl before marrying her, but Pontrelli wouldn't allow that. He assured me I'd be pleased with her looks. Since I didn't care how ugly she might be, I never pressed the matter. Now I regret it.

Avoiding this siren is out of the question until this stupid honeymoon is over, and unfortunately, until we produce an heir. Then we'll have separate wings of the house and I'll never have to lay eyes on her again. I can always fuck her in the dark until she's pregnant. One heir is good, two is even better.

My gaze rakes down her body. The white wedding dress hugs her curves enough to show off her assets. Everything about her is meant to seduce. She looks good, smells good, hell she probably even tastes good.

A real-life temptress. A complication that I don't need.

I shake away that thought, and adjust in my seat, scowling at my body's reaction to this woman.

Temptress she may be, but this time, I'm in charge. I won't be blinded by a woman's charms ever again. Our marriage will play out the way I want.

If I want to fuck her, but never hear her voice, I have every right to shove a gag in that pretty mouth. I can ignore her and still demand she spreads her legs for me when I'm in the mood. She's a mafia princess, she was raised with these kinds of expectations. She'll be obedient. I don't need to worry about that. Don Pontrelli promised me she'd do as she's told.

The limo pulls onto the tarmac, where my jet awaits. Reaching over, I grab the girl's arm and haul her out of the vehicle. She comes willingly, quietly, and a sense of relief settles in my gut. I'm not sure why I half expected her to resist. Out of fear of coming with me, perhaps? Though so far, she doesn't appear frightened of me, just annoyed. Which is not usually an emotion I evoke in females.

Fear and disgust? Yes. Annoyance? No.

She walks in front of me up the stairs and enters the jet, where the flight attendant shows her to a seat, then turns to face me.

The uniformed woman stares, gaping as she takes in my harsh, scarred features. She's obviously a new hire if she hasn't seen my face before and learned to control her reaction. The horror in her eyes makes my stomach churn. Shame pierces my chest. I grit my teeth.

"It's rude to stare," snaps a feminine voice. It takes me a few seconds to realize that my new wife just chastised the flight attendant. My curious gaze bores a hole in the side of her veiled head, but she remains facing forward, ignoring me.

"I-I'm so sorry." The attendant quickly gets back to work, gaze downcast, an embarrassed pink on her cheeks.

With a confused frown, I drop into the seat across the aisle from my bride. Why would this woman—*Elena, that's her name*—defend me? She didn't have to say anything. I'm used to the way people, and especially women, stare at me like I'm the most hideous thing they've ever seen.

Even though some of them, on occasion, like to fuck this monster. I really don't understand the female psyche, nor do I care to try.

The jet taxis along the runway, gaining first speed,

then altitude as it lifts from the ground. The air in the cabin grows thick with silent tension. I should say something, anything, to break this strained silence. But I'm not especially good with words.

"I'm Steff, I'll be serving you both today," says the attendant, saving me from what would likely have been an awkward attempt at conversation with this Italian seductress. "What can I get you to drink, Mr. O'Rourke?"

"Whiskey. Neat." I need something to take the edge off.

"And for you, Mrs. O'Rourke?"

The girl startles at the sound of her new name. I find myself slightly rattled too. She's my goddamn *wife*. *The* Mrs. O'Rourke, until death do us part.

"Mrs. O'Rourke?" Steff prompts when she doesn't respond.

"I'll have a vodka martini, please, and make it dry."

"Coming right up."

Left alone again, I can sense the Italian beauty's eyes on me but not see them. For no rational reason, that irritates the fuck out of me.

"Take off your veil," I demand. "The wedding's over."

There's a long pause, then she unexpectedly snarks, "I thought you didn't want to look at my face."

"I never said that."

"No, you just put my veil back in place instead of lifting it off. What am I supposed to assume by that?"

I grind my teeth. That gag sounds like a good idea right about now. Don Lorenzo told me his daughter would be quiet, meek, and obedient. That's not the vibe I'm getting from her. Apparently he's a fucking liar.

"Take it off." My tone's chilly. "Now."

She huffs. Actually *huffs* at me, like I'm the one being difficult. But she does flip back her veil, revealing an angular face, dark red hair, and blue-grey eyes. Her chin has a stubborn tilt to it, her full lips pursed with annoyance. From her features alone, I'd guess she was Irish instead of full-blooded Italian, until I peer closer and find that Mediterranean sensuality peeking through. As well as that aggravating Italian temperament.

"Your parents didn't send a bag with your things, so there's nothing for you to change into until we reach Key Largo." I'm not sure why I'm telling her this, except in an attempt to ease the tension between us.

She casually nods, as if she already knew that. I'm not sure why she didn't pack herself a bag. She must have known we'd be leaving right from the church. Not that it matters, I'll buy her whatever she needs once we get there.

Actually, why wait? I can use the distraction to pass the time.

"Elena, what size clothing do you wear?"

She visibly flinches, her expression tense for a moment before her irritated mask slides back into place. I search her face, trying to decipher her thoughts. What just happened there? Did she not realize I knew her name? Or is it something else? Immediately, I'm suspicious.

She sits up straighter before answering. "I'm a six, or a small, on the bottom, but prefer a medium on the top."

I grunt, taking notes on my phone. "Small underwear. What size bra?"

"Thirty-four C." Her cheeks flush a distracting shade of rosy pink.

I clear my throat. "Shoes?"

"Eight."

"Colors?"

"Earth-tones."

I glance at her again. "Can you be more specific?"

"You know, I really prefer to shop for myself. If you give me the details of where we're staying, I can—"

"No. You're too late. You didn't bother to pack a bag for yourself, so this is now *my* responsibility. I'm going to make sure you have something other than a wedding dress to wear for a week."

She gasps. "A *week*?"

"Yes." My brow furrows. "Didn't your father tell you our honeymoon would last a week?"

"No. I thought it would be a couple of days, just long enough to... finalize our union."

Realizing what she means, I bark a laugh. "Finalize our union? I think you mean consummate our marriage. Or better yet, *fuck*."

She cringes at my crude language. I don't think she's faking her reaction, she really is a naïve virgin. At least Lorenzo told the truth about that. He made sure I never forgot that I was getting a virgin out of this deal. A pure wife. One to do with whatever I wanted. If anything, he seemed envious, which always left me unsettled.

"Since you're being difficult, I'll just choose whichever colors I like," I tell Elena. "You're mine to dress now anyway. You'll wear what I give you."

She murmurs a word under her breath, but I hear it. "*Stronzo.*"

I level a glare on her. "Yes, I am an asshole. Do yourself a favor and remember that. We're not friends, we're not even friendly. Your father and his men murdered countless people of mine. You're nothing more than my enemy's daughter, and a means to end this bloodshed. I'm not even sorry that I killed your brother."

She cringes.

I revel in her reaction. "It was his death that finally made Lorenzo come to the table and negotiate a peace. You and I had to sacrifice ourselves for that peace, but I don't ever expect us to like each other. Hate me all you want, I don't give a damn. But you will *not* be disrespectful. Are we clear?"

She glares at me, cold fire burning in her stormy eyes. "Crystal clear."

"Good."

The flight attendant delivers our drinks and I settle into my seat, swiping through my phone and ordering my wife the clothing I want her to wear. It takes me the rest of the flight to finalize the transactions and have it all arranged to be delivered tomorrow morning. I may have gone overboard with buying not only clothes and shoes, but perfume, cosmetics, and jewelry. Even some lingerie.

A sick kind of satisfaction courses through me at having this level of control over such an irritating woman. She is my enemy's daughter, and I'm going to enjoy every minute of making her do exactly what I want, all the way down to wearing the black silk panties I chose. Everything on her body will be there because it's what I command.

I crave her hatred, so I may as well give her every reason to hate me. That's the only way this marriage will work. I wouldn't want to confuse her, to have her think that I might be capable of developing feelings for her—because I never will. I'll never like her, much less love her, no matter how many years we are stuck together. This is a lifetime of hell for the both of us. So why hold back?

'Till death do us part.

CHAPTER 3
Ravenna

I feel ridiculous walking around in a wedding dress all afternoon. But as that Celtic bastard pointed out, I don't have anything else to wear. Elena's honeymoon bag is with her...wherever she may be.

All I have is my purse, the only thing that's mine, since even this dress belongs to my twin. My thoughts latch on to the incriminating evidence in my handbag—my ID. Elena and I need to swap our ID cards if this is going to work. Until then, I suppose I can claim that I lost mine. Another lie. They're piling up so quickly, I'm drowning in them.

The situation hits me solidly in my stomach. Dear God, what have I done?

And where the hell is Elena? I can't believe she did this to us—to me. Or should I start calling her *Ravenna* since we're swapping identities? I'm so confused—and tired. Adrenaline has been pumping through my veins all day, another spike hits whenever this Irishman speaks to me, or accidentally brushes his fingers over mine, or looks in my direction. I've had barely a moment out of his suffocating presence.

He's such an asshole. My fight, flight, or freeze response has been on high alert for hours now. I know our families are enemies, so I don't know why I was taken by surprise when he confessed his hatred for me. *Me.* What did I ever do to him besides be born into the Pontrelli family? But men like him enjoy holding grudges for as long as they can. I'm in for an eternity of hell. Who knows what evil things he'll do to me now that I'm his property.

My heart slams against my ribcage when the big brute opens the door to our private bungalow and flips on the lights. It's a honeymoon suite. No privacy except for the bathroom. The bed practically sits in the middle of the floor, covered in rose petals and chocolates, arranged in the shape of a heart.

The romantic scene before me is in stark contrast to the hostile energy sparking between me and my asshole husband. It mocks us. Tentatively, I take a step forward.

I can't believe I'm married. This wasn't supposed to happen, at least not like this. Can I still get an annulment if I chicken out tonight?

Yeah, and jump right back into war, only worse this time because any trust that's been freshly forged between the Italians and Irish will be completely shattered. Irreparable. Forever.

No, I'm stuck in this mess. This is my life now. And I have no one to blame but myself.

The Irishman shuts the door behind me, and I jump at the *click*. The sound is too loud in this quiet space. In the distance, a gull shrieks and the ocean waves *whoosh* along the beach. This should be paradise, not purgatory.

"Are you hungry?" he asks, arms crossed, as he leans against the door frame.

"No." My nerves are so jittery I can barely keep down that single martini I had on the plane.

"Good. Take off your dress."

My mouth falls open. "Excuse me? I don't have anything else to wear. Remember?"

"You won't need anything to wear for the rest of tonight." His pale gaze sweeps down my body. Instead of lust, I see annoyance in his eyes.

"I won't need clothing? Oh... *Oh*. You mean we're going to do...*that*...right now?" My throat constricts. This is all happening too fast.

He looks exasperated. "Yes. As soon as you take off your damn clothes."

"But what if I..." I can't think of a valid excuse to delay the inevitable. I just didn't expect this to happen so soon. But duh, it's our wedding night.

The brute stares me down. He knows I'm stalling and doesn't care. *Insensitive prick.*

I fold my arms, mirroring his pose. "Where are the clothes you bought for me? I don't see them."

"They'll be here in the morning."

I scoff. "You did this on purpose, didn't you? You left me with nothing to wear tonight out of spite."

One corner of his mouth twitches, and it's all the confirmation I need. He's a real bastard, trying to make me feel vulnerable, and uncomfortable, on every *single* level—and he's succeeding. I can only imagine what the rest of this night will be like. I doubt there's a gentle bone in his massive, lethal body. He's going to hurt me, and enjoy every second of it just because this morning my last name was *Pontrelli*. The name of his enemy.

"Take off the dress. I won't ask again."

"You didn't ask the first time," I snipe, almost regretting it, but don't. I'm not going to let this man walk all over me. Call me stubborn—or just plain reckless.

If there's anything I've learned over the years, it's that ultimately, whether you sass back or not, it doesn't matter—either way, you'll get punished. For a couple of years in my late teens, I held my tongue. I did everything I was told and it didn't make any difference, my compliance was never enough to avoid a beating. At least when I say what I want, the beatings come sooner and are over more quickly because of it. I don't have to walk on eggshells anymore, waiting and hoping that I might escape punishment for one small mistake.

If my asshole husband wants to punish me for my disrespect, then by all means, let him have at it. My father couldn't break me, and he's been trying for years, so this man won't either.

The Irish bastard lifts a scarred blond brow, taking me in as if he's seeing me for the first time. He's considering what to do with me, I can see that in his pale blue eyes.

After a few strained moments, he nods, once, as if to himself. He produces a knife from his tuxedo pocket. Flipping it open with a quick wrist moment, he approaches me.

My pulse stutters. Horrified, I stumble backward, my hands outstretched. "Wait. Please. What are you doing?"

Slaps, punches, and kicks, I can deal with those, but

not knives. Is he going to carve me up like someone did to his face? I've heard horror stories about the Irish and their brutality, but I didn't think—

The backs of my knees hit the bed and the huge Celt takes that opportunity to grab me, spinning me around so my back presses to his chest.

I scream.

He tears off my veil, tossing it aside. Grabbing the back of my wedding dress, he slices it open all the way from my neck to my hips.

As my initial shock recedes, I struggle against him. "Get your hands off me, you filthy Irish cocksucker!"

He freezes, my words must have momentarily stunned him. His fingers curl around my neck, and he spins me toward him, dipping his face close to mine. Our breaths mingle.

"*Filthy Irish cocksucker?* Well, well, don't you have a naughty mouth on you?" He's so close that I expect him to kiss me. But he doesn't. "Next time I tell you to do something, you'll do it. Obedience. Respect. Honesty. That's all I ask of you every single day. It's not too much." He gives my throat a squeeze, fear jolts through me. "We're consummating this marriage tonight, as per the terms of the contract. Now tell me, do you want it fast or slow? We can either get it over and done with, which will be more painful, or we can take it slow, which will be more enjoyable for you. I don't mind either way. The choice is yours, *wife*."

I meet his cold gaze, my heart nearly pounding out of my chest. "Just get it over with," I say through gritted teeth.

He searches my face, then releases me. The warmth

of his body disappears as he steps away and pockets his knife, leaving me in the ruined wedding gown. I hold the front to my chest in a futile effort to cover myself, waiting to see what he'll do next. Tight anticipation coils in my stomach as my pulse thunders.

"Have it your way. Now drop the dress, I want to look at you first." His voice rasps against my jittery nerves.

Grudgingly, I do as I'm told this time. If I want to get this over and done with as soon as possible there's no point in delaying any longer. I pull the ruined scraps of fabric from my body until I'm standing in front of him wearing only white satin heels.

Heat spread across my chest, up my neck, to my cheeks. I've never felt more exposed in my entire life. Nor more vulnerable.

His gaze drops from my face to my breasts, then lower, and I battle with the urge to cover myself up.

This is what he bargained for, my body is now his, signed for on the dotted line and paid for in blood. My fate was always to end up just like this. From the day I was born, this moment was inevitable.

With a shuddering exhale, I accept my destiny, and hold my head high.

He extends one giant hand toward me, and I flinch when he palms my bare breast. Steeling myself, I lock my jaw, stare at his chest, and endure his rough touch. His thumb sweeps over my nipple, and it hardens to a peak. I do my best to ignore the fluttery sensations and heat pooling low in my belly.

He can take my body, but he'll never have my pleasure. Not that he wants it anyway.

Reaching out, he palms my other breast too, teasing my nipples until they are both rock hard. Unexpectedly, it feels good. I fight the instinct to arch my back in a silent plea for more.

Then *he* moans.

The sound catches me by surprise. My gaze flicks up to his scarred face. His pale blue eyes burn with unbridled desire, and he bites down on his full bottom lip like he's attempting to deny himself a taste of me. A hint of pink smears his angular cheekbones.

It takes my brain a minute to realize that it's my body, *me*, that has done this to him. Melted his cold, icy exterior, to reveal the fiery blaze beneath. I narrow my eyes. Does he really hate me, or does he hate how much he wants me?

Warmth spreads beneath my skin, but I ignore it, focusing on my resolve. "I chose to get this over and done with quickly. What do you think you are doing?"

The ruffian pinches my nipples between his fingers, and I gasp. Then he gives them a tug. My thighs clench and I stagger. I've never felt anything like it, a sweeping pleasure with a delicious hint of pain.

He knowingly smirks.

Dear God, what new hellish trial is this? Do you have no mercy?

"I want to tell you a secret." He leans down until his breath warms my ear. The scent of whiskey and spice invades my senses. "I don't hate you enough to shove this in your virgin cunt without preparing you first."

Shocked, I angle my head to look at him. The movement brings our lips so close, if either one of us slightly leans in, we'd kiss.

His gaze flicks to my mouth. I swallow hard. Temptation warms his blue irises for a second before they cool. He wants to kiss me, but he won't. Why?

Suddenly, he snatches my wrist and places my hand over the front of his trousers so that I can feel *him*.

My eyes bulge, and fear drives a spike through my chest. That can't be... but it is, it must be. The thing is huge, just like the rest of this enormous man. Not just thick but long. I'm not even sure where the end is at. There's no way that's fitting in me even with *preparation*. Whatever that means.

He moans. "I'll be honest with you, if you keep that up, I'm going to come in my pants."

Horrified, I realize I've been fondling his dick, and I quickly pull my hand away.

He grunts.

"You can't be serious!" I recoil.

His brows draw together. "What—?"

"That *thing* in your pants will split me in two. There's absolutely no way." I vehemently shake my head. "Not happening. Uh-uh. Nope."

He chuckles, the sound surprisingly warm and sensual. His mirth only lasts for a second before he straightens to his full, imposing height, his eyes on mine. That unreadable expression returns to his features.

"There's still time to get an annulment, if that's what you want. Without our two families joined, the peace treaty will quickly deteriorate. I've seen it happen. But if you really want this to be over, then I won't touch you, and in the morning I'll have you returned to your father, intact, so he may marry you off again."

"No," I say much too quickly. The very thought of

being sent back to my father fills me with dread. If I'm rejected, if I mess this all up, Papa will beat me to within an inch of my life. Or maybe kill me, since I won't be of use to him anymore. Actually, knowing him, he'll sell me on the flesh market. He never leaves money on the table.

I shiver at the thought.

This Irishman gently touches my shoulder. "What's wrong? You're shaking. Are you cold?"

"No. I'm fine. I, um... I don't want an annulment." My breath hitches as the rough pad of his thumb caresses my skin. "Don't send me back," my voice is barely above a whisper. "Please. I'll... do whatever you want. I promise."

Cupping my jaw, he tilts my head back until our eyes meet. He stares at me with genuine concern. It's unnerving. Why has he gone from ruthless to caring? Is this some twisted game?

Softly, he asks, "Will you trust me? Just for tonight, I know I haven't earned it for any longer than that—or at all. But if you put your trust in me tonight, I won't let you down. You're my wife and I take that responsibility seriously."

"You won't send me back to my father?" I need to hear him say it.

"No. I won't send you anywhere. You're mine."

"Okay." My relief is probably palpable.

"Did he—?" The Irishman cuts himself off and shakes his head as if he's dismissing a thought. "After tonight we only have to do this a few times each month, when you're most fertile, until we produce an heir. Maybe two."

Children. The thought hadn't even crossed my mind

when I stepped into my sister's place at the altar. Of course he wants children to continue his line, and we're married now, so the sooner the better for the sake of the treaty.

I did not think this whole thing through. And it's too late now. The room spins. I blink until I can focus again.

"That's fair," I say, though my voice sounds distant to my ears.

"Will you trust me for tonight, then?" He strokes my jawline.

I nod. What other choice do I have?

"Good." Releasing me, he grabs the duvet and shakes off all the flower petals and chocolates before spreading it back on the bed. "Lie down."

Swallowing past the lump in my throat, I do as I'm told. I kick off my heels, then lie on my back in the center of the mattress. I anxiously wait for whatever he's going to do next, and pray that it won't cause irreparable damage.

Not that my prayers have been answered at all today.

Mama once told me how painful and humiliating this act is between a husband and his wife. How she escapes into her own mind while Papa takes her body.

I'm not at all prepared for this. I just thought I'd have more time before...

The lights switch off, plunging me into darkness. "What—?"

"Shh, it's okay. I don't do this with the lights on. Just stay where you are and I'll be there in a minute." Rustling fabric follows his words as he undresses in the dark.

I swallow, my throat dry, attempting to get a grip on

my rising panic. The mattress dips, and I push down my welling fear, replacing it with my usual steely resolve when I'm feeling afraid. His hand lands on my thigh and despite my efforts, I stiffen further.

"Relax, *mo stoirín*, I won't hurt you. I'm not that kind of man." He draws soothing circles on my skin. I'm not sure what to make of his change in behavior. Doesn't he want to hurt me? "Trust me for this moment. Give yourself to me." His deep, gravelly voice lulls me into at least trying to relax. "That's it. Good girl. Now touch yourself. Give yourself pleasure."

Embarrassment courses through me. "No. I can't."

"You can. It's dark. Pretend you're alone, that my hands are yours, and you're touching yourself." He guides my fingers to my clit, leaving me to do the rest, as he caresses my thigh with one hand and teases my nipples with the other.

Tentatively, I do as he demands, slipping my fingers through my astonishingly wet folds to play with my clit. I can't believe how turned on I am by all of this—by *him*—I'm soaked.

Beside me, his heat sears my skin. His spicy cologne fills my nose. There's something dangerous, but also alluring about his massive form.

I think I *want* this. I want him. That realization subdues both my fear and resistance as I give in to the pleasurable sensations.

I circle my clit, arching my back in a silent demand for him to do more with my breasts. He reads me loud and clear. His hot mouth claims a nipple, and holy hell if it's not the most amazing feeling ever. I whimper, pressing more firmly against him, and work myself faster.

My orgasm's within reach one moment and gone the next, it keeps building and fading away. I grunt in frustration. I must be overstimulated, overwhelmed. If I can just—

"Let me help you, *mo stoirín.*" His thick, rough fingers replace mine. They feel so good. Undulating my hips, I shamelessly ride his hand.

Yes! If I knew sex was going to be this amazing, I would have jumped on him as soon as we walked through that door. His hands feel so much better on my body than my own. I love the roughness of his palms, the dry heat, his confidence.

Why did mother always tell me sex was a painful sacrifice, a necessary wifely duty? I don't understand.

Reaching out, I find Cian's shoulders and pull him towards me in a desperate need to have him closer. His warmth encompasses me as he hovers over my body. I spread my legs, allowing him better access. He slides a thick finger inside me and my eyes roll back in my head. A couple of strokes has me seeing stars as the most intense orgasm of my life rips through me.

I cry out, needing a vocal release for all of these sensations. My nails dig into his flesh. My entire body trembles beneath him. Then all at once, my muscles relax. Floaty, I go limp as I hover in the stratosphere.

Cian removes his hand only to replace it with cold wetness.

I jolt at the new sensation. "What is that?"

"Lube. Sorry it's cold."

"Why do we need lubricant?" Curiosity has emboldened me, otherwise I'd never ask such a question aloud.

"I always use extra lube to make everything easier. Trust me, we need it."

Always. As in he's had sex before—of course he has, he's a grown man. Even so, the thought of him with another woman feels like slap in the face. He's my first, but I'm his... However many, I don't want to know.

"*Oh*," I sharply inhale when he spreads the stuff over my vagina, working it inside me with one thick finger. Pushing away my troubling thoughts, I moan, giving into the delicious pleasure.

When I start moving my pelvis, demanding more, he slips in a second digit and the stretch burns. Adding more lube, he works me until I relax and it starts to feel good again.

I whimper and moan. He takes pity on me and flicks my clit. That's all I need to send me careening over the edge of ecstasy for a second time.

I'm still trembling when he enters me with something long, thick, and hot. I tense up before remembering the only way I'm going to get through this is to relax.

"I'm ready," I tell him, squeezing my eyes shut. "Take me."

CHAPTER 4
Cian

Every inch I pump into my wife's tight pussy is agonizing ecstasy. Her cunt strangles my cock, the sensation borders on painful, but I'm determined to see this through and soak up every drop of pleasure along the way. I can hardly believe it when I reach her barrier. She's such a good fucking girl that she's never even played with a dildo. My cock is the only thing that's ever been inside her sweet pussy.

That realization consumes me, manifesting a raw possessiveness like I've never experienced before.

I push through and she whimpers. "It's okay, I've got you. Relax. You're doing so well. Just hold onto me, that's right, just like that." Sweat coats my skin. The effort to hold back, to inch into her, taking its toll. But I won't rush this, not her very first time. I'm not a fucking monster. Not in that way, at least.

I'm still amazed at how quickly everything has twisted and turned in the past hour. When she wouldn't obey me, and I had to cut off her dress, I had every intention of punishing her with a quick, impersonal fuck. Who cares if I hurt my enemy's daughter—*ex*-enemy, I have to remind myself.

But then I touched her, and her body lit up, so responsive to my caresses. It made me crave more. Made me realize that above all else, she's my wife. She deserves the respect that goes with that title.

The way she touched my dick, and the fear in her eyes that followed, delivered another blow to my icy resolve. So innocent, so naïve. A ripe, tempting fruit just waiting to be plucked and devoured.

I'm not a good enough man to resist such temptation.

The final straw came when she begged not to be sent back home. I wanted to ask her why she was so afraid of her father, but why the fuck would she confide in me? Though I know something isn't right in that family. Lorenzo is... *off*. But that's not her fault.

I finally had to admit to myself that I don't hate *her*. She never did anything to me or my people. If anything, she's a casualty of war, if not a victim. Taking out my anger and hatred of all Italians on her is unfair. I was being a dick. Which usually serves me well, but perhaps my wife deserves a different approach. Maybe.

Hating her for being a beautiful woman is also unfair. Elena isn't my ex-fiancée. Yes, they both have dark red hair, and that ethereal kind of beauty that's like a siren's call. But Elena isn't *her*. Elena isn't a liar, or a devious, manipulative bitch. She's sweet, sassy, and every kind of temptation I don't need in my life right now.

But I want it. For tonight, I will give into it. Tomorrow, I'll be in control again.

I groan as I finally bury myself balls deep in my soft,

gorgeous wife. Staying still, I give her a moment to catch her breath, for her body to adjust to my invasion. She's panting, clinging to me like I'm her life line, and goddamn does she feel good beneath me, and around my cock.

For the first time since my ex betrayed me, I want to turn on the lights and actually see the woman in my bed. I yearn to watch her face as I fuck her, the tension in her features when she's close, and how she looks when she falls apart. That right there tells me how dangerous this woman is to me. I've known her less than twelve hours and she's already tempting me to deviate from my patterns. To break my own rules.

"Are you okay, *mo stoirín?*" Why the fuck do I keep calling her that? She's not *my little darling*. I need to stop.

"Yes," she pants. "I need you to start moving."

Fuck yes. Her wish is my command.

I pull almost all the way out before slowly, oh so slowly, pushing back inside her hot pussy. She rocks her hips, just enough to drive me fucking wild.

This time, I move a little faster, fuck her a bit harder and deeper. Her moans are music to my ears, a salve to my brutalized soul.

Honestly, a lot of women can't take me, not all of me. I'm too big—it's a fucking curse. But Elena's *moaning*. I'm able to bury my cock all the way in her sweet pussy. It's a miracle. It's like she was made for me. Perfect.

I revel in the feel of her, her amber scent, the small noises that escape her perfect lips. Lips I want to kiss, but that's too intimate. I won't allow myself to fall down that abyss ever again. I'll fuck her, I'll eat her cunt, but I won't kiss her on the mouth. That's where I draw the line. She needs to know about that boundary, and she will soon enough.

All too soon, my spine tingles and my balls tighten. How long as it been since I've had sex? I don't know. Far too long. I usually last longer, but she's so fucking tight and wet.

I'm not going to last much longer, even with all of these thoughts swirling through my head. Sliding my hand between us, I stroke her clit until she's a shuddering, writhing mess.

When she comes, I'm right there with her, emptying my cum deep inside this beautiful woman. I never do this bareback, but she's my wife and I want her pregnant as soon as possible. The sooner we produce a child of our mixed Irish-Italian lines, the more secure the peace treaty will be between our people. We'll be bound by marriage and blood.

She trembles beneath me, clinging to my shoulders, her legs wrapped around my hips. Easing out of her fluttering cunt, I roll to the side and give myself a moment to catch my breath before heading to the bathroom.

After cleaning myself up, I grab a washcloth and run it under hot water. Cloth in hand, I return to the main room and approach the bed. She must be sore. The warmth will help—

A click sounds, followed by a blinding light. I shield my eyes against the glare.

Fuck. Frozen, I stand there, naked, and she has no doubt seen everything I've been trying to keep hidden. My disfigurement.

With a roar, I lunge for the bedside lamp. I grab it,

and smash it to the floor, engulfing the room in darkness once again.

"I told you *no lights*," I snarl in Elena's direction. "Didn't you fucking hear me?"

"I'm sorry," she whispers. Her timid tone infuriates me even more.

"Here. Clean yourself up." I toss the warm washcloth at her, then turn away to find my trousers and shirt. Quickly dressing, I leave the bungalow in search of some fresh air. On my way out, I slam the door shut, hoping my actions clearly communicate that I don't want to be followed.

Not that she would follow me after what she just saw.

I'd intended to keep my body hidden from my wife for as long as possible, but that's now fucked. Maybe it doesn't matter. Or maybe I should have stripped in front of her so she could see the kind of monster she was getting into bed with from the start. Too late now. We've consummated this marriage.

Horrified or not, she's my wife, and she's not going anywhere.

CHAPTER 5

Ravenna

Scars, tattoos, melted flesh...all I can think about is how much *pain* is etched into his skin. Who did that to him? Are those from wounds he received in battles with my family, or was it someone else?

However he got hurt, those scars are obviously a sore spot judging by the look of shame and fear in his eyes, and his anger. I won't forget that sight anytime soon.

Just like I won't forget the way he tenderly... made love to me. That was not fucking, by my limited understanding. It only hurt for a moment, and I'm now sore, but the pleasure outweighed the pain. By a lot. Which is a delightful surprise.

The way he treated me was not at all what I expected. He has a quick switch from asshole, to caring lover, back to total *stronzo*. Moody and unpredictable—that's what I've learned about the stranger that is my husband.

He has an Irish temper, and a sharp tongue to go

with it. But his touch is something that I crave. I'm not sure if that's good or bad.

God give me strength.

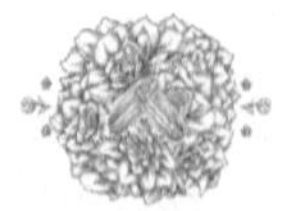

I startle awake, my gaze landing on Cian who sits in an armchair across the room, staring at me. He's dressed in a black T-shirt and dark wash jeans, his hair freshly washed and pulled back at the nape of his neck. The dark circles under his eyes tell me he hasn't slept. But it's morning. Sunlight filters through the gauzy curtains.

"Were you watching me sleep?" I pull the covers up to my chin, awkwardly aware of my nudity in the light of day.

"Yeah," he admits without a hint of guilt.

"Why?"

He shrugs those enormous shoulders. "When was your last period?"

My brows dip. "Why? That's kind of a personal ques—"

"I need to know when you're ovulating and when you're not." His expression's guarded, unreadable.

"Oh." I glance away from him. "I just finished a couple of days ago."

"Then you won't be ovulating while we're here, which means I won't touch you again. Not for another couple of weeks."

That statement grabs my attention. "Why not? I mean... I don't mind if you want to touch me."

"Don't lie."

I sit up in bed and lick my dry lips. "I'm not. If you're worried that I won't want to, now that I've seen your scars, you don't have to wor—."

"Don't!" he snaps. "Don't ever mention my scars again." Rage flashes in his cold eyes.

"I'm trying to tell you that they don't bother me. That I still want you," I argue back.

"Well I *don't* want you!" Cian stands up, pacing the room like a caged lion.

I clamp my mouth shut, enraged that he can be so *terrible* after the intimate night we had together. Did our coming together not affect him at all? Or was I really so bad in bed that he only wants me when it's time to do our marital duty?

That must be it. But it was my first time, what did he expect?

Even with that rationale, hopelessness crushes my chest. My eyes sting. I will not cry in front of this brute. He doesn't get my tears.

Emboldened by fury, I shove off the blanket and stand, proudly showing him everything he absolutely is *not* touching again this week. Whether he wants me or not.

His heated glare drinks in my curves. So, he does want me. With a huff, I saunter to the bathroom, swaying my hips. The big Irishman follows, and I have the immense satisfaction of shutting the door in his face. For good measure, I lock it.

Cazzo bastardo!

Ugh, he makes me so, so… livid!

Maybe I should have given him what he wanted and

cowered in his presence, pretending that his scars frightened me, that I can't bear to look at him. I scoff at myself in the mirror. My brother was about Cian's age and he had plenty of scars too, ones he liked to rub in my face, to try to scare me with when the nasty wounds were still healing. I've seen knife cuts and gunshot wounds, acid burns and shrapnel damage. Physical mutilations don't frighten me. How shallow does Cian think I am?

Actually, I don't care what he thinks of me. He can go to hell.

I take my time in the shower, doing my best to calm down as I wash my hair and body. When I'm finished, I still don't feel like facing him, so I blow dry my hair and moisturize my skin from head to toe. This place has some very nice toiletry products.

Wrapping myself in a plush white robe, I march into the main room, only to find it empty. Well, empty of him. There are about thirty shopping bags on the floor, all with designer logos on them.

The sight brings me to a sudden halt. Lifting one, I peek inside, finding black lacy underwear in my size. Silk. Very nice, and expensive. He must have dropped a hundred grand or more.

Can we say... mixed messages? Ugh. I don't understand this Irish *testa di cazzo* at all. I'm doubtful I ever will.

Dressing in a new pair of linen pants with a silk top, I add a thin sweater and heeled sandals. January in the Florida Keys is not exactly what I'd call warm, but it's a refreshing change from New York's dreary weather.

The bungalow sits right on the beach. Sunlight shines down from a blue sky, waves gently roll across the sand, and palm trees provide spots of shade. I make my way toward the main building and spa. If I'm stuck here for a week, I may as well take myself on vacation.

But first, I need to call home.

I glance around, making sure no one's within earshot before pressing my mother's contact on my phone. She answers after the first ring.

"Sweetheart, how are you?"

"I'm okay. Have you heard from E—my sister yet?"

Mama's silent for a long moment. "No. She's missing. I think she ran away from home."

That just... doesn't seem like something Elena would do. She's a home-body, her books are more precious to her than anything else. I just don't see her up and leaving, especially without taking her most prized possessions with her. And she has no money. She can't survive on her own. So where is she?

"If Elena isn't at home pretending to be me, then where does Papa think I am?"

Another extended pause. "I'm so sorry. I had to tell him the truth. He's a little upset—" Which means he's furious. "—but he does agree that we did the right thing. O'Rourke can never know about the swap. I'm going to tell anyone who asks that my daughter Ravenna is in Italy visiting family."

I inwardly groan, and close my eyes. This is getting more and more complicated. "What happens if she comes home?"

"I'll inform her that she's now Ravenna and she just returned from Italy, and that you're Elena and you married O'Rourke in her place. Everything will be fine."

"Sure." *Doubtful.*

"Oh, and R—Elena, please be your most charming self with Mr. O'Rourke. He's not the type of man who wants a sassy, stubborn wife. Do try to be more like your sweet sister."

I roll my eyes. Like I haven't heard that all of my life. I give her my usual response, "Of course, Mother."

"How are you two getting along?"

"I hate him."

"Oh, sweetheart, I'm so sorry. Arranged marriages can be difficult in the beginning. It took me a long time to adjust to being with your father, but we worked it out. You will too. Just be obedient and have faith. Your husband knows best. Remember that and everything will be fine. Plus, I'm so looking forward to having a grand-baby. Have you two... started trying yet?"

"Yes, Mama. We consummated our marriage last night."

"That's a relief. I'm sorry you had to go through that, but you won't have to endure it often unless he's a pervert. Once you're pregnant he'll leave you alone, and once you give him a few children he'll forget about you all together. That's the way of things. Something to look forward to for sure."

Confusion gnaws at me, but I keep my questions to myself. "Okay. Call me if you hear from my sister."

"Of course I will. Try to enjoy your honeymoon and stay on your husband's good side. Chat soon." She hangs up.

I sigh. Am I weird for having enjoyed the physical pleasures of last night? Maybe I am. That would explain why Cian doesn't want to touch me again, because he didn't enjoy it. Perhaps both men and women generally don't take pleasure in the act? I suppose it's possible. I guess I'm some kind of sexual freak.

Ugh, why am I thinking about that huge bastard when I should be trying to figure out what's going through my sister's head? What is Elena thinking? Why run? I mean, sure, marrying a stranger, especially our enemy, takes courage, but Elena has always been the obedient one. She wouldn't run away. In my gut, I know that's the truth.

Something is very wrong, and I'm not in any position to figure out what it is right now. Once this stupid honeymoon is over, and we're back in New York, I'm going to find out what happened to my sister.

CHAPTER 6
Cian

Housekeeping has come and gone. I returned to the bungalow to find all of Elena's things neatly put away in the closet, the bed made, and the bedside lamp's remains cleaned up. They must have thought we had a wild night. Now all of that evidence is gone.

I sit at the table, overlooking the ocean, and try to get my head on straight. Even with this place cleaned, I swear I smell Elena's amber scent. My palms tingle with the memory of touching her silky skin. My cock grows hard thinking about the way she felt beneath me, and how much I want to bury myself in her sweet cunt again.

Fuck. Fuck, fuck!

She's a siren, my wife, and I want to spend our entire honeymoon wringing every last drop of pleasure from her body. To drink in her moans, revel in her shudders, and fill her with my cum until it leaks from her pussy and drips down her thighs.

The last time I found myself this obsessed over a

woman, it was my undoing. I won't let that happen again —I can't. The next time might actually kill me, as my ex intended but failed to do. I swore then that I'd never be blinded by a woman's wiles again. The more I want her, the more she's guaranteed to be nothing but trouble.

Now I'm married to my worst nightmare—a woman I find desirable. That I can't stop thinking about.

My fist slams down on the table top. Frustration and pent up energy zing through my muscles, demanding release. With a curse, and a sense of defeat, I unzip my jeans, taking my throbbing cock in hand. I don't bother with lube. Instead, I enjoy the friction that brings both pain and pleasure.

I stare out at the beach, unseeing as my mind's eye conjures Elena's image from this morning when she tossed back the sheets and bared herself to me. Her come-fuck-me hair, flushed cheeks, and the way she swayed her hips.

I bite down on my lip, stroking myself faster. Imagining her bent over, that perfect ass in the air, and taking her from behind is all I need to finish.

Cum spurts in the air, spattering my shirt and coating my fist. I don't stop until I've expelled every drop.

What a mess. I clean myself up, tugging off my shirt and tossing it in the laundry hamper. Accidentally, I catch sight of my bare chest in the full length mirror.

I cringe.

Walking toward it, I force myself to look at the damage and the tattoos that attempt to cover the worst of it. But I know what's beneath them.

The stab wounds left short, white marks across my

abdomen. They're crisscrossed with shallower, longer scars from the sweeping cuts of the lashings. My left side is a mass of melted flesh intermixed with skin grafts from when I was doused in gasoline and set on fire.

That pain was the worst. I remember the acrid scent of my flesh burning with a vividness I wish I could forget. But six years isn't long enough for those memories to fade. In fact, I doubt they ever will. One night of terror changed my life forever. Now, I have to spend the rest of my life living in its aftermath.

Resolve hardens my heart. I'll never be at the mercy of a woman again.

Never.

Not that Elena could ever want a beast like me. Who could ever find this wreck attractive or desirable?

My gaze flicks up to meet my eyes in the mirror. But they don't only belong to me, they are the same pale blue as my brother's were. Those eyes, and the matching birthmark on my elbow–that's obscured by a spider web tattoo–are constant reminders of his betrayal.

My ex's treachery was horrible, but my brother's part in all of it was even worse. I lost a part of my soul that day.

Turning away, I change into a new T-shirt, and I zip up my jeans.

Where the fuck is my wife? Then I remind myself that I don't care. She's on this island, not going anywhere. She'll be back when she wants, and I don't give a fuck that she's not by my side.

I groan, raking my fingers through my hair. Hell on earth. That's what this week is shaping up to be and we're not even twenty-four hours into it yet.

My phone rings, and I immediately answer. "Tell me it's urgent and I need to come back to New York immediately."

Wolfe, my right hand man, chuckles. "Honeymoon going that well, huh? Or did you already kill the Italian bitch and you just need help burying the body?"

I bristle at him calling *my wife* a bitch. Then remember that's the phrase we've always used when referring to the woman I'd marry. I shake off my unreasonable anger. "No. Unfortunately the Italian bitch is still alive and well."

"That's too bad."

I murmur my agreement. "You and I both know I can't kill her without the Italians getting all bent out of shape about it. But I don't think they know what they've saddled me with. This one is *not* a meek little thing. She's a walking, talking bull-headed disaster. With a temper like a honey badger."

"A honey badger?"

"Yeah. *Broc meala*. They're aggressive little buggers. Better to avoid them at all costs."

Wolfe laughs—a rarity. "Sounds to me like you've met your match."

"Don't even start." I rub the back of my neck. "Why did you call?"

"I know how you get, so I just wanted to tell you that everything is fine here. Quiet. Business as usual with minimal bloodshed."

I grunt. "Good. Keep everyone in line until my return, especially Finn and Kody. You know how they can get without direct supervision."

"You got it, boss. We're all anxiously waiting for you

to get back so we can start working with the Italians. This is going to mean big business for us."

"No shit. Why else would I agree to *marry* one of them?"

"I don't judge, but I know you like punishing yourself—"

"Shut the fuck up," my tone doesn't hold any heat.

Wolfe snorts a laugh before sobering. "Just be careful, Cian. It seems to me like we're getting a lot more out of this deal than they are, and I don't like that imbalance. Plus they gave you the pretty one. Heard she has a sister that's so ugly they don't let her leave the house."

"Maybe it is too good to be true. Be careful and keep a watchful eye out. Check in with me tomorrow."

"Sure will, boss."

I end the call, pondering what I know about the Pontrelli family. Lorenzo had a son—until I killed him—which left him with two daughters. Neither has any social media presence. When I asked around about the girls, people said they couldn't be any more different. One is the perfect mafia princess and the other is a shrew. No wonder they didn't invite the unfavored sister to the wedding. She no doubt would have caused trouble.

In the extended family, Lorenzo has a brother, Davide, who has three girls. If anything happens to Lorenzo, Davide will step in as don of the Pontrelli mafia family.

A few years ago the city was ruled by five Italian families, until someone took one of them out. The Marino family, the most powerful of them all, disappeared overnight. No one knows who did it or why, but it shook the organized crime world to its core, and suddenly there was something worse to fear than the FBI. A nameless, faceless threat hiding in the shadows.

Some rumors point to Blake Baron being the mastermind behind their disappearance, but he's just a mysterious billionaire, not a criminal mastermind.

At least that's what we've all been led to believe.

Whoever did it, I think that incident helped spur the Italians into peace negotiations with us Irish. They know they're not invincible anymore and the stronger their ties with people like us the better. Instead of fighting each other, they're using us to fortify their position within the city. It's a move that makes total sense. Too bad we had to have years of bloodshed to finally get us here. But in the end, they get an ally, and we get to expand. It's a win-win.

I don't think our arrangement is as out of balance as Wolfe worries about.

Opening up the notes app on my phone, I spend the rest of the day outlining how we're going to expand into potential new business ventures and my vision for my people going forward. I won't be surprised if the Italians unite with the Russians soon as well. Another marriage, perhaps? It would be in their best interests.

Elena finally appears close to dinner time. She's wearing the new clothes I bought her, her deep auburn hair pulled away from her fresh, glowing face.

"Where the fuck have you been all day?" I growl. Apparently her absence put me in a foul mood after all.

She purses her lips and rolls her eyes. If she's the nice sister, I can only imagine what the other one must be like. She's most definitely a stuck up mafia princess.

"Well?" I sit back, knees spread wide, and cross my arms, expecting an answer.

She huffs. "At the spa. Isn't that obvious? My skin is glowing, my shoulders *were* relaxed until you opened your mouth, and I smell like tropical oils."

I narrow my eyes at her, still unused to her snarky comments. Does she have no filter on that mouth? No one talks back to me. *Ever.*

Unsure of exactly how to handle this creature, I stand, taking charge. "Change. We have dinner reservations in half an hour."

"As you wish, your majesty." She bows, a little wobbly, and I peer closely at her.

"Have you been drinking?"

"Why yes, I have. Did you know they serve bottomless piña coladas at the spa?" She contentedly moans, then hiccups. "They are so good. Sweet. Fruity. Boozy. Absolutely delicious."

I scoff. I can't believe my wife has been day drinking. That's completely unacceptable behavior. "Get dressed. Now."

On second thought... She's drunk, who knows what she'll choose to wear to dinner. I stomp over to the closet and paw through the silk and satin dresses, finding an appropriate deep green one for the occasion, and lay it on the bed.

"Wear that."

Returning to the closet, I grab a button down and a tie, then go into the bathroom to change. By the time I come out, she's in the dress, heels on her feet, ready to go.

My chest swells with triumph. Good girl.

I stride to the door and open it. "Let's go."

She scowls at me, seemingly unwilling to budge. Now what's the problem?

With a sigh, I approach where she's sitting on the edge of the bed and offer her my arm. The gentlemanly gesture smooths her ruffled feathers. She loops her arm around mine and we leave for the dining hall.

Spoiled princess... I fucking knew it.

CHAPTER 7
Ravenna

I'm not actually drunk, only a little tipsy from boozy drinks and a day of much needed relaxation. As soon as this ogre accused me of being drunk, I decided to play into it. He deserves to have to go to dinner with an intoxicated wife. Maybe I'll accidentally spill my drink on him, or stab him with my steak knife. *Oops*.

I giggle, and he gives me the side-eye. Good. I hope he's extremely uncomfortable right now trying to guess what's going through my head.

What will she do? What will she say? Who is this girl?

Keep guessing, you overgrown man-child.

Okay, maybe my spa day wasn't actually as relaxing as I hoped. Physically I feel great, but emotionally I'm still angry at this big brute—and at myself.

I shouldn't be here. Being brave and stepping into my sister's place was pure stupidity. There's a reason my parents chose Elena for this arranged marriage and it's not because she's the older twin. It's because she's the one to keep the peace. I'm more likely to blow up this treaty by saying the wrong thing at the wrong time. It was arrogant of me to think I could pull this off. That me marrying this man would be better than the alternative.

So, *so* stupid.

Plus, it's not like I can up and change my personality overnight. Even trying to play nice with this Celt makes me want to scream. Why does he get to be an asshole and it's fine, but when I stand up to him, I'm the one being *difficult*?

Yet, I don't want him to send me home, so I have to find a way to endure. Or maybe we'll just kill each other.

Until then, I take full responsibility that this was my idea and now I'm stuck here for the foreseeable future. For better or for worse, this is my life. I will teach myself to be softer, more charming, more agreeable. I swear it. I'm stubborn enough to pull this off.

Hopefully.

God give me strength.

Or an accident could also befall my husband. I wouldn't mind cutting this marriage short.

"Why are you smiling? What are you thinking about?" he asks as we sit at our table, eyes narrowed with suspicion.

"Acts of God."

He frowns. That expression, paired with his numerous facial scars, paints a dreadful picture. He's so unapproachable. I wish I could say *unattractive*, but I can't. He's no pretty boy, that's for sure. But his raw masculinity has an undeniable appeal. Especially when those icy eyes melt with heat, and he bites down on his plump bottom lip. Dear God, he's strikingly sexy.

I shake my head, dispelling those thoughts, and drink down half my water. That should help clear my head. Maybe I'm more intoxicated than I thought if I can't even sit across a table from this man without admiring his appearance.

Would he be traditionally good looking without those scars? I squint, trying to imagine what he'd look like without them. Defined jawline, high cheekbones, striking pale blue eyes, and full lips. Christ, he's damn handsome. The realization has my stomach fluttering as warmth spreads beneath my skin.

Get ahold of yourself, Ravenna—Elena—whoever you are. Now I'm having an identity crisis on top of everything else. I don't want to be attracted to this Irish brute.

The soup course arrives and we haven't said more than a few words to each other, so I glance at him for inspiration. "I like your tie, that color brings out your eyes."

Lame. Small talk has never been my forte.

Cian, as expected, glares at me like I just offended him.

"What?" I prompt, tapping my freshly manicured nails on the table. Gah, just one look from him and I'm irrationally annoyed.

"Don't lie to me," he grates out.

"It wasn't a lie. That tie is the same blue color as your eyes and it looks nice." I huff. "Can't you just take a compliment?"

"No."

"Well, I guess that's settled then. I won't offer another one. Ever."

"Good."

"Fine." I eat my soup more aggressively than is polite in public, but goddamn does this man rile me up. One word out of his mouth, one facial expression, and I want to strangle him. What's wrong with me? I'm usually blunt, but I'm rarely homicidal. Since the priest pronounced us husband and wife, I've wanted nothing more than to murder this Irish ruffian.

That nice silk tie could do the trick if I can get enough leverage. Maybe I'll strangle him with it tonight, while he sleeps, since I won't have anything more enjoyable to do with my time now that sex is off the table.

"Look at me with murder in your eyes all you want, *broc meala*, you're not the first woman who's dreamed of killing me."

Broc meala? What does that mean? He called me something last night, but I don't remember the exact words. Knowing him, it's probably nothing nice.

I slap my hand to my chest in mock astonishment. "*No*. Really? With your charming personality, who could possibly want to off you?"

Shaking his head, he mutters under his breath.

"What was that? I didn't catch it." I lean in.

His cold gaze collides with mine. "I said it's amazing to think that you're the sweet sister in your family."

That gives me pause. I didn't realize he knew that I had a sister. On second thought, of course he'd do at least some research into the family he'd be joining. Does he know we're twins? Identical twins? The back of my neck breaks out in a cold sweat.

He continues, "People said you and your sister couldn't be more opposite. If you're this... challenging... I can only imagine what a harpy your sister must be."

Challenging? Harpy? Dig your grave deeper, why don't you, Mr. O'Rourke?

"My sister is a perfectly lovely individual," I snap.

He snorts. "I'm sure. Just like your brother was a real nice guy. A perfect mafia prince."

"Of course he was." I have no intention of revealing my brother's true nature to him. He hasn't earned the right to know any intimate details about me or my family.

"You seem really torn up about his death." Cian's tone drips with sarcasm.

"My entire family is devastated by the loss of him." It's the truth. They are, even if I'm not.

"Hmm. And what about you?" He leans forward and lowers his voice. "How did it make you feel last night, knowing that the man who killed your brother was fucking you? Did that get you hot?"

I shoot up, throwing my cloth napkin on the table. "You're a sick bastard, you know that? Excuse me."

I rush from the table, and head straight for the restroom. Stunned gazes and murmurs follow me as I go, but I ignore them. It's not the first time I've been stared at in public. Won't be the last either. The backs of my eyes sting and I just want some privacy where I can fall apart for a moment.

Cian O'Rourke is officially the most insufferable man I've ever met. He's the worst. If he wanted to get a rise out of me, he succeeded.

I push the door open with enough force that it bangs against the wall, then close myself in a vacant stall. Soft music plays overhead. The air has a fresh, sophisticated citrus scent. I lean my back to the door and release a stifled sob.

Guilt eats away at my gut. I'm supposed to be in mourning for my brother. I'm *supposed* to feel something other than relief, joy, and exhilaration by the fact that he's dead. Which goes to show that I'm a horrible person. Though I have my reasons.

For the past few years, Matteo told me that one day Elena would be married and my parents would declare me a spinster, unsuitable for any match. He promised me when that happened, I'd belong to him, that he'd take me for himself and there was nothing I could do about it.

My stomach churns at the memory.

When I pointed out that would be incest, and our parents would never approve, he shrugged as if he didn't care. He said we'd be our family's dirty little secret. He'd already talked with our father about it and gotten his permission. My fate was all but sealed, but I didn't believe him. Not fully.

Papa wouldn't really do that to me, would he?

My stomach threatens to revolt at the thought of Matteo touching me like Cian did last night. Not only because Matteo was my brother, but because of how cruel I know he'd be. Everything I feared from Cian, Matteo would have delivered ten-fold.

He would have cut me with that knife. He would have forced himself on me and laughed when I screamed and pleaded for him to stop.

Another sob breaks free and I hug myself, drawing in deep, shaky breaths. I narrowly escaped one monster only to marry another. Even if Cian isn't as bad as Matteo, they are cut from the same cloth.

It's this world. These men. They're all awful. The

best a girl can hope for is a less evil version of the men she grew up around.

Doing my best to calm down and regain control of my emotions, I wipe the tears from my face and blow my nose. If I'm going to survive Cian, then I can't let him get to me like this. I closed myself off to Matteo, I can do that same thing with my new husband. I guess I just wasn't prepared for how similar they are: large men, scarred, with mean-spirited personalities. They're both monsters.

I married my brother after all. Or at least a man close enough to resemble him in every way that matters.

At least it's me who has to deal with him and not Elena. I'd never in a million years wish this man on my sweet, shy sister. He'd ruin her completely and enjoy every sick second of it.

But me? I'm ready for a fight. We can fight for the next sixty years for all I care. I'm prepared now. That Irishman will never get under my skin again.

I'm so focused on steeling myself against Cian, that when I walk out of the restroom I run right into a stranger's chest.

"Excuse me," I say to him, apologetically.

His large hands land on my shoulders to steady me or himself, I'm not sure. My skin prickles with the sensation. When I try to move past him, his grip tightens and my pulse picks up.

He glances over his shoulder, then at me. "Is that guy bothering you? You don't look very happy to be having dinner with him."

"I'm fine." Crap, I really shouldn't have created a scene earlier.

"Who is he?"

The words stick in my throat. With great effort, I utter them aloud, "He's my husband."

"Well he looks like a real piece of shit." He keeps glancing over at Cian. The guy practically vibrates with aggressive energy, and I suspect he's either drunk or on drugs. No sober man would think it's a good idea to get wrapped up in my and Cian's business.

"Thank you for your concern, sir, but we're just fine." I press past him, and he lets me go this time. I return to the table.

Unfortunately, the guy follows.

"Hey man, you're not treating this lady very nicely. I think you should leave her alone now," the man slurs.

When he drops his hand on my shoulder in front Cian, it's obvious he has a death wish.

Cian slowly lifts his gaze to the man standing beside my chair. It lingers on the guy's hand—which I try to shrug off—before continuing to his face.

I swear the room drops several degrees. I shiver.

"Remove your hand from my wife's shoulder." His voice conveys no emotion, yet it's deadly at the same time.

"Nah, man, this girl is coming with me as soon as she dumps your ugly ass."

I glare up at him. "I never said I'd go anywhere with you."

"Shh, babe, let the men sort this out."

I blink, twice. *Wow. Just wow.*

"Fine." I cross my arms and settle into my chair. At this point, they can kill each other and I'd be happy with that outcome. There's way too much testosterone at this table.

Cian's frigid gaze drops to me and he scowls. "This is all your fault."

I gasp. "*My* fault? How is this my fault?"

"If you weren't so pretty then you wouldn't attract this kind of unwanted attention. Attention that I am now obligated to deal with."

He thinks I'm pretty?

No. That can't be my first thought. It's absurd.

I shrug. "Poor you. Is that what you want, my sympathy? News flash, if you weren't such a dick then people wouldn't think that I need rescuing from you. Ever think of that?"

"Watch your tongue."

"Watch yours." I match his scowl with one of my own.

Seething, Cian unfolds, standing to his full, imposing height. "I told you to get your hand off of my wife."

"Make me. You obviously can't handle a woman like her, but I can, and—"

Cian punches him. His reach is so long that he doesn't even need to move from the other side of the table to lay the guy out. One second he's standing beside me and the next his unconscious body's splayed on the floor. Shocked gasps erupt from the other diners.

The maître d' appears instantly. "I am so sorry, sir. You shouldn't have been disturbed. I'll have this accident cleaned up at once."

As if the guy on the floor is nothing more than spilled wine, several staff people in white uniforms pick him up and carry him away. As soon as the black double doors swing shut, the rest of the diners go back to their meals, and it's as if nothing ever happened. Maybe it's just another Tuesday around here? Who knows.

We spend the rest of our meal eating in strained silence.

On our way back to the bungalow I finally murmur, "You didn't have to hit him."

Cian scoffs. "Oh, I most certainly did. He overstepped."

"How? By touching my shoulder, or by saying you weren't man enough to handle me?"

"Both." Cian glowers. "No one touches my wife without consequence. I should have broken his fingers."

I huff. "That's ridiculous. Besides, why do you care? It's not like we're anything but an arrangement anyway."

He abruptly stops. "Nothing but an arrangement? *Jesus!* While that may be true, you are *my wife*. Mine. We took oaths before God and man, and I will uphold them until I leave this world. We've entered into the most sacred of unions. I don't take that lightly." He looks earnest, but I know he's full of shit. "I'll never let anyone hurt you," he promises.

Lies. A strangled noise escapes my throat. "No, you probably want to carve up my face so that I'm not *too pretty*, so I won't draw unwanted attention from other men and—"

Cian's fingers wrap around my throat as he pulls me toward him, bending down until his face is level with mine. "Don't you dare say such awful things. I'd *never* hurt you."

I swallow thickly. "Now who's lying?"

He searches my eyes, for what I'm not sure, but he must see something he wants. His mouth suddenly crashes against mine. His kiss tastes like lust and frustration.

CHAPTER 8
Cian

I'm lost in the taste of her, in the feel of her, and I don't give a fuck about how unhinged I am right now. Or how I swore to myself I'd never kiss her lips—only to do just that.

She drives me crazy. Everything about her makes me insane, from her sharp tongue, to her death glares, to her pouty lips. I crave to devour her whole, as much as I desperately need to push her away and save myself.

Right now self-preservation is the furthest thing from my mind.

Slowly, hesitantly, she melts beneath my touch, until she's kissing me back. My tongue demands entry and she opens up. A satisfied hum sounds in the back of my throat. I palm her ass, pulling her close so she can feel how hard she makes me just by existing.

No one—not some sleaze in a restaurant or anyone else—is going to steal this woman away from me. I'll mark her in every way that I can, from my lips, to my touches, to my cum.

Without breaking our kiss, I lift her up and she wraps her legs around my hips. I walk the rest of the short distance to our bungalow, savoring the taste and feel of my wife.

Fumbling to get the door open, I finally manage it, then kick it closed behind us. I turn, pressing Elena's back against the door. Unable to resist a second longer, I grind my erection against her hot core.

I need her. Now. With the same urgency that a drowning man needs air.

"Wait." She pulls away from me, and frustration tightens my jaw. "Did you know my brother?"

What? Why is she thinking about *him* right now?

I take a second to clear my head. To cool off enough to answer her random question.

"Yes," I admit, dipping my face to her tender neck for a nibble. "He was a monster, a butcher, and I take pride in having ended his life. I'll never apologize for that."

Her pulse visibly flutters. "You remind me of him," she breathes the admission, so low I almost don't hear her. But I do.

I rear back, shock rippling through me. *What the fuck?* Her comment feels like being doused with ice water.

"Look, I may not have the best personality, but I am *nothing* like him. You hear me? Nothing." I grind my teeth. How can she think I'm anything like that piece of shit?

Though, in all honesty, have I been anything other than demanding and cruel since our wedding? Apart from the sex last night, have I been kind, caring, or generous? Not really.

I shouldn't have said what I did about her brother at dinner. All I wanted to do was push her away—it worked, all too well. Regret sears my chest.

Her soft, pleading voice soothes some of my hurt. "*Show me.* Show me that you're not cruel. That you don't get off on tormenting or threatening me. Show me that you'd never hurt me. Because all I've seen of you so far is someone very much like my brother—and I hated him."

Jesus, Mary, and Joseph, I've really fucked this up, haven't I?

Anger heats my blood. What did her brother do to her? Did he hurt her? It sure sounds like it. My vision tints with red. I wish he were alive so I could kill him all over again.

Stroking her hair, I stare deep into her blue-grey eyes. "*Broc meala*, I will show you that I am, deep down, a much better man."

"Prove it." The desperation in her voice guts me. How can I deny her wish? We're married. We're in this together for life.

"That's a challenge I'll accept." I claim her mouth in a ravenous kiss. She trembles beneath my touch.

Threading her fingers through my hair, she deepens our kiss. She wants this, she wants me, and damn if I have the strength to deny her any longer.

Has my resolve to distance myself from her fallen like a house of cards? Yes, it has.

Do I give a shit? No, I don't.

One look from this woman, one word, and she's under my skin. When I have her in my arms like this, whimpering and writhing against my straining cock, tasting like heaven, I can't think straight. Nor do I want to, consequences be damned.

The full moon's light shines through the gauzy curtains, softly illuminating us. Elena hastily unbuttons my shirt, like she can't wait to feel my skin, scars and all, and I'm drunk on her desire.

Grabbing the front of her dress, I rip it in two, from her neckline to her waist. I bought the thing, I can destroy it if I like.

Her surprised gasp, and full breasts spilling into my hands, are worth every penny.

Playing with her peaked nipples, I suck her bottom lip between my teeth. She moans, grinding her needy cunt against me as her hands explore my chest and shoulders, face and hair. It's like she can't get enough.

"Please," she moans, "I need you inside of me. Now."

I doubt she's ready for me yet.

With one hand supporting her ass, I slip the other between her thighs to find her pretty pussy thoroughly soaked. She's dripping wet.

I groan. Quickly unzipping my trousers, I release my cock and line myself up. I don't know if she can take me or not, but I want to try. Slowly.

She whimpers as I push into her tight cunt. Fuck, she feels like paradise—this is heaven, right here on earth.

"Tell me to stop if it's too much. I can get the lube—"

"More. I need more." She pulls me closer.

Hope rockets through my chest as I give her more. I give her every thick inch of me, and she rocks her hips, moaning in pleasure. She's perfect. There's no doubt in my mind that she was made for me, and only me.

I let myself do something I've never done before with

a woman. I let go. I don't worry about hurting her, or causing damage. The beast within me purrs.

Each powerful thrust draws a gasp from her lips, but her embrace spurs me on. Soon she's meeting me half-way. Her small body takes me beautifully as I fuck her with wild abandon against the wall.

We're drenched in sweat, our breaths mingle, our tense muscles demand release. I flick her clit and she screams out my name, which sends me right over the edge with her.

I bury my cock deep inside Elena, and empty my balls. There's something so primally satisfying about filling her with my cum. I want to do it all over again. Soon.

Pulling out, I drop to my knees, steadying her with my hold on her slim waist. I lift her trembling legs over my shoulders and lap at her pussy, tasting our unique, mixed flavor.

"Oh my god." She tugs my head closer, and I chuckle at how she's insatiable. The vibration has her squirming, panting, and a wicked satisfaction unfurls in me at holding her pleasure in my hands. This time, she's going to earn her orgasm.

"Cian, I need more."

"I know, *broc meala*. I know." Lazily, my tongue circles her clit. "But I want you to beg. That's what I get off on. I want to hear you beg for your husband."

"Please, Cian." She whimpers.

I insert one finger, toying at her entrance. "What do you want?"

"Please make me come."

"I think you can do better than that, wife."

"Cian, *husband*, please, I'm begging you. Make your wife come on your face."

Fuck yes. Warmth spreads through my chest. I groan against her clit.

"That's more like it." Pumping two fingers into her, I flick her nub with the tip of my tongue. "Come for your husband."

Like a good girl, she does as she's told. Fisting my hair, she falls apart in my arms, her release dripping down my chin as I lick her clean.

Standing, I lift her shivering body and carry her to the bed. I remove the remains of her ruined dress. After I shed the rest of my clothes, I join her beneath the sheets. My palm curls around the back of her neck and I kiss her, deeply, reverently.

In the course of forty-eight hours this woman has utterly destroyed me, and I never saw it coming.

She wraps her legs around my hips, and my cock slides home. This time, I make love to her—there's no other way to describe how our bodies come together in perfect harmony.

CHAPTER 9
Ravenna

In the light of day, I thought he'd transform once again into a brooding beast, but he doesn't. Much to my surprise, he remains in bed with me, cuddling, letting me explore his body. The tightness of his jaw tells me he's uncomfortable with it, but he's trying, for me. My heart warms.

The scar that stretches from his forehead to his chin actually doesn't stop there, it continues down to his shoulder where it's obscured by a tattooed patch of four-leaf clovers which bleed into purple bell-shaped flowers that grow from a skull. I trace them with my finger, snuggled up to Cian's side.

"What is this flower?" I ask him, intrigued by the purple bells and the skull.

"Foxglove. It's poisonous. I chose it to remind me that beautiful things can be deadly."

I want to ask for details, but I hold my tongue. "They're pretty. I love purple flowers, especially purple tulips."

"What do you love about them?"

"I guess... their simple grace."

"I see." He lifts onto his elbow, rolling until I'm halfway beneath his massive form. Gently, he smooths my hair away from my face. "There are some things I want to tell you. I don't know why I want to let you in closer, there's just something about you. More than the fact that we're to spend our lives together. I can't explain it." His gaze searches my face, seeking answers.

I know what he means. He gets under my skin too. In both good and bad ways. I'm not sure what to make of it either. Last night I was dead set on shielding my heart against him, until that kiss.

That kiss melted my resolve faster than you can say *whiplash.*

That kiss was my undoing.

He clears his throat, drawing my full attention. "I was engaged once. Years ago. It was a love match. Or so I thought."

I hold my breath, hoping he'll tell me more. I'm desperate to understand him. Every clue he reveals about himself is another piece to the puzzle that is him. I want to see the full picture.

"Long story short, she was in love with my brother, and the two of them wanted me out of the way. They betrayed me. They..." he clears his throat again, and I realize it's a nervous habit. "They did all of this to me." He gestures to his body. "I miraculously survived. Then I killed them both."

Oh. My. God. My heart wrenches. I reach for him, caressing his cheek, but don't dare speak. Afraid that whatever I say will scare him into silence.

"After that, I never wanted to marry. I didn't let anyone close to me ever again. I most certainly never wanted a wife." His eyes squeeze shut. When he opens them, gazing down at me, I see his inner struggle. "But now I have you."

Marrying me has forced him to face his fears. *I'm* doing that. This must be difficult for him. I can't imagine being in love, then betrayed like that, to swear off ever having someone in my life again, only to end up in an arranged marriage with a stranger, who is also my enemy's daughter.

"I don't know what to do with you," he admits, caressing my hair. "You don't know me yet, but I'm the kind of man who's loyal to a fault. I take my vows seriously. I'll never stray from you. I will cherish you, if you'll let me. We obviously have a passionate physical connection. But I don't think I can ever fully trust you. Trust isn't in my nature any more. Maybe with time... but I doubt it."

Guilt coils around my chest, squeezing the air from my lungs. I'm a living, breathing lie. I lied to him the very first moment I saw him, and now there's no way to come clean. We've reached a tentative peace since last night and I don't want to ruin it. There's no way forward other than to keep to my not-so innocent deception.

If I tell him the truth now, he'll definitely feel betrayed, lied to, and he'll return me to my father. Without my virginity, Papa will sell me as he won't be able to marry me off.

I mentally shudder at the thought.

A far worse future awaits me if I speak the truth now. Cian can never know that I've deceived him. It's as simple as that. But from this day forth, I will only ever be honest with him about everything else. He deserves that much.

"I understand." Lacing my fingers through his silky hair, I pull him in for a kiss. "I am also loyal. Fiercely loyal to those I care about. Protective as well."

He entwines our fingers. "I have no doubt about that. When you get upset, you're like an angry badger."

"*What?* I am nothing like a badger. Take that back this instant." I try and fail to hold back my grin.

He smiles, the expression transforming his entire face, softening the edges. My heart skips a beat. "Never. I like badgers."

I laugh. He nips at the corner of my mouth.

My stomach rumbles, drawing our attention.

Heat warms my cheeks. "Dinner was a long time ago and we've been quite... active."

"Yes we have." His smile widens and he rolls off of me to call for room service.

Last night and this morning are a one-eighty from what happened on our first night here. Well, except for the destruction of clothing, and the sex, but that was delicious both nights.

I like this version of Cian much better than the previous one. He gives me hope for a brighter future together.

Maybe this wasn't a huge mistake after all.

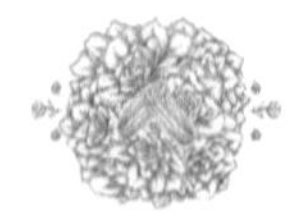

"Do you have any other family?" I ask. We're wearing white fluffy robes at the breakfast table and I've already devoured my weight in pancakes, eggs, and bacon. "I mean, besides your terrible brother."

He swallows a piece of sausage before answering. "Yeah, a bunch of cousins, but we're not close. They're too straight and narrow for my side of the family. Ma died giving birth to us, and Pa spent the rest of his short life in prison. My brother and I were never close. I should have seen his betrayal coming." He glances away.

"Wait, giving birth to both of you? You're twins?"

"Yeah. I'm the oldest, and my brother was always envious of me. He didn't think it was fair that our birth order determined who got to inherit the leadership role." He features harden. "I didn't realize how much he wanted me out of the way until he betrayed me like that."

My heart pinches. My twin and I are so close, I can't imagine either of us turning on the other like that. Family is supposed to have your back, to be your support system, but it sounds like Cian never had that.

While I feel sorry for him, these insights also enable me to better understand him. I have my twin and my cousins, we're close, but Cian has never had anyone. At least, not family.

"Who raised you?" I ask, since his parents obviously didn't.

"My only living grandparent, Grandpa O'Rourke. He was also the Gaelic Devils' leader until I came of age. He passed on a few years before my brother's betrayal. I'm glad he didn't have to witness all of that." He falls silent, pensive.

"Oh?" I prompt. "He may have helped you."

Cian shakes his head. "Nah, he would have called me a damned fool. He never liked Shawn. Which only added to my brother's jealousy. But Grandpa O'Rourke warned me about Shawn once, told me he saw envy in his eyes, but I didn't pay him much mind. So I have only myself to blame for being blindsided like that."

"It's hard to believe when those who are supposed to be our closest allies become our enemies instead." I know it all too well.

Papa and Matteo should have taken care of me. Protected me. Instead, I suffered their abuse. Until now. Marrying Cian is my escape.

"How about you?" he asks. "Tell me about your family."

"Uh. My sister and I are close. We're quite a few years younger than Matteo, so he never really paid us much attention. Unless it was to torment me for his amusement. I'm actually close with my three cousins. They are like sisters to me. The five of us girls always have each other's backs."

"You're lucky to have such a big, close family. I envy that," he admits.

"We're not all close. I mean, my father and Uncle Davide don't really get along outside of family business. And you know how much of a problem Matteo was for everyone, except Papa who was the one to groom him."

Cian glances at me. "Are you saying your brother was a monster because that's what your father turned him into?"

"I don't really know. Matteo was always... different. Mean. I think Papa just encouraged him to be himself."

He leans his elbows on the table, his stare unrelenting. "What did he do to you, Elena?"

My gut twists at my sister's name. Every time he calls me *Elena* it's a reminder of my long list of lies. My biggest lie of all. I hate it.

"As I'm sure you understand," I glance pointedly at his chest, "I don't really want to talk about the details."

Silence hangs in the air between us.

After a moment, he sits back. "Fair enough. How about a truth for a truth? I'll answer one of your questions and then you'll answer one of mine."

That's tempting. Do I want to give him the gritty details? In exchange for knowing more about him, it might be worth it. I hesitate, chewing on a slice of orange, then nod.

"You can go first." How generous of him.

"Okay. Why did your brother and ex-fiancée do that to you? Why not just kill you quickly and move on with their lives?" I mean, from what I've seen, the damage is extensive. They had to have tortured him for days and days.

My stomach twists and I'm no longer hungry. The rest of the orange falls to my plate.

"That's two questions."

I realize he's right. "Fine. I'll roll it into one. Why did they torture you instead of just killing you and being done with it?"

He thinks on that for a moment. "Because my brother, Shawn, was like yours. And I didn't realize it before then, but my ex got off on the same shit." He clears his throat. "I lost count of how many times they fucked in front of me, covered in my blood, while I lost consciousness. It was their ultimate high. They wanted it to last for as long as possible."

My lips part in shock and my stomach heaves. *Oh my god.*

"Cian—"

He shakes his head, cutting me off. "I've answered your question."

"Thank you." I reach across the table, taking his hand in mine and giving it a gentle squeeze. I'm grateful when he doesn't pull away, because right now I desperately need to touch him, to give him whatever small comfort he'll let me. "It's your turn."

"How did your brother hurt you?" His lips press into a thin line.

Of course he'd ask that. I'm somewhat prepared to answer.

I close my eyes against the onslaught of memories, some of them still relatively fresh, some going back years. "He did all kinds of things. When I was eight, he killed my pet rabbit and made me watch. Mostly he liked to hit me. That seemed to turn him on, and sometimes he made me watch him get himself off after beating me. He often threatened to touch me, sexually, but he never did." Thanks God for that.

Cian's pale blue eyes brighten with rage, his neck a deep crimson. "Your parents didn't intervene?"

"They didn't know." I look down at my plate. My statement is mostly true. I didn't realize how much my father knew about what was happening between me and Matteo until quite recently. Before a few months ago, I thought Papa simply chose to look the other way. Now I suspect he put Matteo up to some of those things.

But Cian and Papa have to work together, so they need to get along. I can't jeopardize that peace for my own selfish reasons. What happened with Matteo is in the past. Papa can't hurt me now that I'm Cian's wife.

Abruptly, Cian drags me around the table and into his lap. His huge body folds around mine, his arms caging me against him in a protective, but inescapable embrace.

"Just to be clear, I don't get aroused by pain, *broc meala.* I do get off on being in control, of holding your pleasure captive and having you at my mercy, but I'll never hurt you." His breath tickles my ear.

Relief sweeps through my veins. I trust him. After how he's treated me so far, I believe him.

I nod in acknowledgment. In an attempt to lighten the mood, I say, "My clothes, however, are in danger."

"True." His low chuckle vibrates in his chest, and I relax against him. "But I'll buy you ten dresses for every one that I cut from your body."

"Then you owe me twenty dresses," I tease.

"I do."

I twist in his arms, "What does *broc meala* mean?"

At this question, he simply grins.

I guess we're done with our questions game. For now.

I plant a kiss on his lips. That chaste kiss turns into sex on the table, then another round in the shower. I simply cannot get enough of this complicated, tormented man. As different as we are in some ways, I think we have more in common than either of us realizes.

CHAPTER 10

Cian

The rest of our honeymoon we spend fucking like rabbits, eating delicious food, and talking while in each other's arms. She's so easy to talk to, and a really great listener. I never thought I'd be able to open up about my past, about the pain, but Elena makes it so easy to do it.

I didn't realize how much I ached to confide in someone. Until her. She's crawled right under my skin, burrowed deep.

This isn't me. I don't talk about my feelings. I usually use my fists to express myself, but with Elena all I want to do is be held in her arms and let it all come out. It's a release I never knew I needed.

How did this arranged marriage disaster turn into newlywed bliss so quickly? I don't know, but she's the perfect wife for me.

We both have our own trauma that we carry inside, she just has more grace than I do. After everything her brother did to her, she's still playful, strong, and an amazing woman. The more time I spend in Elena's presence, the more I find myself forgetting about my past. Instead, looking forward to a happy future together. Something I thought I could never have.

She gives me hope. She's an inspiration. An addiction.

These are early days for us and our marriage, I know that, but it seems that fate has finally decided to smile down on me. Just this once. Please, God, promise me this is real. Haven't I fucking suffered enough in my life?

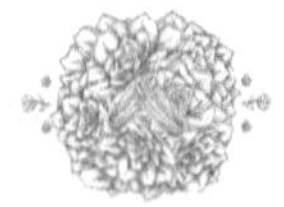

"We're home." I lift Elena's fingers to my lips and kiss them. She smiles at me before her gaze shifts to the massive iron gate and the guard's post. One glance from the man on duty and the gate slowly begins to open.

I try to see my home through her eyes. Cold, fortified, intimidating. My expression drops, realizing that the rigorous security and the massive dark stone house are anything but inviting. Add to that the rough-looking men waiting to greet us, all Irish of course, and I can see why she's worriedly nibbling her lip.

I reassuringly squeeze her hand. "You'll get used to them. They aren't nearly as bad as they look—mostly. But since you're my wife, you have nothing to worry about. I'll always keep you safe."

"It's just that not so long ago we were all enemies. My father's men killed their friends, and these men killed people I've known all my life. It's going to take a while to adjust to this new reality between your people and mine."

"We are no longer two separate people. Your family is mine, and mine is yours." Though I know she's right, and I'm sure that some of my men will have a hard time adjusting too. We just have to take it one day at a time.

We exit the car together, and for reasons I can't explain I'm strangely torn between my men and my wife. For her, I want to always appear kind and attentive, but to my men, I'm their leader, stoic and powerful.

How can I be both types of man at once?

Leaving Elena's side, I approach Wolfe and the men who've turned out to welcome me home. I clap Wolfe on the back and nod in greeting to the rest of them.

"It's good to have you back, boss," Wolfe says. "It's been a long week without you."

"Nothing you couldn't handle, I'm sure."

"True." His gaze slides to Elena, and I bristle. I don't like the way he's assessing her now that she's no longer covered up in a long bridal veil. Now that she belongs to me.

He smirks. "So that's the Italian bitch, huh? Pretty little thing—"

Blinding rage overtakes my every thought.

My punch strikes his jaw. He stumbles backward, shock written across his features. Any other man would have gone down from the impact, but not Wolfe, he's a seasoned fighter and knows how to take a hit—even one as unexpected as that.

"What the fuck, Cian?" He rubs his reddening jaw.

"Don't *what the fuck* me, Wolfe. That's *my wife*!

You'll talk about her with respect. Or better yet, don't talk about her at all, don't even fucking look at her. Have I made myself clear?" I snarl, waiting for Wolfe's reluctant nod before glaring at the other men. They murmur their acknowledgment. "Good."

I drape my arm possessively around Elena's shoulders, holding her close. I give my men one more pointed look, then usher us toward the front door. This is home.

"I don't think that was a good idea," Elena whispers. "Your men will only hate me more if they think you're choosing me over them."

"No they won't. They just needed a reminder to mind their manners. Don't worry, *broc meala,* you're my wife and they will show you the respect you deserve. Now, let's do this properly." At the door, I pick her up, bridal style, and carry her across the threshold. She laces her fingers behind my neck, tugging me down for a sweet kiss. Damn, I needed that.

"Welcome to your new home, darling. I want you to make it your own. Anything your heart desires, you will have it."

"Really?" She glances around before her gaze returns to me. "There's only one thing I want right now."

"What's that?"

"You still haven't told me what *broc meala* means."

Taking the stairs two at a time, I grin down at her, knowing she's going to hate this as much as she loves it.

"*Broc meala* means honey badger."

She scoffs. "You've been calling me honey badger this whole time?"

"Yeah."

"I want a different nickname, or endearment, or

whatever that's supposed to be." She pouts and I tease my nose across hers.

"You're my little honey badger. It's stuck, and I'm not changing it. The description fits too well."

She opens her mouth to protest, and I capture her lips with my own.

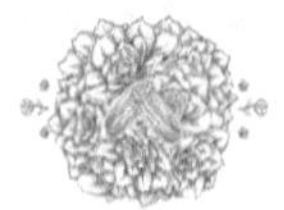

"I've never seen you so pussy-whipped." Wolfe catches up to me in my home office when I leave Elena to soak in the bathtub, alone. Her body needs the rest after this past week. Especially considering what I'm fantasizing about doing to her as soon as she's recovered enough.

I sigh, pinching the bridge of my nose. "I'm not pussy-whipped, I'm married. There's a difference."

"One week with that Italian... *woman*, and you've grown soft. I've never seen you look at a woman the way you look at her. Not since..." Thankfully he doesn't finish that thought aloud. "What's going on?"

I grit my teeth, irritated at having to explain myself. Normally I wouldn't, but Wolfe deserves that much after how hard I hit him earlier. In front of the men, too.

"Turns out I like her. Since I'm going to spend the rest of my life with her, I don't see that as a bad thing. And I haven't grown soft." I eye him. "Do we need to take this discussion into the ring?"

Wolfe and I are quite equally matched in a fight. But

sometimes it's the only way to settle our differences. With fists and blood.

It's his turn to sigh. "No."

"Okay then. Respect my wife, that's all I want. Make sure the men know it too. She's completely off limits to everyone. Don't speak to her, don't look at her, and no one had better fucking touch her."

"You've made that clear." He rubs his swollen cheek.

I nod. "Good. Fill me in on what's been happening around here."

Wolfe launches into every dealing, incident, and rumor that's surfaced these last seven days. I murmur and grunt my responses where necessary, trying to keep my mind on task and off of my wet, naked wife upstairs. That honeymoon wasn't nearly long enough.

"—we have a meeting with Lorenzo Pontrelli tomorrow. On neutral ground, in a private dining room at *Spades*."

Back in New York and right back to work. Why am I so irritated about that? I used to bury myself in my work, sometimes not finding my bed for two or more days in a row. Now, it strikes me as a less enjoyable necessity. I'm sure I'll find my enthusiasm again, once I've broken a few noses and negotiated some new, very prosperous deals. As long as I can return each night to my bed and my new bride.

"Did you hear me, boss? Tomorrow night, eight o'clock at *Spades*."

I wave him off. "Yeah, I heard you. Confirm the meeting. Anything else?"

"That's it for now." Wolfe hesitates before saying, "With all the trouble we were having with some of the gambling dens I'm just glad no one tried to interfere with your wedding. As much as I hate the Italians, we need this alliance. Lost too many good men."

I bob my head in agreement. Someone had been fucking with my business up until a month before the wedding date, then they went silent, and seemingly disappeared. It's possible they met with an accident, or pissed someone else off and were taken out. Either way is fine with me as long as they don't come back round again.

CHAPTER 11
Ravenna

The next day, I explore my new home. Cian's house is more like a military fortress than a cozy living space. Everything is white and grey, stone and stainless steel, it's uninviting to say the least. At first glance, I'm unsure of how I might improve the place, but as I continue to wander, my imagination comes alive with the possibilities.

Of course, I'm not an interior designer, but I know for a fact that I'd like to hire one. ASAP.

This poor house is begging to come to life with some color. A fresh coat of paint on the walls would do wonders. Maybe replace the tile floors with wood?

I round a corner on the main floor and come face-to-face with Cian's second-in-command, who was also his best man at the wedding. Wolfe.

Immediately, I stop. I don't like the way he looked at me when we first arrived. There was something calculating and cold in his eyes.

Similar to how he's looking at me right now from where he stands rooted in place.

"What?" I snap, irritated at how his stare makes me so uncomfortable.

His thick brows lift toward his hairline. "You really aren't timid, are you? Any other woman encountering me alone in a hallway would at least pretend to be polite. For her own sake. It's called self-preservation."

"I don't have any patience for rude men who stare." I fold my arms, partly in annoyance but also to brace myself. Wolfe is not a small man. He's brawny, older than Cian by at least a decade, and radiates danger. Celtic knot designs ink both sides of his neck.

I hate to think of how many people he's murdered, many of them *mi famiglia*.

Wolfe takes one step closer, but I don't budge. "I'm only staring because I'm trying to figure out what spell you've put on Cian. He hates women, especially red haired, pretty ones. Only tolerates them when they're on their backs with their legs spread."

His vulgar words slide beneath my skin. I open my mouth to respond, but he cuts me off.

"Whatever sorcery you've done to him, I want you to know that if he comes to any harm I will slit your throat myself. I'll make all those terrible stories you've heard about us Irish come true for you."

His threats give me pause. He's afraid that *I'm* going to hurt Cian? I'd never do such a thing, at least not intentionally.

"You have nothing to worry about," I assure him. Even if I don't like this man, at least he seems to be utterly loyal to Cian.

"We'll see about that, sorceress." He strides past me, his shoulder bumping mine.

Stronzo.

Relieved that he didn't try to assault me, I continue my exploration, this time being more aware of who's around corners and lurking in hallways.

I poke my head into various rooms. Cian's people must spend a lot of time here since there are multiple entertainment rooms with games or TVs, even a pool hall. It's like a compound headquarters. Which, it actually might be just that.

Several buildings behind the main house hold numerous apartments. I wouldn't dare go into them. But from what I figure, a lot of these men are single and live on the property. The compound is like one big fraternity.

When I enter a new wing of the house and get to a locked door, it piques my curiosity. What kind of room does Cian want to keep under lock and key, away from his comrades?

Glancing up and down the empty corridor, I remove a pin from my hair and bend it into the shape I need to pick this type of lock. Since I learned this skill when I was thirteen, I've always worn my hair either pinned back at the sides, half up, or in a bun. That way my tool of choice is always with me, and at the same time hidden.

My heartbeat pounds in my chest as I inhale deep breaths to keep my hands steady. My senses strain to detect any sudden sound or presence. I certainly don't want to get caught. Not by these people.

So far I've been lucky. No one has ever caught me picking a lock, not even my family knows that I have this skill. If they did, Papa would have taken away all of my hairpins ages ago. He has far too many skeletons in his closets to be comfortable with me snooping around.

The mechanism finally clicks and I turn the handle, quietly opening the door. Victory whooshes through me as I step inside.

Closing the door behind me, I switch on a light, illuminating the mysterious room. Which turns out to be... a library.

Unlike the rest of the house, this space has charm. Floor to ceiling wooden bookshelves occupy three of the walls. Set into the fourth wall is a fireplace and two tall, narrow windows, the only source of natural light. A sofa and two leather chairs occupy the middle of the room. There's even a couple of floor lamps.

It's cozy. The perfect place to grab a book and curl up in front of the fire to read.

Instantly, I'm in love. This is my favorite room in the house.

My fingertips gravitate toward the long rows of spines. I read some of the titles as I pass by them. Business and finance, history, thrillers, there's a bit of everything. Old cloth-bound tomes stand beside mass market paperbacks.

Elena's always been the bookish one, but I read on occasion. I'm just picky, and prefer non-fiction. History's by far my favorite subject, especially New England history pre-and-post the Revolutionary War. Though Elena has tempted me into reading a couple of her epic Romantasy books.

Those were hot. I can see why people enjoy fiction. It's a wonderful escape from reality.

A glass case set into the shelf at eye level catches my

attention. Reading the open title page, I gasp. It's an English first edition of *The Count of Monte Cristo* by Alexandre Dumas, published in London in 1846. The case contains two volumes, which means it's a complete set. Rare, and extremely expensive.

While I don't read a lot of fiction, I absolutely love old books. The older and rarer the better. Something about all the history they've been through makes my heart flutter.

My fingers glide across the glass separating me from these most precious of objects. This edition is sure to have illustrations.

I look around for the case's closure and find a small padlock. That shouldn't be too difficult to open, but maybe the key–

"I warned you about poking around." A deep rumble sounds right behind me, and I spin to face Cian, my heart in my throat. "Now I'll have to kill you."

My gaze collides with Cian's stoney expression. My lips part in shock. He's impossible to read. He did tell me not to poke around, but that was on our wedding day, before we got to know each other. Surely he doesn't mean it anymore.

He places his hands on the bookcase, one on either side of my head, and leans in, trapping me in place.

My pulse stutters, but I'm not sure if it's with excitement or uncertainty.

"Do you have a death wish? Or do you simply enjoy disobeying me, *broc meala*?"

"I..."

He can't be serious. Is he? Have I really overstepped?

"This is my private library. That door is locked for a

reason. But you don't think the rules apply to you, do you? Locked doors are only an obstacle, is that it?" Heat wafts from his huge body.

I swallow hard. He is serious. He's going to punish me for this, isn't he?

"I'm sorry," I whisper, a tremor running through me.

"How sorry?" He presses his body flush against mine, and I can feel the hardness of his cock. My eyes grow round. This is turning him on? Maybe that's a good thing since he told me he gets off on being in control, but not on inflicting pain.

So this is... an act. Foreplay?

Now that I understand the game we're playing, I whimper. "Please. I'm begging you. I didn't mean any harm."

He groans, biting his lower lip. "Fuck, I love it when you beg. Beg for mercy, baby."

"Please have mercy on me." Slowly, I sink to my knees. Keeping my gaze trained on his, I unfasten his dark jeans, freeing his cock. The weight of it in my hand is enough to make me salivate. Lust fogs my senses. "I'm begging you. Please."

CHAPTER 12
Cian

She opens her mouth wide, taking the head of my dick into her warm wetness. Her tongue flicks the underside, then swirls around the ridge. I groan at her tentative exploration, and her courage at trying to suck me into her mouth. There's no way in hell she'll get me all the way in there. Does she realize that?

"Have you ever done this before?" I ask her on a grunt, threading my fingers through her hair.

She pulls away to answer. "Of course not."

"Your mouth isn't like your pussy, *broc meala,* you won't be able to take me all the way in. Not without cutting off your air supply. Even then, I'd have to be halfway down your throat and you're no sword swallower." The thought has my cock twitching, but I don't want to hurt her, or make her feel like she has to do this.

Challenge flashes in her gorgeous grey eyes. "Will you shut up and let me beg for my life, *Irlandese*?"

"What does that mean?"

"Irishman." She huffs. "Now shut up."

I smirk. "Anything for you." I moan as she sucks my throbbing cock past her lips, both of her hands stroke my shaft. She works me in, inch by inch. In and out, in and out, a little more each time. It's fucking excruciating, and a marvel to watch my cock disappear between her lips.

I fist her hair with one hand, my other cups her throat as she swallows me down. My wife sputters and coughs a couple of times, but her resolve never wavers. She relaxes her muscles and tries again, and again, until she's fucking deep-throating me and I'm dangerously close to coming.

Her nose touches my pubic hair, her palms splayed on my thighs. Triumph heats her stunning eyes when she slowly pulls away, releasing me with a *pop*.

"Please, sir, I'll do anything. Please spare my life." Her eyelashes flutter and she sucks my cock down again. All in one go this time.

"Fuck!" I sharply inhale. *Jesus, Mary, and Joseph, this woman will be the death of me.* My hips move of their own accord, fucking my wife's throat. Tears stream down her flushed face. The sight turns me on as I pump into her mouth.

Okay, maybe I do get off on tormenting her, just a little. Mostly I love her determination and willingness. She's perfect for me.

My cock thickens and the alarm in her gaze pushes me right over the edge. I cry out, shooting ropes of cum down her perfect throat. And like a good girl, she swallows it down. All of it.

Finally, I pull out, allowing her to breathe again. She sucks in one breath of air after another, but her eyes show me only victory. She's proud of what she just did to me. Now, it's my turn.

I pick her up, planting her on her feet. "Take off your dress. Now. Or I'll have to buy you ten new ones."

She smiles, hastily doing as I command. I watch with feral satisfaction as she bares herself to me. She's so damn gorgeous that the sight of her physically hurts. My chest clenches. How am I suddenly the luckiest man in the world? When did my fortune change?

Elena saunters toward me. Grabbing her waist, I spin her around so that she's facing the bookshelf. My palms cover her hands as I press them to the smooth wooden shelves.

"Stay right there. Don't move," I growl into her ear.

My fingers glide up her arms to her bare shoulders, leaving goosebumps in their wake. I skim down the sides of her breasts and she shivers. I love how fucking responsive she is, how aware of my every touch, my every move. Pausing there, I weigh her ample breasts in my hands, then roll her nipples between my forefinger and thumb.

She gasps, arching her back into me. "Yes. Please. More."

I groan at her delicious pleading, then continue my path down the silky skin of her sides… hips… thighs, and finally dip my fingers into her pussy. She's so wet, the area soaked, her delicate skin damp.

I find her clit, teasing it with slow circles. Her whimper sends blood rushing straight to my cock.

But first, I need a taste.

Dropping to the floor, I rest my back against the bookcase and nudge her over until she's straddling my outstretched legs. Our difference in height is such that by sitting on the floor, my face is level with her sweet cunt. I lick my lips in anticipation.

She gazes down at me, her tan skin flushed a rosy red. Gripping her ass, I pull her pussy to my mouth and give her an open-mouthed kiss.

"Oh, please god," she moans.

"God can't help you now, *broc meala*, only I can." I flick her clit with my tongue. Tension ripples through her body, her thighs flex and strain. Diving in, I devour my pleading bride.

I show her with my tongue, mouth, and fingers how crazy she makes me. How I can't get enough of her, no matter how many times we satisfy each other. I've never felt lust this intensely before.

"Cian!" she cries out, her hands leaving the shelf to tangle in my hair.

I smother myself between her legs, forcing her to ride my face until she shatters. Her knees give out, but I hold her up, relentless in my mission to squeeze every drop of pleasure from her body.

She screams again. Her tense muscles begin to tremble. Her soft skin breaks out in goosebumps. When she fully collapses, I catch her.

Easing her down into my lap, I gently kiss her, letting her to taste herself on my lips. She moans, gliding her tongue against mine.

Jesus, I'm obsessed with this woman.

With one hand I pull her closer, as the other entwines our fingers, brushing against the plain gold wedding band. One day, I want to replace that with a Claddagh ring.

The impulse startles me. I've known this woman for

less than two weeks and I'm already thinking about giving her my heart. What the *fuck* is wrong with me? How has she gotten under my skin so quickly? Or am I that damn starved for affection, for touch, and acceptance, that I'm fooling myself into thinking she's safe? That she won't grow claws and tear out my heart one day?

I know better than this. I need to protect myself, especially from this siren.

She bites down on my lower lip and I groan. Maybe I'm past the point of self-preservation. Having her in my arms feels too good to ever push her away.

Fuck it.

We're married. Since I don't believe in divorce, this is forever for us. We're in this together for the rest of our lives. If I want to enjoy it, I'm going to fucking enjoy it.

My fears can't control me forever.

Breaking away from our kiss, I flip her onto her hands and knees, then position myself behind her. She arches her back, sending that perfect ass up into the air. I shove my knee between hers, so she spreads her legs wider.

Perfect.

Smoothing one hand over her ass, I dip my thumb into her wetness, teasing her with slow strokes. I slide that thumb up to her puckered, forbidden hole and ease inside. She tenses, holding her breath. I push all the way in before slipping out, then push in again, and again.

A low whimper escapes her lips. Her hips glide back to meet my thrusts.

Cock in my other hand, I position myself at her dripping entrance and ease inside. Her hot pussy envelopes my dick. I continue to fuck her with my thumb as I piston my hips.

"You feel so good, baby. You were made for me, weren't you?"

Her answer is unintelligible. Satisfaction unfurls in my chest. I love the fact that I can render this intelligent, head-strong woman down to nothing but wanton need.

One stroke of her clit is all it takes for her to fall apart. Her pussy clenches around my cock so hard for a moment I see stars. Inhaling deeply, I grit my teeth and ride through her orgasm. Then I take what's mine.

Wrapping my hand around the back of her neck, I press her face down to the plush rug and use my hold to keep her in place as I thrust. Punishing. Unrelenting. I destroy her beautiful cunt with my cock. I let myself go, lose control, and take her like the animal that I am.

She gasps and cries out. Her small body shivers beneath mine. I revel in every sound, in each shudder.

My spine tingles and my balls tighten. I fuck her harder, deeper, until I come with a beastly roar. Her body clenches around me, intensifying my own release.

We collapse onto our sides in a tangled heap of sweaty limbs and ragged breaths. I loop my arms around her, in desperate need of having her as close as possible. She trembles, but I know it's not from the cold.

Intense. That may have been the most intense sex I've had in my life.

How can I possibly keep my heart safe from this woman when she continues to surprise me, and continues to push me into uncharted territory? Every experience with her is like having it for the very first time.

I'm beginning to want everything with her. Even though we did things backwards by marrying first, I want to date her, to get to know everything about this amazing woman.

That's what I'm going to do. Tomorrow night, I'm taking her on a date. A real one, with flowers and everything. It'll be a surprise.

CHAPTER 13
Ravenna

"This is my favorite room," I murmur against Cian's chest, where we lay on the plush area rug in front of the sofa. "I could stay here forever."

"If you love this library so much, then I'll give you a key. Which reminds me... how did you get in here? I'm sure I didn't leave the door unlocked." Cian gazes curiously at me, and my cheeks flush.

"I have a secret. Something I've never told anybody about before." *Except my twin sister, of course.*

"Oh? Do you trust me to keep it, *broc meala?*"

My stomach flutters as I confess, "I do." I mean those words with all my heart. In such a short time, that we've spent mostly together, I've come to trust this big Irishman. He may be all scowls to the outside world, but to me he's *mi Irlandese.*

"Then tell me your secret." He smooths a strand of hair behind my ear.

"I picked the lock with a bobby pin. I learned how when I was thirteen and since then I... do it sometimes."

"Like when there's a locked door in the way of satisfying your curiosity?" He arches a blond brow.

"Exactly."

"You're full of surprises." His lips touch mine in the gentlest of kisses and I melt. "And so very clever. That skill takes practice, and much patience."

"You're not upset, or angry with me?" I wasn't sure how he'd react, but indulgent wasn't my first guess. My father would have been furious, and Matteo would have found a way to use my skill for his own benefit.

"Of course not. I will never be angry with you for telling me the truth. Honesty, remember? I value it above all else. Pick any lock you want, just tell me you did it. Always tell me the truth and we'll have no problems between us."

My breath catches in my throat. I need to tell him who I am. I need to come clean before it's too late.

Isn't it already too late?

My lips part then close, then part again. I must look like a fish out of water.

"What is it, *broc meala?*"

"I have to tell you something." I sit up, my brows pinch together. "But I don't know how or where to start..."

He props himself up on one forearm, his muscles flexing. "Start at the beginning."

"Right. I suppose that would make sense. The beginning." I lick my sore, puffy lips. "On our wedding day at the church—" My phone rings, drawing my attention. It's in my dress pocket. I ignore it, letting it go to voicemail. "At the church, I—"

My phone rings again. Whoever it is really wants to reach me. Urgently.

"I'm sorry. It could be my mother." I crawl over to my phone just as it rings for a third time, showing an unknown number. Cautiously, I answer. "Hello?"

"Ven?" Muffled sobs sound through the line. "Help me. I'm so scared."

My heart twists in my chest, and my stomach drops. "Elena, what happened? Where are you?"

Cian's questioning gaze cuts to me. In that instant, I realize my mistake. Her name slipped off my tongue. But my sister's safety is more important to me than covering up my lies, so I focus on the situation at hand. Consequences will no doubt come later.

"I-I don't know where I am. He s-shoved me out of a van and told me to call home on this burner phone. Can you come f-find me? I'm s-scared."

"Of course. Ping me your location."

"Yeah. O-okay."

My phone chimes and I glance at the pin on the map. "I'm coming for you right now. Just stay exactly where you are. I'll be there soon."

"Okay."

Reluctantly ending the call, I turn to Cian who's quickly dressing. "My sister's in trouble. I have to get to her right now."

"I figured as much." He tosses me my dress. "Send me her location. My men will provide backup."

Relief washes over me. He doesn't ask any questions,

just does what needs to be done. A cage of butterflies opens up in my stomach.

Dressed, shoes on my feet, and phone in hand, I follow Cian to his garage. He opts for a luxury SUV with blacked out windows. Wolfe and some of his other men meet us there, get into vehicles of their own and follow us out of the compound.

The navigation system directs us to Elena's location deep in Brooklyn, as my heart thunders and I scan the dusky streets for my sister. A million questions crown my consciousness. He shoved her out of a van. *Who?* It sounds like she was kidnapped. *Why?*

Has she been held captive the entire week I was enjoying my honeymoon in Key Largo? *Oh my god.* If that's what happened, then she didn't run from her arranged marriage, she was taken, and no one bothered to go looking for her. Papa and Mama just assumed she ran away. I did the same, for the most part.

Guilt pumps through my veins like a toxin.

All of us have let my sister down. We abandoned her when she needed us most. How can I ever make this up to her?

Did this strange man only hold her captive, or did he do other things to my sweet, innocent sister?

My throat tightens, making it hard to swallow. My palms grow clammy.

"There!" I point out the window as soon as a glint of dark auburn hair catches my eye. "That's her. Pull over."

Cian pulls up to the curb where my sister stands under a street lamp in a soiled dress. The same dress she wore on what was supposed to be her wedding day over a week ago. The vise in my chest cranks tighter.

As soon as the vehicle stops, I'm out of my seat, rushing toward Elena. Cian follows, but he's not looking at her, his attention sweeps the area for threats.

"Wait—!" Cian's command comes too late. I'm already at my sister's side, pulling her into my embrace.

She buries her face in my neck as her body wracks with sobs. She clings to me. I hold her tight and move toward the open car door. This could be a trap. Whoever took her could be waiting to ambush us.

I have to get her to safety. *Now.*

Cian's suddenly right beside me, practically shoving us into the backseat. He slams the door and returns to the driver's side. As soon as the SUV starts to roll, I focus my full attention on Elena.

"Elle, talk to me, tell me what happened. I've been worried sick about you." I buckle her in before securing my own seatbelt. "Where have you been? Did someone take you? We thought you ran away."

She shakes her head, more tears spilling down her pale, grimy face. "They did. They took me. I don't know where—"

"Who? Start at the beginning."

She shakily inhales and nods, eyes closed as she calms herself down. "I went to run a last minute errand. I don't even remember what I needed now, but something for after the wedding. I d-didn't even make it back to the car." Her whole body crumples with a sob. "They put a h-hood over my head and I think I was in a van..." She wraps her arms around her middle. "They kept me in a c-c-cage."

"Who are *they*? Did you see their faces?"

"No. They wore m-masks the whole time. Two men,

I think." She sniffles, wiping at her bloodshot eyes. "Only one of them ever spoke to me. That was a man for sure. A big, scary man." For the first time, her gaze takes in Cian. She flinches. "Big and scary like him."

"Do you remember anything else? Any details that might help identify them?"

"I... I don't know." Her voice drops to a whisper. "I was so scared. The big man killed the other guy. He just... shot him. There was so much blood. It kept c-creeping closer and closer to my cage."

I'm not sure what to make of her story quite yet. Why would one of them murder the other? But she's obviously traumatized. I hate to do this, but while it's fresh in her mind, I need to press for details.

"I'm so sorry you had to witness that. Right now I need you to think, Elle, did they make any demands? Did they say anything about a ransom?"

She shakes her head. "Wait. Yes. When they first took me, one of them said 'there'll be no wedding today'." Elena gasps. "They didn't want me getting married. Oh my god! The wedding. What happened? Are we at war with the Irish again? Papa must be so angry with me for not being at the church."

"Shh. Everything is all right." I keep my voice low. "I married him in your place."

"What? Ravenna, that's crazy!"

I cringe.

The SUV lurches to a stop. Cian turns around in his seat and clicks on the overhead light. I blink against the sudden glare.

When my eyes adjust, my gaze meets Cian's icy blues. He scrutinizes me and my sister. His features remain steely as myriad emotions storm through his stare. Interest, disbelief, shock, I read them all like an open book before seeing the flicker of betrayal and pain that disappears beneath his glacial shield. He gazes back at me with pure loathing.

Guilt knocks the air from my lungs.

"Cian, I can explain." My voice cracks. Pulse raging, I reach for him, but he dodges my touch. "Please let me explain."

"You're nothing but a lying, manipulative Italian whore." His words are like a slap in the face. I flinch. Elena gasps.

Cian turns around and starts to drive again, but I soon realize that we're not headed back to his compound. Even so, I keep my mouth shut. What can I say that will make everything better?

"What does he mean?" Elena asks in a hush. She's visibly shivering.

Shaking my head, I remove my coat and drape it over her shoulders. I'm unable to answer her as my heart feels like someone's driving a stake into it. The pain's so intense, it's blinding.

My world spirals around me. Descending into darkness. Guilt consumes me from the inside out. I never should have secretly taken my sister's place. I should have told Cian the truth as soon as possible, it's not like I didn't have an opportunity or two. And as soon as we returned, I should have launched a full scale investigation into Elena's disappearance.

I've failed both of them.

I spend the rest of the ride in silence, until we pull

up in front of my parents' house. A strangled cry tears from my throat. *No, please no.*

Where else would Cian take us other than home?

This isn't my home anymore.

Elena immediately bails out of the SUV and sprints to the front door. She's home. She's safe. But her refuge is my hell.

I stay rooted in my seat, unable to convince my limbs to move. I have a feeling that if I get out of this car, I may never find my way back to my husband again.

"Cian..."

He catches my eye in the rearview mirror. "I never want to see you again, *Ravenna*." He spits my name like a curse. "If you come near me, I'll put a bullet in your head, and two in your heart for good measure. *Get. Out*."

The backs of my eyes sting. He can't mean it. He's been my sanctuary, my hope, the man to unknowingly rescue me from what awaits behind that closed front door. I can't go back to that. I won't survive it.

I reach forward. "Let me exp—"

"Get the fuck out of my car! Now!" His deafening shout rings in the confined space.

"Cian, *please*—"

When he turns around in his seat, he glares at me. There's no warmth or affection in his features. I don't recognize the man staring back at me at all.

This is the face he shows to the outside world, not to me. Being shut out like this hurts.

He really is through with me. I blink. Tears trickle down my cheeks.

With a single nod, I slide out of the backseat. I have no choice now but to face the wrath of my father.

CHAPTER 14
Cian

Elena—no, *Ravenna*—shuffles out of the SUV as I seethe. I should have known she was too good to be true. Once again, I was an idiot, taken in by a woman's beauty and her deceitful tongue. *Liar. Snake.*

When I think of how she got me to open up and talk to her, how she seemed to care about me and my life experiences, my hopes and dreams, I feel sick. Devastated. Fucking stupid.

She fooled me good. If it weren't for her sister's sudden reappearance, I never would have found out I was living with a liar.

What was her end game? Did she really only take her sister's place for the sake of the treaty? I don't know many people who would sacrifice their life like that. It's too selfless. I don't believe it for a second.

She must have a more sinister reason. Is she a spy for the Italians after all? Or just a sick, twisted bitch with her own bloody agenda. Maybe she's a damn psychopath. Who the fuck knows.

All I know is that I'm fortunate to escape now rather than later. Before it's too late.

I probably should have killed her in this car. That's what she deserves. It would put an end to this bullshit and I'd never have to worry about setting eyes on her again.

But for some reason I can't bring myself to do it. Weakness. I'm a weak man, that's why. Weak and stupid.

Just like my ex said.

The back door shuts. The finality of that sound shakes something loose in my chest.

Facing forward, I drive away with such haste that the tires screech. Burned rubber taints the air. I have a visceral need to get as far away from her as possible, as quickly as I'm able.

That snake in the grass. That's what she is, my devious bride. She broke through my barriers so fast that she left my head spinning. No woman wants me just the way I am. She made me believe otherwise, but it's all lies. Smoke and mirrors.

I should have seen all the warning signs along the way. Too sweet. Too innocent. Playing hard to get, only to make me come out of my shell and try harder to be close to her, to be what she needed. To make me think I was what she wanted.

She knew how to play me, like she's a sports star and I'm the field.

I slam my fist against the steering wheel. *So. Fucking. Stupid.*

How did she know that her bull-headedness would

intrigue me? That her boldness would turn me on? Or how her seemingly compassionate nature would get me to open up? Where did she get her information?

Fuck.

Someone has betrayed me to my enemy. Was it Wolfe? He knows me well. Too well. Did he sell out to the Italians? Or is it another within our ranks?

No, it can't be Wolfe. He knows my history, he was there for all of it, but he wouldn't do this to me, would he?

At least this time I learned the truth about the Italian bitch before she decided to carve me up like a Thanksgiving turkey, and finish the job my ex started all those years ago.

My ex is dead. My brother's dead. I have to remind myself of these facts before I fall down a rabbit hole of paranoia. Even so, someone kidnapped Elena—my actual bride-to-be—with the intent of stopping the wedding. That person didn't know she had an identical twin sister. A fact not a single fucking person mentioned when I looked into the Pontrelli family.

Why did her family hide the truth?

Subterfuge.

But what are they after?

At this point, I'm sure that the peace treaty between our people was never supposed to last. How could it?

Damn it, I should have kept Ravenna and interrogated her until she finally, for once, told me the fucking truth. I just let that opportunity slip through my fingers. What was I thinking? *Idiot.*

I drive for a while, as it helps me think. If I go back home, I know I'll drag Wolfe in for questioning, along with half my men, and I can't do that without a clear plan. I need to figure out their motivation for betraying me first. Besides, what if they're loyal, and it was someone from my past who sold information to the Italians?

Another part of me wants to turn around and enter Lorenzo Pontrelli's house with guns blazing. Kill all those fuckers. Be done with it. Including my beautiful wife, but not before I've taken my pound of flesh from her delicate skin.

CHAPTER 15

Ravenna

"Where have you been?" Papa grabs Elena by the throat and shakes her. In the foyer's bright light, the bruises and dirt on her body are clearly visible. She's thinner than ever. Obviously she has been held captive, and mistreated.

But why would Papa care?

"Someone took me. I swear it. I didn't run away." Elena sobs, but she doesn't fight against Father, she knows there's no use.

He shoves her to the floor. "Go to your room. I'll deal with you later."

She scurries away, up the stairs to her bedroom, leaving me alone with our father. He turns his furious gaze on me and I wither. This evening I just don't have the strength to stand up to him, to be strong in the face of his punishment. My heart hurts too much. All I can do is try to hold the shattered pieces together.

Everything I did ended up being for nothing. My initial sacrifice to save the precarious peace treaty between our people means nothing. My escape from here was a temporary fantasy. I'm right back where I started. Only this time, I don't have my innocence to shield me from the worst of it.

I'm no longer a valuable commodity.

"Ravenna." His tone drips with disappointment. "Since you're here, I'm assuming O'Rourke learned of your deception. You've single-handedly destroyed the peace between us. You always were a fuck up." He slaps me across the cheek. The blow sends me staggering backward. "What? No smart mouth on you tonight? Did he fuck the insolence out of you? If I'd known that was all it would take, then I would have given you to my men years ago. Maybe I still will, now that you're nothing but an Irishman's filthy whore."

Mama steps out of the shadows, her arms hug her middle, her face pale. "Lorenzo, don't y-you think you're being unfair? S-she did all that could—"

"Shut up." Papa's punches suddenly rain down on her. She screams. Her delicate body falls to the floor, where her head hits the tile with a *thunk*.

"Stop!" I muster some of my courage and try to drag my father away from my unconscious, bleeding mother. His wrath switches to me, his fists flying at my face, my stomach, my arms.

Each hit sends a shock wave of pain through my body. I crumple beneath his assault, but that doesn't save me. His boot wreaks havoc on my thighs and ribs. My cries for mercy fall on deaf ears. Like they always have.

Once Papa has had enough, he bends, grabbing me by my hair. "Don't ever tell me what to do." He shakes me, agony sears my scalp. "At the church you should have come to me when your sister didn't show up. Your *cleverness* has gotten us into this mess. You're nothing but a stupid little slut. What am I supposed to do with you now, huh? You're worthless to me. If your brother was still alive, I'd let him have you."

His admission makes me gag. Acid burns my throat and nostrils. I can barely see his face through my tears, but his tone tells me he's smiling.

"Now get out of my sight." He releases me with a shove.

I groan, lying on the floor in my own blood. Every inch of my body throbs with pain.

Right now I wonder if I didn't make the wrong choice. Maybe I should have stayed in the SUV and endured Cian's wrath. A quick death would be welcome over this ongoing hell.

But this is my life. Always has been. Always will be, apparently.

For the first time in my life I wonder what it would be like to just give in. To admit there's no escape from here and accept that this is as good as it gets. To let myself die inside.

Wouldn't that be less painful than holding onto hope?

Papa lifts Mama's unconscious body and carries her further into the house. I don't know what he's going to do to her while she's out, and I shudder to even think about it. All I know is that he'll be occupied with her for some time. He always is after he beats her.

Crawling on my hands and knees, I move toward the staircase. The house is quiet, the staff vanishing as they always do when Papa is in one of his foul moods. Lucky them.

One step at a time, I lift myself up the stairs to the second floor, then crawl along the hallway to my bedroom door. Elena steps out of her room across the hallway. She drops to her knees beside me, her hands hovering over my beaten body.

"I-I don't know how to help you."

I do my best to wave her off. "Just open my door. I'll be fine."

She does as I ask, letting me into my room, then helps me to sit on the bed. I take a long look at her, noting how she doesn't appear much better than I feel right now.

She's bruised and dirty. I'm beaten and bloody. What a pair we make. I clasp her hands between mine.

"We'll get through this, Elle. I promise."

"I've never seen Papa so angry," she whispers as if he might hear us and barge into the room.

I smile at her innocence, which causes my lip to bleed more freely and dribble down my chin. Elena has rarely seen father's dark side. For some reason he spares her most of the time. I doubt she witnessed our brother's evil either. She's fortunate, and sometimes I envy her ignorant bliss.

But I have a terrible feeling that our entire family dynamic is about to change. I've seen hints of it since Matteo's death. Papa isn't in control of himself like he used to be. It's only a matter of time before either Mama or I end up dead because of his dangerous temper.

I just pray that Elena is spared. She's too sweet for the horrors of this world. And one of us has to make it out of here alive.

As soon as she leaves me to clean up, I send a text to Cian. I'd rather face him and his punishment than stay here a moment longer.

RAVENNA:

I'm sorry. You have to let me explain why I did it. It wasn't to hurt you. Please come get me, I want to go home.

CHAPTER 16
Ravenna

The next week passes in a blur as Elena tends to me, helping me to physically heal, and reminding me to eat. Depression has descended on me like an unexpected blizzard. I suppose it was that taste of freedom that makes being back here, under my father's roof, so unbearable.

Or maybe it's how Cian and I left things. That pained look in his eyes will haunt me forever.

He never answered my text message, so I can only assume he's leaving me here forever. Washing his hands of me.

"I don't think I'll ever be able to feel like myself again while living at home," I admit to Elena as we eat lunch together in the upstairs sitting room. Well, she eats, while I push my food around the plate. Not hungry.

"And I never want to leave the safety of home again," she murmurs.

"What a pair we make."

Elena's quiet, contemplative. "I'm sorry for ruining

your life, Ven. I should have stuck closer to everyone else, then none of this would have—"

"It's not your fault." I reach over and cover her hand with mine. "None of this is your fault. Someone wanted to stop our family from joining with the Irish—whether that person is one of theirs or one of ours I don't know, but this is not our fault. We're pawns in this game. Nothing more."

"But they won, didn't they? Isn't that why he let me go?" She turns her palm up and squeezes my fingers.

"I'm not sure why he let you go. As to who won, well, we are technically allies with the Irish now. I don't think a little thing like Cian dropping me on Papa's doorstep is going to make him call off this truce. As long as Cian and I are legally married, this alliance stands. It's only a matter of time before we find out if our families are truly joined or not." My free hand drifts to my stomach.

Elena gasps. "Are you pregnant?"

"I don't know yet. I should know in a couple more weeks."

Cian and I certainly had sex enough times for pregnancy to be not only possible but probable. One part of me hopes that I am carrying his child, that he'll be forced to take me back. Unless, of course, that's not enough of a reason for him to do so. Then I'd be stuck raising our child under this roof and that horrifies me into hoping that I'm not pregnant. Who knows what Papa would do to my baby. It would give him power over me, and probably over Cian as well.

I push that potential future from my mind.

"You could always take a test," Elena points out.

"I could. But I'm in no state to go out and get one,

and you're not leaving the house any time soon. I don't want Mama to know yet. I can wait."

"Good point. I hardly want to go downstairs these days. There have been a lot of people coming and going from Papa's office this week, some of them I'm pretty sure are Irishmen. They look big and mean."

My heart stumbles over itself. Has Cian been here? The thought of him passing through this place, going about his business as usual and ignoring me—it stings. Apparently I read way too much into our newlywed relationship. I thought we had a deeper connection, but it turned out to be just sex. I was nothing more to him than a warm place to wet his cock. Outside of that, I mean nothing to him.

This week has proven that. No calls or texts from him. He's simply gone silent, all but vanished from my life like a passing storm.

If only I could forget him as easily as he's forgotten me.

The fact that he has dismissed me so abruptly fills me with anger. The dangerous, explosive kind of rage. I don't like being ignored. What would he do if he was forced to face me? Make good on his threat and put a bullet in my head?

Some days, I want to find out. I want to stare him in the eye when he puts that cold barrel to my forehead and dare him to pull the trigger.

With too much force, I stand, my chair screeching backwards. "I'm going to go take a look for myself. Downstairs," I clarify to a bewildered Elena. "To see if my *husband* is here."

Storming from the room, I make my way down the

stairs to the main hallway. Papa's office is at the far end, overlooking the back garden. On silent footsteps, I march toward his door, only to have it open while I'm several feet away. My breath hitches and my heart stops. I don't know who will emerge from his office. At the last minute, I duck into the living room.

Papa's office door closes with a soft click. Peeking around the corner to get a glimpse of who exited. My entire body shivers with a chill, but I'm not sure why until I see her face.

It's Ginevra. My seventeen-year-old cousin. Her blond hair's disheveled, tears stain her face, and she's walking with her gaze angled down. What is my teenage cousin doing in Papa's office? Presumably alone. What has he done to her?

Nothing involving my father is above board or innocent. There's a reason she was in his office and it can't be anything good.

I'm torn between confronting her right now or keeping quiet and doing that when I don't look like a meat tenderizer met with my face. I don't want to scare her. Much less have to explain to her why I look like this.

My vanity wins out and I let Ginevra go. For now. But my mind races with possible explanations. Perhaps her father decided to let our don punish her for something. Not that I saw a mark on her skin. My instincts tell me the answer to her being here is much more sinister.

My father's an evil man, surely I'm not the only family member he torments for the fun of it.

I spend the rest of the afternoon lingering downstairs, avoiding both of my parents as they come and go, but not once do I spot a single Irishman.

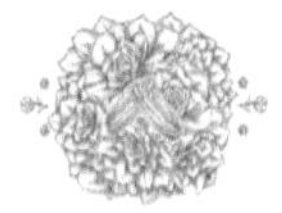

I smooth down my satin dress, my palms clammy. As self-conscious as I am to be out in public with my healing bruises—which are expertly hidden thanks to the best concealer in the world—Elena is a nervous wreck. She keeps dropping her fork and glancing over her shoulder like the boogieman is out to get her. After what she's been through, both the kidnapping and witnessing a murder, I can understand.

Tonight we're seated in a private dining room at *Barbetta*, New York City's oldest Italian restaurant. Its elegant, old-world atmosphere would be comforting, except for Papa's calculating glances, and the fact that he only takes the family out for a nice dinner when he's ready to announce one of his schemes.

He's about to make a move, and we're all his unwilling pawns. Whose life is he going to shatter this time around?

I'm seated with my sister and parents, my three cousins, and my aunt and uncle. Much to Papa and Uncle Davide's disappointment, their only surviving children are all girls. Which means we're commodities to be traded and used for their advantage.

Papa addresses his brother, "Our alliance with the Irish is sealed. They need this arrangement as much, if not more, than we do. They'll keep their word, even with how much Ravenna fucked up."

My head snaps up, but I stop myself from glaring at

Papa. He's right. I messed up. One massive lie destroyed my marriage, my chance at freedom, and my future. I royally screwed myself over. But none of that matters since the peace treaty will stand. In that regard, I did my duty.

Uncle Davide grunts in acknowledgment. "What are we doing about the Russians?"

A devious grin touches my father's lips, making my stomach sink. "I've been in negotiations with the Kozlov Bratva for three months now. They're ready to seal the deal." His gaze lands on Elena. "By marrying one of theirs to my daughter. This time, to the correct daughter."

Elena visibly shrinks in her chair, her eyes wide with horror. My gut twists. The Irish are known to be violent and brash, but they're nothing compared to the depraved Russians. They're animals. They'll eat my sweet sister alive, then pick their teeth with her bones.

"You can't do this," I state before my sense of self-preservation has a chance to interfere.

Silence descends on the table.

Papa's lip curls. "What did you just say to me?"

I swallow past the lump in my throat, square my shoulders, and repeat myself. "You can't do this. Not to Elena."

"I see. Well, since *you're* the don of the Pontrelli family then that must be true." His glare bores into me, but I don't flinch. It's too late to back down now. I'll stand up to him now and take my punishment later.

I glance at Mama. "Please, don't let him give Elena to the Russians."

She shakes her head, silently urging me to shut my

mouth. Everyone else at the table remains quiet, gazes downcast. I'll get no help from any of them. No one dares to stand up to the big bully that is my father and their don. They never have and they never will.

Realizing I'm all alone, I grind my teeth, giving in to the inevitable. Nothing I do or say will stop this from happening.

Papa continues eating, satisfied with his win. "The wedding will take place in two months' time. Buy a dress. The Kozlov's are arranging the rest of the details. They want to make sure nothing goes wrong." His sharp gaze cuts to me. "I'll make sure this time it won't."

The rest of dinner goes by in quiet conversation between Mama and my aunt, and Papa and my uncle. Elena and Ginevra both silently keep to themselves, while I manage to make small talk with my other two cousins, Sophia and Arianna, who are both close to my age.

Once Papa has married off his last daughter, he'll no doubt turn his attention to my cousins. Three more girls to be thrown at our enemies to form alliances, or given as gifts to those he wants to reward.

The entire tradition makes me ill.

I spend the car ride home dreading the punishment I'm about to receive for talking back to Papa. Especially since I went up against him in front of our immediate family. His ego has never been able to handle that kind of blow.

Except when we arrive home, he ushers Mama to their wing of the house, giving me nothing more than a chastising glare. The realization that he's not going to beat me tonight has the air rushing from my lungs.

Suddenly, I'm bone tired.

Elena and I climb the stairs. She stops in front of her door, gazing over her shoulder at me. "I love you, Ven, but you need to stop trying to stand up for me. I know my duty to this family. I'll marry whoever Papa wants and try to make the best of it. So please, stop angering him for my sake. I don't want you to get hurt. You've done enough already. Just stop."

"You know I can't do that," I mutter. "That's not who I am."

"I know. You're bold and brave. But I'll never be those things, and you can't protect me forever."

"No. But I can try."

She gives me a sad smile before slipping into her bedroom. I do the same, being sure to lock my door. It won't keep Papa out if he changes his mind, but at least I'll hear the key turn before he enters. Any amount of warning is better than none.

After some tossing and turning, I manage to sleep soundly for several hours, only to be woken by a sharp pain in my abdomen. With a ragged inhale, I sit up.

I'm alone. Darkness shrouds my room.

The pain comes again and this time I recognize it for what it is. Cramps. I've started my period.

Which means I'm not pregnant.

Devastation mixes with relief in a jumble of emotions. Cian has no reason to take me back now. Which means I'm stuck in this house forever. My only way out of here is forever gone. The last thread ripped away from me.

A muffled sob tears from my throat.

In a moment of despair, I send a text message into the void.

RAVENNA

Please, I'm begging you, don't leave me here.

Of course my text goes unanswered. He's done with me. After five more days , I have to admit that to myself. Cian really has abandoned me and there's nothing I can do to change his mind. But I'm done with remaining silent. The need to explain myself to him overrides any fear of his threats. So I lay it all out in one message after another. Maybe blowing up his phone will finally get his attention. Doubt it.

RAVENNA

I never meant to hurt you. When Elena disappeared on her wedding day, I took her place to ensure peace between our families. And to protect my sister from my father's anger. If a wedding hadn't happened that day, he would have hurt her, and I feared that you would have called off the truce. I wanted to stop the bloodshed.

RAVENNA

I'll admit that I had my own selfish motivations too. Marrying you was my ticket out of here. I never meant any harm. Obviously I didn't know about your past at the time. I understand how my deception looks. I know you think the worst of me. And I know I can't change your mind, but I can tell you my side of the story and why I did what I thought I had to do. I realize now that I should have come clean. I tried to when we were in the library, but then my sister called and everything blew up. I'm sorry for lying to you.

RAVENNA

The connection between us was real for me, and against all odds, I thought we actually had a future together. I know you don't believe me. How could you? But I want you to know that being your wife was the happiest week of my life. Lying to you is my biggest regret. I know you hate me, and that we can't fix this, but I needed to tell you the truth.

There. I told him what I needed to say. Too bad it's too little, too late.

In frustration, at myself as much as at him, I toss my phone on the bed and take a long, hot shower. If only the water could wash away my sins.

Finally explaining myself, even if in a text message that Cian will never read, leaves me feeling both unburdened and adrift. What do I do with my life now? I have absolutely no idea.

Clean, and gravely depressed, I exit the en suite. Only to stop short, when I find my parents in my room.

My pulse spikes. Why are they here? Instinctively, I tighten my robe around my body.

"What are you doing in my room?" My gaze flits between them, coming to land on Papa.

"I've been waiting to find out if O'Rourke knocked you up or not. Seems like he didn't. He's made it clear when I've met with him that he doesn't want you back. He said your usefulness has come to an end." Papa sneers, eyeing me. "Let's hope the next guy who fucks you is more satisfied with the goods."

My pulse thunders in my ears. "What do you mean? I'm still married."

"Marriage is a piece of paper. Since you fucked up and have become my responsibility again, I've been thinking about what to do with you. Can't marry you off again. Not legally. So I'm going to sell you. Tonight."

I gape at him. "You can't—"

He backhands me so hard that my lip splits open again, and I can already feel a bruise forming on my tender cheek.

"*Stop* telling me what I can and can't do. I can do anything I fucking want. Tonight, I want to sell you. You will make yourself pretty. That's final."

"I won't." I blink back the tears in my eyes. "I'm married. I don't belong to you anymore."

"Wrong. You're under my roof, which means you're mine to do with as I see fit. And you're no man's wife, you're nothing but a used whore." He glances at Mama. "Make her presentable or you'll regret it."

Mama nods and I stare at her in disbelief. I mean, she's always followed Papa's orders, but this... She can't go along with this plan. She's my *mother*.

Father approaches me, and I'm too shocked at first to react to his proximity.

Then I'm too late.

He takes my arm. A biting sting is the only warning I get before he empties a syringe into my shoulder. I struggle in vain. The mystery cocktail hits my system two seconds later.

The world tilts. My stomach heaves. I stumble.

"I figured you were going to be a problem. That should calm you the fuck down." Papa's words sound distant, liquified.

This is a bad dream. It has to be.

Through hazy vision, I watch Papa leave. Mama sits me down, then obediently starts drying my hair and styling it.

She does my makeup. All the while she murmurs meaningless, senseless words.

Please, God, wake me from this nightmare.

CHAPTER 17

Cian

"You're pathetic." Her voice taunts me. "One sweet word, one gentle touch, and you fell right into my hands. Did you really think I could love you over him? Your brother is everything. You're nothing. He should have consumed you in the womb."

"Why are you doing this to me?"

"Because I want to, Cian. You're so big and strong. Having you at my mercy, having this kind of power over you, is delicious. Addicting. It gets me hot. I can't wait to fuck your brother in front of you. But we can't have you getting too excited watching us, I don't want you to enjoy it, so..." She grabs my testicles, squeezing and twisting.

I scream in pain.

"Stop!" I jolt upright at my desk, alone, in the dark. I swat the phantom hand away from my crotch. My breath comes in ragged pants. Sweat trickles into my eyes.

The nightmares have returned with a vengeance

these past few weeks, ruining my sleep at night. Which is why I'm dozing off at my desk.

The last thing I remember was working on some accounts in the afternoon, now dusk has fallen over the world.

Groggily, I make my way into the bathroom for a quick shower. Since that awful night that I learned Elena —*Ravenna's*—secret, I've been sleeping on the couch in my home office, only venturing into the bedroom for a fresh set of clothes. Her amber scent still lingers in the room.

This time I skip the clothing and go straight for a shower to chase away my demons, at least temporarily.

Hot, pelting water helps bury my past in the recesses of my mind, which leaves my thoughts open to Ravenna's text messages from this afternoon.

Did I read them? Yes.

Do they change anything? No.

I've been through all of this before—with my ex, Fiona. She was kind, sexy, and adoring. We were madly in love. Until I discovered it was all a lie. Until she wasn't anything like the person she pretended to be for all of those months. If she could deceive me that thoroughly, then Ravenna can do the same.

She *has* done the same.

I'd like to think that I'm wiser now, that I can tell when a woman is lying. But obviously I'm not, and I can't. Ravenna didn't just lie about an insignificant detail, she lied about her *name*, her identity. If she's willing to go that far, what else is she capable of doing?

I've been through this before and I can't do it again.

The first time almost killed me. This time I'm sure it would mean my death.

That is why this stops here, before I get in too deep. I never should have taken a wife in the first place. But what's done is done.

I'll never let her or any other woman into my life again.

Ravenna and I are legally married for the sake of peace between our people. That won't change. But I never want to see my wife's beautiful face again. I can't stand the thought of being in the same room as her, much less trying to live together.

Fortunately, her father seems to understand. I haven't demanded recompense for his daughter's lies and the peace treaty stands strong. She'll live at home with her family, while I'm free to live my life as I see fit. Free of her.

Far away from conniving women who are too good to be true.

I shut off the shower with more force than necessary. Resting my forehead against the tile wall, I groan.

Too good to be true. Too fucking perfect. That should have been a red flag from the beginning.

It was. I chose to ignore it. I just wish I could stop thinking about her, about us, about how goddamn angry I am.

Once out of the shower, I place my dirty clothes in the hamper and wrap a towel around my waist. A knock sounds on the door. *What the fuck is it now?*

"Can it wait?" I call out, drying my hair with another towel.

"No."

Damn Wolfe. He's so fucking impatient.

I open the door an inch and bark, "What?"

"You're going to want to see this." Judging by his tone, I'm *not* going to want to see it at all. In fact, it's likely to piss me off—more than I already am.

"What is it?" I step out of the bathroom and fully into my office, where Wolfe points to his laptop sitting on my desk.

I lift a brow, prompting him to explain what's going on.

"So I've been keeping an eye on the various bratvas, just out of curiosity, and this caught my attention." He wakes up the laptop's screen. "One of them is hosting a pop up event, a flesh auction, tonight on neutral ground. I wouldn't pay much mind normally, except one of the girls is described as a red-haired Italian beauty. I mean, how many beautiful redheaded Italians have you seen around here? So, I took a closer look and found the pictures."

As he speaks, my fingers curl into fists. Rage vibrates through every muscle in my body.

When he brings up the images of Ravenna in lingerie, shackled to a flimsy bed frame, I see red.

"Apparently, her father took it literally when you told him you didn't ever want to see her again." Wolfe shrugs like he's not entirely sure what to do about the situation.

I pin him with a glare. "*That's my fucking wife!*"

"She deceived you, Cian. She's not really your problem any more. Are you sure you care what happens to her?" He eyes me, cool as a fucking cucumber.

"*Motherfuckers!*" With an animalistic roar, I

hurriedly get dressed in today's soiled clothes. "She belongs to me. What about that don't you fucking understand?"

Wolfe chuckles. Bastard.

"What's so funny?" I bark at him. "Never mind. I need to know exactly where she is, and—"

"I already put in the deposit to join the auction. You're bidder number fourteen. You better get going if you want to make it in time."

Tossing on my leather jacket, I shake my head. I swear Wolfe knows me better than I know myself. Of course I'm going to get Ravenna out of there. Nothing can stop me.

"Text me the details." I head out, catching the amused, smug expression on Wolfe's face. He knew this would be my reaction to someone trying to sell what's mine. He also seems to know how much she's gotten under my skin. Damn it.

In the garage, I opt for the fastest car. A motorcycle would be quickest, but I plan on bringing Ravenna home tonight, just not on the back of my Ducati.

Wolfe texts me the location as I zoom out of the driveway.

She's *my* wife.

Mine.

No one fucking touches her but *me*.

My temper has barely cooled by the time I arrive at the pinned location. I want to go in there, guns blazing, and kill every last fucker who saw those photos of my wife online.

But if I'm going to get her safely out of here, I need to

be strategic about it. Recklessness won't do either of us any good right now.

The pop up flesh market is held at an old, abandoned factory on the outskirts of the suburbs. The rough exterior sits in stark contrast to the expensive vehicles parked out front, there's everything from Porsches to luxury sedans. My sports car fits right in with the rest. Which tells me exactly where I stand—no better than the rest of these fuckers. I'll do anything to get what I came here for, just like them.

Inside, the venue bursts with life. Upon entering, I'm given a mask to wear that's the same as everyone else's. Plain and black. As well as a special device for bidding in the auction as phones are not allowed on the premises.

Servers dressed in glaring white uniforms offer drinks in the dimly lit space. At the far end of the stage, a single spotlight shines down on a rusty metal pole.

I'm not entirely sure what the pole is for until the auction starts. The first drugged up girl is dragged onto the stage, shackled to the pole, and instructed to turn this way and that so we all get a view of the goods.

My teeth clench, but I do my best to blend in with the rest of the audience. Some are here as spectators, but it seems most are bidding. The bidder numbers must have been given out at random because I found out about this party late, and there are certainly more than fourteen of us.

It's really too bad that I can't just kill all these fuckers and be done with it. They have no right to my wife.

A sudden pang of guilt hits my chest. If I hadn't abandoned her, she wouldn't be here. She wouldn't be subjected to these strangers' gazes. Since I doubt she'd go along with this auction on her own, who knows what her father did to her to get her here.

Fuck.

When the next woman is led into the spotlight, blinding fury threatens to overtake me. My fingers wrap around the railing in front of me, my knuckles white. My reaction isn't only because of all these men's eyes on my wife's scantily clad body, but because of her broken lip, the swelling around one eye, and the fading bruises on her ribs, arms, and thighs.

Someone is going to die tonight. That's a guarantee. A promise.

Seeing her again fills me with all kinds of mixed emotions. I've had time to think about everything that happened, and on reflection, I may have been in the wrong. I may have judged her too harshly.

Ravenna was trying to tell me the truth in the library before her sister called. I'd warned her enough times about lying to me, and she knew about my past at that point. She had every reason to believe that I'd react badly. But she wanted to confess anyway.

She was willing to put her faith in me, and what did I do? I turned my back on her, shut her out, and apparently delivered her to a monster.

Someone has been mistreating my wife. I won't let that stand.

I punch my bid into the device and watch the number rise as others bid on what's *mine*. I focus, keeping my rage at bay. For now.

There's no way I'm losing this auction, so I skip the suggested bid and type in one million dollars. Some asshole raises me to one point one mil.

Let's play, fucker.

I type in two million.

I'll spend every last penny of my significant fortune if that's what it takes. There's no price too high.

The auction house will take their cut, and the remainder will go to Lorenzo Pontrelli. A dead man walking.

Several seconds pass as my bid remains unchallenged.

Then it changes to two point five million, and I curse.

Scanning the room, I try to find the bastard who's still going up against me so I can drive my fist into his face. When his whereabouts aren't immediately detectable, I type in three million.

And wait.

Then wait some more.

A countdown timer appears on the device's screen. Thirty seconds.

Twenty seconds.

The last ten seconds feel like a lifetime.

I hold my breath. If anyone slides in at the last millisecond and outbids me, they're fucking dead. I'll hunt them down before they get a chance to touch Ravenna.

Five seconds left.

Four... Three... Two... One.

The screen flashes with a three million dollar bid.

I won.

Immediately, I head for the side door to claim my prize.

I hand my device over to the guard in exchange for

Ravenna's room number. That's all the information I need before I'm pushing past him and marching along the dim corridor to room number five, where I don't bother knocking.

I twist the handle and enter with so much force that the door bangs against the wall.

There, chained to a rickety old bed frame, sits my wife. Ravenna. The woman I never wanted to see again. Liar. Seductress.

Mine.

I go to her and drop to my knees, cupping her cheeks. Up close the damage to her face and body are even more pronounced. Her unfocused gaze shows the effects of the drugs coursing through her veins. I deeply inhale, trying to calm my flaring temper.

Someone signed their death warrant when they struck my wife. Was it her father? A guard?

On a growl, I ask, "Who did this to you?"

CHAPTER 18
Ravenna

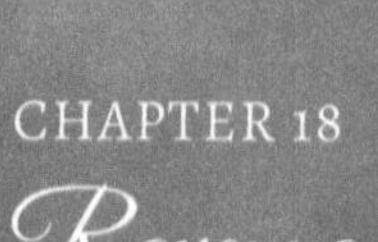

Embarrassment cloaks me. I feel sick to my stomach. I must be hallucinating that the man before me is Cian. Anyone could be behind that black mask. But the drug's effect is starting to diminish and his features are clear. Blond hair, pale blue eyes, strong jawline.

But it can't be him. Cian O'Rourke wouldn't rescue me. He won't even answer a text message. He hates me.

"Who hurt you?" he asks, tearing off his mask and throwing it aside.

It's him.

My shock battles with the shame of what just happened, of being paraded around half naked in front of strangers. Bid on like an object. *Sold* to the highest bidder.

All of it against my will, yet there's nothing I can do about it. My father sold me, now I belong to someone else. I may never see my family, my sister and cousins, again.

I slowly blink. Cian is still there when my eyes open. Why is he here? My brain feels so fuzzy, nothing makes sense, it's all emotion. A mixture of terror, shame, and disbelief.

"Did you come to rescue me?" My words come out slurred. "It's too late. It's over. Someone bought me."

His pale eyes burn with rage. "Yes. *I* bought you. You're mine. You'll always be mine."

"You..." I have to think on his words for a while before they make sense.

He bought me.

He owns me.

But he hates me.

"Why?" My question comes out on a sharp breath. None of this makes sense.

"Because you're *my* wife. Nothing will ever change that." His rough thumbs caress my bruised cheeks. Most of the damage is hidden beneath a thick coat of concealer. It hurts, but I welcome the pain, it helps to clear my foggy head.

"You came for me. After everything, you came to rescue me." Speaking the truth aloud makes it seem more real. Concrete. Irrefutable.

A sob rips from my throat. My body shakes as tears stream down my face.

Cian holds me close and drops his forehead to mine. "Of course I came for you, *broc meala*. You are, and always will be, mine to rescue. I never should have forced you away. I'm sorry."

No matter how hard I try, I can't stop crying. Relief mingles with despair and shame.

My parents sold me at a flesh market. My own

mother prepared me for this auction without so much as a protest to my father. I always thought of us as similar, as we both endured Papa's beatings. But I'm nothing like my mother. I never could have done what she did to my daughter.

And Cian... he came for me. After everything, he saved me.

I close my eyes and let my sobs taper off to hiccups.

Cian speaks against my ear. "Now tell me, who did this to you?"

I focus on his question. I'm about to tell him the truth when I realize the potential ramifications for doing so. At the same time, I can't lie to him. Never again. That's a promise I've made to myself and I intend to keep it.

"I can't tell—"

"You will tell me the truth. Right. Now." His pale eyes bore into mine, unrelenting.

"But if you know, if you act on it, then you'll destroy the truce." I slump. All remaining strength leaves my body.

"I don't give a fuck about the truce. Tell me, or so help me God, I will kill every Italian I set eyes my on."

I see the conviction in his gaze. He's not lying. Cian never lies. Which means I have a choice to make. Either endanger all of my family, my people, or sacrifice just one.

The decision isn't as difficult as I expected.

"My father," I whisper.

"He beat you?"

I nod.

"He sold you?"

I nod again.

"Good girl." Cian presses his lips briefly to mine. Then he stands and exits the small room, leaving me handcuffed and alone. Fear crawls up my spine. Is he going to leave me here?

I struggle against the restraints. They're old, rudimentary handcuffs attached to a chain that's looped around the headboard. I can't stay here.

Now that I can think properly, almost, the room still spins and shifts on occasion like a living beast, I pluck a pin from my hair.

Mama put it up so that my thick mane wouldn't hide my body from the men who wanted to buy me. I'm repulsed by the memory. How could she do that?

Working the pin into the cuffs, I manage to free myself just as the door swings open again.

I go rigid. My muscles coil with tension, ready to sprint away from danger.

Cian reappears. He drags in my father at gunpoint.

I blink twice to make sure that I am not hallucinating. This scene very well could be wishful thinking. A gruesome daydream.

"You can't do this to me, O'Rourke. We have a peace treaty," Papa sputters, face red and eyes bulging. I never realized how much smaller he is than Cian until now. Seeing them side by side, Papa seems like a small, frail man—which he is not.

Cian presses the gun into the back of Papa's head. "On your knees, Lorenzo. Now."

Papa seethes at me, as if this is somehow my fault.

Then, like all bullies, my father folds as soon as he doesn't have the upper hand. Flinging insults at Cian, he lowers himself to his knees.

"Confess," Cian demands of him.

"Confess to what? I didn't do anything, you Irish son of a whore."

Cian's jaw works for a moment before he says, "You beat your daughter."

Papa laughs. "The slut deserved it. And after you see reason and let me go, I'm going to beat her all over again. Maybe I'll even break a few bones this ti–"

Bang!

I jump and scream at the sudden, deafening sound. A few moments pass before I finally realize what happened.

Sticky redness splatters across my legs. Papa slumps, then collapses onto his face. That's when I note that the gun has a silencer, though the sound was still intense in this small space.

A pool of blood grows around Papa's head. He's dead? At least, I think he's dead. Though that seems impossible. Papa is invincible. No one can kill him. Many have tried over the years. He would never die. Until now...

But if death was that easy, someone would have put a bullet in his skull ages ago. They haven't because he's untouchable. Or so I've always thought.

"Ravenna. *Ravenna.*" Cian's voice snaps me out of my stupor. "We have to go. Now."

"Y-you killed him." I point out the obvious, unable to contain my thoughts.

Cian's lips form a tight line. "Yes."

"Are you insane?" Does he realize what he's done? With one bullet he's ruined the treaty.

"Probably."

"You've destroyed the peace between our people. This is a disaster. Why would you do that?" I wrack my brain for any logical explanation but my thoughts keep circling back to the same one.

I swallow hard, my stomach a flurry of butterflies. "You did this for me."

As impossible as that seems. It's the only answer. Isn't it?

Grunting, Cian undoes his shirt and drapes it over my shoulders. I shove my arms through the sleeves. The garment hangs on my form like a tent.

Scooping me into his arms, he carries me through the door. "Yes. I did it for you. And I'd do it again in a heartbeat."

CHAPTER 19
Cian

Insanity. That's the only rational explanation for what I just did. I worked hard for that peace treaty between us and the Italians, only to blow it all with a single bullet to Lorenzo's head. I fucked up, and the craziest thing about it is that I don't even care.

I won't uphold the treaty at the expense of my wife's wellbeing. Which makes me certifiably insane. I didn't even want this woman, or a wife, but now that I have her I'm never letting her go.

Not again. Not ever.

I glance over at her as I drive us home. She stares out the window, her eyes unfocused, and I wonder what drug they gave her. How long will it be in her system? The thought of her drugged and bound has me grinding my teeth, my knuckles white against the steering wheel.

She's obviously in shock, too. What will happen when she's clear-headed again? Will she see me for the reckless villain I am?

I murdered her brother, and now her father, too. She

was not only forced into an arranged marriage with me, but I also bought her at a fucking auction.

I own her twice over.

And I have every intention of keeping her for myself whether she wants to be with me or not.

It's my fault she was put up for sale. That never would have happened if I hadn't ditched her at her family home. An abusive household.

I'm not her hero. I'm certainly not her savior.

Lorenzo always rubbed me the wrong way, but I could never pinpoint why exactly. Now I know how he treated his daughters, probably his wife too. He was just as twisted as his son. Though better at hiding it.

"I'm sorry," I mutter, though I don't expect her forgiveness. "I overreacted that night in the car. Sometimes I see... sinister intentions where there aren't any. You selflessly took your sister's place, and married a stranger, for the greater good. And I punished you for it." I swallow the lump in my throat. "I'm sorry."

Her gaze slides to me. "I wanted to tell you the truth. I really did, but—"

"I know. I made it near impossible, but you tried anyway. You're a brave woman, Ravenna."

Her gaze brightens when I call her by her real name —instead of her sister's. *Ravenna*. I like her name. It suits her much better than Elena.

When we arrive home, I take Ravenna in my arms and carry her into the house. Wolfe's immediately on me, his glance catching on her crimson splattered legs. I have a visceral need to clean her father's filthy blood from her skin. To get every speck of him off of her.

"What happened?" Wolfe cautiously asks, following us through the house.

"I won the auction. Obviously. Lorenzo Pontrelli is dead. I killed him. You'll need to get the car's interior cleaned." That about sums it up.

"Jesus, Mary, and Joseph! Cian, can't you control your temper for one fucking minute?"

I snarl at him. "He beat my wife. He sold her. He confessed, and I fucking killed him. He deserved to die." No regrets.

"Well, now what the hell are we going to do? You can bet the Italians are going to come for us as soon as they find their don's body. They're going to want answers. Or they might just decide to massacre us all. Did you think about that?" He crosses his arms.

I grunt, open my bedroom door and head for the en suite. "I'll deal with it in the morning."

"Why not right now?" Wolfe insists.

"Because my *wife* needs me right now."

"*Jesus.*" Wolfe leaves in a huff. I know he's disappointed in me, but I'll deal with that tomorrow too.

Turning on the shower, I step inside, fully clothed, with Ravenna in my arms. Pink water circles down the drain as we stand in the spray.

I set her on her feet and go about unpinning her hair, then removing her bra and panties. The water reveals that most of her bruises were covered with makeup. She's a mottled mess of faded yellow, dark purple and blue. Lorenzo must have been beating her as soon as she returned home. As soon as I delivered her to his doorstep.

I grind my teeth.

Please, I'm begging you, don't leave me here.

Her text message haunts my memory. My chest clenches.

Lorenzo was tormenting her, and all I did was ignore it. *Fuck! I'm such an asshole.*

As gently as I can, I wash her fragile, battered flesh. She leans against me as I lather body wash over every inch of her skin, then rinse it away with the handheld sprayer. In silence, I wash her hair, rinse it, then condition her long auburn locks. A dark smattering of freckles grace her nose and cheeks, there's even a couple on her forehead.

As much as I shouldn't be turned on right now, I'm only human. She's gorgeous, soft in all the right places, and it's been nearly a month since we were together.

A twinge of emotion sweeps through me. At first, I can't place it. Then I realize, I fucking *missed* her.

Not only physically. Yes, I miss the sex. But more than anything I miss *her*. Being near her, her scent, the way she looks at me across a table. Her laugh. Her sassy remarks and that stubborn tilt of her head.

The way she screams my name when I make her come.

I bite down on my lip. This is neither the time nor place for dirty thoughts, so I ignore my raging hard-on and finish taking care of Ravenna.

Once she's clean, I turn off the water and wrap a fluffy white towel around her body. I take a minute to ditch my soaked clothes before looping a towel around my waist. Then I set her on the counter to survey the damage.

Fresh cut lip. Swelling. Bruises.

Fucking piece of shit bastard. If I could kill Lorenzo all over again, I would. This time I'd make him suffer. Kill him slowly so he could confess to every single one of his crimes against this beautiful woman. Torture him until he begged me for death.

"Is anything broken?" I ask, although I already know the answer from examining her in the shower.

She shakes her head.

"Good. I have some ointment for these cuts." I grab it from a drawer and apply a thin layer to her lip and eyebrow. Then I retrieve the arnica and spread it over her bruises. "I'll get some ice for that swelling."

She silently nods. I'm growing worried. Is it the drugs or the shock that's made her nonverbal? She always has something to say. Always.

I gently cup her face and rest my forehead against hers. Eyes closed, I say, "*Broc meala,* It's my fault that you're hurt. I never should have left you."

The man I was before I married Ravenna would never have felt like this. That past version of myself would believe that she deserved every bruise for lying to me. I would have called it justice. But something about my wife has changed me and I didn't realize it until this moment. Yes she lied, but she didn't deserve this. Any of it.

She sighs. "It's not your fault, Cian. It's mine. If I hadn't lied and pretended to be my sister, we never would have married. I ruined everything, even though I was trying to save it. I made this mess."

The very thought of *not* being married to her, to *Ravenna*—not Elena—guts me. I can't imagine myself with any other woman. Anyone other than her feels... wrong.

Fuck, I can't believe I crave this woman even though she deceived me. It's almost like... I've forgiven her. But how is that possible? Given my past, I don't forgive easily. Or ever. Yet here I am, ready to forgive her completely. Ready to accept her reasons and apology and move on with our lives. Ready to give us a second chance.

Who the fuck am I?

"Actually, I'm the one who fucked this up." I kiss her forehead. "We're married. What's done is done. Our issues are ours to sort out and no one else has any right to interfere."

"Will you ever forgive me?" she asks in a small voice that tears at my heart.

My cynical side rears its ugly head, reminding me that she could be acting. All of this could be one big illusion meant to deceive me, to play on my sympathies, to lure me in only for her to reveal her true, sinister nature.

But that's not rational thought, that's fear.

I shake off my suspicions. I can't keep living my life in fear. What are the chances that both women I'm drawn to turn out to be vipers?

With my luck? Ninety-eight percent or higher.

Shut up, I chide myself.

She pulls away, her gaze downcast. "I understand if you can't forgive me. What I did was horrible. I stole the future you should have had with my sister. You didn't deserve that. Now that I've had time to think about it, my sister might have made you much happier."

"No. She wouldn't have." I tilt her chin up until she

looks at me with those sad grey-blue eyes. "*You* make me happy. You're all I want. And I've already forgiven you. For everything."

"You have?" Hope brightens her tone.

"Yes." My fingers wrap around her delicate throat. "Just never, ever lie to me again."

She sucks in a shuddering breath. "Never. I promise."

"Good. Now we just need to figure out how to stay alive. We could be at war in the morning."

She gingerly licks her lips. "About that. I have an idea."

CHAPTER 20
Ravenna

Cian takes my advice and sets up a meeting with my uncle Davide, Papa's younger brother and next in line to be don. While my uncle is cut from the same cloth as my father, he's not a bully. He's never been wicked or cruel for the fun of it, as far as I know. If anything, he seemed to live in fear of Papa just like everyone else in our family. Hopefully, he'll let Cian explain and they can come to an understanding instead of starting a new war.

While Cian's on the phone sorting out details, I'm in our bed, exhausted. I swear this has been the longest day of my life. Tomorrow might be just as long, but for now, I let sleep take me.

At some point Cian comes to bed. The unfamiliar sensation of having a man beside me temporarily jolts my senses into high alert. But then he pulls me into his bare chest, his spicy and whiskey scent enveloping me, and it's like I never left the comfort and security of his arms.

Like this past month never happened. I doze off.

The next time I wake, it's morning and I'm alone. Cian will have already left for the meeting with my uncle. I cross my fingers that it all goes well. Somehow. God, give us a miracle today.

I shower, then reapply the ointment where needed. Most of my bruises are nearly healed, except for the new ones Papa gave me yesterday when I refused to willingly go along with his plan to sell me. Those ache, and my split lip and eyebrow throb. Even so, I've certainly been in much worse condition than this. And I'll never be hurt like this again, will I?

I can't believe he's dead. Matteo is gone, and now Papa is too. Both of my tormentors have forever been erased from my life.

I'm free.

We're free.

I throw on a pair of comfortable wool pants and a cashmere sweater, then sit on the bed and call Elena. She needs to know what's going on. I'm sure she thinks we'll never see each other again. Did Mama tell her how Papa sold me?

"Ven, are you okay?" she answers. "Where are you? Did a man *buy* you?"

"I'm fine. Cian bought me. He came for me after all. But there's something important you need to know—"

"Papa's dead."

"Yes."

There's a long pause on the line. "Mr. O'Rourke did it, didn't he?"

I hesitate to tell her the truth because the more people who know the more at risk we are of exposure.

But she's my twin and she deserves to know what happened.

"He did, but he was protecting me. He's meeting with Uncle Davide right now, so you just stay put until this is all ironed out. Okay?"

"Okay."

"How's Mama taking the news of father's passing?"

She must be devastated. Or perhaps she feels the same kind of freedom that I do, now that he's gone. He can never hurt her again.

There's another long, weighted silence on her end. "She's okay now."

"That's good. Then—"

"I found her body this morning at the breakfast table. There wasn't any blood, so I think she did it with sleeping pills." Her tone's calm, almost neutral. Distant.

Shock twists through me. Mama's dead? No, that doesn't make any sense, I just saw her yesterday.

Devastation settles like a heavy weight on my chest. She's gone. She took her own life. I try to wrap my head around this information, but it doesn't seem real.

Mama's free now, like me, why would she do this to herself—to us? Both of our parents dead in one night?

Alarm flashes through me, my grip tightens on the phone. "Elle," I say carefully, "are you all right?"

The idea of her being alone in the house with our deceased mother twists my gut. I need to get her out of there, but I can't go anywhere until I'm certain that neither the Irish nor my own people want me dead. Or to use me for leverage against one or the other.

"I'm fine." Her voice drops to a whisper. "I don't

know why but right now I don't feel a thing. It's like there are no emotions left in my body. I'm just numb."

"You're in shock, Elle. Just hold on. I'm going to send our cousins to get you out of there." I can't lose her too. It's all too much.

"No. I don't want to leave. It's safer in here than it is out there. Please don't make me leave. *Please.*" She whimpers.

"Shh, hun. You just stay right there. Okay?"

"O-okay."

With a heavy heart, I hang up. My emotions twist and swirl through me at a nauseating speed. I'm so relieved that Papa can never hurt me again, but Mama... Yes her last act toward me was unforgivable. But I don't feel the same hatred toward her that I do for my father.

She was his victim just as much I was. Now she's gone from our lives forever.

I need to get Elena out of there.

I call my cousin Sophia. She answers on the first ring.

"Soph, I need you to go get Elena. I'm sure you've heard that my father's dead. Mama killed herself this morning and Elle found her body." Those words still seem unreal. "She's in shock. I don't want her to be alone. But I can't go to her right now."

Thankfully Sophia doesn't press for more details or further explanation.

"Oh my god. Of course. We'll go there now."

"Thank you. Text me when she's with you and safe."

"I will." She hangs up.

I blow out a long, slow breath. Even though I'm Cian's wife, I don't dare leave the safety of this room until he returns. I'm sure all the Celts out there are just waiting to rip me to pieces, given half the chance. Cian may have forgiven me, but will they? Or do they still think I'm a threat to them? I won't risk it.

With a sigh, I settle in for a long day of worrying and waiting. And trying to process everything that's happened. There's nothing left that I can do except hope and pray.

CHAPTER 21
Cian

Behind Davide Pontrelli stand two men, bodyguards. His brother Lorenzo has been dead for less than twenty-four hours, so I imagine the Italian's are scrambling to reorganize where their leader is concerned. Has Davide even appointed an underboss yet? A consigliere? I'm guessing not since he's here without either. Which is fine with me. I'd rather negotiate with one man, rather than three.

I also brought two bodyguards, leaving Wolfe on the compound in case things go south. This meeting includes just us six men in a private room at *Spades* restaurant this morning. No show of power by either of us having too many men at our side. Weapons were left at the door, of course, though we both know the other is secretly packing. It's simply the way of our world.

"What's this matter you need to speak with me about so urgently?" he asks from across the table. "I'm a busy man. In case you haven't heard, my brother was murdered last night."

"Yes. I've heard. The late don Lorenzo is why I'm here. I—"

"Everybody out." He motions to his guards in dismissal. "We'll speak in private."

I watch his security detail leave the room before nodding to my men, indicating they should also go.

Once it's just the two of us, Pontrelli narrows his gaze on me. "Let me guess. You murdered my brother."

It's not a question, but I incline my head anyway.

He doesn't seem surprised by my admission. "Well that's a problem. It's unforgivable."

"Unforgivable." I mull the word around in my mouth. "What's unforgivable is the late don Lorenzo beating *my wife*. Selling *my wife*. He had no authority to do either. Ravenna *O'Rourke* belongs to me and only me. He was in violation of our contract."

Davide shakes his head. "You abandoned her, returning her to her father and therefore made him responsible for her again."

I grimace. That was my mistake, but it's no excuse for what her father did to her. "Where she lived has no bearing on the peace negotiated between our people. But I draw the line at having what's mine abused. I had every right to end don Lorenzo's life because of how he treated my wife. And he was in breach of contract by trying to sell her to another man." I lean forward on my elbows. "Would you not kill a man for beating your wife, don Davide? For disrespecting her, and you?"

I hold my breath, hoping this man cares about his own wife a fraction of how much I care about mine. Or that he at least cares about his reputation enough to defend it. A man disrespecting his wife would, by extension, be disrespecting to him. They are one and the same.

Several heartbeats of silence linger between us.

I read his answer clearly in his eyes before he says a single word. He has killed for his wife in the past. Of that I'm sure. But will he admit to it? Will he take my side?

Or will he defend his brother and throw away the peace between us?

The strained quiet stretches as Davide takes out a cigar and lights it, repeatedly puffing on the end as he considers his response.

I keep my mouth shut and wait. Sometimes silence is the best negotiation tactic.

Davide bobs his head, a thick cloud of spicy smoke escaping his mouth. "I would kill any man who dishonors my wife, but this is not the same. The man you murdered in cold blood was my brother and don of the Pontrelli family. I must demand a life for a life."

No fucking way.

"Lorenzo's death was vengeance. You can either accept that and we continue our peace treaty, or else it means war. I have the right to defend my wife—even from her own father and your family's don."

Davide sits back in his chair, studying me through narrowed eyes as he puffs his cigar. Once again, silence stretches between us, and my muscles bunch with tension.

This time, I can't tell what he's thinking. He could decide to go against his word and take me out right here and now. Problem solved. Though that would guarantee more blood in the streets, and no chance of a second peace treaty.

"You killed my family's don. If I let that go, I will look weak." Davide blows out smoke rings. "Luckily, no one knows it was you. Except me, of course. My men are tracking down my brother's killer as we speak. It's better for both of us if they don't end up on your doorstep."

I study his relaxed expression. "I want to keep the peace between our people."

"So do I. Which is why a man will be publicly executed at an event that shows our solidarity."

"What do you have in mind?" I sit back in my chair and it creaks under my weight.

"A fight night. One of your guys against one of mine. The best from our ranks. Better make it a good show to give my people what they want to see. Blood."

"Done."

He leans forward. "There's one catch. Your Irishman has to lose the match. That's my price for keeping your secret."

"Done," I grunt. It's a small price to pay to keep the peace and my secret safe.

Davide nods. "We'll set it up for tomorrow night on neutral ground. I think the Kozlov Russians will accommodate us at *Riot*."

"Agreed. We'll be there." I stand, ready to end this meeting, when a thought strikes me. "Davide, I have a sensitive question for you."

He grunts and inclines his chin, signaling for me to continue.

"Did anyone on your side kidnap Elena Pontrelli in an attempt to stop the wedding, and therefore the peace treaty?"

"No." He taps cigar ashes into a tray. "With the

number of loved ones we've lost these past few years, my people are all on board for peace. If anyone tried to interfere it would be on your side. You should search out that Judas."

"I see. I will." At this point, I have to take his word for it. I don't see any reason for his people or mine to want to stop our alliance. We've both seen too much bloodshed, lost too many good men. Which means the interference came from the outside. This piece of information I keep to myself—for now.

But who could it have been? The Russians? Doubtful as they are seeking their own alliance with the Italians, and so far my people don't have any beef with the bratvas. But there are so many others who could want to stop us. The Albanians, one of the Cartels, maybe even a single person with a grudge. The possibilities are endless. Unfortunately.

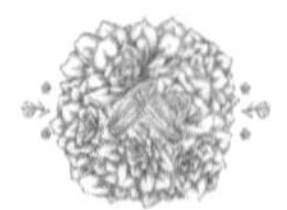

"Cian, you can't do this." Wolfe stands in my way, as if that will stop me from exiting my own house. "Let me do it. Let me go in your place."

I sigh, tired of this argument. "No. That's final. It's also an order."

"Fuck you, you stubborn bastard," he says, but his tone holds no venom, only exasperation. He looks tired.

"Keep my wife here and safe. That's what I need you to do."

Heels click on the tile floor of the entry hall, alerting

me to Ravenna's arrival. "I'm not staying here while you get repeatedly punched in the face."

"Oh?" I lift a brow. "Is that something you'd like to see, *broc meala?*"

She folds her arms. "With how stubborn you're being about this, yes, I very much want to see someone punch you in the face. You should let Wolfe do the fighting. What are people going to think when you, leader of the Gaelic Devils, loses the match to an Italian?"

Wolfe stands in the background, scrutinizing Ravenna. He has yet to warm up to her, much like the rest of my men. Which is fine, I don't want them getting too cozy with her. They need to keep their interactions professional.

I shrug. "They'll know I threw the match."

"Oh really? How's that?" Her hands land on her hips. Fuck, I missed her sass.

"You're so sexy when you're upset with me." I step closer to her, trailing my fingertips along her rigid jawline. I bend down for a kiss and she lets me press my lips to hers. I hum with approval.

"This is the way it has to be. If I put anyone other than myself in that ring tonight, my men will be upset when they lose. But they know me. They know I don't go down easy. They'll see this for what it is—a peace offering in blood."

Ravenna huffs in frustration and I pull her in for another kiss. It's the most sexual contact we've had since her return. Her healing bruises give me pause about touching her anywhere else.

One more lingering kiss.

Then it's time to go.

I point to Wolfe. "Keep her by your side at all times."

His brows reach his hairline. "You're letting *her* come with us?"

"Believe it or not, my wife is as stubborn as I am. There's no point in arguing with her once she's made up her mind about something. Now come on. The car's waiting." I jog out the front door, duffle bag in hand.

There was never any question in my mind about who to put in the ring. It has to be me. The Italians will get the show they want, of one of their own beating the shit out of me, leader of the Irish. And my men trust my authority. Once I lose, and order them not to retaliate, they'll honor my wishes. It's a win-win.

This fight is in the spirit of solidarity. Good old fashion sportsmanship. We all understand that.

The Kozlov Russians agreed to let us hold the fight at *Riot's* underground arena. They will also be there to ensure the peace. No blood will be shed on their turf, outside of the ring. Inside the cage is an entirely different matter.

As the car starts to roll, I pull Ravenna into my side, unable to keep my distance from her now that she's with me again, in my arms. Where she always should have been.

Guilt claws at me as I dwell on everything she's been through since I rashly returned her to her father. I'm not sure I'll ever be able to forgive myself.

She's mine to protect, and I gravely failed in my duty.

Kissing the top of her head, I murmur, "How are you doing?" I don't have to say more than that, she knows what I'm talking about. My question encompasses everything from how she's feeling both physically and emotionally. I also want to know how she feels about her parents' deaths. Everything.

"I'm okay, I guess. Still reeling a bit. My sister's staying with our cousins, but I want her to come live with us after tonight. I need to keep an eye on her after... everything that's happened."

"Consider it done. And the funerals?" A sliver of guilt cuts through my chest knowing that I'm responsible for not only the deaths of her brother and father, but also, in a way, her mother.

If one day Ravenna turns on me, I'll know why. I'll also know I deserved it.

I've destroyed this woman's family. My only hope at making amends centers on treating her sister and extended family well. So long as they deserve it. Ravenna loves her twin, so I'll do what I can to help the girl.

"My aunt is already arranging the funerals. We'll have to attend, but I'm worried about Elena's safety. The man who took her is still out there. Isn't he?"

"My people are continuing to look for him. The Italians and I will have top-notch security at the funerals, so don't worry about that." I pause, gazing down at my beautiful bride. "I'm sorry about your mother. Truly."

She leans into me, wrapping her arms around my waist, and sighs. "I'm so conflicted about my feelings for her. She's my mother, and I loved her, even though she always did what Papa wanted. Even the last time I saw her, she was the one who did my hair and makeup." Her voice catches in her throat. "She made me pretty for the auction. What kind of mother does that? I hate her for doing that, but I still love her. I don't know. It will take me some time to figure it all out. In the meantime, I'm so worried about Elena."

"We'll take care of her. I promise." I hold her tighter, closer.

"Thank you." She rests against me, like I'm her rock.

An hour later, the car pulls into the underground parking garage at *Riot* and we all step out. In another few hours, it will be show time.

CHAPTER 22
Ravenna

"Welcome, family, friends, and allies," Uncle Davide, the new don of the Pontrelli family, addresses the Italians and Irish with Cian at his side. "Tonight we have justice for the tragic loss that we have all suffered. May my brother, and our beloved late don, rest in peace."

Everyone repeats the sentiment. The words taste like ash on my tongue. My father was not a well-loved don among his people. All of this is for show, and Uncle Davide is a good showman, giving the people what they want. He's even nice enough to briefly mention my mother's death, attributing it to her love and devotion to my father.

A ridiculous lie, of course. But it's what everyone wants to believe.

Or is it a lie? Why did Mama kill herself? I suppose it could have been that she didn't know how to live without Papa. Or was she consumed by guilt? Or some other motive entirely?

I'll never know. Her reasons died with her, since she left only the briefest note: *I'm sorry*. Unless she said something more to Elena, but it doesn't sound like they spoke that morning. I'm tempted to ask my sister, though how much more anguish will I put her through? Do I really need an answer? I might, just for my own sense of closure.

Uncle Davide gestures to Cian. "This treachery almost ruined our new treaty with the Gaelic Devils. It almost set us back to a time of war, of blood running in the streets, of all of us losing loved ones again." He lets the too fresh horror sink in. "But we were smart enough to see right through this devious plot. The Irish didn't murder my brother." He points into the ring. "That man did. And tonight he will be delivered the justice he deserves."

Two beefy Italians drag a bound man into the fighting arena. A black hood hides his identity, and he must be gagged because his voice comes out muffled. I haven't a clue who the so-called traitor might be, but my guess is that he crossed Uncle Davide and now he's been made the fall guy.

His life will be taken instead of Cian's. One man's sacrifice will preserve the delicate truce between our peoples.

My uncle gives a grave nod. We all watch as one of his soldiers puts a gun to the prisoner's head, and unceremoniously blows his brains out.

Blood and gore splatter everywhere. Cheers rise up all around me. The people have their vengeance, the issue's solved, and now we can carry on with our lives.

My uncle speaks over the roaring sound, "Now we celebrate!"

The two guards drag the dead man's body from the arena, leaving a smear of bloody gore on the ground. No one bothers to mop up the blood.

I catch sight of Cian shaking Uncle Davide's hand before he meets his opponent in the boxing ring. It's a slightly elevated space with chain-link fencing surrounding the arena. I'm seated with Wolfe in the front row, for the best view of the fight.

Irish versus Italian. The crowd around me goes wild, practically salivating in anticipation of this mostly friendly competition. No one else knows the fight is fixed.

My stomach churns, queasy with nerves. Unfortunately, I know how this has to end, and I don't like it one bit.

The boxers take their corners. Little Italy versus The Beast. Both large, muscular men, and seasoned fighters.

A whistle splits the air.

The fight begins.

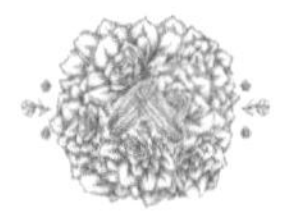

P*ainful.* That's the only word to describe what it's like to watch Cian get hit over and over again. I regret ever saying that I wanted to see this. I take it all back. Each blow to his flesh seems to physically hurt mine. How he's still standing, continuing to endure such violence, I don't know.

This fight seems to be lasting for hours. They're already seventeen rounds into it. Which is absolutely ridiculous.

Wolfe sits beside me in the packed seats, his stoic exterior in stark contrast to my gasps and cringes. While the Irishmen around us shout in frustration, my kinsmen on the opposite side of the room cheer, their bloodlust insatiable.

My soul burns with discomfort. I should be seated with my own people, yet I am now bound to the Celts. My loyalties are torn. Yet, in this moment, I wish Cian would fight back, even though I know he can't, and won't. Not really.

The fighter called Little Italy has numerous fresh bruises forming, one side of his face speckled red, but he's in much better shape than Cian at this point.

My husband takes another hit, stumbles back several feet, but remains standing. *Bastardo testardo.*

I'm beginning to feel remorse over my insistence on coming tonight. The heavy, metallic scent of blood hanging in the air makes me nauseous, and I'm not sure how much more of this I can take.

How much more can Cian take?

Every time he falls, he stubbornly returns to his feet, though each time is slower, more sluggish, than the last. He's gotten his fair share of hits in, his opponent will be hurting tomorrow, that's for sure.

But now his swings are laden with exhaustion, it's clear in every line of his overtaxed muscles that he's spent. Why doesn't he just stay down? What more is there to prove? Especially when he knows he's going to purposefully lose this fight in the end.

I'm starting to suspect that my husband might be a masochist. Does he feel the need to punish himself for some past wrong? Or is he punishing me for my harsh words earlier? If that's the case, I'm ready to tap out.

Come on, Cian, stop this now. Please. I'm begging you.

His opponent delivers an especially wicked right hook, so powerful that blood sprays over the audience on that side of the cage. Which only has them cheering louder.

I cringe with disgust.

Looking to Wolfe, I ask, "Can't you put an end to this?"

"Nope." He glowers. "If he has any teeth left after this, I'm going to knock them out. Stubborn fucker. This should have been long over by now. Those Italian bastards are getting far more out of this than they deserve."

I quickly glance at him, but his gaze remains fixed on Cian. I haven't forgotten about his threats to kill me if I hurt Cian. Hopefully, he doesn't blame me for our current circumstances. Though who else could be at fault? I'm the reason Cian's in that ring and taking this beating.

Guilt slams into my chest.

"I can't watch another second of this. I need to leave. Now." I stand. Wolfe gets up too, muttering curses under his breath as he scowls.

"We can't just walk out of here," he protests, but I ignore him.

We can and we will.

"Leaving gives the wrong impression." He sounds annoyed.

I don't care if *mi famiglia* sees me as weak. I can't watch another second of this carnage.

As soon as we near the exit, a raucous cheer shakes the walls. I glance back to find Cian passed out, lying in the dead man's blood from earlier. His opponent raises his bloody fists in the air and the Italians go wild.

Finally, it's over.

Instead of relief, I'm furious. Turning back, I march toward the fighting platform. I have some choice words for *mi Irlandese*—once he's conscious.

Gesturing at a blood-covered, unconscious Cian, I turn to Wolfe. "Will you get him out of there and bring him home? As soon as he's awake, I'm going to kill him."

"You'll have to get in line, sorceress." Wolfe grumbles, but does as I ask. He and two other men haul Cian from the ring and get him into the car.

I cradle his swollen, brutalized face in my lap. Blood smears my clothing, ruining a nice silk dress, but I don't care. It's an insignificant casualty of this evening. Much like the man who died in that arena for a crime he didn't commit, all to preserve a much more important peace treaty.

We ride in silence as I fume. Cian has the audacity to snore. I glare at him, unamused.

Once home, they get him out of the car and upstairs to bed, where we assess his wounds. Wolfe had the foresight to have the doctor on standby. The older man quickly appears when we decide that Cian needs more than ice and bandages, but stitches too. Not to mention, to make sure he doesn't have a damn concussion after all the hits he took to his head.

None of this helps lighten my mood.

Wolfe helps me give Cian a sponge bath, removing the majority of the blood and sweat from his skin. It's hard to tell how much of the blood is Cian's and how much belonged to the dead man.

The elderly doctor works silently, but efficiently on Cian's deeper gashes. "He has a mild concussion, but nothing to worry about for now. He has quite the thick skull. Let him rest, and let me know if his symptoms get any worse."

"Thank you," I tell the doctor.

Wolfe escorts him out, then disappears around the corner.

Alone with my sleeping husband, my anger and worry marginally fade. I lean down and press my lips to his, relieved that he's alive and not irreparably damaged.

"Are you worried about me, *broc meala*?"

Startled, I jolt upright. "I thought you were asleep, or unconscious."

"I am. Mostly. Sleeping." He cracks open a swollen eyelid, taking me in. "You're covered in blood. Are you hurt?" Fully alert, he struggles to sit up.

I grip his shoulders and try to shove him back down, but even in his weakened state he's so much stronger than I am. Giving up, I fold my arms and glare at him.

"No, I'm not hurt. This is *your* blood, you damn fool."

Relief washes across his rugged, bruised features. His shoulders slump and he relaxes against the pillows.

The corners of his lips twitch. "Damn fool, huh? So you do worry about me."

"I'm half-tempted to kill you myself after what you put not only me, but Wolfe, through. Watching you get beat to a pulp is not my idea of a good time."

A deep chuckle rumbles in his chest. "Wolfe can stomach it. And I warned you not to come."

"That's completely beside the point," I grumble. "Don't you dare turn this around on me. You're the one who insisted on taking that beating. You could have ended that fight long before you were knocked unconscious, but you didn't. You're a goddamn masochist."

Heat rises up my chest and neck, and I clench my fists. This man infuriates me by simply existing.

Cian grunts. "So I might be." His gaze flashes with interest. "But you... you care about me. Act mad all you want. You're only upset because you care."

I open my mouth, only to snap it shut a moment later. How can I argue with that? I mean, I could argue, but we'd both know it was a lie, and I promised never to lie to him again.

"That's what I thought." He drags me on top of him, his mouth claiming mine. His kiss bold, desperate, and a challenge in itself. He's daring me to try to reject what's growing between us. "You're so sexy when you're mad at me, baby," he murmurs against my lips.

"Cian," I chide, trying to climb off of him. "You're supposed to be resting. Doctor's orders."

"Yeah. Mm-hm." He nuzzles my neck as his hands slip beneath my skirt, resting on my thighs. "It's over and we've come out of it alive. And together. I don't want anything to ever tear us apart again."

I gaze into his pale blue eyes, seeing the sincerity in them. "Neither do I. Promise me, *Irlandese.*"

"I promise to never let you down again. You're mine and I'm yours, until death do us part."

"Until death." I seal our promise with a kiss.

CHAPTER 23

Ravenna

The frozen winter ground must have given the grave diggers a challenge. I sympathize with them as I stand before Papa and Mama's coffins, with Elena at my side, in the frigid weather. Today the cemetery is full of Italians, *mi famiglia*, the truce is too fresh for Cian to be here in person, though I know he and his security men lurk at the perimeter.

This is a family event, so I'm under my uncle's protection. As the new don, Uncle Davide is the ultimate authority now and I feel much safer with him than I ever did around my own father. So I'm not worried for myself.

It's Elena that I'm concerned about. My cousins and Aunt Rosa had to literally drag her out of their house this morning. Now she stands beside me, quiet, but in a vacant kind of way. She should be crying over the loss of our parents. She's always been sweet and emotional like that, not hard as stone like she is right now.

As far as I know, Mama and Papa never abused her. She was our brother's favorite. He doted on her while he harassed me. Even though we're identical twins, our personalities are so unique to each of us that we have always been treated differently.

I don't know why I've always been everyone's punching bag. Because I can take a hit? My strong personality hasn't done me any favors, that's for sure.

Whereas Elena is the type of sweet that makes everyone treat her like a fragile object. She's pretty, agreeable, and docile. Her tone's always polite. She's the perfect princess in every way. Everything a mafia man wants in his ideal wife.

Though she's different now. Being kidnapped, and witnessing two deaths, changed her. Understandably. But I'm afraid that I'll never get my twin sister back, that she's as dead as our parents even though she walks among us.

That fear makes me feel so alone. I've lost everyone but my sister. I can't lose her too.

I'm not uncaring toward our mother and father, but even as the priest says his words, I can't summon up a single appropriate emotion to express. I struggled with the same when we lost our brother. Does that make me a bad person? Am I somehow as rotten as my brother and parents, but don't know it?

Maybe that's why they beat me. They could see a reflection of themselves in me and they hated it.

We're supposed to love our parents—even if they are terrible people. We're born with that expectation ingrained in us. I'm not sure when my love for them turned sour, but it did at an early age. Yet, even after everything they put me through, I feel guilty that I despised them both.

My father had been terrible to me for years, so it's no shock that I'm relieved that he's gone. But Mama... I thought we were on the same side. Until she completely betrayed me the night of the auction.

She never even said she was sorry. Unless that's what her suicide note meant? I don't know. I'll never have any concrete answers.

I'm not sure how else to feel as I stand here. I'm not going to lie to myself about my feelings toward them. Nor will I gaslight myself into believing the past is anything other than what it was.

Mentally shoving away my self-analysis, I bow my head and lace my fingers with Elena's. As the caskets are lowered into the graves, many people step forward to toss flowers and other mementos to be buried with them. We follow their example. I toss a white rose into each of their graves, finally feeling a twinge of sadness and sympathy for my mother. Nothing but loathing for my father.

I can't imagine the horrors she faced being married to Papa. Perhaps I should forgive her weakness, because would I have acted any differently married to a man like him?

He broke her. Given enough time, he would have broken me too.

Maybe. Maybe not. Either way, I don't have to find out.

Relief settles over me as we amble toward the waiting car. It's over. Not only the funeral, and burial, but also the past twenty-one years of my life. My childhood is gone. My brutal adolescence is done. The traumatic beginnings of my adulthood are over.

I'm free of those who tormented me my entire life. That realization seems surreal.

Given the stress of the past week and a half—being auctioned off, my father's death followed by my mother's suicide, narrowly avoiding another mafia war, then Cian's fight—I attend the reception hosted by my aunt and uncle for the minimal amount of time possible.

I suffer through all the condolences, trying to sound like I'm grieving that my parents are six feet under. When all I can think about is how my sister and I are free of them. Free of our toxic upbringing.

Wrestling with my guilt takes a toll as well. By the time I can escape, I'm exhausted and want to go home.

I go in search of my sister, finally finding her staring at the floor in a corner. "Elle, you're coming home with me. Grab your coat."

She silently nods. We head for the door, but we're intercepted by our cousin Sophia.

"She's welcome to stay with us indefinitely," Sophia glances between us. "Mama said it's the least we can do."

"Wait here," I tell Elena. Pulling Sophia aside, I lower my voice in the crowded room. "I appreciate everything you've done for her, but Elle is my responsibility. I want to keep her close and make sure she's going to be okay. I'm worried about her."

"Me too." Sophia chews on her bottom lip.

I frown as I gaze at my twin, who continues to stare at the floor. "Please tell me your father isn't going to uphold the plan to marry her off to the Russians. She wouldn't survive it."

Sophia wrings her hands, catching my full attention.

She's struggling to find the right words, to be diplomatic. What is she so concerned about?

"Spit it out," I tell her. "You know you're not good at keeping secrets from me."

A wry grin briefly flits across her lips. "True. And no, Elena doesn't have to worry about the Russians. Now that Papa's the don, it makes more sense for our alliance with the Russians to be through our immediate family. Which means..." She glances away. "Which means it falls on my shoulders, since I'm the eldest."

"Oh, Soph." I grab her shoulders and pull her in for a hug. "I'm so sorry. I don't wish those brutes on anyone."

She hugs me back. "I don't know if it will be that bad. I get to start dating my fiancé soon, so my experience won't be anything like yours. I'll at least get to know him before our arranged marriage happens. Besides, you survived the Irish, and we thought they would be horrible. Remember all the terrible stories the aunties used to tell us about them?"

I snort. "The aunties are terrors. But you're right, I might even find happiness with Cian. He's nothing at all like I expected—mostly. I mean he is huge and can be mean, he has a temper too, but there's so much more to him. I hope your Russian match goes as well as mine."

She stares at me for a moment. "You had to pretend to be your sister—who got kidnapped—then your husband ditched you when he found out, only to have your parents try to sell you on the flesh market. No offense, but I hope my marriage match goes *way* better than yours."

I laugh, drawing startled glances, and immediately sober. "Fair enough."

My cousins, uncle, and aunt know most of the details of what recently happened to me, but everyone else is in the dark. Which is where they will stay. I don't want anyone spreading gossip or half-truths. My parents' memory should be untainted by their last few actions in this life.

The official story is that Papa was murdered at the auction house, where he was conducting business, by an opportunist with a grudge. That man was executed before everyone's eyes on the night of the fight. Mama couldn't live without him and took her own life. Elena and I are now orphans who've suffered a tragic loss.

Only Uncle Davide, my sister, and myself know the truth of my father's death, and that's how it's going to stay. If any other Italian learns that Cian pulled the trigger, we'd be back at war in an instant.

That secret will die with us.

"In all seriousness, are you sure you're okay?" Sophia studies my face, searching for clues of the truth. I haven't confided in her, or anyone else, about all the past abuse from my father. I'm too raw to talk about it. Elena would never divulge my secrets, so I'm not concerned about her revealing anything to our cousins.

"I'm not okay, but I will be. Until then, I need to be strong for my sister."

Sophia glances at Elena. "Yeah. Given everything you know about Cian, can you imagine him married to her instead? I mean, that's how it was supposed to happen."

An uncomfortable sensation slithers through my stomach. I don't want to even think about my twin with my husband. He's *my Irlandese*.

Shaking off my unease, I consider her question, but the answer's obvious. "They would have been a terrible match."

"I guess it was fate that you ended up taking her place." A soft smile graces her lips.

"I suppose so." All the what-ifs plague my mind for a moment before I push them aside. "I'm taking her home with me, but if anything changes, or it doesn't work out, I know she can always come here. So thank you."

"Of course. And I'll text you when I find out which Russian I'll be marrying next year."

"You better." I hug her again, then usher a zombie-like Elena out the door.

Her eyes widen with fear as we step onto the sidewalk and a black SUV pulls up to the curb. It's the most emotion I've seen from her in days.

Cian exits the passenger side, then opens the back door for us. I push my reluctant twin inside, noting how her whole body shakes, and I don't believe it's from the chilly late winter air.

"What's wrong?" I ask in a hushed tone. "We're safe now."

She shakes her head. "We're not. Safety is an illusion. Anything can happen to us in this car, anyone can get at us. And... they're *Irish*, how far do you really trust them? Don't forget they murdered our brother."

I swallow down my shallow but reassuring response. She's suffering from some sort of post-traumatic stress, which is completely normal, but I don't know how to deal with it. How do I make her feel better when she's right, safety is not only an illusion, but often fleeting.

We're never guaranteed anything in this world other than eventual death.

God, I sound morose.

But I'm not going to sugarcoat anything for my sister either. That won't help her get better.

"I trust Cian with my life." It's the truth. The rest of his people, I'm not so sure about.

"I don't." She peeks at him. "He's big and scary. He killed Papa and Mama too. I don't understand how you can like him even a little."

"I know him," I attempt to explain. When she doesn't answer, I ask a question that's been on my mind for a while. "Did Mama speak to you the morning she died? Do you know why she did it?"

Elena's silent for a few breaths. "No. Not a word. The new maid brought me breakfast that morning and told me they found my father's body last night. I ran downstairs to find Mama. I looked all over, no one had seen her in a while and they assumed she was in her room grieving. That's when I found her body. And that note."

I hold her hands. "I'm so sorry you had to go through that. That's awful."

A pang of sadness hits me hard. I guess Mama really couldn't live in this world without Papa. Even though he was her abuser too.

Elena whispers, "The man you married did this to our family."

"I know. I wish I was sorry, but I'm not. You saw how Papa hurt me, and how Mama helped him. I'm not sorry Papa and Matteo are gone." Finally, I voice the hard edged words. A sliver of guilt pierces my chest. "I'm sorry Mama couldn't embrace a future free of Papa."

"Me too." She sighs. "I wish we could both go far, far away from here."

"I know." I drop my arm across her shoulders. "You'll be fine. You are safe with me. You know I'll protect you with my life, don't you?"

"Of course I do." She rests her head against mine as we head home.

CHAPTER 24

Cian

"Please, Cian, I can't breathe." My ex squirms beneath me, trying to free herself from the hold I have on her neck. Her pleading only makes me squeeze harder. I've lost count of the number of times I've fantasized about wringing the life out of her. The way her skin would redden, her lips turn blue, and her eyes bulge.

I want to watch that spark fade as her gaze stares blankly at the ceiling.

"Cian—" She slaps me.

My eyelids fly open.

The scene in front of me shifts, the bedding becomes a starker white. The red hair splayed across the pillow is a darker shade than before.

I blink. And Ravenna materializes before me.

My hand strangles her long neck.

Her blue-grey eyes are wide with terror.

Tearing myself away from her, I scramble out of bed. I stare back at her as she sputters and coughs, trying to catch her breath, and massages her rapidly bruising throat.

What the fuck have I done? This isn't a dream. It's a living nightmare.

Disgust—at myself—slithers through my chest. I hurt her. That realization hits me like a boulder.

I stand next to the bed, paralyzed. I have no idea how to deal with this situation, with the ramifications of my actions.

Fists at my side, heart pounding, I insufficiently mutter, "I'm sorry."

Unable to bring myself to meet her gaze, I stumble into the bathroom and turn on the shower. I need to clear my head. How much of that was a dream versus reality? I rake my fingers through my hair. Gripping tight at the scalp, I tug.

Fuck! I really fucked up, there's no doubt about that.

I step into the shower's spray as my mind races with possible courses of action. Ravenna deserves a better apology, and an explanation, at the very least. My intention wasn't to kill *her*. It was a dream.

How am I ever going to make her feel safe with me again? I'm no better than her brother and father. I could have killed her this morning. Accident or not, it doesn't matter.

I punch the wall. The tiles crack and cave in. My knuckles split from the impact. The pain helps clear my mind. Then, the shower door opens and I'm reeling again.

Startled, I glance at Ravenna. Healing bruises mottle her naked body. A deep red rings her neck, and guilt smashes into me like a wrecking ball.

I did that. I hurt her.

I'll never forgive myself and neither will she.

"Cian." Her voice draws my gaze to her eyes. She searches mine, then takes a step closer.

"Stop!" I shuffle backward. "Don't come near me. I'm dangerous. I almost murdered you and would have if you hadn't woken me up. I'm so sorry—" My anguished words falter.

"I forgive you, *Irlandese.*" Her use of that endearment paired with those three words, leave me confused. She can't possibly forgive what I've done. Doesn't she realize how serious this is?

Ravenna steps closer, crowding me until there's no more room to retreat. She cups my cheek. Her other hand slides up my chest to the back of my neck. On her tiptoes, she pulls me down for a gentle kiss.

"I'll never let anyone hurt you like *she* did." Her breath brushes against my lips. "This isn't the first time you've spoken her name in your sleep. Let her go, Cian. For me, let go of her memory. I don't want another woman in our bed, even if she is a ghost."

Fiona has plagued my nightmares again, in a way she hasn't in years. They started back up when I abandoned Ravenna and they haven't stopped, even though I have my wife back.

"Let me help you forget about her." Ravenna drops to her knees and takes the head of my cock into her warm, wet mouth. My fingers automatically fist her hair. I can never deny this siren anything.

"You don't have to do this." I groan as she takes me deeper. "*Jesus.*" Her mouth feels so good, heavenly.

Pulling back, she releases my cock with a *popping*

sound. "We haven't had sex since... before everything that happened. I know we both needed time to heal, but I'm not waiting a second longer. I need to feel you in me. Please."

That's all she needs to say before I'm lifting her from the tile floor, pressing her back to the wall, and giving her what she desires. My mouth crashes down on hers in a desperate need to taste, claim, devour. When she moans my name, my restraint snaps.

I line my throbbing dick up with her entrance and thrust. She cries out as I bury myself deep in her pussy. For a long moment that's where I stay, sheathed, surrounded by the woman I'm falling in love with. I revel in the feeling of her body. My thumb slips between us, and circles her clit.

"I'll never be able to forgive myself for hurting you, baby."

Her soft gaze claims mine. "It was an accident. You were having a nightmare, which is something you can't control." She loops her arms around my neck. "I don't want to live in the past. Step into the future with me, Cian. Let's leave it all behind. Can you do that?"

"I can try." I rest my forehead on hers. "No, I can do better than that. I'm done living in the past, too. All I want is us and our future together."

She exhales against my lips. "We can have that. Now fuck me."

A weight lifts from my shoulders. My chest grows lighter, airy. Heaven sent this woman to me. An angel. My very own angel.

CHAPTER 25
Ravenna

"If you could find the man who kidnapped her, then she wouldn't be terrified all the time," I tell Cian over breakfast, as I sip my Earl Grey latte. "She might leave her room, or even the house. She can't go on living like this. Are there any clues? Any leads? It's been weeks since Elle's moved in with us."

Even though our honeymoon is long over, we're still in that phase. Enjoying each other's company, we take breakfast in the privacy of our room every morning. I love having Cian all to myself for a while before he goes to work. Which he does for a few hours before we have lunch. And by *lunch*, I mean mid-afternoon sex in his office. My husband's insatiable appetite matches mine.

Since that morning he accidentally tried to strangle me to death, we haven't spoken of it again. Not because we're trying to avoid the subject. If anything, an easiness has entered our relationship, a harmony that wasn't there before. We're open with each other. Real with each other in a way that has my heart singing every single moment we're together.

Cian sighs. "Whoever he is, he's gone. Vanished without a trace, and we haven't heard so much as a rumor about him. I'm sorry. There's nothing more we can do."

"Didn't the apartment give you any clues? What about the police report?" I'm unwilling to let this go. We need answers.

"All we found out was that the apartment was rented under the name of the dead man. Police identified him, and we looked into his background. For all the good that did. Turns out he was dying of a terminal illness, on one last vacation here to New York City before he died. The man was from California. He had no connections to any gang or criminal organization. No one has any idea how he ended up involved in Elena's kidnapping. The place was wiped clean. No prints or anything to tell us who the other man was. Any trail he might have left has gone cold by now."

I set my cup down. "That's just... frustrating. Are you sure it's where my sister was held captive?"

"I saw the cage they kept her in." He grimaces. "For now, there's nothing more we can do. I'm sorry. Of course we'll be vigilant, but that's all we can do for now. I'm sure the bastard will come at us again, another way next time, and that's when we'll catch him."

"Are you telling me there's nothing to do now but wait?" I don't know how long I can remain on pins and needles.

"That's right. I'm sorry, for all of our sakes."

Disappointment hits me right in the chest. If there's nothing more we can do, then that means Elena will live the rest of her life in fear of pretty much everything. Fear of being taken and held hostage again, of being used as a pawn to get to one of us. Fear of leaving the house. Of living a life.

That's unacceptable. But what do I do now?

"Is that therapist doing her any good?" he asks, sucking on a piece of orange.

I shrug. "Not that I can tell, but these things take time. It could be months or even years before she sees the benefits."

Cian grunts.

"Although..." Considering an idea, I chew on a piece of toast. "All of her bad memories are tied to this city. What if we get her out of here, far away from this place? Maybe give her a new identity and put her somewhere safer? Do you think that would make a difference?"

"It could. It's worth a try." He eyes me. "Where would she go?"

I don't even have to think about it, the answer's that obvious. "Italy. We have a lot of family there. Enough that she could blend in and disappear among them all. I'm sure someone would be willing to take her in for a while."

"If that's what you think she needs, then I'll have the jet fueled up and ready to go. Just say the word."

I smile like a love-sick fool, unable to hold back how happy this man makes me. He always says the right thing. Does the right thing. And it's all for me and those I care most about.

Am I falling in love with my husband?

"Why are you smiling like that?" he asks, right as my phone chimes with multiple texts.

"You. You make me happy." I pick up the device, and groan.

"What is it? Someone I need to kill?" He teases.

I roll my eyes at him, but inside, my stomach flutters. "No one to kill—except maybe Sophia's fiancé. She's texting me about their date last night. The man either ignores her or criticizes her for what she eats. I want to punch Nikolai Kozlov in the face."

Cian laughs, a sound I immensely enjoy every time I hear it. "Do you want me to start a war with the Russians for your cousin's sake?"

"Absolutely not. You're unhinged," I mutter with a smile.

He flashes me a wolfish grin, then drags my chair across the floor until I'm as close to him as possible. "I'm unhinged for you, *broc meala*."

His seductive kiss causes my mind to blank. Suddenly, nothing else is important, there are no pressing concerns. My entire world begins and ends with his taste, his scent, his warmth.

This man who rescued me from a fate worse than death, who chose me over peace, holds my heart in his hands. I moan into his mouth.

"If you keep making that noise, I won't make it to my office this morning," he warns, but I know it's an invitation, a tempting offer.

Reluctantly, I pull away. "You need to go downstairs. Now. Wolfe accused me of monopolizing your time and attention the other day."

"Did he? That bastard." Cian shakes his head, but his tone holds no heat, only amusement.

"But it's true, isn't it? Are you neglecting your duties

because of me, Mr. O'Rourke, leader of the ruthless Gaelic Devils?" I tease.

His grin returns. "Of course I am. You're my wife. You're supposed to be my primary focus, steal all my attention, and infiltrate my every thought."

My heart leaps. "I don't think your men agree."

"Fine." He sighs. "From now on, I'm giving Wolfe additional responsibilities so he spends more time working and less time complaining about you."

I giggle. "*That's* your solution?"

"Damn right it is." He stands. "I'm going to offload half of my work onto him so I can spend those hours between your legs and in your arms."

I quietly grin at his back as he leaves our bedroom. He *wants* to spend time with me. That realization makes me giddy, hopeful.

We've spoken many deep, meaningful words to each other since he rescued me, but words are words. Actions speak much louder, and are more sincere. His actions give me hope for a happy future together. Maybe even for love someday.

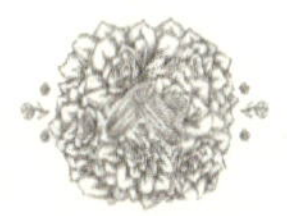

"Elena, please come out of your room. I'm begging you." I knock again at her door. "It's just dinner with me and Cian. No one else will be there. I promise."

"I can't. Don't you understand? He's so big, mean, and scary looking. He *ruined* our family. Plus, I don't like the way these Irishmen look at me. I'm not leaving this room—ever."

I groan in frustration. Recently, Cian and I have been so wrapped up in each other that I feel guilty about not paying enough attention to my sister. Besides her therapist, who comes to see her twice a week, Elena won't allow anyone else into her room. Not even me, and that hurts.

Her meals have to be left in the hallway. She manages to slip out and grab the tray when no one's around.

I understand why she's holding a grudge toward Cian, she has every right to her feelings, and maybe I'm crazy for not hating him. But if I had to choose between my father and Cian, I'd choose Cian. If the choice was between my brother and my husband, again I'd choose Cian. There's no world in which I wouldn't choose to be with the man who makes me happy every single day.

But he doesn't make Elena happy. All she sees is the blood on his hands. Her trauma's all wrapped up in him.

Even so, I'm trying to find peace between them. Tonight I thought I'd try to lure her out with a nice family dinner.

Which is not going as I imagined. Am I delusional to try? Maybe.

Will Elena always see Cian as the enemy? Probably. I sigh.

"Fine. I won't bother you anymore." My forehead rests against the wooden door. "I love you, Elle. I'm so sorry for everything."

With another heaved sigh, I turn away and head to the dining room. On my way, I pass by one of the compound's recreational rooms, which brims with conversation and laughter. These Irishmen are a rowdy bunch, but they don't bother me as much as they used to anymore. I'm starting to grow accustomed to their culture.

Similar to us Italians, they are family focused. Many of these men are related to each other either directly or distantly. Cian's clan is composed of four main family lines, him being the last of the O'Rourkes until we have a child. He's distant relatives with the McIvers, and somehow the Cullens and Teagans share the blood of an ancient Irish king. Apparently that's enough for them to call each other family.

I don't dare ask for clarification due to the fact that these Celts haven't warmed up to me at all. They seem even more uncomfortable now that Elle's living here too. Like one Italian woman wasn't bad enough, now they have two in their midst.

Maybe bringing my sister here was a bad idea.

Two men spot me as I walk past the doorway, and they immediately lower their gazes. Cian really did put the fear of god into them. I just hope they don't hold it against me forever. The respectful distance they keep from me serves as a constant reminder that I'm an outsider, a stranger.

On entering the dining room, I find Cian slouched in a chair. He straightens up, peering at me with a questioning expression. He's cleaned up more than usual tonight, his wild hair secured at his nape, clean shaven, and he's wearing a dark blue suit with a pale colored tie. He would appear more businessman, and less Irish mobster, if not for his facial scars.

"She's not coming," I inform him, taking a seat.

"I'm sorry." He sounds sincere, though he's losing patience with Elena. He hasn't said anything about it yet, but I can tell by the way he clenches his jaw when we speak of her.

"I'm not sure how to—"

The door bursts open. Elena stands on the threshold wearing a soiled, mismatched pajama set. Dark circles surround her haunted eyes. Her hair hasn't been brushed in weeks.

My lips part in shock at her appearance.

"I..." her voice croaks. "I'm sorry." She takes one look at Cian and bursts into tears.

Standing, I hurry to her side and wrap my arms around her trembling frame. "Shh, it's okay. I've got you." Tossing Cian an apologetic glance, I usher my twin from the room. "Come on. We'll eat in your room."

We make it back to her bedroom without running into anybody. Thankfully. As soon as we're inside, her ragged breathing evens out.

Firmly closing the door behind us, I dial the kitchen and inform the staff of our change in dinner plans. Then I send a quick, apologetic text to Cian. He responds instantly with a kissy emoji—which makes me smile.

"I'm sorry, Ven, but I can't be around that man. Or any of these men." Elena hugs herself as she stares out the window that overlooks the backyard. This time of year, the landscape is just beginning to bud with Spring. "I've been working on it with my therapist, but I don't think that will ever change. It's not just how many of our people they murdered. Large men *terrify* me. They all remind me of the man who kept me in a *cage*."

"I understand, I do." I plop down on her unmade bed. "I've been thinking—and don't take this the wrong way—but maybe you need to leave the city. Or even... this country."

She faces me, her bloodshot eyes alight with curiosity. "Where would I go?"

"Italy." I lick my lips. "I'm not trying to get rid of you, so don't start thinking you're too much of a burden or anything. Getting far away from here might be good for you. Of course, I'd visit—"

"Yes." She settles beside me. "I want to go. I *need* to go. I'm going crazy here, but didn't want to say anything, afraid you'd think I'm ungrateful. You've done so much to help me. But I need space. I need to find a way to help myself."

I pull her in for a hug. "I'm so glad we're on the same page. It's settled then. I'll make some calls and hopefully you'll be on your way to Italy soon."

Her sigh of relief tugs at my heart. "Thank you."

A knock sounds at her door, and her entire body goes rigid. I smooth my hands down her arms. "It's just dinner."

"Right." She visibly swallows. "Okay."

I go to answer the door, letting in the staff member who's kind enough to bring up our food, and my stomach drops at Elena's reaction. She's frozen in place as the old Irish butler sets the tray on her table.

The man couldn't be intimidating if he tried. His hands shake with a tremor as he removes the tray cover. I've spoken with Cian about letting him retire and live out the rest of his life in peace. Apparently, the ancient man *is* retired, and this is what he's decided to do until he drops dead.

Some of these Irishmen take loyalty to a whole other level.

As he leaves, my concern falls on my twin. She hasn't made any progress at all.

She's right. At this point, she does need to figure out how to help herself, because I'm all out of ideas. I just pray that she heals. Somehow. Someday.

CHAPTER 26

Ravenna

Two weeks later, it's time to say goodbye to my sister. Finding relatives in Italy, willing to take her in for as long as necessary, took longer than I expected. Not only did I have to find her a place to live, but also guarantee she'll be protected and well hidden. I'm now confident that she'll be safer over there, away from this city, and given a new identity to travel under. A fresh start.

Uncle Davide was understanding enough to lend us a couple of Italian bodyguards as Elena's escort. They're men, but they aren't *Irish* men.

"I'll miss you so much." I hug her tight for what must be the hundredth time this morning. "When you're ready to come home, just tell me and I'll be there in an instant to get you moved back here."

"I will. But don't hold your breath. I'm not sure I ever want to set foot in this city again." Her gaze flits around the tarmac as if she's expecting a viper to strike her out of nowhere.

"I understand." I do, but it still hurts to see my sister leave. I miss her already.

God, please help her, and keep her safe in Italy.

I watch her warily board the jet, a piece of my heart going with her. Cian, who had been giving us space, comes up beside me, wrapping his arm around my waist. I breathe him in, taking comfort in his unique scent.

Now, all of my immediate family is gone. Either dead or traveling thousands of miles away. Tears well in my eyes, and seeing them, Cian tugs me closer.

"We can visit her whenever you want. Just say the word, *broc meala,* and we'll be on a jet."

I nod, clinging to his arm. When it begins to rain, we head back to the town car, where I watch the jet taxi, then take off, disappearing through the low cloud cover.

My heart constricts. A deep sense of loss pools in my chest. Why does her leaving feel so final? Like I'll never see her again?

Beside me, Cian sighs. "You're strong, capable, and have such a big heart, Ravenna O'Rourke. You welcome my touch, and can stomach the look of my scars. You make me happier than I've ever been in my life." He laces his fingers with mine.

"You know I—"

"I'm not finished yet. What I want to say is, I'm so very grateful that you took your twin sister's place at that altar and became my wife. I can't imagine my life any other way."

My breath catches, my heartbeat fluttering at his sweet words. I know he forgives me for deceiving him in the beginning, but I didn't know, until now, that he's actually *grateful* for the outcome of my deception.

Thankful that my rash decision has led us to each other, and exactly where we're supposed to be.

He glances out the window. "Marrying your sister would have been a disaster for all of us."

Once again, that queasy, pained sensation slithers in my stomach. Cian is mine, *my* husband, and I don't want to think about him with my sister or anyone else.

"She was different before she was taken," I say in her defense.

"But she's always been timid, right?" Cian's features darken. "At least that's what your father promised me. A timid, quiet wife."

I nod. "She's always been the shy one."

He lifts my hand to his lips, gently kissing my fingers. "Well, turns out I like my wife *difficult. Challenging. A real harpy.*"

I laugh as he repeats the words he unknowingly called me on our honeymoon, when he thought he was speaking about my twin instead of me.

"I'll show you a real harpy, Mr. O'Rourke." I climb into his lap, straddle his thighs, and playfully bite his neck.

His head falls back with a moan. He palms my ass, dragging my body closer to his. "Fuck yes, Mrs. O'Rourke. That's exactly how I like it."

A delighted shiver runs through me. This man has owned my body for a while now, but I'm beginning to suspect that he also owns my heart.

I think I'm falling in love with my husband.

"I need you to hold that thought," he says. "We have somewhere to be."

"We do?" I'm not aware of any other set agenda

today apart from seeing Elena off. I can't believe she's really gone.

"Yeah." He doesn't elaborate.

The car rolls forward, and I climb off Cian to settle into my own seat, wondering where we're going. Gazing out the window, I realize we're driving further into the airport instead of toward the exit. Two minutes later, we stop beside a helicopter.

I shoot Cian a questioning look.

"It's a surprise." He takes my hand, kisses my fingers, then helps me out of the vehicle.

A porter grabs two suitcases out of the trunk and carries them to the waiting helicopter. When did my sneaky husband pack for us?

Curiosity sears through me as we're helped into the chopper, our seatbelts secured, and given headsets so we can speak to each other over the roar. Then, in a matter of minutes, we're airborne.

I admire the breathtaking views as we fly over New York City. Headed east.

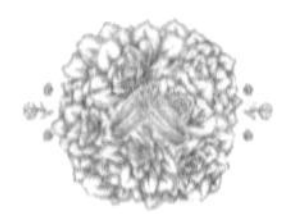

We arrive at Martha's Vineyard airport, where an SUV picks us up. I gaze out the window at the island's unique architecture and historical monuments. I'm enraptured as we pass light houses, churches, and vibrantly colored Victorian Gingerbread cottages. New England's history is one of my favorite subjects to read about and explore. Martha's Vineyard holds special interest since it's one of the oldest settlements.

But surely my history fascination isn't why we're here. It's also a popular vacation spot. Though not normally this time of year when we have chilly, rainy weather.

We travel along a narrow road that leads to a cottage beneath budding trees. As I exit the vehicle, salty air mingled with the fresh scent of Spring teases my nose. The gentle sound of lapping water catches my attention.

I round the house, Cian lumbering behind me, to find that we're right on the water. A short staircase leads to a sandy beach, with blue-green waters beyond.

Cian wraps his arms around me from behind. "One day, I'll bring you back here in the summer when it's warm enough to swim and sunbathe. This time I wanted us to explore the area while there are fewer tourists."

"Oh? What do you have in mind?" I'm curious about our itinerary.

"Let's talk inside, it's starting to rain again." He takes my hand and leads us into the adorable cottage. It's cozy in a modern rustic sort of way.

I set my purse down on the entry table, then step into the main part of the house. Cian flicks on the lights and my heart stills, before beating double time.

"Cian..." I gasp his name.

Purple tulips decorate every horizontal surface from the kitchen countertops, to the dining table, to the sofa's credenza. They're everywhere, I breathe in their sweet floral scent.

I enter the space, spinning in a slow circle to take it all in. He remembered. I told him once, what seems like a long time ago now, that these are my favorite flower. I never in a million years expected him to remember, much less do something like this.

Cian clears his throat, drawing my attention to him. "It's not too much, is it?"

Is he really asking that? I launch myself at him, and he catches me, chuckling. Our lips meet and I pour my gratitude into this kiss.

"They're beautiful. Thank you. This is the sweetest thing anyone has ever done for me."

His smile transforms his features from harsh and rugged to devastatingly handsome. "I aim to please."

"You've more than succeeded." I gaze in awe at the countless vases of purple tulips. They range in color from pale lavender to deep plum. I love them all. "So, how long are we here?"

"Just through the weekend." He drops a kiss on the top of my head, then moves to the kitchen island. "I thought we'd spend our time visiting these places."

Intrigued, I follow him, finding numerous informational pamphlets on the marble countertop. Picking them up, I shuffle through them. They're all historical attractions and tour schedules.

My gaze flits to Cian. He's watching me with interest.

My brow furrows. "You want to go... sightseeing?" That's the least Cian-type activity I can think of doing.

His pale blue eyes light with amusement. "Correct me if I'm wrong, but I'm pretty sure all of those New England history books you have piled on your nightstand aren't there for decoration. You're always reading about the area, I thought you might like to see it in person. More than just Manhattan."

My lips part in shock. I didn't realize he paid that close attention to me and my reading habits.

A frown creases his brow. "If that's of no interest to you, we can always—"

"No, I want to. I just didn't think that you would find any of this interesting." I don't want him to be bored out of his mind.

His features soften. "I'll be perfectly happy listening to you talk about all these places and the bits of trivia you've read about."

"You're sure?"

"Positive. Stop worrying so much, *broc meala*. We're on vacation. We're going to spend our days exploring this island, and our nights cozied up by that fireplace." He tilts his head toward the stone hearth.

I relax, taking him at his word. It just feels so strange to be put first. To have a whole weekend planned around what I find interesting, without having to feel guilty about it.

Stepping closer to my husband, I beam up at him. "Thank you. This is..." My heart warms. "I can't wait to do this, I'm so excited! Martha's Vineyard is one of the oldest British colonies, after Plymouth and Massachusetts Bay of course, and I've been dying to visit one day."

"Good. Now go get ready, there's a tour of some old church starting in an hour." He kisses me once before sending me off.

Giddy, I go in search of the single bedroom and my

suitcase. I'll have to dress warmer if we're going to be out in the elements.

This is a dream come true. The island's only accessible by boat or plane, and although I could have taken the ferry over from Cape Cod, my parents never agreed to let me go. Plus, I don't know anyone who enjoys history as much as I do, and I've never really wanted to go alone.

With this trip, Cian's given me much more than he realizes. Purple tulips, a chance to indulge my interest in history, and a distraction from incessantly worrying about Elena's flight to Italy.

CHAPTER 27
Ravenna

Our getaway was lovely, but as soon as we're home, I realize how much I miss Elena. This place isn't the same without her. Even though she refused to leave her room, I knew she was close by and that proximity eased some of my worry. Now she's on the other side of the Atlantic.

I check in on my sister, probably one too many times, to make sure she's settled in okay. Elena arrived safely at great aunt Antonia's house in Parma, Italy. There, she's under Pontrelli protection for the duration of her stay. I hope our extended family takes good care of her.

"You're crowding her from four thousand miles away." Cian arches a scarred brow.

I set my phone on the bedside table and snuggle into my husband's tattooed body, taking comfort in his heat. "I know. It's just that she's the only close family I have left now that my mother, father, and brother are all gone."

His muscles flex, turning to stone. "I'm sorry I had to be the one to take them from you," he says quietly.

I sit up, peering at him. That's an apology he said he'd never give me. But I'm sure I heard him right. My pulse flutters.

"I'm in no way trying to make you feel guilty. They were messed up people and my life is so much better without them. I can't even begin to..."

"I know." Cian clenches his jaw. "For you, I'd kill them all over again if I could. But I'm still sorry that I took your family from you."

"Thank you for that." I lean down to kiss him when my phone chimes five times in a row with incoming text messages. I reach for it.

SOPHIA

He did it to me again.

SOPHIA

I'm supposed to be on a date with Nik right now and he just texted to postpone. Again!

SOPHIA

I'm starting to think he doesn't like me.

SOPHIA

How am I supposed to marry a man who doesn't like me? To spend the rest of my life with him?!

SOPHIA

Is it me? Did I do something wrong? You're married. What do men want?

"That *stronzo*," I murmur, angry on my cousin's behalf.

"Who pissed you off?" Cian asks, arm resting behind his head and his scarred, tattooed chest on full display. My mouth waters. I tear my gaze away from his delicious muscles.

"It's that Russian that Sophia's engaged to marry. He stood her up again, and she thinks the problem is *her*. This is how men make women doubt themselves. It's despicable. She's done nothing wrong. I wonder what she can do to get his attention and hold onto it?" I muse. If his wandering attention is even the problem. From what I can determine, he's just a jerk.

"She could always date another man. Irish, Italian, Russian, it doesn't matter, we're all possessive of what's ours. If that doesn't get his attention then he's not into her at all."

I stare at him in disbelief. "She can't do that! Her father would murder her for being unfaithful. The Russians would probably call off the deal. It would destroy them all, and my cousin would be caught in the middle."

"You forgot to mention that they'd kill the man she dated too. Hmm, maybe that's not a good idea."

"You think?" I laugh when he reaches out to tickle me for my sassy mouth. "What if he's not into her? What if that's what's going on?"

Cian shrugs. "They'll have to make the best of it. Arranged marriages aren't based on love or attraction—only duty." He pulls me onto his chest. "You and I got lucky, *broc meala*. We like each other. Attraction isn't an issue. And someday, we might even..." His breath tickles my ear. The ghost of the words he's left unspoken hang in the air between us. *Someday... we might love each other.*

So he feels it too? This giddy sensation. The way butterflies swarm inside my stomach when he touches me, looks at me, kisses me. I thought I was alone in my deeper affections, but now I'm beginning to think they're mutual. His emotions for me could run deeper than duty and vows. Deeper than protecting what's his.

He rescued me in my darkest hour. Before that, he went with me to save my sister, no questions asked. He listens when I speak. He values whatever, and whoever, I cherish.

It's a one-eighty from our animosity-clouded beginning. Sure, it's been bumpy since then too. But something has shifted in our dynamic since the auction house.

Then shifted again after that cage fighting match. And once again following that nightmare-induced morning.

Am I too optimistic to think that we might have smooth sailing from here on out?

I want a life and relationship that I love. After all the hardship I've been through, I just want happiness. Being in Cian's arms makes me think that God has finally answered my prayers.

My husband nuzzles my neck. "What are you thinking about, baby?"

"Nothing. Everything." I can't help the smile that forms on my lips. "I should respond to Sophia before she spirals any further."

"Take your time. I have some work I need to get done." He crawls out of bed, then bends down to plant a kiss on the top of my head.

Naked, he saunters to the bathroom and I take my time enjoying the view. Taut ass, rippling muscles, dark ink covering his myriad scars. My insides warm. I have absolutely no shame in admiring my husband's physique.

Damn. I already want him back in bed.

As if he knows I'm having dirty thoughts about him, he glances over his shoulder at me and winks. I melt into a puddle of goo.

CHAPTER 28

Cian

Call me a selfish bastard, but I enjoy having my wife's full attention again. She's no longer constantly fussing and worrying over her twin sister. Though the concern she showed toward her gave me the sense that she'll be a wonderful mother. One day. Soon, I hope.

Having Elena in my house showed me that she would have been the wrong bride. We would have been a disaster. I thought I wanted the meek, sweet sister, but now I know otherwise. Ravenna was meant for me in every way possible, and even though she originally deceived me, I'm grateful I ended up married to her instead of her twin.

Smart. Sassy. Bull-headed. She's perfect.

She's also a distraction. As I knew she would be.

I think about her even when she's not around, like right now. Walking down the street at night near this cemetery, I should be vigilant. Instead I'm preoccupied with thoughts of my wife's charms. Not only her physical assets, but also the way she makes me feel... is it happiness? Hope? Something akin to those emotions.

I feel young again. Free. My wife manages to take me back to a time before my mistakes of the past, before the trauma, pain, and hatred. A time before my scars. I don't know how she does it.

She's ruined me in more ways than she'll ever know. I let her go once, and I'll regret that for the rest of my life. She's mine. Forever and always. I hope she understands what that means.

I love the woman, there's no doubt in my mind about that. One day I'll tell her, but now's not the right time. I want it to be perfect, memorable.

I've yet to find the perfect moment to confess my feelings. The right moment, but also the right words. I don't want to fumble.

Clearing my throat, I consider how I might phrase those three short but significant words. I've never been so nervous about speaking a single sentence before.

I'll want to practice.

Someone smashes a glass bottle as I round the corner of the cemetery's iron fence. I sense their presence before I see them. Turning, I find three men following me. They slow as I come to a stop. Yeah, definitely tailing me. But why?

I take in their buzz cut hair, muscular builds, and distinct features. *Russians.* There are several bratvas in the city, so it's impossible to tell which one these men belong to, unless they're going to tell me. Which is unlikely.

We stare each other down. They widen their stances. I fold my arms.

I probably should have brought Wolfe or one of the other guys with me tonight, but my plans were to visit the Pontrelli family graves—alone. In private.

Seems like I picked up a tail along the way. Opportunists?

The three Russian punks crack their knuckles and fan out to divide my attention between them.

The one wearing all black speaks first. "They call you The Beast, and I can see why—you're one big, ugly fucker."

I've been called that and worse so many times in my life that his insult rolls off my back. Mostly. Except for an inner voice that whispers, d*oes Ravenna see me that way too?*

I hate that I have that insecurity. It haunts me.

"We heard you got the shit kicked out of you by Little Italy," says the one wearing a bomber jacket. He snickers as he shuffles closer.

So that's why they think I'm easy prey. Because I lost a fight. One I was honor bound to throw.

I scowl. Dumb fucks.

The third one's dressed in white athletic gear. He hovers near his bomber jacket friend, but I can tell he's eager to strike. His shifty gaze and tense muscles practically scream his intentions before he moves.

I make a come hither gesture, and they pounce. Bomber and Athletic rush me as the guy in black opens his switch blade.

One punch and Bomber hits the ground, out cold. I elbow Athletic in the nose. *Crunch.* A wellspring of blood follows the loud sound, drenching his white clothing in a deep crimson. The violent sight satisfies a primal part of myself.

Those clothes were too white anyway. Glaring.

This is what they wanted to see, right? They wanted to go up against The Beast and be able to tell the tale to their friends. Too bad for them, only one of them will walk away from this tonight.

The guy with the knife comes at me, slashing his blade in quick, jerky movements. He's trained, but not well. He's also too confident, thinking that since I'm unarmed—at least to his knowledge—that I pose no threat.

Foolishly, he's under the assumption that a knife gives him an advantage.

I jerk backwards, dodging his slashing arcs. Pivoting, we dance around each other for a few seconds. Just long enough that I start to predict his movements.

He jabs the blade at me.

I catch his hand and crush it, breaking his fingers.

His screams land on unsympathetic ears.

The sound cuts off when I take his head between my hands and break his neck. His body crumples to the ground.

When I glance around, Athletic is nowhere in sight. Bomber hasn't moved, so he's either knocked out or dead. Or too afraid to move. I don't really give a shit which.

Five strikes of my boot do the job of caving in his skull. Now he's dead for sure. Message sent.

I leave their bodies on the sidewalk for their people to find and clean up. Hopefully their *pakhan* will take it as a warning not to fuck with me again.

With that inconvenience out of the way, I continue

into the cemetery. It's quite a hike to the Pontrelli family plot. The short, wet grass whispers beneath my boots. Twisted, budding trees dot the landscape. My breath fogs in the chill night air. Spring is supposed to be approaching, but fuck all if it feels like it.

Using my phone's flashlight feature, I find the graves I seek.

Lorenzo Pontrelli. Matteo Pontrelli.

Ever since Ravenna confided in me about her abusive family, I've been itching to visit these assholes one last time. She told me about her brother on our honeymoon. It wasn't until later that I found out how her father treated her at home.

If they were alive, I'd kill them both again, slowly, painfully.

Unfortunately, they're already dead, and reaching into the afterlife isn't in my skillset. But I can do the next best thing.

Unzipping my fly, I take my flaccid cock in hand. "I hope you can feel this all the way down in hell."

With a grunt, I piss on their graves.

You deserve so much worse, you motherfuckers.

CHAPTER 29
Cian

"You miss your sister." I observe the way my wife perks up at my statement. It's been obvious for weeks now that Ravenna's having a hard time with the distance between them. They really are that close. That kind of family bond is beyond my experience, but I like the fact that she has it with her twin.

Ravenna sets her hairbrush down on the vanity, and turns to face me. "I do miss her. This is the longest we've ever been apart."

I walk up to her and slide my fingers through her silky auburn hair. I'll never get enough of the simple joy of touching her—her hair, her skin, her palm in mine. Her body curled against me as we sleep at night.

"I want a honeymoon with you. A real one this time, with my wife *Ravenna*, not her twin sister Elena." My hand curves around her delicate throat, feeling her pulse. "I was thinking we could go to Italy. You could spend time with your sister for a couple of weeks, then we could have a week in Rome all by ourselves. What do you think?"

"What do I think? Yes! Please. I'm ready to leave right now." She jumps up and hugs me.

I laugh, then bend down and capture her lips with mine. "We'll leave tomorrow."

"You already made all the plans?"

"I figured the chances of you saying *yes* were pretty high. Turns out I was right. Now go pack."

She bounds toward her closet. I swat her ass on her way by, and she rewards me with a giggling yelp.

My chest squeezes. I love making this woman happy. I want to do just that, for ever and ever.

Happy wife, happy life. Whoever first said that was on to something good.

I head downstairs to finish up some business. Wolfe's waiting in my office when I get there. His brawny arms crossed, and he wears a familiar scowl.

"Who pissed in your cereal this morning?" I ask him, moving around my desk.

"You did."

I glance up, and growl, "Is that so?"

"Yeah. You're leaving me to find a new security lead, while you go off to Italy with that Italian b—"

"Choose your next word wisely, Wolfe, I'd hate to have to cut your tongue out," I warn.

He sighs, jaw muscles flexing. "I'm just trying to warn you that you're going to lose your men's respect if you keep putting your wife first, spending all day and night with her, and neglecting what you've built here."

"I'm not neglecting anybody." I run my fingers through my hair. "I know it's been chaotic since I married, but when I return from my honeymoon we'll get to business. I value your judgements, Wolfe, you're a good man. But right now, I need you to take care of business while I'm away. Can you do that?"

"I can."

"Good. Now go find us a new security lead among the men so poor old Seamus can retire. He's too fucking ancient for the position anyway. I know he wants to spend more time with his own wife and their garden. Choose us a good, trustworthy man."

"I will." With a frown, he leaves my office.

Perhaps I have shoved too much work onto Wolfe. But he's the only man I trust not to take this new responsibility as a sign to seize control and push me out. We've been through too much together. And at the same time, he's right, I am living in a newlywed haze. Which is something I never expected to experience. It won't last. Not forever. While it does, I want to enjoy every moment with Ravenna.

So fucking bite me if I neglect my men and the business for a couple of months. It's Wolfe's job to take care of things when I'm not here, that's why he's my second in command. Once I'm back, I'll return to work as promised.

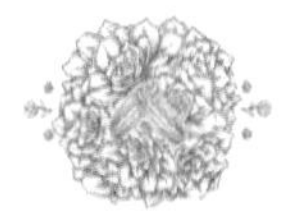

Alone together on my private jet, Ravenna and I barely sleep. We spend the long flight across the Atlantic making love, talking for hours, and generally indulging in each other's company. I'm so obsessed with my wife that I'm not sure I'll ever get enough of her. Maybe that's how it's supposed to be.

Perhaps this is true love. She's stolen my heart and I'll never get it back. I'm fine with that. Glad even.

We land on a private airstrip outside of Parma, Italy. From there, we travel by car to our hotel in the colorful city. Warm air and golden sunlight greet us as we arrive in front. The hotel porters grab our luggage from the trunk before the driver pulls into traffic.

Taking Ravenna's hand, I stride through the wide double doors and enter a marble lobby with towering ceilings. A hush settles over those relaxing in nearby seating areas. Suddenly, I sense too many eyes on me. Wide with horror, shifty with fear.

A woman to our left gasps, muttering something in Italian before she scurries toward the hotel bar. We're given a wide berth as we approach the reception desk.

I clear my throat, which feels too tight. Heat crawls up the back of my neck. I hate how uncomfortable I feel in public when everyone stares. Unless I look in a mirror, I generally forget about my scarred appearance. Until I'm around strangers who not only remind me of my deformity, but judge me for it.

I wish I could gouge out their eyes.

Ravenna squeezes my hand and takes charge, rattling off rapid-fire Italian to the staff. She glares at anyone who dares stare too long at my face. Once we have our room key, she leads us toward the elevators.

"*Uscite!*" she snaps at the people in the elevator. They take one glance at us and do as she commands, exiting the elevator.

I love my wife, but I especially adore her when she's angry. Especially when she's furious on my behalf.

We step inside and the doors slide shut. Ravenna huffs out a sigh. "Rude. Can you believe how awfully—?"

I grip the back of her neck and draw her in for a ravenous kiss. My tongue slides into her mouth, our tongues tangle. Her soft moan goes straight to my cock.

I'm grateful of how she looks at me, seeming to see past my scars and into my depths. She gazes upon me like I'm a person instead of a frightening beastly creature. For that alone, I'll always be in awe of her.

"You're the sweetest woman I've ever known," I murmur against her lips.

"I told you I'm protective of those I love." Her eyes widen, as if she's surprised the word slipped out.

Love.

My heart skips a beat. "I know, *broc meala.* I'm a lucky man to be on that short list of people."

She smiles up at me. "Yes, you are."

I swat her ass in retaliation for her sassy mouth. She rewards me with a squeak and a giggle. But all can think about is how she just confessed to loving me.

I cage her against the elevator wall. Leaning down, I gaze into her soulful eyes. "I love you, too."

Her breath hitches, all humor erased from her expression. "I love you more."

"Don't bet on that." I kiss her forehead, inhaling her amber scent.

She fucking loves me. I swallow hard. Elation thrums through my chest.

The elevator dings, the doors open on our floor. Taking her hand, my heart so full it could burst, we find our suite at the end of the short hallway. I wanted a nice place for our honeymoon, so I booked the best room in the place.

On entering, I take in the airy space with marble columns, soft linens, and an excellent view of the city. This will certainly do until we head to Rome.

"What do you think?" I ask Ravenna, who's already making herself at home.

She plucks a grape from the table's centerpiece and pops it in her mouth. "I could live here forever."

And I would be happy living wherever my wife wants to be. She loves me.

CHAPTER 30

Ravenna

Our second honeymoon delivers on everything it promised us. I spend my days in Parma visiting with Elena in the confines of our relatives' house since she refuses to leave the safety of these walls. I'm still worried about her mental health, but she does seem to be calmer than she was in Manhattan. For that, I'm grateful.

My nights are spent wrapped in Cian's arms. Every morning I wake up and love him more than I did the day before. He knew how much I missed my sister without me having to say a word.

We spend an entire week in Parma where I visit with my sister until it's time to continue our travels. Saying farewell to her this time isn't as soul crushing. I know she's only a flight away. Plus, she seems to be doing better.

Cian and I travel to Rome for a whirlwind trip of sightseeing, luxury hotels, and being so wrapped up in each other that the strangers around us may as well cease to exist. Even their stares and gasps at the sight of Cian don't get under my skin like they have before. I simply shoot them withering glares, then we continue on with our day.

We're six months into our marriage, and I've never been happier. I hope this honeymoon phase of our relationship never ends. I want Cian to gaze at me like I'm the center of his universe for the rest of our lives.

I'm so caught up in our blissful honeymoon that my early morning cramps take me by surprise. Pain doesn't belong in this perfect fantasy life that I'm living in Rome.

With a groan, I climb out of bed and hurry to the bathroom. Sure enough, my period has arrived right on time.

A lead weight drops in my stomach and my shoulders slump. I'd hoped... Well, I'd hoped to be pregnant by now.

For the first few months we were together, I figured my body wasn't ready yet. After being beaten and drugged, I had a lot of healing to do, so I didn't worry about the fact that my period kept arriving every month. But recently we've been having so much sex, and this trip has been so relaxing that I was sure it would finally happen.

But it hasn't. Once again I'm not pregnant.

Securing a tampon in place, I find a pair of panties and slip into a silky robe. I down a couple of Tylenol to deal with the pain. My good mood completely ruined, I settle onto the sofa and stare out at the dawn.

"Why are you up so early?" Cian appears in the

bedroom doorway, his blond hair tousled by sleep. He's so big his frame easily fills the space.

"Cramps," I state as an explanation. Drawing my feet up, I hug my knees.

"Oh." His tone comes out flat, and I see the flicker of disappointment in his eyes before he looks away.

That sight sends me spiraling. My eyes sting as my face grows hot. Before I can stop them, silent tears spill down my cheeks.

Cian glances at me in alarm. He rushes to my side, frantically trying to figure out what's wrong. "Do they hurt that much? What can I do? Tell me what to do."

I shake my head. "It's not the pain, that's fine. It's—" I avert my gaze.

He cups my chin, lifting my chin until I meet his eyes. "Tell me what's wrong, *broc meala*. I'll do everything in my power to make it right."

My chest clenches. "It's just that..." I sniffle. "I'm not pregnant. Shouldn't I be pregnant by now?"

"Oh, my sweet wife." His gaze softens. "Not necessarily. These things can take time. It will happen when it's supposed to, I promise."

"You're not... disappointed?" I stare hard at him and demand, "The truth. You know there can be no lies between us."

He sigh heavily. "I'm not disappointed in *you*. I'm impatient and eager to start a family with you. But I could never be disappointed in you." He hauls me into his lap, curving his body around mine. "I want everything with you. And I want to give you everything your heart desires. Especially a child. But I will learn to be more patient."

I snuggle against him, feeling cherished. "What if I can't give you a child?"

"Then we'll be happy without children."

"But what about the treaty between our families? Only an heir, a child of our bloodlines will secure the truce forever. Until then, it's fragile."

"I know. But that kind of pressure isn't helping either one of us relax and get pregnant, is it?"

"I guess not."

"Besides, the truce and our families shouldn't obligate us to anything. I want you, Ravenna O'Rourke. What's important is *us*. Nothing else. Do I make myself clear?"

"Crystal clear."

He grunts in approval. "Good."

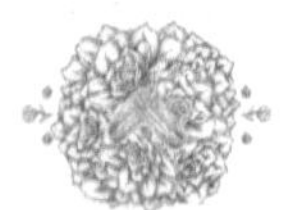

"Where are we going?" I ask as the limo drives us to the outer edge of Rome. We're clearly leaving the city behind, but our hotel room's booked through tomorrow.

Cian chuckles at my concerned expression. "Don't worry, I'll have you tucked in bed by midnight at the latest."

I glance out the window again. It's not even sunset. Though we're heading out much too late for a day trip.

"You're really not going to tell me where we're going?"

"Nope." He thumbs through his phone. "But I am going to have to blindfold you soon. We're almost there."

Before I can search for clues out the window, thick silk fabric drapes across my eyes. My world goes dark.

My heartbeat pounds against my ribs. "Is this really necessary?"

"It is," Cian's deep, gravelly voice speaks into my ear. He's much closer than he was a moment ago.

Right now, I'm at his mercy. A delicious shiver rushes across my skin.

The car slows to a stop. As soon as the door opens, I strain my other senses for any hints as to where we are. Cian's calloused hand wraps around mine as he helps me stand, then he leads me across a hard-packed surface.

We're greeted by a stranger with a heavy Italian accent. "Welcome, Mr. and Mrs. O'Rourke. Please come aboard."

Aboard? At first I expect a boat, but as we walk forward, there's what feels like a short ramp, then we're being seated in a cushioned bench. There's no telltale rocking, we seem to be firmly planted on earth.

All of a sudden, the ground shifts, lurching and rocking. With a startled gasp, I reach for Cian, and hold onto him to keep my balance. With one arm, he plasters me to his side.

"What's happening?" My stomach feels weightless as we rise into the air. A warm summer breeze caresses my face.

To answer my question, Cian removes the blindfold.

My breath catches in my throat as I take in the scene before me. We're in a hot air balloon, cruising over trees, headed toward Rome in the distance.

Inside the small space, we're seated at a table. A chef, who I vaguely recognize from television, begins to cook our meal at a tiny kitchen against one side of the carriage. Heady aromas of Italian spices drift by on the breeze. The only other person aboard is a server, who bobs his head at us and pours wine.

Cian murmurs in my ear, "Do you like it?"

I gape at him. "Like it? I *love* it! Are we really having dinner as we fly over Rome at sunset?" The whole idea seems too wild to be true. Yet here we are.

He chuckles. "I wanted to do something especially memorable for our last night of our honeymoon."

"This is truly amazing. Thank you." I reach up and kiss him before turning my attention to the breathtaking view. "It's so beautiful."

"I couldn't agree more."

I glance at him, but he's gazing at me instead of the glittering city. Heat blossoms on my cheeks. My heart skips a beat, then flutters like the wings of a hummingbird.

I love how Cian makes me feel like I'm the center of his world. Being with him is the opposite of how I felt growing up, always being either abused or disregarded. Told I was too opinionated, too stubborn, too much of everything that my parents didn't want me to be.

But Cian doesn't treat me that way. He seems to adore what I've always been told are my negative qualities. He makes me feel seen, validated. I can be myself without apology.

It's refreshing. I didn't know how badly I needed it, until this moment.

Up here, soaring through the sky, we sip wine as the master chef serves us an eight course meal, all while admiring the sights of the city from a completely new angle. Golden rays of the setting sun light up the stunning architecture. This is an experience I'll never forget.

CHAPTER 31

Ravenna

Returning home feels like waking from a dream. I stare at the foreboding, heavily guarded compound, noting the distinct differences between this place and all the beauty of Rome. The place I call home is masculine, stark, and downright depressing at times.

That needs to change.

I glance at Cian and announce, "I'm redecorating." Though *re*decorating is too subtle a word. This space has never seen a decoration since its original construction. Maybe not even then.

"I was hoping you'd make this place your home too. It's about time."

"After spending so much time in gorgeous Italy, then coming back to this..." I motion toward the compound.

He gazes out the car window. "Yeah, it's functional and secure, but that's about it. I don't even know if someone can make this place visually appealing. Or inviting."

"A professional can. Plus, I have some ideas too. But first, is there anywhere in the house that's off limits?"

"Nope. Every area in the main house is yours to do with as you please. If need be, we'll build a new structure for the common areas."

"That's not necessary." I hold his hand as the car rolls to a stop. "I just want to rearrange a bit, so that the common areas are confined to the left wing of the house instead of in the main section. That way we'll have more privacy."

"I like privacy." His brow furrows in thought. "What do you think about leaving the compound as-is and buying a place in the city? I know being this far away from your cousins is difficult for you. We could get a brownstone or a penthouse in Manhattan, anywhere you'd like."

"Are you serious? I'd love that." My pulse speeds up as I consider the possibilities of moving back to the heart of the city. "Can we? Really?"

"Of course we can." He drops a kiss to my forehead before climbing out of the car. I follow him, coming up short when I notice Wolfe waiting for us by the door. He has another man with him.

The man looks vaguely familiar, like I've seen glimpses of him in passing, but I don't know his name. He's tall, broad, and well-groomed. Dark brown eyes scrutinize us beneath his trimmed black hair. His darker features stand in stark contrast to his pale skin. He's obviously Irish, just a different coloring from all the red-tinted brown haired men and dirty blonds around here.

"Cian, it's good to have you home." Wolfe pats my husband on the shoulder, then gestures toward the semi-stranger. "Brendan Dunne is our new security expert. Lad's quite talented, who knew?"

"Welcome to your new official role, Brendan."

"Happy to be promoted, sir."

Cian drops his arm around my shoulders. "I don't believe you two have formally met, so let me introduce you to my wife Ravenna O'Rourke."

I nod and smile at the man.

"Nice to formally meet you, Mrs. O'Rourke." His attention immediately returns to my husband. "Mr. O'Rourke, I look forward to getting to work. I've already tested the current security system and have some ideas on how to improve it. There's new, upgraded technology we can install. But that can all wait until you're settled in from your travels, of course."

"That won't take me long. I'll see you in my office in two hours and you can show me what you've got."

"Yes, sir. I'll be there." Brendan gives a curt nod before leaving us.

Wolfe eyes me as he speaks to Cian. "Hope you had a relaxing honeymoon and you're ready to get back to work. Things have been a bit more exciting around here since you left."

"Walk with me. What's going on?"

I linger behind them, half eavesdropping, half studying the foyer and considering the pros and cons of moving. The only con I see is Cian being further away from his men.

Wolfe and Cian head in the direction of his office. "We had a bit of a skirmish with some new Irishmen in town. The Monahans. Ever heard of them?"

"I haven't." Cian's voice echoes down the hallway.

"Well they're trouble. Skirmish almost got us killed."

"Tell me everything. Spare no detail." His office door clicks shut.

We just entered a peaceful time between the Irish and Italians, don't tell me we'll be at war with some other Irish mob soon. Hopefully a skirmish is like a misunderstanding or something easily resolved. Thought it doesn't sound good.

Even after a long day of traveling, I'm not tired, so I dig right in to searching for real estate for sale in Upper Manhattan on my phone. Brownstone or penthouse? Newly renovated or fixer upper? The place needs to be large enough to raise a family as I want this to be our forever home. There are so many details to figure out.

CHAPTER 32
Cian

As I promised myself and Wolfe, once I returned home from my second honeymoon with Ravenna, I'd dive into work. This skirmish with the Monahans monopolizes my attention as soon as I sit down at my desk. Apparently, there was a misunderstanding over turf lines. They tried to open a gambling den on a property that I control, and when forced out, they didn't take it lying down.

Shots were fired, but thankfully no one was seriously injured. This time.

We're in a time of peace, and I intend to keep us out of any mob wars that might pop up. Including this one.

"Tell me about the Monahans," I urge Wolfe.

He claims the seat across from me, arms folded over his chest. "I looked into them. They're relatives of the old Flanagan family, and it seems like they're taking over that turf. Clearly they don't know where the border line's drawn."

"Or they're testing the boundaries."

Wolfe nods. “Could be. Three brothers lead the Monahan family. The eldest living one is Cormac, who has quite the reputation as a ruthless motherfucker. His younger brothers are Liam and Killian. There’s a nephew too, the son of the deceased brother. They’re fresh off the boat from Ireland. That’s about all anyone knows about them.”

“That’s a good start. Keep an eye on them. We need to hold firm to our borders, don’t give the Monahans an inch. Also, make sure they know we have the Italians to back us. That should give them some perspective of who they’re fucking with.” Hopefully, they won’t want to fuck with us.

“Will do. Do you want me to arrange a meeting with them?”

Considering that option for a second, I shake my head. “Not yet. Hopefully we can both peacefully coexist.”

“All right.” He runs his hand over his shaved scalp. “Had a hell of a time trying to replace Seamus. Most of our guys don’t know shit about computers. Never expected to find out Brendan had such brains. I guess we all underestimated him because of that pretty boy face and crisp suit.”

“So you think he knows his stuff?” I wouldn’t have guessed it of the Dunne lad either. He’s always been the quiet, serious type. Didn’t think he was especially bright though.

“He’s already run circles around what Seamus installed. We’ll finally get a real security system around here.”

“Good.”

Wolfe settles back in his chair. "One other thing. After you're finished with Brendan and the security system, we need to go over the accounts. I think a betting ring in Harlem is skimming money. The Italians might be lax about such things, but we sure as fuck aren't."

I suppress a sigh. It's going to be a long day. Never a dull moment in this line of work.

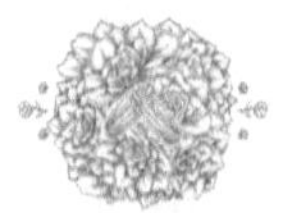

"Are you sure your heart's set on a brownstone?" I ask Ravenna over dinner. We still wake up with each other in the mornings, but our days are mostly spent apart. Our evenings have been drifting in separate directions as well, so I insisted on us having dinner together tonight.

"Yes, definitely. I mean, we can look at some penthouses if you want. I have a list of interesting ones, but if I want to be close to my cousins then we should move into my old neighborhood. Plus, those old houses feel like home to me, I can't imagine living in a different style of architecture We can renovate to update it if need be."

I give her an indulgent smile. "If that's what you want, then put together a list and we'll schedule the viewings around my work obligations."

"Okay. I can do that." She swallows a spoonful of soup. "Text me the dates you aren't available and I'll work around those."

I grunt out an affirmative. Reaching across the table, I entwine our fingers, hardly able to believe that we're taking this leap together. Buying a new home is no small feat. I'm looking forward to having a place that's all ours. A home for our family. Putting down roots.

Ravenna hasn't brought up children again since our honeymoon. The question surfaces in my mind sometimes though. Why isn't she pregnant yet?

Is it her? Or is it me?

Then I remember that we've been trying to conceive for less than a year. Patience. It will happen in its own time.

The timing will be even better once we've settled into our new home. That's the ideal scenario in which to welcome our first child into this world.

We finish eating, and I'm about to escort my wife upstairs to our bedroom when my phone rings. Glaring at it, I tell Ravenna, "I have to take this, and it may be a few minutes. I'll see you in bed."

"No rush." She presses a kiss to my lips, then heads upstairs.

I answer the call. "Niall Bane, do you have what I asked for on the Monahans?"

"Good evening to you too, cousin."

I cringe. "We're not family."

"Hm... last I checked my mother and your father were siblings. That would make us cousins. Though you only ever contact me when you need something—nope, wait, that definitely sounds like something family would do."

"We don't live in the same sphere. So I don't consider us family."

He chuckles. "Our spheres cross more than you'd think. Just because my siblings and I have legal day jobs doesn't mean our hands are any cleaner than yours, O'Rourke."

"Yeah, I doubt that. Your father made it clear he wanted nothing to do with mine." The resentment still burns. Aiden Bane is the reason my father spent the remainder of his life in prison. So no, I don't consider the Banes family.

"Well, they're both dead. So what we do is up to us now. Anyway, I have that information on the Monahan family."

"And?"

"They ran a gang in Belfast called the Irish Hammers. After getting into too much trouble there, they escaped and made their way to New York. These guys are the real thing. Seasoned Irish gangsters. Don't mess with them. It's a good thing you have ties to the Italian mafia now, so they can watch your back. The good news is the Monahans are new in town. They don't have any real connections or allies yet, which makes them vulnerable. At least for now. Funny thing is, they're now calling themselves the Monahan Group."

"Sounds like a financial firm."

"It does. But they're far from anything corporate."

I take a moment to process this information. "Do you have a full dossier on the Monahan brothers?"

"I do. Emailed it to you," he pauses for a long second, "I also emailed it to Blake Baron. He's taken an interest in them too. Which isn't surprising since he's interested in everything that goes on in this city. But I thought you should know."

I grunt. The Monahans really are serious players if Mr. Baron is also looking into them.

"Well..." Niall sighs. "See you around sometime, cousin. Or just call me up when you need another favor."

"Thanks." I mean it, but he's already ended the call.

I'll look through the information Niall sent me on the Monahans tomorrow. But if they're as dangerous as they seem, then I might have to set up a meeting and see if we can come to an understanding before we start fighting over the limited space that New York offers.

Maybe they'll welcome a peace treaty between us. Or maybe they'll try to cut us out.

CHAPTER 33

Ravenna

"Enough about me and my complaining about Nik," Sophia says. "How's Elena doing? Is she feeling any better since you last saw her in Italy? She'll be at my wedding, won't she?"

"I'm sure she'll be there. She's still visiting family in Italy and trying to figure out what she wants in life. Overall, I think she's feeling better." I take a sip of my Earl Grey latte.

In truth, to my knowledge, she hasn't left our great aunt's house for any length of time. Though she does seem less depressed these days when we chat on the phone.

"Lucky girl," Ginevra sips her tea, her blond curls framing her face. "I wish I could go live with family in Italy and do whatever I want with my life."

Arianna chides her, "It's not like she's partying all the time, Gin. She's recovering from the loss of her parents. She's grieving in Italy, not having fun."

Guilt slithers through my stomach. Elena has been

grieving. While I've been having the time of my life with Cian this past year. My parents' deaths feel like they happened years ago instead of months.

Sophia reaches across the table where we're sitting in a coffee shop on the Upper East Side. "How are you doing with it all? You always seem so pulled together, I sometimes forget that you lost your parents too."

"I'm okay. I think we all grieve in our own ways and my sister and I are very different people. I've really been occupying myself with this renovation."

"Oh, that's right. How's it going?" Arianna leans forward, her expression expectant.

I'm more than happy to change the subject. Since Cian gave me the go-ahead to find us a forever home, we spent the rest of the summer viewing places all over Upper Manhattan. We finally settled on a gorgeous old brownstone in desperate need of repair. The up side being that we can renovate it to be perfect for us and our lifestyle. As well as our future family. So that's what we're doing.

"That designer Aunt Rosa recommended is a miracle worker. We just heard back from the city and our design plans have been approved. Construction starts next week. I'm so excited to finally see some progress. The sooner we get started, the sooner the work will be done and we can move in."

"I think it's smart not to live there while construction is happening," Gin says. "It's so loud and dusty. Plus all those strangers going in and out of your house." She pulls a face.

"I completely agree." Fishing my phone from my purse, I announce, "I wanted to show you all some photos. The designer texted me some mood boards this morning. I'd like your opinions."

We go down the interior design rabbit hole for the next hour. I'm glad they want to be part of the process since I value their feedback. Especially Arianna's. She has an amazing eye for design. I wouldn't be surprised if she decides to go into some type of work that involves aesthetics. *If* her future husband will let her work. That's not always a guarantee in our world.

When I'm finished visiting with my cousins, a grouchy Wolfe drives me back home. Every time I have to go somewhere, he's my assigned driver and bodyguard, or as he refers to it *babysitter*, which is way below his pay grade. But he's the only one Cian trusts enough to leave him alone with me.

With the drive being over an hour each way, he's always exceptionally grumpy when we go into the city from the compound. He should be much happier once I live closer to my cousins.

"Fucking asshole, where'd you learn how to drive!" he shouts out the window, flipping off a driver at the busy intersection.

Groaning, I do my best to ignore him. He's never any fun when he's in one of his moods. Which means he's never any fun.

"This is why I hate driving in the city," he grumbles. "Too many fucking people everywhere."

That's Cian's lament too. I'm still shocked at how well my husband managed to tour Rome and all the crowds on our honeymoon, especially during the summer season. The fact that he wants to move into the city where the houses are jammed together, with all the hustle and bustle, still has me in a state of shock. He really has changed since we've been married.

Maybe Wolfe could use a woman in his life to cheer him up. Some men need a partner to make them happy. He's certainly not enjoying life as a bachelor.

I glance up at the rearview mirror. "Wolfe, do you have a girlfriend?"

His gaze snaps to mine in the reflective glass. "What the hell kind of question is that? You're not looking to set me up with one of your Italian cousins are you?"

I snicker. "Of course not. You're much too old for any of them."

He scowls, grumbling under his breath.

"What did you say? I didn't catch that." I lean forward.

"I *said*, I'm in my forties, that's hardly ancient."

"True," I agree with him. "So why don't you have a girlfriend or a wife? Or even... a boyfriend? If that's your preference."

I don't know what it is about Wolfe, but I absolutely love getting a rise out of him—when I'm not busy avoiding his sour moods. If I'm not careful it might turn into a hobby. He's much too easy to provoke, and I'm ninety percent sure he won't murder me for annoying him.

He scoffs. "Not that it's any of your business, but I'm too damn busy to have a woman in my life right now."

"Cian's just as busy and he's married," I point out.

"Yeah, well he didn't have a choice, did he?"

Ouch.

"No, but he's happy. Or haven't you noticed?"

"Yeah, I've noticed," he mutters. "He's so damn

happy I have to chain him to his desk to get any work done. Metaphorically speaking of course."

"Is he more focused when I'm out of the house? Do you think that helps?" I'm asking because I'm genuinely curious.

Wolfe grunts and shakes his head. "Nope. He's more agitated when you're not home. All the men complain about it."

"Really? I thought he'd be able to focus more without me around."

"Nope. It's a dangerous world out here. When you're not at home, you're not safe."

"I'm perfectly safe with my bodyguard—you. Don't you agree that we're safe?"

His gaze scans the streets. "Anything can happen out here. You're safe one minute, then dead the next. You'd do well to remember that, sorceress."

I glance up again, surprised by his strange nickname for me. I can't tell if it's a type of endearment or an insult. Wolfe doesn't exactly like me, so I assume the latter.

"You're a ray of sunshine, you know that?"

"Just saying it like it is."

"And managed to avoid my original question." I lean further forward in my seat. "What's the real reason you aren't in a relationship since we both know the excuse of you're too busy is bullshit."

He glares into the rearview mirror, our gazes lock. "I was there when my mother became a widow. Then I lost my sister to this world's darkness. I'll never risk putting a woman through that, especially one that I claim to love."

My lips part, forming an O.

Wolfe tears his gaze away, his jaw muscles tense. I

settle back into my seat, silence hanging between us as I digest his words. I didn't know he had a sister. What happened to her? How old was he when his father died?

So many questions that I know he won't answer.

With the house renovations seeming to take an eternity, the holiday season and our one year wedding anniversary pass in the blink of an eye. We spend a few weeks packing, eager to move, but trying not to get ahead of ourselves.

Who knew the permit process would take *months*? Then all the inspections, the delays, the bribes that had to grease a few wheels. Sourcing everything I wanted, design decisions... At one point, I wanted to scream, cry, tear my hair out. But we made it through.

Then one day I wake up, it's February, and our move in day.

I'll admit, I am not really going to miss the compound. This step forward in our relationship feels like a piece, one I didn't even know was missing, has finally fallen into place. We have our perfect home in the city. This is the start of our true married life together.

First marriage. Then a home. Next a family.

The renovated brownstone displays the perfect mix of old and new. We have a primary suite with two dressing rooms, and an en suite bathroom. A smaller attached room reserved for a future nursery. It can be accessed from our room as well as from the hallway. A guest room, and several other bedrooms to accommodate us as our family grows.

On the ground floor, Cian has his home office. We've also created a library, complete with a fireplace and two stories of bookcases. Very similar to the library at the compound, but now he won't have to keep the door locked to keep it private.

Setting up a new household comes with the need for staff. We've hired a chef, housekeeper, and cleaning service. All with ties to the Irish mob, of course. They may as well be extended family.

The place only comes with a two-car garage in back, so Cian has had to pare down his collection of cars, leaving several of them at the compound. One space is taken by the town car I ride in on a regular basis, the other spot houses Cian's vehicle de jour. Sometimes his motorcycle, other times a sports car or an SUV. The man loves his cars.

We arrive at the house as soon as the moving and decorating crews have finished. Cian sweeps me into his arms, as if I weigh nothing at all, and carries me over the threshold.

"Welcome home," he says, taking in the grand entrance.

I kiss him. "What should we do first in our new home?"

"Bless it, of course." He carries me up the stairs to our bedroom. Tonight will be our first time sleeping here. He sets me on my feet. "Take hold of that bed post."

"Why? What are you going to do?" My pulse flutters in anticipation.

He flips open his switchblade, his grin wide. "Let's have some fun. Like old times."

"Mr. O'Rourke, if you ruin this dress, you'll owe me ten new ones."

His smile widens, crinkling his eyes. "They're already hanging in your closet. Now do as you're told, *broc meala*."

I playfully huff, but turn around and wrap my hands around the bed's corner post. Cian wastes no time cutting my dress from my body, just as he did on our wedding night. The poor fabric's sliced and torn, until I'm left in only my underwear and heels.

He palms my ass cheeks, a sound of appreciation rumbles in his chest. Then he does something he's never done before. The cold edge of the blade scrapes along my skin, leaving a trail of goosebumps in its wake. He skims it up my sides, follows the curve of my breast, he teases my nipple with the unforgiving steel.

I gasp. My nipple pebbles.

Cian nips at my throat. "Beg for me, baby. You know how I like it."

A whimper escapes my lips. He teases the other nipple with his blade. His free hand drags my panties down my thighs, then his fingers draw lazy circles around my clit. I'm so turned on that a shudder rattles through my body.

"Please," I murmur.

"Tell me what you want."

Slowly, he drags his blade down my stomach. Its blunt edge replaces his fingers, teasing my clit. The sensation, tinged with danger, has me rolling my hips, silently demanding more.

"Please," I say again. "Please make me come. I'm begging you, husband. I need you."

He grunts with approval. "Beg me on your knees."

Carefully, so as not to cut myself, I drop to my knees. He's still fully clothed, so I unbuckle his belt and drag down his zipper. Freeing his erection, I hold his heavy cock in my hands, and gaze up at him through my lashes.

"I need you," I say.

"Show me how much you want it."

Maintaining eye contact, I open my mouth wide and suck on the head of his dick like it's my favorite hard candy. He hisses when I flick my tongue. Carefully, with intention, I take in every inch of him.

His body shivers, his blue eyes darken with lust. When I have him all the way down my throat, I hum.

"Jesus!" Cian pulls me off of him. I hide my triumphant smile as he drops to his knees, and spins me around so I'm facing the bed again. I love it when he loses control like this. Love that I can drive him wild with desire.

From behind, he lines himself up and presses inside my pussy. I push back against his cock. He curses under his breath, and I grin—until I feel the cold steel of his blade slide between my legs.

Oh god. He works my clit with his knife.

Cian fucks me with punishing thrusts until my thighs quiver and an explosive orgasm rips through my body. I hold onto that corner post for dear life because he's far from finished with me.

Angling my head back so I can see his face, he removes the blade from my clit. With deft swipes of his tongue he licks the knife clean.

The erotic, unhinged sight sends me over the edge again, and I come on his cock.

I scream his name as he fucks me through this orgasm before finally pumping me full of his cum.

Chests heaving, we collapse in a sweaty mess, both of us spent.

Easing his cock out of my pussy, he scoops me into his arms and settles onto the bed. He cradles me close, where I fit perfectly under his arm. I rest my arm across his expansive chest.

This is pure bliss.

We doze for a while. Content in each other's company. Happy in our new house. This place is already worth the wait. I sense it in my bones, it feels like *home.*

Cian eventually breaks the silence. "You should know, I have to go out of town next Saturday."

I glance up at him. I wish we could stay in our little space, wrapped up in each other forever, but the outside world always seems to demand attention.

I sigh. "But that's Sophia's engagement party."

"I'm so sorry, *broc meala*, I forgot to put that on my calendar. I can move the meeting."

"Is it important?"

"I'm meeting with a supplier in Florida, but I can reschedule."

"Is this the new supplier you've been trying to find a time to meet with for the past two months?" I prop myself up on one elbow, and he nods. "Then don't cancel. It's fine. Sophia's party will be small. Just family and close friends. There's no real reason for us to go together. However, the wedding is a different story. You have to come with me to that."

He smiles up at me. "I wouldn't miss it for the world."

"Promise?"

"I swear it." He flips me over, peppering open mouth kisses down my chest, across my ribs, and on my hip bone. When he glances up at me, I part my legs, giving him access to what he wants. A wolfish grin on his lips, he dives in.

Oh dear God, this man knows how to use his tongue.

CHAPTER 34
Ravenna

Sophia's engagement party is not anything like I expected. Half the city must be in attendance tonight, there's enough food to feed an army, and the entire house is decorated to show off the Pontrelli family's vast wealth. It's garish. Embarrassing even. I'm so glad I'm not in the spotlight of tonight's festivities.

Poor Sophia. What are the Russians going to think of all this? Will they be impressed? Doubtful.

Though as I question that, already intoxicated Russians stumble into each other, speaking loudly, all throughout the room. They seem delighted by all the free booze.

To think, if Papa was still alive, Elena would be the soon-to-be bride on display this evening. The thought makes me cringe. My sweet sister wouldn't survive these brutes. I'm sorry Sophia has to deal with them, but my cousin and I are much more alike. She's no wilting flower.

I've seen her a couple of times tonight, from afar

through the thick crowd. Once most of them have cleared out, I'll have a moment alone with her to chat. Though, I'm not sure if I should be offering my congratulations or my condolences. Nik never did warm up to her and their wedding's right around the corner.

I spot her a third time as she weaves through the crowd. She does look stunning in that red dress. It compliments her deep brown hair. Hopefully her fiancé appreciates what and who he's getting—once he gets to know her.

Most of all, I hope he's kind to her and treats her with respect. That hasn't been the case so far, but maybe he'll change after they're married. Cian has changed so much in the past year. It can happen. He's proof.

"There you are!" Ginevra appears at my side, Arianna close behind her. "We thought you went home early."

"I'd never leave without saying goodbye. I'm hoping to catch Sophia alone for a second, but she's been completely swamped all evening." I grab a glass of champagne from a passing server. "Cheers."

Ginevra and Arianna clink their glasses to mine. They're both technically underage, but at home our family has always bent the rules. Especially during celebrations.

"Come on. Let's get out of this crush." I lead the way upstairs to the landing that overlooks the massive foyer. It's much less crowded up here.

Arianna leans against the railing. "I know it hasn't been easy for my sister, but I hope this ends up being a good match between Sophia and Nikolai. Her wedding will set the tone for the rest of us. I'm up next, and surely

Papa is already scheming. The aunties told me they think he'll want to connect us to the Baron family next, but I hope that's false gossip."

"The Barons." I frown. "I hope your father knows that's a terrible idea. Blake Baron's an anomaly in our world. Mysterious and untouchable. You'd do much better marrying an Irishman."

Arianna scrunches her face, and Gin laughs.

I pretend to be offended. "What's that look for? The Irish are perfectly attractive men."

"They're big and scary." Arianna shudders. "Somehow you managed to get the biggest, scariest of them all, yet you're happily married. I don't think I'd have that kind of luck."

"You never know until—"

"Put me down! You *monster*!" Sophia's scream tears through the hallway below.

A man—not Nikolai Kozlov—carries my cousin over his broad shoulder. He rumbles a laugh as she frantically struggles against him, then he swats her ass.

Arianna and Gin gasp

I blink, shocked at the crude display.

He's kidnapping Sophia, strolling right through the front door, and no one's attempting to stop him.

Arianna and I look at each other in horror.

"Did he—? Who was that?"

Gin answers. "Roman De Luca. I noticed him staring at Sophia earlier."

"Well he can't just *take* her like that! She's engaged to Nik." I can't believe this is happening. Where is my uncle? Where are the Russians?

"Actually, it's worse than you think." Arianna's pale as a ghost. "Roman De Luca really is a monster."

Uncle Davide steps out of a doorway and gestures for us to come down. I follow my cousins downstairs and into his office, where Aunt Rosa joins us.

"What is the meaning of this!" My aunt shouts at her husband once the door has closed. "You better start speaking."

Uncle Davide holds up his hands in surrender against his wife's fury. "I had no choice. Roman De Luca and I came to an understanding. Sophia is no longer engaged to Nikolai Kozlov. She will marry Mr. De Luca instead. Everything will be fine."

"Everything is *not* fine!" Aunt Rosa glances at us. "You girls go join the party. You don't need to be involved in this. This is between me and my husband."

Quickly, we scurry from the office as Aunt Rosa lays into Uncle Davide. We climb back up to our perch on the landing. The hairs on the back of my neck stand on end, prickling with awareness. My bodyguard is watching us.

Arianna grabs my shoulder, turning me to face her. "Roman De Luca murdered his first wife. Now he has Sophia. We have to do something. She's in grave danger."

"Are you sure? Your father seemed... less concerned."

"I'm sure. He either doesn't know or doesn't care. We have to help Sophia before it's too late."

My mind races, seeking a solution. Uncle Davide didn't try to stop Roman and we know they have an understanding. One that Sophia didn't agree to by the look of things. Disappointment and anger flares in my veins. I thought my uncle was a better man than my father, but it seems I was wrong. Uncle Davide is just as quick to sell his daughter as Papa was to put me up for sale.

What can we do? How do we stop this?

Cian's out of town, so he can't help us. I don't trust any other man but him.

"We're going to have to save Sophia ourselves," I murmur. "But first..." I glance around until I spot Wolfe sulking in a dark corner. He's been my shadow all evening, as that's his job. Unfortunately, he won't let me go after Sophia on my own. He certainly won't help me confront Roman De Luca.

Which leaves me no choice but to get him out of the way. How does a person incapacitate a huge Irishman? I purse my lips in thought.

I don't have the time to drug him. Hitting him over the head seems insufficient. I don't want to do anything that would risk his life. He's going to be furious with me, and hate me even more after tonight, so I'll have to do this as gently as possible. Or say screw it and go for maximum effectiveness.

"But first *what*?" Arianna presses. "I can't read your mind."

"First we have to deal with my bodyguard. I'm open to ideas on how to get rid of him for tonight. Not permanently," I clarify.

"Can't we just give him the slip?" Arianna points to a window. "We can climb out through there."

I shake my head. "You don't know Wolfe. He has a sixth sense when it comes to guarding people. I'm worried that he's already suspicious, and I'm only *thinking* about getting rid of him. As soon as we move, he'll be on to us. Trust me. I need something he won't see coming. Something... unpredictable."

Ginevra moves closer to me, her voice low. "How about something extremely *predictable* instead?"

"Like what?"

She whispers, "Like you're in trouble. Like someone's trying to take you from the party. Bodyguards go rabid over that type of thing. Naturally."

A slow smile forms on my lips. "Gin, you're a genius."

She beams at me.

"So... what's the plan?" Arianna surveys the foyer below us.

"You two go save Sophia. I'll stay here and deal with that bodyguard." Gin glances over the railing at him. "Do you have his number?"

I nod.

"Good. Give me his number. I'll call him, but then hang up. This is all going to happen real quick. As soon as he's distracted by the phone, duck down and hide. I'll go down there and tell him I saw someone forcing you into the basement. Once he enters the basement, I'll lock him into that creepy room we used to play in as kids."

"Gin, that's terrible," Arianna chides her, but doesn't seem opposed to the plan.

She shrugs. "Sometimes you have to do terrible things to get what you want."

"Let's not waste another minute. Think of Sophia, Arianna, she's in danger." I need her on my side, totally committed if we're going to pull this off.

"Right. This is for the greater good. Let's do this."

I share Wolfe's contact with Gin. She presses his number and it rings.

Wolfe briefly glances up at me, taking note of my location I'm sure, before his phone steals his attention. The crease between his brows deepens as he stares at the unknown number.

That's all I see.

The next second, Arianna and I sprint through an open door. By the time Wolfe looks up again, I'll have disappeared.

A commotion downstairs tells me Ginevra's already put the rest of her plan into action. A loud, masculine voice booms, "Everybody move!"

We're hidden away for the moment. Now we need to figure out the next steps of our plan.

"Try calling Sophia. We need to find out where she's going."

Arianna dials her sister's number, but it goes to voicemail. She tries to reach her again and again, to no avail.

"She's not answering. What are we going to do?" She frowns in thought.

With Wolfe out of the way, we're free to leave. "We should get to the car. If she calls, I want to be ready to go to her. If only we'd gotten away earlier, we could have followed them."

"Too late for that now." Arianna pokes her head out the door. "It's all clear. Let's go. Follow me."

Like two thieves, we sneak down the back staircase to the first floor, then slip out the door to the garage. The car Wolfe drove me here in is parked in the private driveway.

"We're going nowhere real fast if you don't have a key." Arianna and I approach the car.

I pull the fob from my clutch. "Security measure. I always carry a key fob so if anything were to happen to my driver, I can drive myself out of danger. Cian's big on safety measures."

We get into the car, then wait. There's nothing else we can do. Maybe this is a stupid idea. We can hardly rescue Sophia if we don't know where Roman's taking her, can we? There's no guarantee that they're headed to his house. Wherever that may be.

Arianna sends Sophia one text after another.

I wish I knew someone who had the technology to ping Sophia's phone. Or that in all these years we had thought to share our location with each other. Hell, I'd even take jewelry with a tracking device in it at this point. Anything that would let us know where Roman De Luca is taking my cousin.

I could call Brendan, he's set us up with all sorts of fancy new security systems, but I don't want to get him involved. How would I explain what happened to Wolfe?

Arianna's phone vibrates in her hands. She answers it. "Sophia, are you okay?"

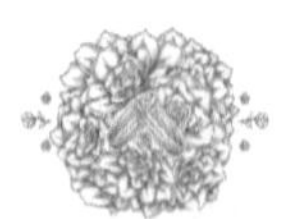

"Make a left up here. Not from this lane, from the other lane!" Arianna screams as I swerve through traffic.

"Sorry. I'm not used to driving. Now where?" I glance at my cousin. She's focused on her phone and the little pin icon that points us to Sophia's location in Connecticut.

As she's navigating for us, my phone keeps chiming with calls and texts from Wolfe. I don't dare answer a single one of those until this is all over. I'm probably giving the man a heart attack, but if he wasn't such a grumpy bastard I might have placed more trust in him. Then he could be the one driving late at night in questionable weather.

As we near the state border, the weather gets worse. Snow flurries obscure the highway. The temperature plummets. If this keeps up, we might not be able to reach Sophia tonight.

Which is unacceptable. She could be dead by morning.

Maybe that's an overreaction since Mr. De Luca did said he'd marry her, stealing her away from Nik and the Russians. But I've learned never to take a man for his word. They all lie. I don't trust Roman De Luca any further than I can throw him.

Plus he *murdered* his last wife. I'm not letting that happen to my cousin.

"Oh no!" Arianna gasps, shaking her phone.

"What?" My gaze darts to her. "What's wrong?"

"It's gone. It was just there. Now it's gone."

"What's gone?"

"The pin on the map! Her location. She was moving one minute and the next... *poof*, gone!"

"Okay. Just calm down. We're in the middle of a storm, so I'm not surprised. We have her last known location. Get us there and we'll figure out what happened." My grip tightens on the steering wheel. The windshield wipers struggle to keep up with the worsening blizzard. God, what is this weather?

Once we get off the highway, the main road leads us to an area of large estates. Sprawling mansions with gated entries, and acres of land are covered in fresh, white swirling snow.

"This must be it." Arianna glances up at a formidable gate as I slow the car. "Sophia's pin was right beside this place when it disappeared."

Turning into the driveway, I stop at the entrance and roll down my window. Frigid air and freezing rain mixed with snow blast in the vehicle. Arianna gasps at the sudden cold.

Ignoring the weather, I press the intercom. No one answers.

I press it again.

"What if they won't let us in?" Arianna asks, her teeth clattering. "I don't know about you, but I can't climb those walls in this dress, especially in this weather."

"If they don't let us in, we'll make a new plan. Hold on." I press the button for a third time, annoyed. If they don't answer soon, we're going to freeze to death out here.

Static crackles, then an irritated male voice says, "Mr. De Luca doesn't see visitors at this hour. Come back in the morning."

The crackling cuts out.

I press the button again, and again. My stomach drops with disappointment. Frustrated, I sigh.

"They're not going to let us in," I state the obvious.

"So what's plan B? Are we scaling the walls?" She casts me a doubtful look. "Or can we slip between those bars on the gate?"

The wind has picked up again, obscuring the sight of everything further than five feet away. I roll up the window and crank the heat on high, then evaluate the situation.

We're in evening dresses and high heels. Neither one of us thought to bring a coat on our hasty departure. If we get out of the car, we'll more than likely die in this blizzard. Who knows how long the walk is from this gate to the house, it could be half a mile or more, too far to risk.

Damn.

"Is there a hotel nearby?" I ask.

Arianna taps on her phone. "Crap." She types some more. "I can't get any search results. My phone says I have service, but it's not working."

I try my own phone, but nothing will load. Even when I attempt to send a text to Wolfe it fails to go through. We're on our own.

Defeat settles heavily across my shoulders. "We're going to have to stay here for the night."

Arianna's gaze snaps to mine. "In the *car*?"

I nod. "If we stay inside where it's warm, we should make it through until morning. There should be emergency supplies under our seats."

I reach beneath mine, pulling out a small bottle of water, a flare, and a thermal blanket. Arianna discovers the same under her seat. Thanks goodness Cian's some kind of boy scout.

"Better than nothing. Maybe we won't freeze to death," she mutters.

"I'm so sorry about all of this."

She glances over at me, a rueful smile on her face. "What an amazing rescue attempt. I wouldn't hire us, that's for sure."

"It's not over yet. This is just a setback. In the morning, hopefully the storm will pass, then we'll get into that house and save Sophia."

CHAPTER 35

Ravenna

Glaring sunlight woke me up this morning. Miraculously, we survived the blizzard in the car, and although I feel dead tired from a restless, uncomfortable night's sleep, I'm ready to see this rescue through to the end.

On the plus side, the weather has cleared, we're alive, and I can pick the gate's lock if they won't come down from the house and let us in.

The downsides? I can't walk far in these heels, and both of our phones' batteries died. They're charging but it may be a while.

Starting the car, I blast the heat. Once it's nice and toasty inside, I roll down the window and press that damn intercom again.

Immediately a voice comes on the line, "De Luca residence. How may I help you?"

I scowl at the polite voice. Like they don't know we've been out here all night long?

"My cousin, Sophia, is a... guest. I've come to visit her."

"I'm sorry. There's no one here by that name." The crackling abruptly cuts out.

"Damn it!" I roll up the window, then smack my hands against the steering wheel. "I'll show that *stronzo* how serious I am. Wait here."

"Where are you—?"

Getting out of the car, I slam the door closed behind me, cutting off Arianna's question. Fury heats my blood.

I march through the snow to the gate. Up close the bars are actually fairly wide apart. No so far that a large man would fit through them, but I certainly can. Angling my body, I step through the gap, my heels sinking into the snow.

I better make this quick if I don't want to lose my toes to frostbite.

On the inside, I find the old fashioned padlock. Plucking a bobby pin from my disheveled hair, I pick the ancient lock. At this point, I don't even care if a security team shows up. I'd gladly give them a piece of my mind.

When the mechanism releases, I manually swing the gates open wide enough to drive through.

Back in the car, I put it into gear and step on the gas. The vehicle lurches forward. About a quarter mile ahead stands Mr. De Luca's formidable mansion and our destination.

"How did you get the gate open?" Arianna asks in awe.

"Picked the lock."

"I didn't know you could do that."

I shoot her a sideways glance. "We all have our secrets."

Not even bothering to park, I pull up to the front door and cut the engine. We rush to the entrance. As soon as a housekeeper opens up to see who it is, we elbow our way inside.

"Stop! Come back here!" The woman screams as we dash up the stairs.

My heart hammers as we climb the stairs. We get to the first landing, when a man appears in the hallway. Roman De Luca's impeccably dressed in a dark suit, his short black hair perfectly styled. Menacing dark eyes stare us down. He's every bit as intimidating as I imagined.

"What are you doing in my house?" he demands.

I should be afraid. Arianna and I are in a stranger's home—a dangerous stranger. But I'm too livid to back down, or to take any type of sensible approach.

I confront him head on. "You kidnapped my cousin. I want her back."

"Is that so?" he drawls.

"Yes. Now where is she?"

He folds his arms. "Get out of my house. You're trespassing."

"I'm not leaving until we see Sophia!"

"I said get out!" He snarls.

A door in the hallway suddenly opens, and Sophia flings herself at Arianna. They embrace as relief washes over me. She's alive. Now we just need to get her away from this man.

I glare at him.

He manages to look bored, like we're nothing but a minor inconvenience. A hiccup in his daily routine.

"What happened to you last night?" Arianna asks Sophia.

"I fell through some ice and into a lake."

That catches my attention.

"Are you okay?" Arianna asks before I manage to utter a word.

"I'm fine. Roman rescued me." She sneaks an appreciative glance at her rescuer.

Now *that's* a shocking turn of events. I gaze at the brooding man with interest.

He scowls. "I'm very busy. Conclude your business and get out."

"Give me my cousin," I snap at him, "and we will happily leave you alone."

"I can't do that."

"Can't or won't?" I challenge him.

He sneers at me. "Both. You wanted to see that she's alive, and there she is. Now get out."

Frustrated by the entire situation, I try to reason with him. "Fine. I'll pay you for her. How much do you want?"

Men like him only understand two things: Power and money.

Chuckling, low and dangerous, he steps closer to me, but I hold my ground. Cian's much bigger and scarier looking than this man and he doesn't intimidate me. I'll never cower before a man again.

"I don't want money. I don't want anything you could possibly have to offer me. And if either of you interfere here again, your family will never find your bodies. I have no issues making enemies with the Pontrellis or the O'Rourkes, or anyone else for that matter. So leave. Never come back."

Sophia speaks up. "You're such a tyrant. These are my best friends, you can't throw them out of the house. Not while I'm supposed to live here too."

Surprise flickers across his features, mirroring my own reaction. Obviously she's unafraid of her kidnapper.

He studies Sophia like he's seeing her in a new light.

"You think I'm being unreasonable?" he asks her, frowning as if he's considering that idea as valid.

"Did my use of the word *tyrant* tip you off? Or are you simply that intuitive?" Sophia sasses at him.

I swallow a chuckle. I'm so proud of my cousin for standing up to this brute.

Roman's dark eyes light with amusement. In a second it's gone. But I know what I saw. Worse, I recognize his reactions to Sophia for what they really are. He likes her.

He stole her from Nikolai.

He rescued her last night.

He finds her sass amusing.

This man would never admit it, not yet anyway, but he *likes* Sophia. And when a man like Roman De Luca sets his sights on a woman, the world will burn down before he'll ever let her go.

I glance at her. She gazes at Roman with a mix of irritation and intrigue.

Suddenly, I sense that I'm intruding where I don't belong. Sophia's not in danger. Not from this man.

Relief settles into my bones. This situation could have turned out very differently. But these two, I can already see them as a couple. There's way more spark between them than Sophia ever had with Nik.

We're allowed to stay, and she invites us into her bedroom, telling us all about what transpired last night.

She's safe. That's all that matters.

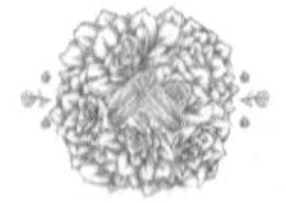

Riding in the car with Wolfe has never been more strained than right now. After being released from my cousin's basement, which Gin ended up getting in trouble for with her parents, he tracked us down to Roman's house.

Arianna went back home with her father's people, while I'm stuck with Wolfe. He's never been especially sociable, but now he won't talk to me at all. He barely glances my way. Keeping his head down, jaw clenched, he drives me home.

"I said, I'm sorry." My third attempt at an apology goes over as well as the first two.

Wolfe shrugs. I don't think there's a forgiving bone in this man's body.

I sigh. Maybe I should have handled that situation differently. Regret slithers across my skin. I didn't mean to hurt him, or to make him my enemy. Too late for that now.

Wolfe pulls up to the brownstone and opens my door for me, but refuses to meet my gaze. Anger radiates off him in waves.

I slide out of the back seat. I'm almost to the front

door when Wolfe speaks, startling me after the long, silent car ride.

"You dropped this," he murmurs in a clipped tone.

I turn toward him, arm outstretched to take whatever it is from him, and pause. A gold shamrock pendant dangles from his fingers. The four leaves are encrusted with diamonds, an emerald stone in the center. It's beautiful, and looks expensive. Too bad someone lost it in the snow.

"That's not mine." My hand drops to my side.

"It fell out of your purse."

"No it didn't. I've never seen that before in my life. Someone must have dropped it." Why is he pushing that jewelry on me?

"Fine. Whatever." He lets the pendant slip through his fingers and sink into the snow. Brow furrowed, he gets back into the car and drives off.

I stare after him, guilt ripping me in two. If only I could figure out how to make amends.

The necklace catches my eye. Even if it's not mine, I can't leave it out here, it's much too pretty. Picking it up, I study the piece. Eighteen carat gold. Diamonds and emerald on a four leaf clover attached to a gold chain. Whoever lost this will be sad. I tuck it into my clutch for safe keeping.

As I walk through the front door, I'm surprised to find Cian home. Did he change his plans and come back early?

I've never seen Cian's pale blue gaze alight with so much fury. He knows. Wolfe must have already told him about what happened last night.

Fists clenched at his sides, I can tell he's desperately

trying to control his temper. But I don't want his control, I want his understanding.

I set my clutch on the entryway table. "I didn't have any other option. Wolfe would have stopped me from going to Mr. De Luca's house."

"Exactly!" Cian snarls. "His job is to *protect you.* No one else. You! To hell with everyone else if your life is in danger."

"That's where you're wrong," I snap, my own cool-headedness hanging on by a thread. "I'd *die* to protect those I love. That includes my cousins. You weren't there, you didn't see how Roman carried her out of the house over his shoulder, and everyone stood around, watching. Not a single person—"

"It doesn't matter!"

"Yes it does! Not a single person tried to stop him. You don't know what it feels like to never have anybody interfere. For no one to stand up for you when you need it most. To save you from the monsters of this world." I jab my thumb at my chest. "I will not idly sit by and let my loved ones get hurt!"

"Roman De Luca is a dangerous man," he growls.

"Exactly! I wouldn't have tried to save Sophia from him if he weren't." Why can't he understand my perspective?

"What you did was reckless." He turns away from me, raking his fingers through his long blond hair that's loose around his shoulders.

"I'd do it again in a heartbeat. I have no remorse." It's the truth. Although, what I had to do to get Wolfe out of the way pains me. He didn't deserve that.

"*Jesus, Mary, and Joseph!* You're going to drive me to

an early grave, woman." Cian faces me again, his cheeks and neck tinged pink. "You make protecting you nearly *impossible.* What the fuck am I supposed to do with you?"

"Understand why I did what I had to do. Love me for who I am. Please." All I want is his understanding. Is that too much to ask?

His features soften. "I *do* love you."

"I love you too. I understand why you're upset, but I'm not going to apologize for my actions." I hug my middle, fighting against the burn behind my eyes. I'm so damn tired. "I was beaten for years of my life and no one ever stepped in to stop it. They were all too scared of my father. I'm not scared, not any more. After what I've been through, I'll never sit by and let anything happen to someone else. I *can't.*" My voice breaks. "The things Roman could have done to Sophia... I couldn't live with myself if I let him. I *needed* to make sure she was okay."

Cian's arms envelope me, encompassing me in his protective embrace. His warmth and spicy scent surround me as he pulls me into his chest.

"Shh, *broc meala.* I'm only angry because I could have lost you, and I wasn't here to be by your side to rescue your cousin. I should have been here. I should have gone to that engagement party with you. I'm sorry I wasn't here when you needed me."

I wrap my arms around him, my cheek pressed against his chest. "Would you have gone after my cousin with me?"

"Of course. I would have taken twenty men and stormed De Luca's mansion."

I let out a soft chuckle. "You would have started a war with him."

"Meh. I don't care, as long as you're happy." He smooths his enormous palm over my hair. "I know you love your family. Having never been close to mine, then betrayed by my brother, I forget what that feels like. But yes, I understand the burning need to make sure my loved one is safe. I'm sorry I wasn't here."

"You don't need to apologize. I'm sorry I made you worry."

He sighs. "I'm sorry for being angry."

"I understand why you were. If anyone deserves an apology it's Wolfe. Do you think he'll ever forgive me for having one of my cousins lock him in a cellar? For ditching him like that?" I pull back enough to gaze up at Cian. "He didn't say a single word to me on the ride home."

"Winning his forgiveness might be the toughest battle of your life. Wolfe's still holding onto grudges from more than twenty years ago."

"Hm. I figured he was that type of man." My heart sinks.

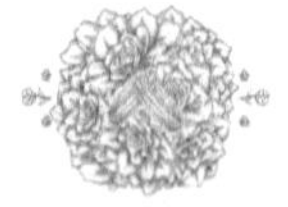

A few days later I let myself into the house, and run into Brendan in the foyer. He's on a ladder, doing some work beside the door.

"New security system installation?" I ask, always curious what he's up to in our home.

"Just some upgrades, Mrs. O'Rourke. Installing a new motion sensor for this room." He continues working while he gives me the necessary details without further elaboration. He's always succinct.

"Is that really needed?"

He gives a one shoulder shrug. "This way the camera for the door only turns on when there's movement. The last one was faulty, unreliable. No use recording this area when there's no one here."

"Makes sense. Thanks for doing that."

"Have a good day, Mrs. O'Rourke."

"You too." I'm about to head up the stairs when Cian appears on the main floor hallway.

"I need to speak with you." He doesn't sound too happy.

"Oh? About what?"

He tilts his head toward his office, and I follow him inside. We kiss in greeting, then he settles behind his desk, back to focusing on business. Apparently business that somehow includes me.

"Wolfe called." He eyes me and my chest tightens. "He doesn't want to drive you anymore. Doesn't want to be your bodyguard either. I'm sorry, but I'm going to give you a new driver and guard."

"That's fine." I round the desk, sitting my ass on the hard surface. "There's no love lost between me and Wolfe. He's never going to forgive me, and I don't want him to spend his days doing something he hates."

Wolfe's been especially short-tempered and unfriendly. Understandably so.

Cian releases a relived sigh. "Okay. I didn't know how you'd take that news. I didn't want to upset you."

"I'm really fine. Wolfe's grumpy on the best of days, you can only imagine what he's been like since the... incident."

"Oh, I can imagine." He chuckles. "You injured his pride and he's going to lick that wound for a very long time."

"I know, and I'm sorry for it."

"I don't think you fully understand. Wolfe used to be an assassin, freelance, a hitman for hire. He was damn good at it too. The very idea of him getting bested by three young women and locked in a cellar... Well, I'm surprised he feels he can show his face anywhere. The story spread like wildfire through the men." Cian's hand settles on my thigh. "Of course, the first man to try to tease him about it ended up in the hospital. So the others have been quiet since then, but they all know what happened. You sort of damaged Wolfe's reputation."

My stomach drops like a lead weight. I hadn't realized what I'd done would have these kinds of repercussions. No wonder Wolfe hates my guts.

"Is there anything I can do to make this right?" I ask Cian.

He shakes his head. "I doubt it. Sorry, *broc meala*."

Unease swarms in my gut. I'd hoped by now that the Irish would at least tolerate me, instead of treating me like an outsider. I'm beginning to think my status here will never change until I have a half-Irish child. Even then, *I* might not be accepted by them, but I'll have family ties through my offspring. But will that ever come to be?

CHAPTER 36
Cian

After going through the Monahan brothers' dossiers, several months ago, I decided to take action. Neither my people nor the Italians needed to get tangled up with these newcomers. I sent a text message to the number my cousin Niall acquired for me, supposedly it was Cormac Monahan's personal contact. But my message went unanswered for months.

All through the house's renovation, and the drama with Ravenna's cousin, Sophia being taken by De Luca. Which ended up being fine, until it wasn't. They married earlier this summer, but now they're going through a sort of falling out. I try not to get involved unless Ravenna insists.

Business has been going well, we even plugged that money leak in that Harlem gambling den.

But hearing back from Cormac Monahan brightens my day. It means I can finally move forward on this front.

CORMAC MONAHAN:

We'll meet. O'Malley's bar. Wednesday. Six PM.

A relieved sigh pushes past my lips. Meeting with these men is the first step toward negotiating peace between us. Though they've been quiet recently, until we have a deal, I'm counting my blessings.

Too many times in the history of this area have Irish gangs ended up in feuds with each other. Those wars only end once every member of a gang has been wiped from this earth. We're better off finding a way to work with the Monahans instead of against them.

I've waited a good long while for this meeting. Immediately, I send a confirmation text to Cormac and give Wolfe an update with instructions. We have one chance to make a good impression. We can't fuck this up.

A knock comes at my door, drawing my attention. It opens, and Ravenna peeks inside before I have a chance to respond.

"Are you terribly busy?" she asks.

I smile at my wife. "I'm never too busy for you."

"I know, but I always like to ask." She returns my grin, and steps inside. "I saw the doctor earlier today."

I practically fly out of my chair in my haste to go to her. My hands skim her body, seeking the slightest injury or reason she'd have to go to the doctor—and not inform me about it first.

"What's wrong?" My tone comes out harsher than I meant.

She grips my forearms to still my wandering hands. "Nothing's wrong. Actually, I'm as healthy as can be."

"Then why visit the doctor?"

"Because, given our ages and general health, I should be pregnant by now and I'm not. So I finally decided to see if I had any fertility issues." Her gaze catches mine. "I don't. There's absolutely no issue with my reproductive organs."

I hold her around the waist. "That's good."

"It is. It just means... I'm not the reason we haven't started a family yet."

Seeing her point, I frown.

"Well that's—" I clear my throat. "I'll schedule an appointment to get checked out."

I had considered that the problem might be me, though I didn't want to think about it. Now that I have to, the answer is pretty obvious. The things my ex did to me... She very well could have left me damaged in a permanent way.

I might not be able to give my wife a child.

That realization punches me in the gut. I tighten my grip on her to steady myself as the room spins.

"*Cian*, are you all right?" Ravenna's worried face floats before my eyes. "Cian?"

I blink several times to clear my head. Gradually, the world rights itself.

Grunting, I say, "Yeah. I'm okay."

Releasing her, I drop into a nearby chair, my head in my hands. What if I can't give us a family? What if I'm damaged beyond repair? Will Ravenna still love me when it will only ever be the two of us together, no children and no grandchildren?

"Cian, talk to me. What's going on? I didn't mean to

make this awkward. Or to hurt you in any way." She smooths back my hair.

I look up at her. "You're not. I'm fine. We'll figure this all out."

Worry fills her blue-grey eyes. "If you're sure you're okay."

"I am." Taking a deep breath, I sit upright. "How's your cousin doing?" I'll talk about anything for a change of subject, even Ravenna's dramatic extended family.

Roman and Sophia seemed happy when we attended their nuptials. When they came back from their honeymoon all hell broke loose. Since then, Sophia's been living at her parents' house and Ravenna spends a lot of her time visiting.

Apparently, Roman did something unforgivable, but I don't have the mental capacity to get too involved with all of that when I'm trying to keep my own empire alive and thriving.

What I do know is that the peace between the Italians and the Russians is precarious at best. But that all went up in smoke as soon as the engagement between Sophia and Nikolai ended.

Are all families such a handful? Do they always have this much drama going on?

Will I ever get to have my own children and find out?

For a moment, I wonder about my cousins. The Bane family, like all good Irish Catholics, has seven children—my cousins. All adults now. But I can only imagine the kind of insanity that goes on in that household.

"Sophia's heartbroken. I'm not sure she'll ever be okay again." Ravenna settles on my lap. "I have half a mind to kill Roman De Luca. Though word is no one's seen him. He's become a complete recluse. If I ever see him again, I'll stab his eyes out."

I chuckle. "Remind me to never get on your bad side. You're a vicious woman, *broc meala*."

"You love me for it. Admit it." She loops her arms around my neck.

"I admit it. I love you." I kiss her forehead.

But will love be enough to keep us together if I can't give her children?

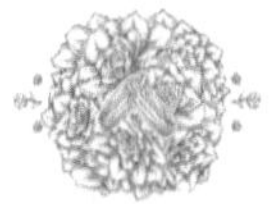

From the outside, O'Malley's looks like a dive bar in a rough part of town. Inside it's not much better. The place reeks of cheap booze and body odor. Even the thick cigar smoke doesn't manage to mask the less pleasant scents.

As soon as I enter, all eyes turn on me and the two men I brought along. I'm used to stranger's stares at this point, as my frame not only fills the doorway but I have to duck to enter. Then, of course, the jagged scars across my face demand attention.

Several people quickly glance away, while others take their time sizing me up. I hate how often some of the larger guys see me as a challenge they're compelled to take on. They see me and immediately think it's an opportunity to prove themselves. To who, I'm not sure. Themselves, maybe?

It never ends well for them. Their fragile egos ultimately take as much of a beating as their flesh.

Today, one such massive guy approaches me, looking me up and down, his gaze barely touches on the two guys behind me. My fingers curl into fists, ready for what's coming next.

"Are you Cian O'Rourke?" he asks, openly studying my scars.

Narrowing my eyes, I nod.

"Come with me." He turns and leads us further into the bar.

Not what I expected to happen. But I'm far from out of danger's reach, so I keep my guard up as I follow him into a private back room.

He stops my two bodyguards from entering. "They stay out here."

I consider the risks. I'll be vulnerable in there without backup. Ultimately, I'm on Monahan turf and what they want goes, so I tell my men to stay put. They know to take this guy out and charge into that room if anything unsavory happens.

I enter alone. Chairs surround several round tables, and I realize it's a gambling joint. Currently not in use.

Three Irishmen sit at a single table. When I approach, they stand.

The man in the middle immediately catches my attention. His height and form rival my own, but it's the multitude of white scars across his neck that draw my eyes. Someone tried to decapitate him and almost succeeded. Instead leaving his flesh ruined for all to see.

A sense of intimate understanding grips my chest.

I meet his green gaze, striking beneath his thick black hair. A tailored, dark suit gives him an even more formidable energy. He's a bit older than me, but I wouldn't want to meet him alone in a dark alley.

He's flanked by two men who hold a close resemblance to him. I'm guessing all three are the Monahan brothers. Which means the most powerful men of their gang are right here in this room. I'd never take that risk. Wolfe and I rarely appear in the same place at the same time, especially under potentially dangerous circumstances. Leadership must be preserved or my men will fight among themselves until a new one rises to take charge.

While the man in the middle is my height, the other two aren't much shorter. One stares at me with a scowl. He has reddish-blond hair, and dresses more casually in a black button down shirt with dark slacks.

The third man smirks at me. Easy going. Though I see the glint of death in his blue-green stare. He's dressed in a Henley with dark jeans and a blazer.

"I'm Cian O'Rourke."

"The one they call The Beast?" asks the sour-faced one.

I nod my confirmation.

He looks me up and down before he introduces himself and his brothers. "I'm Liam Monahan. This is Killian," he gestures to the smiling one, "and that's Cormac."

I bob my head. "Pleasure to meet you. You seem to be settling well into New York City."

They sit, motioning for me to do the same. We're left alone in this room, me facing them. Could they take me out right now if they wanted? Probably. Though that's not why we agreed to meet. No guns drawn, let's hope it stays that way.

Liam, the perpetually grouchy Monahan by the looks of him, speaks again, "We came to an agreement with the Flannagans, as they're family, and our only interest is in taking over their small empire."

For now. Until they get greedy enough to fight for more turf, more money, more power.

"As long as you don't mess with us, we'll stay out of your way," he states.

I grunt. "Apparently there's some confusion over our property lines. If you recall our skirmish last year?"

"That was our mistake," Liam admits. He unfolds a large piece of paper on the table. "This is the map from Old Mister Flannagan. It seems to need updating."

I look it over, noting where the Flannagans handed over a chunk of land to the Italians a few years ago in exchange for some favor or another. That turf was turned over to us when I married Ravenna.

Liam hands me a marker. "Draw it in for us."

I catch his dark brown gaze, sensing a trap. I could easily create any new border that I want. They'd never know the difference if I took five blocks from them or twenty.

Glancing at Cormac, their leader, though he hasn't uttered a word, I read the challenge in his eyes.

"Go on," says the youngest Monahan, Killian. His friendly grin seems superficial at best, predatory at worst.

That's when I realize this is, in fact, a test. The map before me is an old one, but they have a newer version somewhere. They'll know if I'm honest or not. But they want me to think they're ignorant.

Tricky Irish. Though I'm mildly amused that they think they can trick one of their own people.

I uncap the marker and draw the new boundary line exactly where it should be as three pairs of watchful eyes bore into me.

Done, I toss the marker on the map.

Cormac studies my handiwork, then nods.

"We thank you for this," Liam says, seeming to answer for Cormac. I'm beginning to wonder if the man is mute. Those old wounds on his neck could have caused permanent damage to his vocal chords.

Either way, I don't want my men getting mixed up with the Monahans. In a relatively short time, they've proven themselves not only dangerous, but cunning. A deadly combination. Certainly a hornets nest I don't want to kick.

"We're in agreement of the turf lines, then?" I need to make sure, to hear them say it.

Again, Liam answers. "We are."

"Good. My men and I have partnered with the Italians, they protect—"

Liam cuts me off. "We know all about the war between your people and the Italians. You married a woman from the Pontrelli family to bring peace. That's quite the sacrifice, especially to take on that burden yourself. Very honorable, too. Because of that, we believe you don't want another war with anyone."

I dip my chin. "That's correct."

"Then we don't have to worry about you coming after our slice of the city?" He warily eyes me.

"I don't want it. You have my word." Peace is more appealing to me than more... of anything. Though telling them that would make me appear weak, so I keep that thought to myself.

Liam glances at Cormac and they have some kind of silent conversation. All the while, Killian stares at me, unrelenting. Honestly, the guy's starting to annoy me. But I don't let my aggravation show. I won't let them get under my skin.

Cormac rises, offering me his hand. I stand up, and shake it.

"We'll be in contact if anything else arises." Liam also shakes my hand.

Killian flashes me another of his creepy smiles as he leans back in his chair.

With that, I'm shown out of the room. A short meeting, but I guess we all got our points across.

Though I have a feeling this won't be the last time I cross paths with a Monahan.

CHAPTER 37

Ravenna

The scorching Italian summer sun beams down on us. Today we're all gathered for Sophia and Roman's *second* wedding. Somehow they made up. Seems like they'll get their happily ever after, after all.

After the ceremony, everyone mingles. I find Elena hovering on the outskirts of the crowd.

"Do you think you'll come home now?" I ask her, picking up from our earlier conversation when she told me she was doing better, feeling happier these days.

"Actually, I wanted to talk with you about that."

"Yeah?" Hope blossoms in my chest. I'd love for us to live in the same city again. I miss her. She's been gone for far too long.

"I'd like to stay in Italy indefinitely." She squeezes my arm when my smile drops. "I'm happy here, Ven. This place has become my home in a way that New York will never be. That city is tainted for me and I never want to go back."

"I see." Disappointment hits me hard. "What do you plan on doing here? Do you want to marry, start a family of your own?"

She grimaces. "No. But I have my hobbies. I like to read, and I'm even thinking about writing a fantasy novel."

"Oh? We've never had a novelist in the family." As long as she doesn't just wither away in our great aunt's house, I'm happy for her and her pursuits.

"I'm actually pretty excited about it. It's an epic Romantasy. I know you don't read much fiction, so don't worry I won't make you read it."

"I don't read a lot of fiction these days, but I'd still love to read your book. I'm sure it will be brilliant."

A faint blush touches her cheeks. "Maybe. We'll see. I'm not sure if anyone's first book is any good."

"All that matters is you're happy, Elle." I mean every word.

She grins. "For the first time in a long time, I am. I'm content with life. How about you?"

"I'm content." I haven't confided in my sister about the challenges I've had around getting pregnant. Or the feeling of being shunned by Cian's Irishmen. Nor the sense I have at times that I'm drifting through life and one day I'll wake up an old woman with nothing to show for the years I've lived on this planet.

Worse, it's been many months since I told Cian that I'm healthy, and not the reason we haven't had a child yet. He keeps insisting that he'll get checked out by the doctor, but at this point I've given up asking him about it. Does he not care, or is he afraid to learn the truth?

I understand him well enough to know that he's most

likely afraid of letting me down. I wish he knew that's not possible. Even if it's only the two of us forever, I'd be happy with him. Though he won't believe that.

We regularly have sex. So that's good. Outside of the bedroom we've fallen deeply into our individual routines. I wouldn't say our honeymoon phase is over, we're crazy for each other, especially between the sheets. More importantly, my heart still skips a beat whenever he looks at me like I'm the center of his universe.

"I thought you'd have a million Irish-Italian Catholic babies by now," Elena teases, unaware of my internal frustrations.

I force a smile. "We're still working on that. One day. Hopefully soon."

"What else have you been up to?"

"Not much, honestly. I miss the days of renovating and decorating our home. That kept me busy. I'm not sure what to put my efforts into these days."

"Is there anything you want to do? Anything you're passionate about?" She plucks an hors d'oeuvre from a passing tray and pops it into her mouth.

In all honesty, I'm passionate about making a comfortable and beautiful home for me, Cian, and our children. I'm *passionate* about raising a family. Which has completely stalled out.

With no hope of starting a family on the horizon, I think it may be time that I turn my focus onto something else. But what would give me a sense of fulfillment?

"I'm not sure yet," I answer. "Don't worry about me, I'll figure it out."

Someone taps their wine glass, the ringing sound draws everyone's attention. "Let's eat!"

Cian finds me and we join the newlyweds at their table for the wedding feast. Elena follows behind us, takes one glance at where Cian settles beside me, and she chooses the chair furthest from him. I hate how her eyes light up with fear every time he's around. He's done nothing cruel to her, in fact he barely pays her any attention at all.

Perhaps it's the what-ifs that plague her mind. What if she hadn't been kidnapped? She'd be the one married to him instead of me. She'd be his wife, and she'd hate it.

CHAPTER 38
Cian

"I want to get a job," Ravenna announces a couple weeks after we return to New York from Italy. Her words take me completely by surprise. For a long moment, I stare at where she hovers in my office entrance.

"Why do you want a job? We don't need money, you don't have to work." I'm confused. Don't I provide enough for her? Isn't she happy with what she has? If she wants a job, then I must have somehow failed her. Is she not happy with me?

"I know. And honestly, I feel a little bad potentially taking a paying job away from someone who needs it. But I'll donate everything I make to charity. I'm going stir crazy. I need some kind of routine, structure to my life. I'm not involved in your business and I don't want to be. I want to do something normal—and legal."

I frown at her, not understanding where this is suddenly coming from. "What type of job do you want?"

"Well, I'm not qualified for much. Most of the things

I've looked into require at least some college education, but I talked with Aunt Rosa and she has a friend of a friend who is looking to fill a simple secretary position at a modeling agency. It's nothing glamorous. I'd mostly be getting coffee, running errands, and doing other odds and ends until I've proven I can take on more responsibility. That's if I can even get the job. I have an interview on Wednesday."

I lean back in my chair, arms folded. "You've been busy, haven't you?"

She flushes a pretty pink beneath her tan. "I wanted to have a potential plan in place before talking with you about it. So you know that I'm actually serious, and this isn't a whim."

"Oh, I take you very seriously, *broc meala*, you should know that by now. It seems like this has been on your mind for a while." I study her.

"Sort of. I really came up with the idea when we were in Italy. But I've been feeling restless for months."

Standing up, I go to her and cup her cheek. "All I ever want is for you to be happy. If you think this job will make you happier, then do it. I'll give you anything this world has to offer, as long as it's in my power to do so. But if you ever feel like I'm letting you down, say so."

"You've never let me down," she says sweetly.

We both know that's not entirely true. I let her down when I abandoned her at her parents' house. And now I'm afraid I'm letting her down by not giving her a child. I need to get myself checked by the doctor, though I'm dreading that, so I keep delaying. What if all of my fears are confirmed? What if I'm infertile?

My darling wife could drift into the arms of another

man, one who can give her the family she desires. Which would be my fault, since I can't fulfill her needs. She thinks I'm unaware of it, but I've seen the yearning in her gaze when she sees a child. The way she slows down when we walk past the room that's reserved for a future nursery. Not having a family is slowly killing her inside.

If she finds another man, I'll have no one to blame but myself.

Then I'd have to kill that man. But doing so would destroy Ravenna. Her being with another man would destroy me.

Sometimes I feel like our nearly perfect marriage teeters on the brink of disaster. If I talk with the doctor and they confirm that I'm infertile, what will that do to us? Will that be the beginning of the end?

I try to push away my negative thoughts. Worries and fears won't fix anything. Besides, I should have more faith in my wife, and in *us*, but I'm not perfect. Far from it.

Gently kissing Ravenna, I ask, "What's the name of the agency?"

"Bane Modeling Management."

I grunt in amusement. "I see. Are you sure you don't want to find work that has something to do with your interest in history?"

She wrinkles her nose. "No. History is my escape, I read it to relax. I'd never want to work in that field."

"Very well. If this job is what you really want, I can deliver it to you on a silver platter. You don't need to ask your aunt for this favor."

"Oh? How?" Her beautiful face brightens with intrigue.

"One of my cousins owns that agency. I'll talk with him. He'll make sure you get the job."

Her eyes light up with so much hope that my heart skips a beat. I love making this woman happy.

Years ago, I thought I loved my ex-fiancée, Fiona, but any feelings I had for her pale in comparison to how I adore Ravenna. This is love. True love.

I just hope it's enough to keep us together through the hard times. Every marriage has some difficult ones, right?

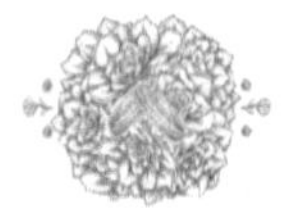

Connor Bane, my cousin, made good on his promise to get Ravenna hired. When I told her the news last night, she jumped on me, which led to some very enthusiastic sex. If I'd known a regular, minimum wage job would make her this excited, I'd have suggested the idea myself.

Rinsing my hair under the shower's scalding spray, an image of my wife in the pencil skirt she bought for this job appears vividly in my mind. Today she's heading into work for her first day. Even though she'll be out of the house for hours, I want her thinking of me. I can't wait to find my wife, lift up that tight skirt, and pump her full of cum.

I'm not going to let her clean up afterwards so that my cum coats her thighs all day long. My cock hardens at the thought.

I shut off the water. Wrapping a towel around my

hips, I go in search of Ravenna. She should be in her dressing room getting ready.

Sure enough, her door's ajar. I peek through the opening, not yet alerting her to my presence. She's wearing a blue blouse with a black skirt that hugs every curve. Her hair's pulled up into a bun, pinned in place. Her legs look a mile long in those high heels.

As if she has a sixth sense, her gaze snaps to mine in the full length mirror. She smiles, invitingly.

I push open the door. Immediately I'm hit with the scent of vanilla and ylang-ylang.

My head spins, dark spots appear before my eyes, and I can't breathe. I'm drowning in that cloying odor. An invisible enemy strangles me as I struggle to remain conscious. My knees give out, hitting the soft carpet.

"You have no idea how easy it was to lead you on, Cian. How pathetic you looked, always doting on me, saying you loved me." Fiona's unique perfume wafts into my bruised and bloody face. Vanilla and florals.

"Remember that first time when I was supposed to be visiting my parents in Ireland? I was actually at a cabin with your brother. While you told me how much you missed me on the phone, I was screwing the hell out of Shawn. You're pathetic. No woman will ever take you seriously, much less love you."

"Cian! Cian! Can you hear me?"

I suck in a harsh breath. My vision clears, but I cringe at the scent. Ravenna's in front of me, holding my face between her hands, worry mars her beautiful features.

"I'll be okay," I murmur, trying to sound reassuring, but my voice comes out strained.

"What happened? One moment you seemed fine and the next you collapsed. I'll get the doctor—"

"No." I hold her wrists, and climb to my feet. "I don't need a doctor. It was a... one of those attacks."

Her brow furrows even more. "A panic attack? What set it off?"

I deeply inhale, instantly regretting it. Trying to calm my pounding heart, I say, "Your perfume. It's new. Where did you get it?"

"My perfume? It's not new, I found it in a drawer. I don't remember buying it, but I thought today—"

"It's *her* perfume. Her signature scent that she always wore. Ylang-ylang with vanilla."

"Her... as in your *ex*? Fiona?"

All I can do is nod, my teeth clenched against the offending smell.

She hugs me, her cheek pressed to my bare chest. "I'm so sorry. I didn't know. I'll shower and throw that scent away. I don't even know where it came from."

"Don't. You'll be late for work."

"I have a minute. I'm not spending my day wearing *her* perfume." Opening her dressing room window to try to air the room out, Ravenna hastily goes into the bathroom.

Feeling like I've been gut punched, I sink into her vanity chair. The fresh air helps clear my head further.

What are the chances of Ravenna purchasing the exact same scent that Fiona wore? If she even did buy it.

Is my ex haunting me from the grave? Why now?

CHAPTER 39
Ravenna

By the time the holiday season rolls around, I'm settled into my new job. It's nothing to brag about, as I mostly run errands for my boss and her personal secretary. I have been to a few modeling shoots, which are like stepping into a whole other world at the studio. When we're doing those, I'm pretty much the gofer for everyone. I like to think of my position as keeping everyone's basic needs fulfilled at all times. Preferably before they even ask.

Plus, I'm appreciated. Which is a bonus to my self-esteem that I didn't expect.

When I told my cousins about my new job, they were happy for me too. For the first time in years, I feel like I'm actually doing something with my life.

At first I thought having to be at work every morning at eight sharp would be a challenge, but now that I'm used to it I'm thriving on the structure of a set schedule. Monday through Friday, eight hours a day, I know where I'll be and what's expected of me. The weekends are my own time. Most of those are spent with Cian, my cousins, and some me time.

Christmas Eve and Christmas Day the agency closes for the holiday, so I have two extra days off this week.

When Finn pulls the car up to the house after work, Cian's returning from his day too. We meet at the front door and he leans down to kiss me, lightly, with some reservation, and I sense he's preoccupied.

He lets us into our home. I'm about to head upstairs to change into something more comfortable when he calls my name. The torment in his voice stops me in my tracks. I turn to face him.

"What's wrong?" I study his unusually pale skin, the tightness in his shoulders, and the way he seems to draw himself inward.

He clears his throat, a sure sign that he's nervous about what he's going to say. "I don't want this to ruin our holiday, so may as well get it out now rather than let it fester. I got checked by the doctor today. I'm damaged. The torture... There's only a slim chance of me getting you pregnant." His tone drops. "I'm so sorry, *broc meala*."

I reach for him. "It's okay. I've had a feeling that might be the case." I hug him tight. "I'm so sorry for what you went through, that this happened to you. But we'll be okay."

After a moment's hesitation, he envelopes me in his arms. His body shudders with either relief or tension, I can't tell.

He's put this off for so long that I never thought he'd get checked out. Now I understand why. As I suspected, he's been afraid of letting me down. Doesn't he know that I love him no matter what challenges we face, as long as we strive to overcome them together?

"This doesn't ruin our holiday, *amore mio*. I'm glad you talked to the doctor and now we can modify our expectations."

Though I don't blame him at all, because it's not his fault, a piece of my heart breaks. This is the confirmation that I've secretly been avoiding thinking on. I might never have a baby.

That realization sinks into my soul. An excruciating sorrow settles in my chest.

He holds me tighter, and I do the same, as if we're each other's life lines in a storm. "But we may never have children. It might be the two of us forever. No kids, no grandkids. Can you live with that?"

"Can you?" I pull back enough to see his face. "Am I enough for you?"

This is the worst case scenario, and in all honesty it's not terrible. I'm so in love with my husband. We're happy together.

His eyes soften. "Of course you're enough. You're more than enough for me."

I smile up at him, my heart swells. "You're enough for me too."

He makes a doubtful face.

I take a moment to gather my thoughts. "I'm serious. Yes, I've always wanted a family, especially with you. But if that's not something God will give us, then I'm grateful he's given you to me. I love you." It's the truth.

"I love you too." He rests his forehead on mine. "I don't want to give up trying for a child. But now we know what to expect."

My heart skips a beat. This isn't the end, it's just a bump in the road.

"Exactly. I don't want to give up either. If it happens, it happens. It may take a miracle, but I'll pray for that. In the meantime, all I want is you."

Tension leaves his body all at once. "You're my life, *broc meala*."

"And you're mine."

I'm working in the office today, helping my boss with the flurry of new model applications. Apparently, the start of the new year always brings in a flood of new hopeful models. New Year's resolutions and all of that.

On my way to grab a pitcher of water and ice, I round a corner and collide with a brick wall. At least that's what it feels like. Two hands reach out to steady me as I regain my balance.

Then my gaze travels up, and up, and up. Amused blue eyes stare down at me. Dirty blond hair, tall, broad... handsome. Stranger. I've never seen this man before.

Taking a step back, I demand, "What are you doing in here?"

One corner of his mouth lifts in a casual smirk. "I work here."

"No you don't."

"Hmm, pretty sure I do. Is this Bane Modeling Management?."

"Well, yes," I sputter. "What's your position here?"

"I'm Scott's new assistant. He's a photographer."

"I know who Scott is."

The man holds out his palm. "My name's Devlin. Devlin Doyle."

Hesitantly, I shake his hand. At first, I assume he's a plant. That Cian found some Irishman to take a job here and keep an eye on me. But why do that at all, and especially after all these months. That doesn't make sense.

So, the more reasonable explanation would be Devlin's exactly what he appears to be. An Irish-American, with no affiliation to my husband or his gang, who now works at Bane Modeling Management.

Cian's cousin owns this place, so if he wanted to keep tabs on me that would be easy enough. Not that I think my husband's the spying type. He simply goes over the top at times in an effort to keep me safe. Which I appreciate—mostly.

"And you are?" Devlin prompts.

I shake myself out of my meandering thoughts. "Ravenna O'Rourke."

"Nice to meet you." His gaze appreciatively flits down my body. The fact that he's checking me out makes me uncomfortable.

"Excuse me." I move past him, going about my work.

Thankfully, with one last lingering glance at me, he leaves to go do his own job.

I release a heavy sigh. The last thing I need at work is a giant, flirty Celt who reminds me entirely too much of my husband. Sure there are plenty of gorgeous male models around every day, but I've never been tempted to spare them more than a glance.

This Devlin fellow, however, makes me uneasy. I think it's his striking resemblance to Cian.

CHAPTER 40
Ravenna

"Some little bee told me that you have a particular liking for Earl Grey lattes. So cheers." Devlin holds out a drink cup from the coffee shop around the corner, presumably of the beverage he just described.

When I don't take it from him, he sighs. "Look, this is my attempt to apologize for the other day. I think I came on a bit too strong. I didn't mean to make you uncomfortable. You're a beautiful woman and it's impossible not to notice, but that's no excuse. I obviously over stepped. I'm sorry. Please take this latte as a peace offering, Ms. O'Rourke."

"*Mrs.* O'Rourke," I correct him.

His brows lift. "I see. Again, my apologies."

"Thanks." To be polite, I take the offered beverage and set it on my desk. There's no way I'm drinking from that cup. Call me paranoid, but he could have spiked with anything from Rohypnol to a deadly poison.

No thank you.

Devlin grins, then straightens to his full height. "Got to get back to work. See you around, *Mrs.* O'Rourke."

I wave an unenthusiastic goodbye.

As soon as he's out of sight, I go and empty the cup down the break room sink.

One of my co-workers, Susan, appears in the doorway. "Hey, there you are."

"Sorry, were you looking for me?" I rack my brain, trying to remember if there's something specific on my schedule for right now.

"Don't worry. It's not work-related." She coasts into the room. "Several of us are going for drinks on Friday after work. Do you want to join us? It's just to the bar a couple blocks over."

So far, I've been working here for several months and have yet to be invited to any social gatherings. "I'd love to!"

"Great!" She grabs a cup of coffee, adds two packs of sugar and disappears back to the work area.

I'm a little distracted throughout the rest of the day thinking about the end of the week and finally, hopefully, making some friends among my co-workers. It's not that they've been mean or anything. They just seem like a close knit group. Not all of them, but the few women in the agency that I really like and respect.

Besides my cousins, I don't really have any friends. My family has always been enough and I never sought that kind of connection elsewhere. Until now.

Plus there's something novel in the idea of having friends who live in the normal world. Women who aren't connected to one crime family or another. Who live their lives by their own rules, work for a living, and get where they want to be on their own merit. It's something I find intriguing, and I deeply respect these confident women. I'd love to be more like them.

I wrap up my work day and head to the elevator. Finn and Kody will be waiting for me in the car, ready to drive me home. I'll have to figure out what to do with them on Friday. Knowing them, and my husband, they'll have to wait around for me, then take me home afterwards.

I step into the elevator, along with several other people leaving work at the same time. Devlin spots me and gradually edges closer by squeezing his huge frame through the dense crowd.

"How was your day?" he asks, gazing down at me.

I tense beside him, trying my best not to be nudged any closer to his body. We're already stuffed in here like canned sardines.

"Fine. Thank you." I don't ask about his day because I'm trying not to encourage his attention.

"Good to hear. Are you going straight home after work? I suppose your husband's waiting for you."

"He is," I confirm.

"Lucky guy," Devlin murmurs low.

I ignore his comment.

The elevator finally reaches the ground floor and everyone rushes out. A massive, sprawling marble lobby separates us from the multiple revolving doors.

I hurry to the exit, but Devlin's long strides quickly catch him up with me. Even so, I don't bother slowing down.

"Do you have any kids?" he asks.

"No."

"So you're a career woman?"

"Something like that." I walk through the doors and emerge on the wide sidewalk. This time of day especially, the area's bustling with activity. Mostly people leaving work.

Devlin steps in front of me, blocking my path to the waiting car. He hasn't touched me, which is smart, since Kody, my bodyguard, hovers nearby.

He watches, waiting for any sign that I need him. Subtly, I shake my head, signaling him to stand down. This man isn't a threat. Especially out here on a busy sidewalk where a million people can see us.

Oblivious, Devlin shifts closer. "Look, I'm just trying to be friendly. I'm new in town and this city's rough. You seem nice. Unlike a lot of the other women at this agency. Not a ton of guys work here, you know?"

I soften toward him the tiniest bit. I know exactly how it feels to be the outsider, the newcomer.

"I'm not trying to be mean. It's just that I'm happily married."

He takes half a step back. "I'm sure you are. I'm not trying to seduce you." Devlin holds up his hands in surrender. "Really. Sorry if I came across that way. I just want to be friends, or even friendly co-workers. Nothing more."

"Oh. Sorry. That's not the impression I got from you." A faint heat settles on the back of my neck. I can't believe I completely misinterpreted this situation, and his intentions.

"Fair enough. So, will you give me a chance to be friendly? Just as co-workers? Maybe gossip in the break room from time to time?"

I smile with relief. "Sure. I guess."

"No harm in that, is there?"

"I guess not." I glance around him at my waiting car. "I need to go. Have a good night."

"See you tomorrow."

I wave and head to the car. Finn and Kody give me curious glances but they don't ask any questions and I don't offer an explanation.

CHAPTER 41

Cian

"This couldn't wait until morning?" I gripe at Wolfe, who's standing in my home office. It's well past midnight. I had to leave the warmth of my bed, and the soft comfort of my wife to come downstairs for this spontaneous meeting with him. "You could always use your phone, you know."

"Best done in person," he grunts, sitting in the leather chair opposite my desk. "Finn and Kody were too afraid of your reaction, so they came to me about it."

Finn and Kody? My wife's driver and bodyguard?

My heartbeat picks up, driving the remaining cobwebs of sleep from my mind.

"What's going on?" I growl.

"They saw a man walking with your wife out front of her building today after work. He chatted with her for a while before she got into the car. Apparently, they seemed rather friendly with each other. He wasn't a stranger to her." Wolfe leans forward, elbows on my desk. "Also, the man had the look of the Irish, not Italian, so he's not her family. Not one of our guys either."

Immediately my mind conjures up all kinds of possible scenarios, but only one lingers, manifesting in a full blown vision. Was she flirting with this man? Worse, is she cheating on me?

A dangerous heat crawls up my neck.

We've been married for two and half years now, and my greatest fear has come to life. She didn't take a job because she was bored, or needed a sense of purpose, she took it to meet another man.

How long has this been going on?

Are they planning to run off together?

Is she already pregnant with his child?

I shove my fingers through my hair, grip tight, and tug on my scalp. I'm going to drive myself crazy with these questions. I need answers. Right. Now.

I stand up so fast that my chair topples over, crashing to the floor. A startled Wolfe eases back in his own seat.

"What are you going to do with this information?" he asks.

"I'm going to confront my wife." I lumber out of the room, up the stairs, and enter our bedroom with such force that the door bangs against the wall.

Ravenna clicks on the light, blinking at me in confusion. She takes in my wild expression and starts to move toward me, reaching for me.

"Stop!"

She halts in the middle of the bed. "What's happening?"

"That's what I want to know." I can't hold back my glower.

Her furrowed brow deepens. "What?"

"Who is he?"

"Who?" Her gaze shifts around the room, as if these walls will give her more insight.

"The man from work," I grind out.

Her expression changes from confused to annoyed. "You mean the man who I was talking to outside my building this evening? I assure you, Finn and Kody must have blown that encounter out of proportion if this is your reaction."

"Who the fuck is he?" My fingers ball into fists.

"Nobody. We work at the agency and occasionally cross paths. That's all."

I'm not buying it. "What's his name?"

"Devlin Doyle." She slumps back on the bed. "For god's sake, Cian, did you really wake me up in the middle of the night to question me about a co-worker? You don't actually think—" She cuts herself off, her gaze sweeping over me from head to toe. "Are you accusing me of cheating on you?"

I clench my jaw. It's all the answer she needs.

Ravenna grabs the battery powered bedside clock and hurls it at my head. The thing narrowly escapes my skull, crashing against the far wall.

Pink blossoms in her cheeks. "How dare you?" she shouts at me.

"How dare I?" I feel my own temper rising and do nothing to suppress it. "You're the one chatting up strange men in front of everybody."

"Chatting up strange men? Really?" She glares. "Let's address what this is really all about. What's really going on here."

"Oh? And what's that?" I narrow my eyes at her.

"You don't trust me because you can't let go of what happened with your ex."

I flinch as though she struck me. Her words burrow deep, right into the heart of my tainted soul.

She's right. I have no reason not to trust her. Not now. Not after everything we've been through together. But I can't shake off the past, no matter how hard I try. My fears are so deeply rooted that they're impossible to pluck out.

When I don't respond to her accusation, she says, "For the *millionth* time, listen to me. I'm. Not. *Fiona*. Her and I are *nothing* alike. I'd never cheat on you. I'd never hurt you like that." She sighs, the fight leaving her body. "You need to see a therapist. I hoped you'd do that on your own, but that's just not happening. You need to talk to someone about this, Cian."

I shake my head. "I don't need a damn therapist. What happened is not anyone else's business."

"Can't you see that it's a poison to our marriage?" She says so low I have to strain to hear her. "It will ruin us. We can't go on like this forever. The nightmares, your suspicions and inability to trust me. You need help."

The sadness on my wife's face causes a spike of pain through my heart. She's right, of course.

But I can't imagine talking to anyone, even a stranger, about what happened to me. I'd be too raw, too exposed, and worst of all, they'd see me as not only weak but stupid. I was tricked into thinking I was in love with a woman. Betrayed by not only her, but my very own flesh and blood. So damn naïve that they should have just killed me.

Supposedly, it wasn't all a lie. Right before I killed Fiona with my bare hands, she said she loved me in the beginning. Then she met my brother and fell for him. That the heart wants what it wants, and I shouldn't hold that against her. She even said she was sorry as the light left her eyes.

Even though Ravenna and I have been married for a few years now, I keep worrying, in the back of my mind, that she's going to change, like Fiona did. She'll love me up until the moment that she stops loving me.

I've been waiting for that moment since the second my wife got under my skin.

Maybe I should just accept that she'll be my ruin one day. Until that time, I should treat every moment with her as my last.

"Did you hear me?" she asks, studying my closed off expression. I've been standing here like a statue, processing, thinking.

I nod. Some of the tension leaves my shoulders. "You're right. I'm sorry."

"Will you see a therapist?"

"I can't."

The sliver of hope falls from her features. "Oh."

"I'm sorry," I say again. Annoyed at myself for being unable to give Ravenna the one thing that will make her happy, I leave the room. Defeat tangles with remorse in my chest.

Back in my office, Wolfe's dozing in his chair. He yawns. "How'd it go?"

I glare at him. "When you're married, you can ask me that question."

He grunts, seemingly unaffected by my irritability. "What are you doing now?"

My phone in hand, I type out a text message to Brendan, my head of security. Without looking up, I tell Wolfe, "Taking precautions."

"Normally that sounds like a good idea, so why am I getting a bad feeling?"

I spare him a glance. "I'm having Brendan install tracking chips in all of Ravenna's purses. That way I'll always know where she is."

"Did you tell her about your plan?"

I sigh. "No. And don't you speak a word of it to her either."

"No worries there. I don't even like the woman. Just make sure she doesn't find out or there will be hell to pay. She's that type."

Annoyance flares through me at Wolfe passing judgements about my wife. "You can go."

He bobs his head in acceptance of his dismissal.

Even at this hour, Brendan replies to my message. He'll have it done by the end of the week.

I toss my phone on the desk. Am I overstepping by placing tracking devices on my wife? Perhaps. But I'd rather have the peace of mind of knowing where she is, than dreading the unknown. My imagination gets away from me at times.

The jealous, possessive beast within won't leave me alone. If I don't do something to ease my mind, I'll spiral into the pit of darkness where my fears live. They'll dig their claws into me, unrelenting, until I lose my goddamn mind.

I wish I wasn't like this, but it can't be helped.

She says she'd never cheat on me. This way I know for sure.

It's a win-win.

CHAPTER 42
Ravenna

At work the next day, I'm unfocused, groggy from the late night fight with Cian. Especially since after going back to sleep, I woke up again early this morning to another of his nightmares. They had been better for quite a while. The perfume incident set them off again for a couple of weeks. Now we have another round of his night terrors because of this situation with my co-worker, I assume.

On top of all that, I'm upset at him for not seeking professional help. It's been years of this and when it's good, it's great. But when he declines like this, letting his demons consume him, our relationship feels the strain. We both suffer.

I also hate the fact that he dreams about *her*. His ex. She has a stronger hold over him than I do, and she's been dead for what? Close to a decade?

Call me jealous. I loathe sharing him with another woman, even if she's only in his nightmares.

"Good morning, Mrs. O'Rourke." Devlin stops by my desk, pulling me from my thoughts.

"Good morning." My tone's brisk.

He notices. "Rough start to the day?"

"You could say that."

"Oh? What's going on?"

"Nothing."

He frowns. "I thought we decided to be friends yesterday. Has something changed since then?"

"Yes." I sigh. Being rude doesn't come naturally to me, but at times it's necessary. "We can't be friends. I'm sorry, but you need to find some other nice co-worker in the building to chat and have coffee with. This isn't working for me."

"Oh. Okay." Devlin looks like a whipped puppy, and I feel bad. But I'm not letting anyone get in the way of my already complicated marriage. The truth is, Devlin simply isn't that important to me. He's not my family. He's not a friend, either. So he certainly shouldn't be the cause for a middle of the night meltdown for my husband.

Thankfully, Devlin goes away without making a fuss. I hope he takes the hint, which was not very subtle, and leaves me alone from now on.

I'm sure he can make other friends at work.

The rest of the week, Devlin only says hello in passing, which is a relief.

Friday rolls around, which I've been looking forward to ever since Susan invited me out. I check in on my boss to make sure she doesn't need anything else from me before I grab my purse and meet up with Susan, Jade, and Lisa. The three of them are inseparable. A clique I've been dying to socialize with since I first met them.

We ride the elevator down together. They gossip with each other, and I kind of feel like I'm just tagging along to one of their weekly social rituals.

Outside, we walk the short distance to the bar, our stilettos clacking against the concrete sidewalk. I gave Finn and Kody a heads up about this evening. They have eyes on me from across the street, but have been specifically instructed not to draw attention to themselves.

Susan finally speaks, including me in their conversation. "What do you think about that guy Devlin? Handsome devil, isn't he?"

"He is," I admit. "Though kind of clingy. He gives me a weird vibe."

Jade speaks up, "I know what you mean. He's always flirting with me, but it comes off as creepy rather than sexy. I'm not sure why. Now, I avoid him."

"You guys don't like him?" Lisa asks, glancing around at all of us. "I'm supposed to go on a date with him this weekend."

"Really?" I'm surprised, since Devlin has insisted that I'm his only friend at the office. Maybe he puts me in a different category because I'm married, whereas all these women are single.

Jade scrunches her nose. "Don't date him, Lisa, you can do better than him."

"He's strange," Susan says, "but imagine having a hunk like that in bed? I wonder if he's that large... everywhere."

"Still not worth it." Jade shakes her head, opening the door for us at the bar.

We're seated at a cocktail table in the swanky little establishment. I buy the first round of drinks, partly because I want to make a good impression on them. But also out of generosity. They should keep as much of their hard-earned money as they can.

The conversation drifts from work gossip, to personal life matters, to celebrities, until we finally end up on the subject of the agency's owner and popular model.

"Now Connor Bane? I'd totally jump into bed with him," Jade states. "That man is *fine*."

Susan sips her cocktail. "Maybe you should ask him out. You've only had a crush on him for years. Everyone knows he's single right now."

It's interesting hearing their opinion of my husband's cousin. I don't dare tell them about that connection, or about how Connor gave me this job in the first place.

Jade giggles, obviously tipsy. "Connor isn't the type of man you ask out. You have to catch his attention, then he'll ask you out. Just watch me, one of these days he'll see me and he'll come after me. It will be an epic workplace romance."

"I've heard he doesn't date other models or anyone from work," Lisa adds.

"I'll be the exception."

Susan laughs. "If you say so. Personally, I think we're looking for love in all the wrong places." She glances at me. "You're married. How did you and your husband meet?"

For a couple of seconds, I blankly stare back at her, at a complete loss for words. I'd never thought about explaining my relationship to someone from the outside.

If I tell them it was an arranged marriage, they'll think I've lost my mind. Or that I need rescuing.

Jade arches a perfectly shaped brow. "Well?"

"I..." To give myself a couple more moments, and time to pull together a lie, I down the rest of my drink. "How about another round?"

They nod and I signal for the server. While we wait for our next round to arrive, I launch into my quickly made up story. There's no avoiding it now.

"He was a friend of my family, but we didn't know each other very well. He's a few years older than me. Then one day, everything changed. My parents died in a tragic accident, and Cian was there for me. We fell in love, and the rest is history."

Jade gasps. "Oh my god. I'm sorry for your loss. But that's *so* romantic."

"You're so lucky you didn't have to date a stranger," Lisa says. "At least a friend of the family is a known quantity. You get to know him by proximity."

I hum a noncommittal noise.

"So you're happily married?" Susan asks as our drinks arrive.

I nod. "Quite."

"That's good because, take my word for it, you do not want to reenter the dating market if you can help it. I was in a three year long relationship that totally blew up. Even after three short years out of the scene, I feel like I'm trying to navigate a whole new world of men." She glances around the table. "Is it just me or have men somehow gotten worse than they were a few years ago?"

"It isn't you." Lisa snorts. "They're terrible. They

either want a situationship or a mommy. I'm not up for either."

"Amen," Jade chimes in.

We're in the middle of another conversation when Devlin walks through the door. He spots us and waves, but none of us acknowledge his presence. This doesn't deter him. He grabs a beer at the bar and makes a beeline for us, pulling up a chair at our table.

"Hello, ladies."

I'm beginning to realize that he has terrible social skills. The strange thing is, while he's not uncomfortable, but everyone else around him is. Poor guy. No wonder he has a hard time making friends.

Jade empties her drink. "Well, I think I'll call it a night."

Devlin doesn't get the hint. "How about one more drink? I'm buying."

"That's okay," I say, trying to smooth over the situation, but also leave as soon as possible.

He glances at Lisa. "Come on, I just want to hang out for a few minutes."

"Okay." She folds. Which means we're all stuck here because none of us would leave her on her own. Not tonight. Her date with Devlin this weekend is entirely another issue.

He grins, having won, then orders us another round of cocktails. Jade and Susan exchange a loaded glance. They're not happy to be pressured into this. Neither am I. Lisa shrugs like there's nothing she can do about it.

So we hunker down and make the best of it. Devlin dominates the conversation, going on and on about his boss, Scott, and how the man is such a womanizer. We all know this, of course, which is why we steer clear of the man. The agency's newer models aren't always so lucky.

Finally, I glance at the time on my phone and decide I've had enough. "Oh my god, it's already seven o'clock, we need to hurry if we're going to make our dinner reservations."

Jade and Susan glance at me with understanding in their eyes. This is our excuse to escape.

Lisa seems lost.

"Oh? Where are we having dinner?" Devlin asks, perking up.

"Sorry," I tell him, "but it's a reservation for four and the restaurant's sold out." I gather my belongings. "Ladies, we can take my car. See you at work on Monday, Devlin."

Thankfully, he doesn't press for any more details—or follow us.

Susan, Jade, Lisa, and I head for the door as a unit, hurrying to get out of there and away from our co-worker. To see this charade through to its end, the four of us squeeze into the back seat of my waiting car.

"Drive," I tell Finn. Kody shoots me a questioning glance but I shake my head at him. He shrugs, as if he really doesn't care for an explanation to this turn of events.

"Are we really going to dinner?" Lisa asks.

"No. But, I mean, we could. If you all want." I look to Jade and Susan.

"I'm game."

Jade nods. "I'm starving."

It's settled then. I get us a table at *Spades*.

CHAPTER 43
Cian

With a growl, I flip through the photos on my phone for the tenth time. No matter how many times I look at them, the facts remain the same. Ravenna told me she was going out for drinks with a few of her female co-workers. She lied.

Across from her sits a man. He smiles at her. She laughs at something he said. So do the other women at their table, but in every photo his eyes are on my wife. He barely pays any attention to the others.

The jealous creature within me comes to life. Dark thoughts overtake my mind. I can't hold back the onslaught.

This right here is the proof I dreaded. My fear becomes a reality. Another man has Ravenna's attention. What else has she given him? Her body? Her love?

Does she plan to give him her future too?

I slam my phone down on the coffee table hard enough that the screen cracks. *Damn it.*

Since Brendan sent me these photos a couple of hours ago, I've been sitting in the living room, stewing, waiting for my wife to come home. All possible scenarios have occupied my thoughts. I've considered multiple ways to confront her, and how those could go over. I should remain calm and talk to her, give her the benefit of the doubt, a chance to explain.

But when the front door clicks open, all rational thought flees my brain. I'm reduced to nothing more than a jealous, possessive beast of a man. Ruled by instinct. Dominated by fear and insecurity.

And I'm angry as fuck.

Standing, I stalk toward my unsuspecting wife. I can't stand the thought of her leaving me. Her betrayal tears my heart to shreds. Guts me and leaves me to die.

She's wearing a form fitting dress that hugs her beautiful curves. Hair up in an intricate bun, that exposes her long neck. She's sin incarnate.

"Hi," she says, setting her purse on the entry table.

I don't answer her. Instead, I pull out my switchblade and flick it open. The metallic sound echoes in the hall.

"Cian?" she questions, wariness mars her gorgeous features.

I grab hold of her arm and pin her between me and the wall. Her innocent gaze only fuels my anger, so I spin her around.

My blade rests at the back of her neck. In quick slashes, probably not being as careful as I should be, I cut the dress from her body. But I don't stop there, I cut away her bra and panties too.

Breathlessly, she says, "You owe me ten new dresses."

I grunt in response. Wedging my knee between her thighs, I spread her legs wide. She arches her back, sticking out her perfect ass, inviting me in.

Pocketing my knife, I smack her pussy. Once, twice, three times in quick succession. She gasps and tries to straighten up, but I hold her in place by the back of her neck.

"Cian?" She weakly struggles against me, but I'm too strong for her to escape.

"Shut the fuck up," I growl in her ear.

"What—?"

Lining my raging hard cock up with her pussy, I press inside. Ravenna whimpers. She wiggles in my hold, but I keep her still, pumping into her cunt with harsh, angry thrusts.

This isn't sex, it's a punishment.

As I use her body, images of her with *him* drift through my mind's eye. Has he taken her from behind like this? Does her greedy pussy swallow him whole? Has she come home to me with his cum in her cunt?

The more I imagine them together, the harder I fuck I her.

She doesn't say a word. She just takes, like she's repenting for her sins.

The foyer fills with the erotic sounds of slapping flesh. My grunts, and her whimpered moans.

When I'm close, I murmur in her ear, "Does he fuck you like this?"

"Wh-what?"

"Do you moan his name?"

Ravenna tries to break my hold on her, but I have her

pinned between my body and the wall. "What are you talking about? Have you gone insane?"

Maybe. Quite possibly.

"Devlin," I spit out his name. "How many times have you fucked him?"

"I'm not doing this. Get off of me!"

Pulling her into me, my cock buried deep, I cum in her pussy. As soon as I'm finished, I push away, giving us both some space.

She rounds on me with fury heating her grey eyes. Her slap lands across my face. It stings. "If you ever treat me like that again, we're through. I'm not fucking Devlin, or anyone else. I'm not cheating on you. But, obviously, you don't believe me. And you know what? I don't care. You need to get your shit together and straighten yourself out. Don't fucking touch me again until you do."

With that, she storms up the stairs.

Guilt immediately slams into my gut. *Fuck*, what have I done?

As suddenly as the feeling came on, it recedes. She's blatantly lying to me. I have evidence right here that this Devlin guy's into her. If she's not fucking him now, it's only a matter of time before she does.

Isn't it?

Or am I fucking delusional? Am I making a mess of everything?

I want to trust my wife. I do. But I can't.

I want her to be happy. But even if I can't give her what she wants, I also can't let her go so she can find it elsewhere. She's *mine*.

I've never claimed to be a good man. I'll fucking lock her up if necessary.

I'm almost at the end of my rope.

In an attempt to give her the benefit of the doubt. Just this once. I consider that maybe Ravenna isn't the problem. She could be faithful to me, like she insists, while Devlin tempts her to betray me.

I snarl. My fist collides with the wall, which cracks. I don't give a fuck who he is, he's a dead man.

CHAPTER 44
Ravenna

"Roman and I are doing great, thanks for asking." Sophia sips her drink. We're seated in a quiet little coffee shop in an upscale neighborhood. It's that sweet spot in the afternoon when the morning customers have already come and gone, but those in need of an after lunch caffeine hit haven't come by yet.

"I can't believe you're going to be a Junior in college after this summer. Where has the time gone?" I muse.

"I know. It's kind of crazy."

Luckily, making small talk with my cousin doesn't require much effort. On the outside, I'm serene enough, but inside I'm awash with havoc.

Cian's been a ruthless beast all weekend. I doubled down to get my point across to him and have been sleeping in one of our guest rooms. What he did to me in the foyer is unforgivable behavior. I've been understanding and tolerant, but he's way out of bounds if he thinks he can warp our sex life into something dark and twisted.

That was the furthest thing from making love I've ever experienced. Even on our strained wedding night he was more compassionate than that.

"Okay, what's troubling you?" Sophia asks, drawing my attention back to her. "You're much too quiet."

I sigh. Everyone thinks my marriage is perfect. I guess I've fostered that illusion because most of the time it is great, and I've wanted to be a beacon of hope for my cousins. None of them have had easy beginnings to their relationships, but they've all seemed to work it out in the end.

I guess Cian and I haven't gotten to our end yet. We've flirted with, but haven't managed to achieve, our own happily ever after. I'm beginning to wonder if it will happen for us.

"How did you and Roman move past his betrayal?" I ask her. "What he did was... disgusting." I have a lot more words for it than that, but I figure one is enough to get my point across.

She hums, thinking. "It was. I guess what made all the difference was him facing his demons in the end. He confronted the darkest parts of himself, even though it was difficult for him, but he did it for me. I was worth it to him, for him to go through all of that. If he hadn't, I don't think I could have forgiven him. But he put in the effort. He changed."

"I see." Unfortunately, Cian has no interest in putting in the effort. He won't talk to a therapist. It's like he revels in tormenting himself. I'm afraid his demons have too firm of a hold on him and one day they'll drag him under. He's drowning in them.

"Is there something going on with you and Cian?" Sophia asks, cocking her head to one side.

"Yeah, but I don't think there's much to do about it." I wave off her concern. "We just need some time. Everything will be okay."

"If you say so. Just remember that you don't have to deal with any of his crap. You're not stuck with him. If you need a place to stay, or anything else, I'm always here for you."

"I appreciate that."

She pats my hand and smiles. "I'm serious."

"I know." Knowing that I have her at my back does help lighten my mood. Even so, I change the subject. "Are you ready for Gin's wedding next month?"

"Yes. But I don't know why she decided to have it in London. I mean... it's fake. Why not do it locally? New York has plenty of gorgeous venues."

I shrug. "Arianna's planning the whole thing. Since they're trying to make it look real, I guess that's a good enough reason for the extravagance of a destination wedding."

"That makes sense. I'm still worried about her though. She's in way over her head."

On that, we can totally agree. Sophia ended up happily married to an Italian mafia man, while Arianna caught the eye of a Russian bratva leader, but sweet Gin has gotten herself mixed up with a man who has the most sinister reputation. Blake Baron has no heart. Everybody knows that.

I'm afraid my youngest cousin will come out of this

situation with Mr. Baron utterly destroyed. Surely a brutal man with no heart could never give Gin the love she deserves.

At least we'll be there to pick up the pieces. There's nothing else we can do.

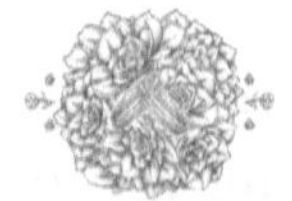

On Monday morning, I've just returned from grabbing coffee for my boss, when I hear a commotion in the general office area. As I cautiously approach, several of my co-workers shoot me worried glances. That should be a hint as to what's going on. But I'm still shocked when I round the corner to find Devlin and Cian staring each other down.

My stunned disbelief quickly turns to fury. I'm absolutely livid that my husband has shown up at my work to confront my co-worker.

Devlin turns to me. "You didn't tell me your husband's a jealous animal."

"Don't speak to my wife!" Cian snarls at him.

"Go fuck yourself—"

Cian punches him. Even though Devlin's about the same size, the man's lived a much softer life than my husband. He goes down like a tower of bricks, out cold.

Gasps sound all around us, but no one dares to intervene. Cian stands over Devlin's prone form, breathing hard, fists clenched like he's waiting for the other man to get up so he can hit him again.

I've had enough of this.

"Get out of here." My tone's deceptively calm. I'm too angry right now to shout. "Go home."

Cian finally glances at me. "I'm going to kill him."

"If you ever lay a finger on that man again, I'll leave you." I mean every word. Not because Devlin is important to me, he's not, but because Cian can't act like this without consequence.

"Why? Because you—?"

"I'm not even going to answer that absurd question." My unrelenting gaze bores into his. "Your behavior is not only inappropriate, but downright embarrassing."

"What is going on here?" My boss, Ms. Ryan, walks into the office and my stomach sinks. She takes one look at Devlin on the floor, and my deranged husband hovering over him, and calls for security.

"I can explain," I tell her. "It's a misunderstanding."

She nods, as if she already knows what's going on here. "I know who you're married to Mrs. O'Rourke. I'm sorry, but for the safety of everyone at this agency, you're fired."

I blanch. She can't mean it. I'm losing my job because of Cian's jealous actions?

Cian steps forward, all intimidation. "You can't fire her. Get Connor Bane on the phone, he'll straighten this out."

Ms. Ryan isn't impressed by his attempt to go over her head. "I'll be sure to have Mr. Bane give you a call." She turns to me. "You have five minutes to pack your things and leave the premises."

"I'm sorry," I tell her, and her gaze softens. She's clearly sympathetic, even though she's doing what she has to do.

I grab my stuff from my desk, glaring at Cian when he tries to help. The rest of the office remains silent as everyone gawks at us. I'm never going to live this down. Maybe it's for the best that I'll never see any of these people again. It's too embarrassing.

Head held high, I march out to the bay of elevators. Cian follows, but I barely spare him a glance. He's single handedly ruined not only my day, but my entire work life. I only got the job here because his cousin owns the place. There's no way in hell they'll give me a good reference after Cian assaulted my co-worker.

Hell, we're probably going to have charges filed against us. I'm not sure if Devlin's the type of guy to take a payoff to keep quiet. Will Cian even offer him money? Or will they have another round of this bullheaded insanity in a courtroom?

"I apologize," Cian murmurs. "This is my fault and I'll straighten it out."

"You'll do no such thing," I snap at him. "You got me fired. Fired! Because you're obsessed with the idea of me having an affair with my co-worker. When in reality, nothing has happened with him or anyone else. Ever. Do *not* talk to me. I don't like you right now."

The elevator doors open and I step inside. When Cian attempts to join me, I stop him by holding my palm out and say, "Don't."

He grits his teeth, but stays firmly planted on the marble floor as the doors close.

On my way down, I text Finn to have him bring up the car from the garage and pick me up. I haven't decided where to go yet. Not home. I can't deal with my home life right now.

After debating about the other possibilities, I settle on one of my favorite coffee houses on the Upper East side. The quiet, soothing atmosphere is exactly what I need as I sip my Earl Grey latte and ponder my marriage, my work, and the future.

Honestly, all of it's looking rather bleak at the moment.

CHAPTER 45

Cian

Ravenna's cold shoulder feels like the deepest, darkest winter of my life. She only speaks when spoken to, rejects my touch, and we haven't shared a bed in weeks. I don't blame her. Not at all. This is all my fault.

Though every time I try to apologize, to beg for her forgiveness, she shuts me down. Or worse, walks away, leaving me on my knees. All alone.

Every morning I wake from haunted dreams, only to be plagued by worries and fears that today's the day my wife leaves me for good. As much as I can't live without her, I can understand if she decides she's through with us.

No matter how hard I try, I can't believe her innocence. One part of me knows she's never cheated on me and never would, while a demon inside me insists that I'm being fooled. It whispers that she's not only unfaithful, but a liar and manipulator.

I'm going crazy.

The days pass in a blur. I'm having trouble telling reality from delusion—I think. My fears eat me alive, consuming me. At night they only get worse.

In the darkness, my own fearful thoughts have the voice of my ex and my brother. They whisper in my ear when I'm trying to sleep. Shawn's condescending laughter echoes in my bedroom. Even though Ravenna threw away that vanilla and ylang-ylang perfume, I swear I smell it on my sheets and pillows.

What is happening to me? I don't believe in ghosts—at least I didn't until recently.

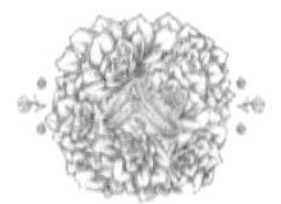

It isn't until July that Ravenna and I are finally forced to be in each other's company. We have to attend Ginevra Pontrelli's wedding in London.

The flight across the Atlantic starts out with the same energy we have at home. Distant. Solemn. Then Ravenna speaks to me for the first time in ages.

"If we could get out of going to this wedding, I would, but we can't. So we'll just have to make the best of it." She gazes out the jet's window. "I will *not* have us make a spectacle of ourselves, so we will act like a happily married couple. No exceptions. Once this plane lands, we will start pretending. Have I made myself clear?"

"Crystal clear," I use her own words, but she doesn't seem to realize it. Or she doesn't care. My gut twists.

"Good."

I plan on behaving exactly as she wants, once we've landed. Until then, I have my wife right where I want her. Alone with me, my own captive audience.

Getting up, I move to the seat directly across from her and sit down. My hands land on top of her thighs. She flinches, her gaze snaps to mine.

"What are you doing?" she demands to know.

I lean forward. "I'm sorry—"

"We've been through this before." She grits her teeth, then continues, "You keep saying you're sorry then you go right back to your bad behaviors. You can be as sorry as you want, that doesn't change anything. You need to get help."

"I know. I have an appointment with a therapist when we return."

Her brows lift. "You do?"

I dip my chin. "I don't know what's happening to me and you're right, I need professional help." Admitting to that galls me, but I'll do anything to keep my marriage from falling apart the rest of the way.

Ravenna deserves better. So do I. I need to find a way to tame my inner demons before they destroy what we have together.

Her tone softens, "I'm glad that you finally see that for yourself. I'm proud of you."

The vice around my chest eases a fraction at Ravenna's approval.

"I—" Sunlight breaks through the cloud layer and a sparkle at her neck catches my attention. She's wearing a necklace, but it's half tucked beneath her dress's collar. Even so, it looks familiar. "That pendant..."

I reach for it, but she clutches it first and pulls it free

from the fabric. I stare at the diamond Shamrock with an emerald in the center.

No, it can't be.

Suddenly, I can't breathe. The jet's walls close in on me. My vision blurs as the world tilts.

"Cian?" Ravenna's voice sounds so far away.

I blink a few times and my head clears. "Where did you get that pendant?" I demand, low and deadly.

She jolts back into her seat. Obviously surprised by my change in tone. But I don't care as my thoughts scramble to make sense of my current reality. Suspicions flare up like an uncontrollable wildfire.

She glances down. "This? I found it on the sidewalk. A long time ago."

I draw away from her, trying to contain my rising temper. "Don't fucking lie to me."

"I'm not." She scowls. "I found it on the sidewalk outside our house. Wolfe said it dropped out of my purse, but since it's not mine, he must be mistaken. I thought about leaving it there, but decided it's too precious to toss away. No one ever came for it, so I locked it in my jewelry box. When I was packing for this trip, I came across it and thought I'd wear it." She frowns in confusion. "Why?"

"Because that's Fiona's necklace. I gave it to her for her twenty-first birthday."

I can't make this marriage work if she's going to keep tormenting me with pieces from my past. What the fuck is going on?

CHAPTER 46

Ravenna

The trip with Cian to London was torture in many ways. We shared a bed for the first time in weeks, but weren't intimate. I barely managed any sleep with the way he thrashed around every single night. With spending so much time apart, I hadn't realized how bad he's gotten.

At home I could smell that vanilla and ylang-ylang perfume wafting from his bedroom. I assumed he retrieved the bottle from the trash and spritzed it on his sheets as a way of tormenting himself with reminders of *her*. Jealousy ate away at me.

I loathe the idea of competing with a dead woman.

Cian hates Fiona. But given some of his behaviors, I began to wonder how much he also still loves her. There's a fine line between hate and love, isn't there?

Yes, she betrayed him—tried to kill him—but I suspected that put Fiona on some kind of twisted pedestal. He's clearly not over his ex. Though I can't figure out if he continues to pine for her ghost, wrapped up in his guilt for murdering her, or if she so deeply damaged him that he's traumatized for life.

I come back to the same question over and over; why wasn't he like this the first year of our marriage? He was wonderful then. But there's been this slow decline into what I can only call *madness*.

Why? What's changed?

I glance over to where he's dozing in the car ride home. The poor man hasn't had a decent night's sleep in forever. Too long. Sleep deprivation is more dangerous than many people realize. The mind can start playing tricks on you. Is that what's happening to him?

Opening my purse, I take the Shamrock pendant from where I keep it in the inside pocket. As soon as Cian told me it belonged to Fiona I removed it, and haven't worn it since.

I offered it back to Cian, but he cringed away from the thing like it was a poisonous snake. If we hadn't been on a jet, I'm sure he would have chucked it out the window.

I rub my thumb over the jewelry. I suspect it's a piece of a larger puzzle. Too much of a coincidence to be anything other than sinister.

If Fiona were alive, I'd think she was trying to infiltrate our lives. To leave pieces of their past in various places, all for Cian to find, just to haunt him.

But she's dead. And I don't believe in ghosts or spirits.

The car pulls up to the house. Although I hate to do it, I nudge Cian awake. "We're home."

He grunts in response.

Wolfe opens the car door for me, and I slide out, followed by my husband. As I climb the front stairs, my gaze slides back to Wolfe. He's the one who found the necklace. He has also been in Cian's life since before Fiona. Which means he lived through that entire situation. He knows what she was like, had access to things like her perfume and jewelry.

Does Wolfe have a reason to never let Cian forget about Fiona? Did he intentionally plant that pendant on me, knowing at some point I'd wear it and Cian would instantly recognize it? Perhaps. Though I don't understand his motive.

He catches me looking at him and scowls. Ah. Maybe he's set on destroying our marriage. He doesn't like me, but perhaps I underestimated just how much.

As soon as we enter the house, the stench of vanilla and ylang-ylang assaults my nose. I used to like that scent. Now I can't tolerate it.

Spinning around, I block Cian from stepping through the doorway. "We're not sleeping here tonight."

He pauses on the step. "We aren't? Why?"

"Because the place reeks. I'm going to call in a cleaning crew and get this entire house done from top to bottom. Will you book us into the Four Seasons?"

"Yeah." Cian secures our lodging arrangements while I make sure all of our luggage stays in the trunk.

Wolfe seems disgruntled by the change in plan, but he's never happy, so I'm unconcerned. Though I closely watch him as we get back into the car and he drives us to our new destination. Suspicion coils around my chest.

We check into our hotel room, and have our things

brought up. I order room service as we haven't had a proper meal in a few hours and Cian looks like he's about to pass out. Even so, he won't settle down and allow himself to sleep. I suppose his nightmares are so bad that he'd rather avoid them. But this can't go on forever.

I fetch the little pillbox I keep in my purse for emergencies. There's a bit of everything in there from gentle Aspirin, to sleeping pills, to prescription strength pain meds. Taking out two sleeping pills, I offer them to Cian with a glass of water.

"What are these for?" He warily eyes them.

"They'll help you sleep. Take them. Now."

He shakes his head. "I don't want to sleep. Can't do it anymore."

"You need sleep," I insist. I'm beyond worried about him. "It will be dreamless, I promise."

That makes him reconsider. Reaching out, he plucks the pills from my palm and downs them with a mouthful of water, then settles into bed.

Within seconds he's out. His features relax in his sleep, so peaceful and serene. Even his body remains still —not thrashing or jerky like so many nights recently.

While he rests, I make arrangements to have our house cleaned, everything laundered or dry cleaned, and consider having the local priest do an exorcism on the place. Would that be going too far? I doubt it. So I do in fact schedule for the church to do a ritual cleansing of our home.

Cian sleeps all through the rest of the day and night. He's still asleep the next morning, so I let him be. He's breathing, so he's still alive. Obviously, he needs the rest.

When he wakes up, I'll tell him my theory about our

mystery person's malicious intent to plague him with the ghosts of his past. As farfetched as that seems, what else could possibly be going on?

CHAPTER 47
Cian

Waking up, I'm more clear headed than I've been in ages. I lie still, attempting to clearly recall everything that's led up to this moment. My mind replays everything, but backwards.

The nightmares in London, Fiona's pendant around Ravenna's neck, me punishing Ravenna for my own demons. The photos, our fights, vanilla and ylang-ylang, my apologies, her cold shoulder...

Guilt slams into me.

She's right. We can't go on like this, and the problem is me. I'm ready to admit that now.

"You're awake." Ravenna's soft tone coats me like salve. "Do you feel better?"

Sitting up, I nod.

"That's good. I didn't know when you'd be awake, but I ordered dinner for you anyway. It's fresh and warm if you're hungry."

I clear my throat. "Thank you." Glancing around, I

vaguely remember how we arrived here, but not the reason behind booking a hotel room. Even though I'm the one who made our reservation.

Getting out of bed, I join Ravenna at the table, where we silently eat dinner.

"Why aren't we at home?" I ask between bites of filet mignon. "My memory's a little foggy."

She pats her lips with the napkin. "I'm having the place cleaned, aired out, and exorcized."

"Exorcized?" Does she believe we're being haunted?

"Yes. While I don't believe in ghosts, I figure it can't hurt." She sips her wine. "When we arrived home, the place reeked of that perfume. I couldn't stomach staying there. Not until it's cleaned. And... I have a theory."

"Oh?"

Setting down her wineglass, she pins that beautiful blue-grey gaze on me. "Someone in our household is trying to drive you crazy, and they've succeeded. They're using reminders of Fiona to haunt you. Whoever they are, they must have known her quite well. Who else would have access to her perfume and her jewelry?"

"You think someone's doing this on purpose?" I take a minute to wrap my head around that idea.

"Absolutely. These things aren't coincidental. Someone wants to put you in a vulnerable, off-center state of mind. I think they're also trying to drive us apart. Though I'm not sure about their end game."

"I agree that those two things are too much of a coincidence. But the only person around me who knew Fiona that well..."

"Is Wolfe," she states in such a way that I believe she's given this a lot of thought.

"Yeah." I chew on another bite of meat. "Except he wouldn't do this to me."

She frowns. "How can you be so sure?"

"I just..." Fuck, I hate sounding naïve, but Wolfe? We've been through so much together. "I just know. It isn't him. Wolfe saved me from Fiona and Shawn. He's not about to torment me with my ex all these years later."

Ravenna releases a long sigh. "Then I'm out of suspects."

"I'll look over the security footage with Brendan. I don't think it's someone from the inside. If someone is planting things around our house, then they must be breaking in. Or in the case of that pendant, leaving it on our front walkway."

"I guess that's possible. It would be easier for someone with access though," she points out.

I grunt in agreement. "We did thorough background checks before hiring any of the staff. As for my men, none of them knew Fiona *that* well. If it was my brother's things around the house, then I'd turn my suspicions on them."

Ravenna's quiet for a moment as we continue eating dinner. Her explanation of what's been going on makes complete sense. Even so, it's no excuse for my actions. I'm hesitant to apologize to her again, except for the fact that she's treating me differently tonight. She hasn't been this open in far too long.

I decide to get to the point and tell her the one thing that may break through her reserved demeanor.

"I'm serious about seeing a therapist. I know I told you on the jet, but even though we've sort of figured out what may be happening, I'm still going to go. I want to be the best version of myself, for both of us. It's become clear to me in the past few weeks that I do need professional help. I fucking hate to admit this, but I can't figure this shit out on my own." I swallow down my wine.

I hate feeling so damn vulnerable, incompetent, and unable to fight my own demons.

Ravenna reaches for my hand, entwining our fingers. "It's not weak to admit that you need outside help. In fact, it's the opposite. You're strong enough to seek out help in order to vanquish your inner demons."

I hate the thought of her viewing me as *broken*. Though, neither her eyes or her smile hold a hint of pity. She actually believes that by seeking out a professional, I'm showing my strength. Not weakness.

The vice around my chest loosens. I'm going to get professional help, hunt down the person responsible for fucking with our relationship and gut them, and above all else, I'm going to make this up to Ravenna.

I've majorly fucked up twice in our years together. The first time when I abandoned her at her family home. The second time when my jealousy and suspicions overtook me and I did horrible things.

There won't be a third time.

CHAPTER 48

Ravenna

"I'm touring Italy with Gin. That girl does not take *no* for an answer," Elena tells me on the phone.

"You mean you're with Gin and Blake?" I ask. Why would Gin be in Italy by herself when she was so recently married?

"Nope. Just us girls. Apparently, Blake's on her shit list, and Gin's getting her revenge on him. I'm helping her, too. In all honesty, I'm glad for a reason to get out of the house and see a slice of the world. We've been staying at the best hotels and you wouldn't believe the food we've eaten. Gin knows so much about the culinary arts. We've been putting the top tier restaurants to the test."

"I'm happy that you're having a good time." A trip like that seems very outside of Elena's comfort zone but maybe she's finally decided to rejoin the world. Ginevra's so full of life, I hope she'll be a good influence on my sister.

Though a fallout with her husband this soon into

their fake marriage concerns me a bit. Not that I'm one to give marriage advice, or pass any judgements on other people's relationships.

I wish I could tour Italy as a way to deal with my problems. Instead I'm back at home. No work life. No normal friends. Still no family of my own.

At this point, I'm hesitant about bringing a child into our lives. Until we have a stable relationship again, I don't want to start a family. Though I'm wondering if any marriage is always stable. Maybe the ups and downs are simply part of life.

Cian's been doing better since we had the house not only cleaned, but aired out. The entire atmosphere of the place has changed for the better.

We've both been discreetly trying to uncover who's behind the perfume and that necklace. Cian reviewed the security footage going back weeks, but hasn't found anything of note. With a, sort of, rational explanation behind it all, he's been much calmer and more focused.

And true to his word, he's been seeing a therapist. Which makes me greatly relieved—not to mention hopeful. I know progress will take time, but that's okay.

Unfortunately, all evidence points to an outside intruder being the one behind the mysterious Fiona haunting. So why haven't they been caught by our security system?

"Ven, are you still there?" Elena asks, and I realize I've been zoning out.

"Yeah, sorry, just a lot on my mind."

"Do you want to talk about it?"

I sigh. "Not really. No. Look, I should go. You have

fun and try to keep Gin from getting into too much trouble."

"I will. Love you."

"Love you too. Bye." I end the call and flop back on the chaise in the library. I feel like I'm back to square one on trying to figure out what to do with my life. If I had even an ounce of the talent of my cousins, I'd be thrilled. Sophia's a junior getting her Art History degree. Arianna's turned out to be quite the event organizer, she even did Gin's wedding, and it was beautiful. Even Gin, the wild card, turns out she's a brilliant chef in the making.

Meanwhile, I'm unemployable and no closer to starting a family.

"Ugh." Okay, I can't sit around the house all day and wallow. I text Finn. I'm going out.

For some peace, I decide to stroll through Central Park. It's still warm, but the air holds a crispness, a gentle cooling breeze, that hints at the coming autumn.

Finn waits at the car, while Kody shadows me, staying far enough away to be discreet, but close enough to offer his protection. His gaze scans the area like every jogger or mom with a stroller could be suspect. Without a destination in mind, I amble along.

I come to a crossroads and startle when I hear my name.

"Mrs. O'Rourke!"

Turning, I find Devlin waving at me, a grin on his face. Not the reaction I would have expected, given how the last time I saw him my husband had punched his face. Devlin does strike me as the easy going, forgive and forget type. So maybe this greeting isn't too unusual?

He jogs over to me, his breath escaping in white whisps. "Hey."

"Hello," I say, my tone laced with caution.

"I've been meaning to get ahold of you but I don't have your number."

"Oh?"

"Yeah. So... I never filed assault charges, and I managed to smooth over everything at work with your boss. Have you heard from her?"

"I haven't. And why didn't you file charges?" I'm more surprised than anything.

His smile wavers. "I thought you'd be happy about that. You don't actually want me to put your husband in jail for assaulting me, do you?"

"No, of course not. But you had every right after what he did to you."

Devlin waves me off, as if he's used to it and gets punched in the face quite often. Maybe he does?

"That's all in the past now. No hard feelings, you know?"

I nod, even though I don't know. If I were him, I'd be pissed.

"Anyway, I can put in a good word for you at work. That is... if you want your job back."

I brighten at that. "I would like to return to work at the agency. Would you really do that for me?"

"Sure." He chuckles. "We're friends, remember? Friends help out friends."

Friends. Sure. Okay.

"That's very kind of you."

"No problem at all. Hey, I have to run, but let's do

coffee once you're back at work." He jogs off before I can get in a single word.

Why isn't he worried about Cian coming after him again? I feel like I'm missing something crucial, but for the life of me I don't know what. His actions don't make sense to me.

At the same time, I'd be thrilled if he can get me rehired.

I'm sure my paranoia's misplaced. Maybe he's just a nice guy? Those do exist, right?

CHAPTER 49
Ravenna

"Why did you meet up with Devlin in the park today?" Cian asks as soon as he comes home, finding me in the living room, curled up on the sofa with a fascinating book about the Revolutionary War in my lap.

I scan my gaze over him. He seems calm, though there's a hard set to his jaw. Inwardly, I sigh. We're not about to launch into a jealous fit again, are we?

Marking my place in the book, I sit up. "We ran into each other. He offered to get me my job back."

Cian slowly nods. "I brought that up with my cousin, and he said the decision rests with your boss. I hoped she'd call you by now."

"She hasn't yet. But maybe she will. I can't really get a job anywhere else without her reference. At least, not easily."

"I know. I'm sorry I fucked that up for you. I was being selfish." He sits beside me. "All I ever want is for you to be happy, *broc meala*. I'm so sorry for all the ways

I made you unhappy. For the way I drove you away and almost ruined our marriage. I love you."

"I love you too." Tension leaving me, I reach for him. "I forgive you. For everything."

He's made progress just by taking that first step into therapy. Overall, he seems calmer, more centered than he has been in a very long time. Though that change came about as soon as he got some decent sleep and we had the house cleaned.

I forgive him for everything he did. At the same time, and not to make excuses for him, but he was sleep deprived and someone seemed to be triggering him on purpose. I'm still not sure who it was. Wolfe? Or someone else? We don't have any solid clues yet.

At least they have stopped. We haven't had any of Fiona's belongings randomly show up recently. Which has me thinking that it is someone close to us, someone in this household. We could fire the staff and start over, but what if it's one of Cian's men? We simply don't have time to interrogate them all.

Wolfe remains my prime suspect, but Cian doesn't want to go down that path.

So instead, we wait and hope they'll eventually reveal themselves. Or go away and leave us in peace.

How malicious is their intention? I don't understand what they gain from haunting Cian with his past. Obviously, it's more than a prank, having caused so much damage, but to what end?

"I want you to have your job back," he admits. "You were happy working at the agency."

"I was. I'll have to face all my co-workers again, and I'm sure the gossip will be over the top, but it will pass."

"I'm sorry about how I embarrassed you." He frowns. "I won't fuck up like that again."

"That's all in the past now, and I don't want to linger on it. We can't change what happened, we can only do better in the future." I mean it, I'm willing to turn over a new leaf. We both need it.

"True. Speaking of doing better..." He hauls me into his lap. "I did something that I can never apologize for because I can't accept your forgiveness. I don't deserve it. But I can promise that I'll never, ever treat you so disrespectfully again."

I turn around in his lap, straddling his thighs. "Is that a promise?"

"It is."

"You're repentant of what you did?" I hover above him, my gaze latched onto his.

"I am. I'll get on my knees and prove it, if you want that from me."

"Hmm. What if I do?" We haven't had sex in much too long. I held firm to my resolve that he wouldn't touch me again until he went to therapy, until he sought out professional help. Which he's done.

Now that I have him back, I want him. I want *us* again.

"As you wish, baby." Taking hold of my waist, he lifts me up only to set me down on the edge of the sofa. He drops to his knees between my legs. His gaze locked on mine, he peppers hot kisses from my knee up the inside of my thigh. When he reaches my center, he teases my clit through the thin fabric of my panties.

I arch my back, desperate for more. My fingers tangle in his silky soft hair as I pull him closer. It's not long until

I'm riding his face. A moment later, I cry out his name as I come apart.

Cian lies on the floor and drags me on top of him. Leaning down, I kiss him, showing him every ounce of pent up lust I've kept hidden away. It comes flowing out of me.

"My turn," I say, sitting up. Clutching his shirt collar, I yank it hard, sending buttons rolling across the floor.

He chuckles. "Are you going to buy me ten new shirts to replace this one?"

In answer, I bend down and tease his nipple with my tongue. He groans. I leave a trail of kisses across his tattooed chest as my hands work to free his cock. I stroke his length, spreading precum over his head, then sink down on him. Slowly. It's been a while and the stretch burns.

"Oh, fuck," he moans.

When he makes a move to switch our positions, I slam my palms down on his shoulders. "You're exactly where I want you, *Irlandese*."

He groans again. Taking my hips he thrusts upward, fucking me from below. He can't seem to resist being in charge, even when I'm on top. I love it.

My head falls back as I brace myself against his muscular chest. I meet him thrust for thrust, our tempo going from slow and steady to fast and sloppy. We take every ounce of pleasure the other has to offer—then demand more.

"Cian!" I come around his dick, my pussy milking him.

With a roar, he slams into me, burying himself deep.

He fills me with so much cum it seeps out and coats my thighs.

I collapse onto his bare chest. Our ragged breathing the only sound in the living room.

"You're not spent yet, are you, *broc meala*?" His breath warms the top of my head.

My murmur's unintelligible. I feel like my entire body's been steeped in lead, even the thought of moving a single finger is exhausting.

Cian rolls us over, bracing his weight on his forearms as he peers down at me. "You're the most beautiful, stubborn woman I've ever laid eyes on. After all this time, I still can't believe you're my wife."

In my contented state, all I can do is offer him a lazy grin.

He kisses the tip of my nose, then my lips. Sliding down my body, he feasts on my pussy until I'm begging him to fuck me again.

I love this man with all my heart.

CHAPTER 50
Ravenna

Tragedy has struck my family again. My uncle Davide is dead. While the loss of him is greatly felt by all, it could have been worse. That terrible day, I could have also lost both my aunt and Gin. Thank God they're safe. Although I can't help but wonder how Aunt Rosa is coping. She's a much stronger woman than my mother was, so I think she'll grieve but ultimately be okay.

Aunt Rosa's home hosts the after funeral service. The place is packed with mafiosos and their wives. Everyone from the other family's leaders, to foot soldiers have turned out to pay their respects and mourn.

But there's one face I don't immediately recognize. A newcomer. He's tall, almost as tall as Cian, but completely the opposite in coloring. His skin's a deep bronzed tan, with wavy black hair, and the most stunning blue-green eyes I've ever seen. A short, trimmed beard adds a kind of maturity to his look. He'd appear more boyish without the facial hair.

He glances my way, then does a double-take. His dark brow furrows. Seeming to make up his mind, he stalks my way.

"Ravenna," he cautiously says, though it's far from a question.

"Yes. Ravenna O'Rourke. I assume you know my sister." I offer my hand and he shakes it.

"I do. I'm Maximo Pontrelli." He has a smooth Italian accent.

"Nice to meet you. So, I'm guessing we're distantly related."

He bobs his head. "We are. Our fathers were cousins."

"Which makes you my second cousin." I muse.

"That's correct. I'm deeply sorry for your loss. I did not know don Davide well at all, but my father spoke highly of him. I did make a study of the family tree a while ago. You had a brother who also passed on, I believe."

"Yes. Matteo." I try not to grimace as I speak his name. I haven't spared my dead brother a thought in a very long time.

"Right. Had he lived, he would have been don after your father's passing, and certainly after your uncle's early grave. Since you have no more male relatives in this country, it seems I'm next in line."

"Next in line... to be don of the Pontrelli family?" I clarify.

"You seem surprised."

"I am."

"Why, may I ask?"

"You're so... young. Probably the youngest don we've ever had."

He grunts, though he doesn't seem irritated, just confirming my assumption. "That may be true. But I have prepared to be don all my life. My father raised me and my brothers to take on this responsibility. I assure you, I'm ready even though I am younger than most expect."

I'd wish him luck, but that seems inappropriate. I just hope the other dons don't eat him for lunch. It's a tough city and the families don't often welcome outsiders into positions of power, even if they are blood relatives. To them, this man hasn't proven himself at all. He's a wild card. He's going to have an uphill battle carving out a reputation for himself while holding on to the power he's been handed on a gold platter.

"Well, welcome to New York," I finally say. "I'm sure we'll cross paths again."

"It was nice to make your acquaintance." He wanders off, speaking to others in the room.

"Who is he?" Cian's deep voice rumbles behind me.

"The new don Pontrelli." I face him. "Which means he's your newest ally."

Cian's gaze follows Maximo around the room. "Do you think he's even thirty years old?"

"Barely. But he seems serious and mature enough."

Hopefully he's not hiding some psychotic or deranged behaviors under that handsome façade. Everyone thought Matteo was a charming young man, because they never saw beneath the surface to his rotten soul. I pray to god that Maximo is nothing like my brother. Our family wouldn't survive it.

Keeping true to the whirlwind that is my life these days, my boss calls that weekend, confirming that Devlin did put in a good word for me.

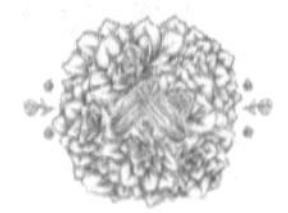

"Mrs. O'Rourke, I'd like to hire you into a new position at the agency. If it's agreeable to you."

"Yes, I'd love it. I accept!"

"If only all of my employees were as happy to come to work as you." Ms. Ryan chuckles. "I haven't told you what the position entails yet."

"Oh. Go ahead." Honestly, it doesn't matter. I'd mop floors on my hands and knees if that's the job, and do it without complaint. I just need a sense of purpose.

"Apart from... that incident, you're a diligent worker. I'd like to offer you the position of my personal assistant. Heather's on maternity leave and doesn't know if she'll be rejoining the workforce, so I'm hiring her replacement. Does it interest you?"

"Yes. Just send me a list of my duties and I'll be there Monday morning."

"I'll email you the details. I look forward to working more closely with you, Ravenna." She hangs up, leaving me grinning at the wall like I've lost my mind.

I have a job! I'm even being promoted. Didn't see that coming.

Cian steps into the room. He takes one look at me and his features soften. "Good news?"

"Yes! My old boss offered me a job as her personal assistant. I'm heading back into the office on Monday."

"That's excellent. I'm so proud of you." He seems sincere.

I beam up at him. "How about we go for a celebratory dinner tonight?"

"I'll book us a reservation."

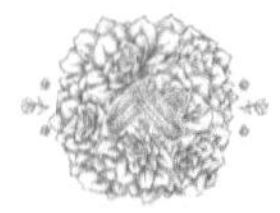

After all this time, I think I'd be immune to how people stare at my husband's scars. News flash: I'm not. The way people openly gape at him as we make our way through *Spades* to our private table fills me with fury. It's so rude.

More importantly, I notice the tinge of pink crawling up Cian's neck. He's still affected by it, too.

Gritting my teeth and glaring, I'm grateful when we finally sit down at a secluded table with a wonderful view of the city. We're back in our little bubble again, where it's just us and we can ignore the rest of society.

As soon as I sit down, I notice the purple tulip centerpiece. I don't recall my favorite flower on any of the other tables we passed.

"They're a custom request," Cian explains, studying the menu. "I wanted to make tonight special."

My stomach swoops and dives. This was a last minute reservation, how on earth did he have time to put in a custom request?

I lean forward to better smell the floral arrangement,

noting lavender and foxglove among the tulips. "That's so sweet of you. I love them."

A grin touches his lips as he lowers the menu. "I want to earn your happiness every single day. I've been thinking about that a lot lately. Now that my mind isn't so cloudy, I like to envision our future together."

"Oh? What does that look like?" I'm extremely curious about how Cian sees us.

He clears his throat, indicating he's nervous. "I see two possibilities. One where it's just the two of us loving each other every day, traveling to any historical sight that intrigues you, and retiring in a lakeside cottage."

"Mmm, that sounds pretty fantastic. What's the other possibility?"

Our server appears, taking our drink orders. A merlot for me, and a whiskey for Cian.

As soon as we have our privacy again, he reaches for my hand and continues, "The other version's very similar, except in this one we adopt a baby."

My heart lurches. "You'd be open to adopting?"

Many people in our world aren't willing to do such a thing. Most men are too concerned about their legacy, about passing on not only their name but their bloodline. Therefore adoption is out of the question unless it's an orphaned close relative.

Cian dips his chin—an affirmative. He raises my hand to his lips and kisses my fingers. "For your happiness, I'd do anything. I know you've taken this job at the agency to fill a void. To give your life a sense of purpose. You deserve to be a mother, *broc meala*. I'll do anything in my power to make that happen."

I'm at a loss for words. He's serious. I feel so giddy, so full of hope that I could float away.

"Would you be willing to try some medical solutions before looking into adoption?" I tentatively ask. Unsure, since it can be invasive.

Call me old fashioned, but my deepest desire is to have *his* child. I want a mini Cian running around.

"Yes. Anything." He leans forward, brushing his lips against mine. "I'll make an appointment for us next week."

My chest swells. Finally, after all of our trials and tribulations, I have my *Irlandese* back—the man I originally fell in love with.

CHAPTER 51
Cian

I'm at the compound with my men, going over some revenue numbers. Wolfe's worried that one of our gambling den dealers has sticky fingers. What he's been reporting versus the amount of traffic the place gets isn't adding up. I hate it when someone in my employ gets greedy. That's when things turn messy.

"Besides the numbers being off, do we have any proof of who's doing the stealing?" I ask. Throwing around accusations without solid proof puts everyone on edge.

Brendan speaks up. "I checked the security cameras. Somehow the one in the office, that's supposed to show the safe, has been moved so that's now a blind spot. I've fixed it. I also installed a hidden camera on the opposite wall, and on the main floor pointed at his station. We'll have that proof soon enough."

"Good," I grunt.

"The footage we do have reveals that some of the men have been bringing women in there to fuck."

Brendan pulls out his phone. "I took screenshots of their faces."

I glance at Wolfe. "Find out exactly who, and remind them of the rules. They want to screw someone, get a damn hotel room. We're running a gambling den, not a brothel."

Wolfe says, "We should also change the lo—"

My phone chimes with the sound I set for notifications from Ravenna. Holding up a hand, I pause the conversation, and read her text.

RAVENNA

I have to work late tonight. See you later. We need to stop by Gin and Blake's place. His birthday party's tonight. xox

I frown at my phone. What's keeping her at work? Did something unexpected come up, or does her new job have less defined hours than her previous position?

And I'd forgotten about that birthday party. Blake Baron doesn't strike me as the type of man who celebrates his birthday, or has parties. But his wife sure is. Now that they're back together.

CIAN

I'm working late too. Have some business to sort out at the compound. See you at home later.

I sign off with a kissy face emoji. She hearts my reply. My heartbeat thumps faster as warmth spreads through my chest. I suppress the smile on my lips as I look back at my men.

"Wolfe, continue with what you were talking about," I say, just as my phone pings again.

UNKNOWN

This is Devlin. Your wife's running away with me tonight. She's had enough of your shit. Don't try to stop us.

My heart stops. Rage and shock crash through me like a thunder storm. I stand up so fast my chair topples over and crashes to the floor.

What the fuck? This can't be real. I blink, but the message remains.

Ravenna just sent me a text saying she'll see me later. Nothing in her tone sounded off. She sent me exes and ohs. We've been good together lately.

My brain rapidly tries to make sense of what's happening.

Getting this text from Devlin is completely out of the blue. Ravenna's not running away with him. She's mine. I'm sure he's a lying snake.

He'll find out soon enough who he's fucking with, and regret it. I want that piece of shit as far away from my wife as possible.

Marching out of the room, I bring up Ravenna's number and press the call button. It rings.

"Come on, pick up," I mutter.

It rings again, and again.

I desperately need to hear her voice. She might be in danger. What if she refuses to go with him? Will he take her by force?

I'm not waiting around to find out.

With a curse, I sprint from the building to the garage

that houses the majority of my vehicles. This time, as I go to rescue her, I choose the Ducati. Straddling the black beast, I bring the engine to life and peel out of the garage.

I try her number a couple more times, but she doesn't answer.

Then I call Kody. He doesn't answer either.

I try Finn. Same thing.

What the fuck is going on? Where is everybody?

I speed up, running a red light as horns blare and drivers curse. But they don't matter.

I hope to fuck I'm not too late.

CHAPTER 52

Ravenna

"What's going on, Devlin? My boss said you needed me for a project of some kind?" I enter his office. Since I last worked here, he's also been promoted and now has his own space. It's quite the upgrade from the main office with all its cubicles.

"Yes. Please come in. Close the door behind you."

I quickly peek back at the hallway. It's after hours and the place is pretty much empty. Even my boss, who usually stays late, grabbed her coat and left a few minutes ago.

Closing the door, I approach Devlin's desk. "Tell me about this project."

"It's quite simple actually." His head bowed, he shuffles papers around as if he's stalling or distracted. "Have a seat."

"Will we be here long?"

"I'm not sure yet." Finally, he glances at me. "It depends on how quickly we can get through this."

"Okay." I take the vacant chair and make myself as comfortable as possible.

Honestly, I'd rather be home. This time of year it gets dark early. Today has been especially gloomy and drizzly outside. All I want to do is curl up with a warm cup of tea and a book until Cian gets home. Then we have to head out to Blake's party, but there's no need to stay long.

Devlin rounds the desk, coming closer until he's standing in front of me. His features aren't as relaxed as usual. He's devoid of his carefree, boyish attitude. Whatever he wants to talk about must be serious.

I straighten up, just as he leans down and places his hands on the arms of the chair, trapping me. My breath hitches. The hairs on the back of my neck stand on end. My gaze snaps to meet his.

He's much too close.

"What are you doing?" I demand.

"Stop playing with me, Ravenna. I love the cat and mouse game, the playing hard to get, but I've had enough of it," he growls, his tone completely unlike him.

I blink at him, bewildered. "What are you talking about? I assure you, I haven't been playing any games with you."

"Yes you have." His breath heats my face.

I jerk back, but I can't go far. How am I going to get out of this? If I scream for help, no one's going to hear me. They all left.

I swallow thickly. "What do you want?"

"*You.*"

"If you touch me, my husband will kill you." I hope that danger's enough to warn him off.

He smirks, a very strange expression for Devlin. "We'll see."

My pulse spikes with alarm. What is he going to do to me? My mind swims with depraved images. We are all alone in his office, and he has me trapped. No one will hear my screams. By the time Cian finds me it will be too late.

Then, two things happen almost simultaneously.

The office door bangs open.

Devlin grabs me around the neck and presses his lips to mine.

I struggle against him, but it's like pushing against a brick wall. He hauls me to my feet, and shoves his tongue halfway down my throat, as I try to fight him off.

With a chuckle, he finally removes his mouth from mine. "I know you like a little rape fantasy role play, *mo stór*, but we have company."

"Wh—" I gaze over my shoulder. My pulse flutters. He's come for me.

Cian stands in the doorway, frozen. Gun in hand. He's obviously stunned, even though his expression's guarded, unreadable.

"Cian!" I spin around and try to go to him, but Devlin wraps his arm painfully around my waist. He pulls my back to his chest.

"Don't play all innocent, *mo stór*. Your husband can clearly see what's going on between us."

"There's nothing going on between us," I snarl at him. "Let me go!"

He fists my hair. "Not in a million years. You promised to leave your husband for me. Don't back down now. Tell him about us. Confess."

I gawk at Devlin. Why is he lying? Why is he making up a past between us that we don't have?

"I'm not leaving—"

Cian cuts me off. "How long has this been going on?" His voice sounds hollow.

"A few months now," Devlin answers.

"No! That's not true. He's lying, Cian. This is all a *lie*." My voice breaks on that last word. I need my husband to believe me, to see through whatever Devlin's trying to do to us.

But with each passing second the fissure between my husband and I grows wider, deeper. I can feel it in my soul.

"You're such a good actress," Devlin murmurs. "I guess you'd have to be to string Cian along for so long. Though was it really that hard to do? I mean, you're gorgeous. He must know that he doesn't deserve you. Just look at him and those nasty scars." He sneers. "You deserve someone easy on the eyes."

Cian's expression shifts from unreadable to rage in a millisecond. He trains his gun on us. My stomach drops. Fear curls around my ribcage.

"Cian. *Amore mio*, you have to believe me," I beg.

The rage vanishes, replaced with something that breaks my heart. Defeat. Loss. He harshly shakes his head, as if trying to clear it, then takes a step toward us.

"Believe me," I plead. "This is a trick. You know it is."

Devlin pulls me flush against him. "Do you know how many times I've fucked her on this desk, Cian?"

"He's lying!" I cry. "Don't listen to him."

Devlin chuckles. "Are you really going to believe her

after all the lies she's told you? I know about her trading places with her twin sister. She told me all about it."

I've never told him, or anyone at work, about that, so how does he know? How does he have that information?

He continues, "She's been lying to you since day one and she never stopped."

"Cian, don't listen to him," I beg again. He has to believe me. Why is he just standing there? "Please, put the gun down. Get me out of here. I want to go home."

His gaze dances back and forth between me and Devlin. He seems torn. He doesn't know who to believe, and that's crushing my soul into tiny shards. After everything we've been through, I thought he completely trusted me.

But Devlin somehow knows his weak points. He's opening up old wounds. Playing on my husband's fears. Twisting everything around in his mind.

How is this happening? Who the fuck is this snake and why is he trying to destroy my marriage?

CHAPTER 53

Cian

"Cian, *please*," Ravenna begs. "Trust me." Her sultry voice grates against my raw nerves. I want to believe her, to trust that she's telling me the truth. I know Devlin's a piece of shit. So why don't I shoot him and take her home where she belongs?

Because this is exactly the scenario of how I found out about Fiona and Shawn. They were at his office, in front of his desk. I walked in on them kissing. Fiona immediately denied it all, even pretended to fight against my brother. They threw all kinds of accusations at each other.

She said she'd never leave me, that she loved me. While Shawn insisted they'd been at it for months and she belonged to him.

He even called her *mo stór*.

I saw the triumph in his eyes that night. He'd taken what was mine. After all those years of being envious of me, he finally had his revenge. He'd taken what I thought was most precious to me. He'd won.

Fiona begged and pleaded for me to believe her. She told me my brother was the villain. That he held her against her will.

I had to choose a side. Either I trusted her or believed him. Suspecting how much my brother hated me, I only had one choice.

Like an idiot, I was taken in by her lies. As soon as I rescued her from my brother, she turned on me. Together, they overpowered me and knocked me out. It had been a perfectly orchestrated trap.

I woke up tied to a chair with a hot poker searing my bare chest. My own screams echoed in the torture room.

"You're pathetic!" She cackled. "I can't believe you fell for that. Please, Cian, please," she mimicked herself. "I mean, how stupid can you be? Everything was right there in front of you. Plain as day."

I snarl, returning to the present. To where Devlin holds my wife against him like a doll. She struggles, but her much smaller frame leaves her at a disadvantage. If she's even trying to escape him. Jury's still out on that.

Who do I believe?

He calls her *mo stór*. She struggles and begs just like Fiona did all those years ago. I swear I even smell her perfume, vanilla and ylang-ylang.

My chest constricts, so tight it hurts. The memory of burning flesh wafts through the air, I can still smell it mingled with Fiona's perfume. My skin prickles with the sensation of ants crawling all over my body. A splitting headache spreads from behind my eyes as I try to detangle past from present, Fiona from Ravenna, and Shawn from Devlin.

My heartbeat pounds in my chest. I can't do this again. It's a trap.

No way in hell can I believe either of them. Not him. Not her.

Last time, after escaping them and their torture chamber, I shot Shawn in the chest. Then, slowly, making it last, I strangled Fiona to death. Wolfe disposed of their bodies.

He never pressed for details of what happened. Instead, he immediately got me to a doctor who cared for my infected wounds, stitched me up, and set me on the path to physically healing. My psyche was, and still is, a different story. The nightmares plagued me for years, coming back again and again.

I don't want a repeat of the past. This time, I won't let it happen. I'll nip this fucked up shit in the bud.

I refuse to repeat my past mistakes.

Taking aim, I slowly, intentionally, pull the trigger.

CHAPTER 54

Ravenna

Behind me, Devlin's body stiffens with expectation. Cian's expression darkens. He's more than angry, he's murderous. I see it plainly in his pale blue eyes. All of his softer emotions vanish until he's nothing left but iron and steel. Then suddenly he shows no feeling at all.

In a low voice, Devlin speaks into my ear, "It's finally over. I'm sorry I had to do this to you." He releases a contented sigh.

BANG!

One gunshot, the single bullet whizzes past my ear, finding its mark in Devlin's chest. His body jerks from the impact. He releases me and staggers backward until he bumps the desk.

Even though he knew it was coming, his expression reflects shock. He touches his chest, then studies his bloody fingers. Confusion mars his face before it turns a ghostly shade of white. Mouth slack, he sinks to the floor. His eyes close.

Relief crashes through me. It's over. Finally. Cian saw reason and rescued me. He took my side, and I regret ever doubting him.

Facing him, my heart beating out of my chest. I have every intention of throwing myself into his arms. But I take one look at his cold gaze, at the gun pointed at me, and my lips part.

"Cian?" I don't understand why he's aiming that weapon at me. What's going on?

He shakes his head. The movement's harsh. It hits me like a slap to my face.

He doesn't trust me. He didn't take my side.

Disbelief rattles through me. What more does he want? How can I possibly prove myself to him?

Cian stalks forward, and I startle. I fight the instinct to step back, because I refuse to fear my husband. He'd never hurt me.

He stops, pressing the gun to my temple. "We're over. I don't ever want to see you again. If you come near me, I'll blow your fucking brains out."

All words stick in my throat as I tremble beneath his wrath. I squeeze my eyes shut, half expecting him to shoot me now.

But he would never hurt me.

Heavy footsteps leave the room. When I open my eyes, he's gone.

Rapid, shaky breaths fill my lungs. A cold sweat drenches my neck. I try to wrap my head around what just happened, and fail. Miserably. This can't be the end of us. We can't be over. Not like this, this is all wrong.

Against my better judgement, I go after Cian. We will not end like this.

I search the hallway, the elevator, and the stairwell exit. But I've wasted too much time processing and he's nowhere in sight. I'll have to catch up with him at home.

He's threatened my life once before, when we were first married. I believed him then. I thought he'd actually hurt me. After our years together, I know he's threatening me out of anger and self-preservation. Would he kill me? Truly? No. I can't bring myself to believe that he would go that far.

On my way down in the elevator, I send a text to Finn, telling him I'm ready to be picked up. Oddly, he doesn't reply.

Stranger still, when I make it out of the building into the cold, rainy night, the car's not there. I fidget while I wait. Five minutes tick by, then ten. Traffic and people go about their business all around me as I huddle near the side of the building. I would wait in the lobby, but I didn't expect Finn to take this long.

Something's wrong. Very, very wrong.

Did Cian order them to go home and ditch me here? I have to find out.

Heading back inside, I take the stairs down to the valet parking garage where Finn parks as he and Kody wait for me to finish up with work. With most employees already gone for the day, few cars are left in the garage.

I spot the town car easily enough. Even from this distance, I see two figures in the front seats. Why are they just sitting there?

Irritated, and still shaky from everything that happened in Devlin's office, I quickly approach the vehicle. I need to get home to Cian as soon as possible.

The tinted windows obscure my view, so I pull open

the driver's door. "Finn, what are—?" The question dies on my lips as horror wraps around my insides. "*Oh my god.*"

Both Finn and Kody have their seat belts on, keeping them strapped in place. Blood drenches the front of their shirts. Their throats cut.

They're dead.

Shock and grief ripple through my body. Of all of Cian's men, I was closest to them. We saw each other almost every day. I can't believe they're gone. Who would do something like this to them?

I slam the door shut, and spin around, my gaze searching the garage. Is the killer still here?

The place is as silent as a wintery tomb.

Devlin must have done this. Why? Murdering my driver and bodyguard seems unnecessary. Was he afraid I'd call for help and they'd show up? Possibly. It's the only logical explanation. He made sure we weren't going to be disturbed.

Unless... Cian...

No, I can't start down that train of thought. Cian is *not* the villain, he's the victim.

Even if he thought Finn and Kody knew about my supposed affair with Devlin... and thought they were hiding that information from him... would he kill them?

In a fit of murderous rage, would Cian do this to his own men?

I'd like to believe him incapable of such an act, but I'm not one hundred percent sure of anything at this point. If he's tipped so far over the edge that he'd do something like this, do I really know him as well as I think I do?

All of a sudden I'm not as confident about confronting my husband. What if he meant it this time? What if Devlin pushed him too far and there's no coming back to sanity? Do I risk my own life to find out how far Cian will go?

I hug my middle. Dizziness overcomes me as the world tilts. I steady myself against the car.

I can't stay here. Going home isn't an option either.

Turning away from Finn and Kody's dead bodies, I stagger out of the garage, and into the freezing Manhattan night.

My thoughts tormented by uncertainty, I walk through bustling streets with no real destination in mind. I should call someone, but who? How do I explain what happened? My cousins... then I remember that everyone's gathered at Gin's house tonight for her husband's birthday party. Her place isn't that far away.

I glance up for the first time in too long, only to discover that I'm no longer in the heart of the city. The busy streets have vanished. They're now darker, and nearly deserted. How did I get here? How long have I been walking?

Quite a while if the ache and blisters forming on my feet are any indication. I shouldn't be here. Not alone.

Sensing a presence behind me, I spin around. My breath catches in my throat. A hooded figure looms over me. There's a clicking sound, then a blade glints under the street light.

"Give me your purse. Now," a male voice demands from within his hood.

Am I seriously being mugged?

My heart beats against my ribcage, my hands tremble.

"I said now. Or I'll cut you."

This day has been too insane already, I don't want to tempt fate and end up dead in a dumpster. So I do as he says and hand over my purse.

"Take off your coat. I want that too."

"But it's freezing out here," I protest.

Menacingly, he steps closer. "Take it off."

I strip off my heavy winter coat. He snatches it and runs off, leaving me in the cold with nothing. No purse, no phone, no shield against the elements.

As if I pissed off God, the sky decides to open up. Freezing rain pelts my skin, soaking through my dress in a matter of seconds. The deluge plasters strands of hair to my face.

I was going to hail a cab to Gin's place, but with no money on me, I'll have to walk. Without my cell phone, I can't call for help.

Arms folded, head down, I briskly make my way toward her place. Already having been mugged, I assume it won't happen again before I reach my cousin's home. Like lightning doesn't strike twice in the same spot.

Though being stripped of my belongings, I feel more vulnerable than ever, like prey as I walk the city streets.

By the time I find her address, my feet burn with raw, open blisters. I'm so cold my teeth rattle. My skin and face went numb long ago.

With the last bit of my energy, I open Gin's front door and stumble inside. The party draws to a halt, stunned gazes stare at me, but I can't find it within myself to care that I've caused a scene. Exhausted, and stricken with grief, I barely feel it when someone wraps a warm coat around my shoulders. Voices speak to me, but I don't quite understand the words.

I think I'm in shock. It took a while to set in, but it makes sense.

Devlin turned out to be the villain. Now he's dead.

Cian doesn't trust me. He says he'll kill me if I go near him.

Finn and Kody... so much blood. Who murdered them?

Some random guy mugged me in the middle of a street, because obviously I wasn't traumatized enough from tonight's events.

Overwhelm consumes me. I break down and finally cry.

CHAPTER 55
Ravenna

Of course my cousins were extremely concerned as I told them about what happened yesterday. Gin settled me into a guest room and I slept like the dead, until waking up with a jolt this morning. If I had my phone on me, it would be blowing up with notifications from work.

How do I explain Devlin's body in his office? Or Finn and Kody in the garage? Or how I've seemingly vanished from the face of the earth?

What a mess. A tragic, terrible, mess. All for what?

In the end, what did Devlin gain? He's put my marriage in more trouble than ever before. He's gotten under Cian's skin. But ultimately, he got himself killed. I don't understand his motive. What did he actually end up accomplishing? And who was he? Cian and him didn't have a past, as far as I know. I'd never met Devlin until that day at work.

Then I remember how he apologized. He knew Cian

would kill him, he accepted his fate, but also felt remorse for what he'd done.

These puzzle pieces don't fit.

A knock sounds, startling me from my thoughts. "Yes?"

The door opens and Ginevra pokes her head inside. "It's me. How are you feeling?"

"I'm not sure. Okay, and not okay at the same time. Confused."

She steps into the room and closes the door behind her. "I bet. Hopefully, this will help you sort things out. Here." She hands me a brand new cell phone. "Blake managed to get your number transferred to this one last night. A lot of your contacts and stuff as well. You'll still need to download and login to any apps."

Guilt fills my chest. "Sorry for ruining his birthday party. I didn't mean to crash in here like that. That was sweet of him to do this for me, but I wish he'd put it off and enjoyed his party instead."

Gin giggles. "Are you kidding? An urgent tech problem, especially in order to get out of a social situation, is Blake's dream come true. I've never seen him so happy. I think recovering your stolen cell phone data was a better birthday gift than anything else he was given."

"That man's a strange one." I see the humor, but can't bring myself to smile.

She shrugs. "He's just antisocial."

Her obvious happiness with her husband makes me glad for her. At the same time, my chest squeezes with longing for Cian.

"Tell Blake *thank you* for me. From the bottom of my heart." I take the phone and pull up Cian's number, then frown. "What do I do if he doesn't answer?" I speak more to myself than to Gin.

She answers anyway. "You could always confront him in person. Though... that might be dangerous."

"He needs to cool down. If I give him some time, he'll come around. That's what happened before, when I lied to him about my name." When my father beat me, then tried to sell me to a stranger.

He's dead, I remind myself. That's all in the past. I'm safe this time.

Now that I think about it, would Cian have come for me if I hadn't been put up for auction? I shudder at the memory. Do I have to be in danger for him to forgive me? Is that the only thing that gets through to him? I hope not.

Gin reassuringly rubs my arm. "In that case, I'd call him, text him, and send him an email. If those don't work, after a week I'd show up at his door and not leave until he agreed to see me."

"Oh really? Is that what you'd do if a man ignored you?" I can't help but tease, even in my solemn mood.

She laughs. "Well, no, not exactly. If you want to do what I did, then you should hop on your private jet and spend millions of his money in Italy until he finally decides to track you down and bring you home."

I huff a laugh. "I guess that's not my style."

She sobers. "It's not. You're much more practical. Cian's in the wrong here, just so you know that. You didn't do anything bad. He'll either get it through his head, or you're better off without him."

"I know. Thanks." I tap the phone. As it rings, Gin leaves the room, giving me privacy.

He doesn't answer. Surprise—not really.

I call again, this time it goes straight to voicemail which tells me he declined my call. *Stronzo.* I swear that man infuriates me at times. Times like this, when he's a *bastardo testardo.*

I leave a voice message. "It's me. I know you're upset, but we need to talk. None of what happened last night made any sense. Devlin made all of that up, but why? What did he accomplish? You know I'm faithful to you. You're the only man I'll ever want. I love you. Call me back. Please."

I'm too inpatient to wait around for him to call, so I also send him a text message. A few actually, as I think more about the Devlin situation.

As I go over it again and again, each time I feel like I'm missing a significant piece of information. I know Cian. I really do. He should have come into that office, shot Devlin, and rescued me from that creep.

But something went very wrong. I just can't figure out what.

CHAPTER 56

Cian

The truth is I love my wife, otherwise I would have killed her too. I couldn't bring myself to do it. Gun pressed to her head, finger on the trigger, I couldn't go through with it.

I love her too much to harm her, even though she betrayed me in the end. I knew she would—eventually. Why would she choose me when she could have a whole man? One who's not scarred and ugly. One who can give her a family.

I'm not that man. These past few years, I've fooled myself into thinking I was, or that I could be what she deserves. But I'm not.

That truth hurts.

My phone floods with Ravenna's voicemails and text messages. I delete one after another without reading or listening to them. The thought of hearing her voice is more torment than I'm willing to put myself through.

She gutted me. I'm lost without her. I'll never recover from this, from her. So I push her from my mind.

I have other problems to worry about right now. Wolfe and I eventually found Kody and Finn's bodies in the garage beneath the agency's building. I went looking for them as soon as I left that office. Wolfe met me there, and we eventually found them. Dead.

Did Ravenna know her lover slit their throats and left them there? How cold-hearted is she to let him do that to those boys? Goes to show that you never really know a person when they can surprise you like that.

Wolfe helps me remove Kody and Finn's bodies from the trunk of the car, and place them in a walk-in refrigerator where they'll stay until funeral arrangements are made. I need to break the news to everyone about their deaths.

As for Devlin? Fuck him. His corpse can rot in his office for all I care. I made that mess but I'm not cleaning it up. The cops can piece together that scene and do their investigation. I don't care.

Luck was on my side last night. Somehow, the building's security camera system was offline. My guess is Devlin took it down so there'd be no footage of him murdering Finn and Kody, then forgot to reactivate it.

His oversight worked in my favor. Anyone can guess as to who killed Devlin, but without evidence no one will know for sure. His death will be filed as another senseless office shooting. Probably by a disgruntled co-worker or vengeful ex.

I didn't leave any DNA or prints behind. As for Ravenna, hers have every reason to be all over that place, since she works there. Although she may be questioned, since she was the last one to see him alive. If she even shows up to work this morning.

Not that I care. She's not my responsibility anymore.

"I'm calling it a night," Wolfe says as we head back to the car. We've both been up all through the night. Dawn spread its gloomy glow across the sky hours ago.

I nod. "Drop me at my motorcycle and I'll drive myself home."

"Sure thing." He sends a worried glance my way. "Do you want to tell me about what happened last night?"

"No." My firm tone puts an end to this conversation. I don't want to talk about it. It's humiliating enough that Wolfe saw me through the fallout after Fiona. I'm not putting either of us through that a second time.

The best thing I can do is pretend Ravenna's dead. She died last night, taking my heart with her. Good thing I don't need that organ.

We ride in silence to where I left my bike near the modeling agency. As expected, the place is crawling with cops. Paramedics load a body into the back of their vehicle. Onlookers gather round to gawk. Even the news crews are in full swing, reporting on what little they know, sensationalizing every bit of it. Vultures. I'm sure the *Big Apple Buzz* will make a mint off this story.

I'm about to get on my Ducati when my phone chimes with a different sound from Ravenna's tone. This time, it's Brendan texting me, so I don't ignore it.

BRENDAN:

Urgent. Meet me at the compound.
ASAP.

I scowl at the message, tired. What the fuck is going on now?

Starting up my bike, I head north to the compound. Brendan always gets straight to the point, no filler needed, so I don't demand an explanation. If he states it's urgent, then it is.

Security lets me through the gate and I drive around back to park in my sprawling garage. I plan to swap the motorcycle for a car on my way home, especially now that it's raining. My clothes are soaked through.

Crossing the distance of the garage, I enter the house through a side door and head straight for my office. That's where Brendan will be waiting.

I hope to fuck whatever the problem is can be sorted quickly. I'm dead on my feet with exhaustion.

As soon as I enter my office, an odd sensation crawls beneath my skin. On instinct, I reach for my gun.

But I'm too late. Some big fucker hits me in the side of my head. The brief disorientation gives him enough time to disarm me, then hold me at gunpoint with my own weapon. *Motherfucker.*

"What the fuck are you doing?" I snarl, facing him. Only to realize he's a stranger. "Who the fuck are you?"

In answer, he tilts his head to the other man in the room. Brendan.

He sits behind my desk, a gun held casually in one hand. "Thank you for coming so quickly. Please, sit down."

I glower at him, remaining right where I stand. I wasn't expecting an ambush this morning. "What's going on here?"

"Your time is over, O'Rourke. This is the way of our world when the strong overcome the weak. I'm taking over your empire. All that you had is now mine."

"My men would never put you in charge."

"They already have."

How in the fuck did I not see this coming? Brendan, my security guy, has been scheming to overthrow me? For how long? He's been with us for years.

"They'd never make you their leader." I sound more confident than I am about that statement.

"No? Let me explain why they chose me. Let's see... there's the bit about you paying too much attention to your Italian bride. You negotiated peace with the Monahans when you should have taken their turf before they had a chance to settle in. They were weak without allies and you have the Italian mafia at your back, and therefore no good reason not to use them. So disappointing that you didn't. Last, but certainly not least, is your unstable mental health. Not the good kind of unstable where you might make a bloodbath out of the Monahans or anyone else who oversteps. No, unfortunately, you're simply incompetent." He sneers.

Did I really fuck up that badly?

Brendan smirks. "Though I guess I'm to blame for some of that."

"What do you mean?" I cautiously ask. I need to keep him talking until I get a clear idea of what the fuck just happened, and how this came to be. Why now?

"Let me enlighten you. You don't know me, not really, but I know all about you. My sister told me even the most intimate details. Driving you insane was actually easier than I thought it'd be."

His sister? A lead weight sinks to the bottom of my stomach. "Fiona?" I guess.

Brendan nods. "Very good. I see you're catching on

quickly. My name's Brendan Gallagher, but I changed it to Dunne before I left Ireland."

So he's Fiona Gallagher's brother. She told me about him a few times, how he was mostly away at a private school in Switzerland. The last thing I'd ever expect is some rich boy showing up here to join the Gaelic Devils.

Brendan sits back in my chair, making himself comfortable. "My sister and I were close. She confided in me about everything, all the way down to how she and Shawn trapped and then tortured you for their pleasure. Then one day, I never heard from her again. When I learned that you were alive, I knew what had happened. You murdered my sister."

I have nothing to hide, so I nod.

"I dropped out of school, changed my name, then came to New York. With bits and pieces of information I had from Fiona, it was easy enough to befriend those close to you. Pledging, then proving myself to you was easy, considering I'd do anything to get inside the Gaelic Devils. After that, all I had to do was wait for my chance. In the meantime, why not torment you with my sister's memory?"

All at once, the pieces fall into place and I see the complete picture. "The perfume and the pendant. That was you."

"They were a start. Did you know that olfactory memory recall is often the most vividly emotional kind? Spraying my sister's perfume all over your house was one of my more brilliant ideas. The pendant you gave her, resurfacing around Ravenna's neck, I thought to be a poetic touch. But the real fun and games started when I put Devlin into play."

My gaze narrows on him. "Devlin was your man?"

He snorts a laugh, but I don't see what's so funny. "You could say that. He was sick, dying of a terminal illness. So when I offered him a quicker death, and his family a million dollars, he jumped at the opportunity."

If that's true, then it was all a lie, a setup to drive Ravenna and I apart. The confrontation in the office was orchestrated to remind me of Fiona and Shawn. Brendan's been pulling the strings all along.

"What have you done," I snarl at him. He's destroyed my marriage.

"It's called vengeance." He sneers. "Since the day I found out you strangled my sweet sister to death, cutting her life way too short, I vowed to take you down. It's taken years of planning. I thought I had you when I stole your bride-to-be, but I didn't see the whole identical twin swap coming. That was my bad for not thoroughly doing my research. That set me back *years*. I had to regroup and find another way to get to you. Finally, I did. Do you have any idea how much power and control your security administrator has? How much access?"

It's a rhetorical question so I don't bother answering him. I clench my teeth and seethe.

"I've dipped my fingers into almost every aspect of your life—until that too smart wife of yours caught on. She wasn't on to *me* specifically, she thought it was Wolfe. Even so, I had to step back and play my other angle. Devlin. He did such a convincing job. To think he failed to make his career as an actor. Anyway, we're finally arriving to the moment I've envisioned for *years*. You, alone, and at my mercy."

"Fuck you."

He smirks. "You're not my type. Your wife however... I love a feisty red-headed beauty. Did you know the poor thing spent the night on the streets?" With his free hand, he pulls out his phone and sets it on my desk. "Thanks to those tracking devices you insisted I put in her handbags, I have her location right here. She's in an alley, out in this weather all alone. Don't worry, I plan on coming to her rescue. I'm taking everything from you, Cian, and that includes her."

"If you lay a finger on her—" I take one menacing step forward.

"Spare me the threats. You're in no position to threaten me." He nods to his man. "You've lost."

A fist flies at my face, then all I know is darkness.

CHAPTER 57
Ravenna

I sit in my cousin's guest bedroom, annoyed that I can't reach Cian, even though I've been trying for the past two days. I even broke down and texted Wolfe. No word back from him either. They all hate me for something I didn't do. It's infuriating. Most of all, I hate this sense of helplessness. It's soul crushing.

My phone pings with a notification, and I immediately reach for it, then stare blankly at the screen. It's an alert from my period tracker app saying I'm one week late. But that can't be right...

Everything has been so stressful lately. I think back and realize I haven't felt my usual PMS symptoms, except for tender breasts. I kept thinking that would go away once I started my period. Now I'm a week late?

I do the math, and my app is correct. I'm exactly seven days overdue.

Oh my god.

Oh. My. God.

Quickly, I send a text to Gin.

She doesn't bother knocking before she barges into my room a few minutes later. Her wide eyes staring at me in shock and wonder.

"You think you're pregnant?"

Trying to remain calm, I stand up and point to the packages she's holding. "That's what those are going to tell me."

"Oh, right! Here." She hands me both pregnancy tests, then flops down on my bed to wait, grinning with excitement.

I head into the bathroom, my hands shaking as I open the packages so I can pee on a stick. The results seem to take forever. Each second ticking by is a slow thrum compared to my rapid heartbeat.

If they're negative, then I'm fine. It's just another disappointing month. But if they turn out positive, and I'm pregnant... Do I want to bring a child into this world right now?

On the wall clock, the second hand meets the twelve. Finally, it's time.

I glance at the tests where I left them by the sink. Two pink lines. I blink, but the result stays the same.

"Ravenna?" Gin knocks on the bathroom door.

In a state of shock, I open it. She looks at me and I nod.

"You're pregnant!" She squeaks, hugging me close.

I'm so shocked, I'm not sure how to react. Cian and I have tried to have a baby for years. I'm not sure when it happened, but I reached the point where I gave up thinking it would ever be a reality. Now... I'm pregnant.

Ginevra glances at my face. "Are you okay? You look kind of pale."

"I'm just..." I lick my dry lips. "I'm pregnant."

"Yeah, we kind of established that fact. I think you need to sit down for a minute." She leads me to a chair. "I'll get you some water. Be right back."

I stare into space while she's gone. This is the worst possible time to find out I'm carrying a child. I'm homeless. My marriage is in shambles. In nine months I'll be bringing a baby into this world. Alone?

I huff out a sigh. No, not alone.

Cian might hate me right now, but he's going to be a father. I'm done being ignored and shoved aside. He has a responsibility to this child.

Gin returns with a water glass in hand. I take it, down half the contents, then stand with purpose.

"I need to borrow a dress."

She's shorter than me, and much curvier, but I'll make it work. I don't have time to wait around for my own dress to be washed and dried. I'm going to confront my husband—today.

Gin gasps. "You're going after him, aren't you?"

I bob my head.

She claps her hands and smiles. "You can borrow the car and our driver. I'll get you something to wear, though you probably want to shower first."

Glancing at myself in the mirror, I cringe. She's right. I look terrible.

As I head into the bathroom to shower, Gin leaves to get everything else ready.

I wash my body and hair in record time, my thoughts jump between what I'm going to say to Cian and the fact that I'm finally pregnant. Back and forth, until I'm toweling off and drying my hair.

Gin's left me a dress on the bed, along with a pair of leggings and a warm winter coat and scarf. I get dressed, then pin my hair up. Using the makeup she left on the vanity, I conceal the dark circles under my eyes before swiping on some mascara and lipstick. I want to look my best, like I haven't been crying my eyes out for the past two days.

When I'm ready, and step out of the room, Gin's waiting for me near the stairs. We walk down together to the car she's generously provided.

She gives me a reassuring hug. "Go get him."

"I will." I'm going to find Cian and not leave until he stops being impossible.

CHAPTER 58

Ravenna

First, I stop by the house and let myself in with the electronic keypad. The place is eerily quiet. No one's around, not even the staff. I check all the rooms. "Cian? Are you here?"

No one answers.

If he's not here, then he must be at the compound, or one of the clubs, but I'll check our old home first.

Back in the car, I give Gin's driver the address and we head north. As we approach the massive gates, they swing open, inviting us inside the secure grounds. The car stops at the front doors and I get out, glancing around for Cian. If he is here, he hasn't bothered to come out to greet me.

"You may go," I tell the driver. "Thank you."

The car rolls down the driveway, leaving me here. If I need another ride, I can always get one of Cian's men to take me where I need to go. Or I can borrow one of his cars.

"Mrs. O'Rourke," Brendan calls as he rounds the building. "What a pleasant surprise."

I warily eye him. He's usually not this friendly. "Is my husband here?"

"He is. Come. I'll take you to him." He kindly grins.

"Thank you." I start up the stairs, then frown when Brendan gestures toward the side of the main building.

"This way. He's not in the office."

"Where is he?"

"I'll take you to him." He sets off on the gravel path, leaving me no choice but to follow. "We've had a challenging time trying to find you. It seems some vagrant got hold of your purse."

I halt. "How did you know my purse was stolen?"

"We didn't. Mr. O'Rourke had tracking devices installed in your handbags. When we tracked it, we were led to a street person on a park bench who claimed they found your bag in a trash bin."

Of course he'd put trackers on me. I scoff. "Why were you looking for me? All Cian had to do was answer a single one of my calls or texts and I could have told him where I was."

"Is that so?" Brendan takes a moment to digest that information, no idea why. Surely Cian told him I've been attempting to contact him, right?

Brendan continues walking, and I catch up with him. We enter a smaller building that I've only been in once. Old, abandoned car parts and tools take up space in the front room. At first glance, it's nothing more than a storage shed, but through a thick metal door lies the *other* room.

Brendan's keys jingle as he finds the right one for this lock. I'm half curious, half apprehensive.

"Is Cian questioning someone?" I don't know if I want to interrupt him if he's doing *that* type of work.

"Mmm," Brendan murmurs, noncommittally, as he opens the door. "After you."

Cautiously, I enter. The central space is set up for interrogations. A chair sits over a large drain in the middle of the room beneath a single hanging light. This concrete floor has seen so much blood and gore that it's discolored—more so near that drain. I'm relieved to find the single chair unoccupied.

Two holding cells are situated off to either side. They're open to the main area so anyone being held captive gets a front row seat to whoever's being questioned.

I turn to Brendan. "Where—?"

"Ravenna!" Cian shouts, immediately drawing my attention to one of the holding cells.

I rush to him. "Cian! What's happened? Why are you in there?"

"Leave. Now. Get out of here!" He gazes over my head. "If you touch her, I'll kill you."

Brendan slowly approaches us. "I already told you my plans for her. You should be more concerned about yourself."

I face Brendan. "Release my husband this instant."

Dark amusement blossoms in his eyes. "So bold. Fearless, aren't you? I can't wait to break you."

My lips part, but no sound emerges. I'm anything but fearless. I don't know how this happened, but Cian's being held prisoner by his own men. Brendan seems to be in charge now. How? Why?

Dread slithers beneath my skin. The danger of my situation sinks in just as Brendan grabs a handful of my hair and pulls me away from Cian. Pain sears my scalp. I claw at his wrists, but he doesn't care, even as I draw blood.

He pats me down with his free hand, stealing my new phone from my pocket. It's the only thing I have on me.

"Let her go!" Cian reaches through the bars, his glare pinned on Brendan.

"I was hoping you'd come for O'Rourke," he murmurs in my ear. "He's the best trap I could have laid for you." He licks the shell of my ear. I cringe. "Got you, little vixen."

"If you know what's good for you, you'll let us go, then run far, far away," I warn, despite being at his mercy.

He laughs. "That's not how this is going to play out. I'm in charge here. You'll be a good girl and do as I say. For now, I need you to behave." He drags me by my hair to the cell beside Cian's. Tears sting my eyes, a sharp pain splinters my skull. Then he shoves me to the cold, hard floor. Rusty hinges screech as he locks me inside.

"I'll be watching." Brendan points toward a camera mounted high on the opposite wall. With one last glance at us, he leaves, securing the outside door behind him.

"Are you hurt?" Cian crouches down, gaze alight with fury and concern.

I crawl to him, resting my shoulder against the bars

that separate us. "I'm fine. Tell me what in the hell is going on."

In light of Cian's imprisonment, what I came here to speak with him about can wait. I need to know what's happened, so we can rescue ourselves before this goes any further. Before one or both of us end up dead.

"Brendan's behind it all—everything from the perfume and jewelry, to Devlin. He's been the one making me think I'm being haunted by Fiona. He drove us apart," Cian explains, his tone both furious and defeated.

"Why?" What does Brendan have to gain?

"He's Fiona's little brother. He wants vengeance."

Oh. That explains a lot. "You didn't know she had a brother?"

"I did. But he was much younger, away at boarding school, and I never met him. I certainly didn't expect him to infiltrate the Gaelic Devils on a many years long revenge scheme."

It seems Fiona and Brendan were quite close if he essentially gave up his life to avenge hers.

Cian rests his forehead against the iron bars and sighs. "I fucked up—again. I should have trusted you, but that scene Devlin created in his office was exactly how I found out about my brother and Fiona. Brendan gave him detailed information, everything from how Devlin restrained you to what he said to me. He even called you *mo stór*. Shawn called Fiona that. I should have seen it for what it was, but... I didn't. I was too blinded by my memories, by my fears. That's no excuse. I should have seen through the lies. I should have known you were telling me the truth. Even Devlin, though a snake, wasn't the true villain. Brendan used and manipulated him."

So that's why Devlin apologized in the end. He really was sorry for his part in all of this.

I reach for Cian through the bars. "Shh. Now you know that I was never unfaithful to you, that's all that matters."

"That's not all that matters. Don't fucking forgive me." Angrily, he pulls away, pacing his cell. "I didn't trust you. Worse, I thought terrible things about you. I was so fucking close to killing you, Ravenna, don't you understand?"

"I do understand." I rise to my feet. "Brendan gaslit the hell out of you. He used your PTSD, your *trauma*, and twisted it to his advantage. You can't blame yourself for what he did to you. You were caught in his trap, that doesn't make you an awful person or make your actions and decisions unforgivable. Quite the opposite." I point toward the door. "Brendan's evil. He deserves a slow, painful death for what he put you through. I blame him, and I'll never forgive what he did."

Cian stops pacing and stares back at me. "He's also the man who kidnapped your sister the day of our wedding."

Shock ripples through me. I hated Brendan before this moment, now I *loathe* him with my entire soul. He's responsible for not only Cian's ongoing trauma, but Elena's too.

Brendan's the reason my sister fled this country and went into hiding, the reason she won't come home. He's why my husband had a mental break. He tried to ruin our marriage and nearly succeeded.

He says he wants to avenge his sister's death, but that's not what he's been doing. He's sick, *twisted.* Taking too much delight in ruining other people's lives. A master manipulator playing his game until someone puts a stop to him.

"I want him dead," I state in a cold, hard voice.

"You and me both, but in case you haven't noticed we don't have the upper hand at the moment." He glances around his cell. "We need to get out of here. Brendan's set on taking you for himself, and I won't let that happen."

I shudder at the thought of Brendan's hands on me. "I can get us out of these cells, but that lock on the door will be challenging. Plus, he's watching us. I don't think we can escape from here."

As soon as Brendan sees what we're up to on the camera, he'll put a stop to it.

Reluctantly, Cian nods, agreeing with my assessment of our situation. "We'll have to wait for an opportunity. Until then..." He clutches the bars separating out cells and sinks to his knees. "I have wronged you in so many ways. I've taken our beautiful, sacred marriage, and twisted it into something unrecognizable. I'm as much to blame for ruining our marriage as Brendan."

"Cian—"

"Don't. I know you want to soothe me, to say you forgive me, like you always do. But I need you to know how desperately sorry I am for everything I've put you through. From abandoning you at your father's house, to threatening your life. For accusing you of cheating, for punishing you with sex, and for making you lose your job. I've pushed you away again and again, fucked up over and over, but you keep coming back. I know I don't deserve you."

"That's not—"

"It is true," he practically snarls. "You're a saint for putting up with my shit, and you should have given up a long time ago, but I'm glad you didn't."

His voice drops so low I have to lean in to hear him. "As much as I don't deserve your forgiveness, I must ask for it, because I can't imagine my life without you. You're the love of my life, my anchor, you're the person who makes me whole. You're the beauty to my beast."

I reach through the bars and caress his cheek, gently tracing his scars with my thumb.

"If you give me another chance, I swear on my soul that I'll make everything up to you. I'll never doubt or question you again. I'll treat you with the love and respect you deserve every single day." He gazes at me with longing and hint of hope in his pale blue eyes. "You hold my heart in your hands, b*roc meala*. Do with it what you will."

My chest flutters, warmth spreads through my veins. Yes, he's been terrible at times, but I've never stopped loving him. He doesn't seem to understand all the *good* he's done to me, he only sees the bad. Someday, he'll see our relationship from my perspective. In time.

I promised us both that I'd never lie, so I tell him the truth. "I love you."

He searches my eyes for several long seconds. His palms cup my face. "I love you more."

"I'll love you forever, *amore mio*. I want us, together, until death."

"If that's what you really want, then you have me, body, heart, and soul. From now until forever."

I nod, and his shoulders loosen with relief. He blows out a shaky breath that tells me how afraid he was that I'd finally had enough, that I didn't want him anymore.

I lean slightly forward, and it's the sign he needs. His lips crash against mine with heart-wrenching desperation. I kiss him back, pouring all of my longing and hope into it. More than anything in the world, I just want *us*.

Putting minimal distance between us, he grunts. "These damn bars are in the way. I've missed you so much. I thought I'd never see you again."

"You can't get rid of me that easily," I tease him.

He eyes me. "Why did you come?"

I briefly press my lips to his. "I came because I'm far from finished with you, Mr. O'Rourke. We're married, and this is *not* how our marriage is going to end. I came to talk some sense into you."

And to tell you we're going to have a baby. I keep that to myself, for now. We're going to get out of this alive. When that happens, then I'll tell Cian he's going to be a father.

Right now we need to focus on saving ourselves and each other, so we can have our happily ever after.

CHAPTER 59
Ravenna

Brendan and a small group of men, who I vaguely recognize, take Cian from his cell and cuff his hands behind his back. Discretely, I pluck a pin from my hair, hiding it in my palm. As expected, they handcuff me as well.

We're brought out of the building to a couple of waiting SUVs. It's night. A biting November wind chills my skin. I firmly hold onto the bobby pin. It's my only chance for escape once the opportunity presents itself.

Cian's shoved into the backseat of one vehicle, while I'm separated from him and deposited into the other car. Brendan follows me inside, occupying the seat next to me.

As we roll out of the compound, I wonder why Cian's men turned on him. Is it all of them, or just some? Did Wolfe become a traitor too?

Knowing Brendan's behind everything, I'm pretty sure my suspicions of Wolfe were misplaced. If that's true, then where is he? I'd think Wolfe would be charging in here to rescue Cian. So far, no such luck.

"Where are you taking us?" I ask Brendan while staring straight ahead. I don't want him to see the fear in my eyes. He's the type of man to get off on that kind of power trip. Something about him reminds me too much of my brother.

He pulls me onto his lap. I struggle against him, but lose my balance with my hands secured behind my back. He steadies me by gripping my shoulders. One palm slides up the side of my neck and he cups my cheek. I glare daggers at him.

"You have so much fight in you, Ravenna." His minty breath washes across my face. "You remind me of my sister. Fiona was so full of life before *he* took it all away from her. Don't you see? All I want is revenge. You'd do the same if you were in my shoes."

"I'd never do what you did to Cian. I'd never torture someone like that," I spit at him.

"Yes, you would." His nose brushes mine. "In fact, if you could, you'd do that to me. Wouldn't you?"

I open my mouth to respond when his lips crash down on mine. A strangled protest leaves my throat, my eyes wide. Snarling, I bite his lip, satisfied when I taste a coppery tang.

Brendan jerks his head back. Blood trickles down his chin.

Wiping it away with the back of his hand, he grins. "We're going to have so much fun together. But first, I need to make you a widow."

Alarm shoots through me. "How are you going to do that?"

"Wait and see, little vixen." He cocks his head to one side. "Really, it shouldn't make much difference to you. You were arranged to marry the leader of this crew, to unite the Irish and Italians. Nothing will change except you're getting a new husband. Me. I'm the new leader, and I'm Irish. But unlike O'Rourke, I know what a bitch like you is good for. You'll be pregnant with my child as soon as possible. Then we'll do it all over again, and again. I'm going to keep you pregnant for years. Seven, twelve, twenty children—I haven't settled on a number yet."

I recoil on his lap. "You'll never get close enough to me for that."

"No? You should know that I have no qualms about rape. You can scream all you want, but I will fuck you. As soon as I do away with O'Rourke, we're signing that marriage certificate, and you'll be mine. It's your *duty* to spread your legs for me whenever I want. Besides, there's no such thing as rape in marriage."

Ew. What a disgusting asshole.

For probably the first time in my life, I keep my mouth shut. He's told me everything I need to know for now. He's going to murder Cian. I have to stop him. It's as simple as that.

The SUV pulls into a deserted parking lot. Is this it? Is Brendan going to shoot Cian and leave his body here? Why not kill him at the compound where his death could be hidden? Unless Brendan wants the whole world to see what he's about to do.

We get out of the vehicles. "Walk," Brendan demands.

We're both marched toward a bluff, then down

several stairs to a walkway. Traffic hums below us. Moist, frigid air clings to my lungs.

The walkway emerges onto a long, narrow bridge with ancient pillar lights. It's not built for vehicles, and this time of night there aren't any pedestrians on it either. We're all alone up here above what I recognize as the Harlem River.

We don't have much time left, do we?

I remove the rubbery tip from my bobby pin with my nails, then insert one end halfway into the lock. I bend it to a ninety degree angle. Doing the same on the opposite side, I feel the shape of the pin, envisioning it in my mind's eye, until I have the desired, sharp S-shape.

"Cut it here," Brendan instructs his goons, and they get to work cutting away the chain-link safety fencing on one side of the bridge. Without it in place, only a short metal railing prevents a person from falling into the rushing current below.

Realizing what he's going to do, I face my captor. "Please. You can't—"

"I can and I will." He speaks up so everyone can hear him. "I've thought long and hard about an appropriate ending for you, O'Rourke. I considered all the usuals—gun, knife, strangulation, etc. Then it hit me. I want you to suffer like Fiona did. Suffocating, while you're completely helpless."

While he talks, I devote my attention to picking the handcuff lock. I only need one hand free. Just one.

The pin slips between my freezing fingers. I still. For a second, I think I've lost it, but it's stuck in the cuff of Gin's fur coat.

Deeply inhaling to steady my trembling hands, I

patiently maneuver the pin until I apply just the right amount of pressure. Doing this behind my back messes with my head. Everything is upside down and backwards. I should have practiced this more.

"See you in hell, you fuck," Cian snarls at him.

"You can bet on it." Brendan grabs my arm and pulls me into his side, the jerky motion releases the locking mechanism. I'm free. "Now we're going to watch O'Rourke drown. I can't think of a worse way to go. The pain as your body fights for oxygen must be excruciating. To know that there's no way to save yourself must be even worse. Say goodbye."

"Cian—" I start, but one of Brendan's goons shoves my husband over the short railing. His hands are still cuffed behind his back. He'll drown. "No!"

Punching Brendan in the balls, I free myself from his hold. He curses and doubles over.

So he does have a weak spot. I wish I'd tried that earlier.

As I sprint away from him, he reaches out and grabs my coat. I let the oversized garment peel away from my shoulders and down my arms.

One of the goons makes a grab for me, but I'm already mid-swan dive over the railing. Then I'm falling, falling, falling. The rushing water rises up to swallow me whole, knocking the air from my lungs.

CHAPTER 60

Cian

My life flashes before my eyes, but the images that linger aren't those of my brutal past. Instead, I see Ravenna's smiling face, hear her sweet laughter, feel her touch against my skin. It's not only the past that drifts through my mind, but the future too. A future we'll never have together. I see sunshine illuminating a field of flowers where Ravenna playfully chases two little red haired girls.

At that moment, I'm completely content. I know true happiness.

With a contented sigh, I let it all go. I found my peace. Now where the fuck is that white light that's supposed to usher you into the afterlife? And why does my chest hurt so much?

The pain grows more acute.

Searing agony splits me wide open. Sound assaults my senses. I'm so fucking cold.

Then I'm coughing, emptying water from my lungs. I drag in one breath after another, the oxygen stings, burns, and causes my body to convulse in another coughing fit.

"Y-you're a-a-alive."

My gaze snaps up to find a drenched Ravenna beside me. She's shaking, her teeth clattering so loudly I clearly hear them.

She's alive.

"*Broc meala.*" Sitting up, I pull her into my chest, wrapping my entire body around her small frame and hold her tight. I never want to let go of her again.

Clinging to each other, we shiver on a frozen river bank. The last thing I remember is being pushed into the water. Did they throw her in too?

"How did we survive?" I ask.

"I j-j-j—" Her teeth violently rattle. We need to get someplace warm.

Lifting her, I carry her up the bank to the street above. We're in a quiet neighborhood.

Considering how much she's shaking and the fact that I can't feel my limbs, I'd say we need medical attention. Neither of us have a phone or ID on us. I'm not sure if I can trust any of my men. We're kind of fucked.

What we really need is a safe house. Luckily, I know just the place.

I spot an older vehicle parked on the side of the road. Wrapping my fist in my sodden shirt, I punch out the back window and unlock the passenger door. I settle Ravenna into the seat before going around to the driver's side. No alarm and easy to hot wire—my favorite kind of car.

As soon as it starts up, I crank the heat and speed toward the city.

"Are you okay?" I glance at my wife. "Ravenna?"

She nods, but I don't like the blue tinge to her skin. She's still shaking. We need to get her out of those wet clothes. I speed up.

New York really is the city that never sleeps, so there's traffic even at—I look at the clock—three in the morning.

"Stay with me. We're almost there," I tell her, though she seems to be slipping in and out of consciousness.

By the time I pull up in front of The Manor in Manhattan, and park on the sidewalk, she's out cold. I don't bother to cut the engine before rounding the vehicle and gathering her into my arms.

The Manor's staff meets me in the lobby. They take one look at us and a flurry of activity follows.

We're checked into a suite where a medical team shortly joins us. They carefully strip off our clothing and replace them with The Manor's logo-embossed black flannel pajamas. I'm given warm liquid to drink and a blanket. They hook Ravenna up to an IV and place a heating pad on her chest before wrapping her in a comforter. All through this, I never leave her side.

We're settled together on the bed. The medical team diminishes to a single nurse who regularly checks in on Ravenna throughout the night. Worry coils through me.

As exhausted as I am, I can't sleep. I spend the rest of the night watching Ravenna doze and hope she'll be okay when she wakes up.

My near death experience rattled something free in me. I've gained a clarity of perspective I never thought possible. When I think of everything I've put Ravenna through, I want to go back and beat the shit out of my past self.

What the fuck had I been thinking? My priorities were in all the wrong places. My fears, my demons, much too powerful.

From now on, I'm going to do better. I silently make that vow to myself.

Somewhere around dawn, sleep claims me, only to be jolted awake, disoriented and sweaty. It's too damn hot in here. I untangle myself from the blanket cocoon, then strip off my flannel shirt.

"Cian?"

I turn to Ravenna, surprised and delighted to find her awake. At some point the nurse removed her IV. I must have slept through that. One glance at the clock tells me it's mid-afternoon.

I drop to my knees beside the bed. "Ravenna, how do you feel?"

She stretches, yawning. "Like I've slept for a million years. Where are we?"

"The Manor. The safest place in the city." It's a refuge for those in the underworld.

"Oh." She sits up. "I've heard of this place. Arianna and Dimitri hid out here for a while once."

I hum in acknowledgement. "What happened last night? I remember going into the river and that's it. Did you escape Brendan or did he toss you in after me? How the fuck did we survive?"

She looks a little sheepish as she says, "I escaped and jumped in after you."

"What?! Are you insane? You could have gotten

yourself killed." I suck in a deep breath, an attempt to calm down. "Tell me *exactly* what happened."

She holds her head high, chin at that stubborn angle I love so much. "I freed myself from the handcuffs. They pushed you into the river, so I jumped in after you. It was the only way to save you from drowning. Somehow, by God's mercy, I found you in the water, dragged your heavy ass to the shore, and managed to get your cuffs off too. Then I beat on your chest, and screamed at you, until you came back from the dead. I think that about sums it up."

I'm so conflicted my head's about to explode. "First of all; don't *ever* risk your life like that again. Not for me, not for anyone." When she opens her mouth to argue, I cut her off with a sharp look. "Second; you're one hell of a woman, *broc meala*, and I'm the luckiest man alive to be married to you. Thank you for saving my life."

Her features soften. "You're welcome. It seems like we saved each other last night, because I don't remember how we got here."

"I stole a car and drove us here. Not nearly as heroic as jumping into a half-frozen river in the middle of winter." Drawing her close, I capture her lips with mine, overcome with gratitude and relief.

The bedside phone rings. Reaching over, I pick it up. "Yes?"

"Sorry to bother you, sir, but there are some people in the lobby who insist that you're here and won't go away."

I tense. "Who?"

"Dimitri and Arianna Kozlov. Roman and Sophia De

Luca. Blake and Ginevra Baron. If these people are not known to you, I will have them—"

"Send them up."

"Yes, sir. Right away." The call ends.

"What's up?" Ravenna asks.

"Your family found us."

Her brow furrows. "Oh no, they must be worried sick! Gin's probably been waiting to hear from me and when she didn't, she sent out a search party."

A few minutes later, a knock comes at the door. I answer it, and our quiet escape turns into a frenzy of greetings, questions, and explanations.

All of it going well enough until Ginevra blurts out, "Is the baby okay?"

What baby?

I follow Gin's gaze to Ravenna. A slight blush appears on my wife's cheeks.

"What baby?" I growl, and the room goes silent.

Ravenna glances around at everyone before her gaze settles on me. "Surprise, we're having a baby." A weak grin appears on her lips.

My fingers ball into fists. "And you knew about this *before* you jumped into that river?"

"I did."

"What the fuck were you thinking?" I roar.

"I'm not letting this child grow up without a father!" she shouts back.

We stare at each other, neither willing to back down. I want to shake her for her recklessness. She didn't only put her life in danger, but that of our unborn child.

Then it hits me. She's pregnant. We're starting a family. It's a miracle.

I swallow hard. "We're really having a baby?"

"Yes. I just found out. That's part of the reason I went looking for you. I'm never letting you go. You're my *Irlandese*. Forever and always."

I don't care that everyone's watching us. I sweep Ravenna into my arms and kiss her until we're both panting. I've never been this fucking elated in my entire life.

"We did it, we're finally pregnant," I whisper in awe.

She searches my eyes, a question in hers. "You're not afraid that it's another man's child?"

"No." I kiss her nose. "I'll never doubt you again. I promise."

"Aw, look," Gin says. "They kissed and made up. I love happy endings."

Roman, Blake, and Dimitri have formed their own huddle away from their wives. They catch my eye, and I already know what they're thinking.

This isn't over yet.

I can understand, and maybe even forgive Brendan for trying to kill me, but he put my wife and child in danger. That's unforgivable. I'll rip this city apart until I find him and end him.

CHAPTER 61
Cian

Half eaten lunch dishes litter the table before us, even though it's far past afternoon. Through the windows, dark storm clouds spit on the city streets as the sun sets with an eerie glow. For the past few hours we've been sorting through what information we have available to us.

Early today, Brendan spread word far and wide about how he killed me. He may as well have placed an announcement on the front page of the paper. Everyone knows of my supposed demise. We're dead. We plan to stay that way for as long as possible.

The Manor staff have been very accommodating of our special circumstances and requirements. They've delivered us clothing and other essentials. Most importantly, they've remained tight-lipped about the fact that we're under their roof. Hidden away.

Blake scrolls on his phone, reading the text. "My little birdies—" his informants "—say your gang is divided. Some followed Brendan, while others have fled the compound. Ah, it seems your man Wolfe is gathering them to him as we speak."

"And where's that?" I ask the man who seems to know everyone's business in this city.

"Two sources sent word that they're on Monahan turf."

I scowl in thought. "Do we think the Monahans will get their hands dirty and help us overthrow Brendan, or are they only providing a safe house for Wolfe and the rest of the men?"

Dimitri speaks up, "Do you need the Monahans? I thought the reason for you two marrying," he glances at Ravenna, then back to me, "was to unite the Pontrelli family and your Gaelic Devils. If you need men, isn't Maximo Pontrelli supposed to have your back?"

"He's supposed to," I confirm.

"I've just heard back from him." Roman scowls. "He says because you're dead, his consigliere and underboss advise against involving them in an Irish turf war. But, he's offered to help with the aftermath. He'll smooth things over with the authorities once this is over."

"I suppose that's better than nothing." Though it's far less backing than I expected.

"Fuck them," Dimitri spits out. "You don't need them. The Kozlov Bratva will be at your side and we'll get this over with tonight." He squeezes Arianna's hand as she gazes worriedly at him.

I'm disappointed, to say the least, that since Maximo Pontrelli thinks I'm dead, he's unwilling to stand by the treaty's terms agreed on by his predecessor. I'm also not about to tell him I'm alive and well. The more people who know that, the sooner the rumor will start spreading.

Wolfe may have already sought help from Maximo, and when turned away he went to the Monahans.

In my mind, this reconfigures who I'm aligning myself with and who I don't give a fuck about. Maximo better never come crawling to me for help. I'll return the favor by lining some politicians pockets and call it good. The Monahans, however, have just gained another ounce of my respect. I'll owe them big for this—assuming we all survive.

"I need to contact Wolfe. We need to coordinate with him, the Monahans, and Dimitri's brotherhood. Most of the traitors will be at the compound, including Brendan. We should have enough men to surround it and take it by force."

"If that's the plan, then I have toys I'd like to play with," Blake says. "You don't mind a little structural damage to the place, do you?"

"Not if it's necessary. Just don't hit the garage."

"Deal," he drawls.

"I'm going to call Wolfe. It's time." I march over to the landline phone and dial his number. The first time I call, it goes to voicemail. He probably thinks it's spam. So I call again, and again. Normally, I'd leave a message, but in case his phone isn't with him, I don't need anyone else hearing what I have to say. Or discovering I'm alive.

On the fourth try, he finally picks up with a snarled, "*What?*"

"Good to hear your voice, too."

A long pause crackles through the line. "I knew you weren't fucking dead." Wolfe laughs.

"Thanks to Ravenna, but that's another story."

"Is she still alive too?"

"Yes. We're both fine. Listen, is it true you're with the Monahans?"

"Yep. Those Italian fucks didn't offer much help, so I figured I'd look closer to home. Cormac and his guys are ready to help us take back what's ours."

I hum in appreciation. "We have the Kozlov Bratva with us too."

"Then Brendan and his fuck-face traitors don't stand a chance. Are we going tonight?"

"Yeah. Here's the plan..." I fill him in, trusting Wolfe to work out the finer details with Cormac and his brothers.

While I'm on the phone with Wolfe, Dimitri gets word to his brotherhood. Roman just smuggled in a nice assortment of weapons he's willing to let us use—automatic guns mostly, some semi-automatics, and grenades. We're leaving the big stuff to Blake.

Ravenna curls her hand around my bicep, drawing my full attention. "Come back to me in one piece, *amore mio*."

"I've already died once in the last twenty-four hours, I'd say chances are slim for that to happen again."

Her brow creases. "I don't think that's how death works."

"Death will be plenty busy tonight without looking my way. I'll come back to you. I promise."

"You better." She rises onto her toes, her lips finding mine. I deepen our kiss, my tongue slides against hers, and I softly moan. I'll never tire of her taste. Or her amber scent.

Reluctantly, I draw back. "Stay here and keep everyone safe. We'll be back by dawn."

"I love you."

"I love you with all my heart and soul, *broc meala*."

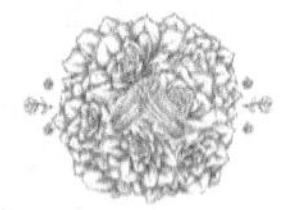

Never in all my life did I think I'd be in this position; breaking into my own compound. The bright side is I know the security system, it's defenses, and the camera positions. I knew exactly how I'd get by all of those if I were breaking in on my own. With the Monahans, Russians, Wolfe and my own men at my back, we're going to set off alarms. No way around it. The key is to get inside as quickly as possible.

Working together, a couple of us take out the security guards, while others scale the wall like spider monkeys. We're inside in ten seconds flat.

Part of me is relieved at how easy that was, and the other half is annoyed. Once this is over, the entire grounds will get a new, much more secure system. One that's professionally installed, not whatever this shit Brendan saddled me with. I'm also adding wire or spikes to the top of the wall.

As soon as we're inside, area lights begin to turn on, illuminating the main house and parts of the grounds. Any moment now, the enemy will come pouring out to meet us. Fucking traitors.

Blake, the crazy fucker, brought an RPG. He carries the rocket launcher over his shoulder and advances into the compound. Taking aim at the main apartment complex, he fires.

One wall partially collapses, taking out a corner of the building. The damage isn't extensive, but it's enough to have everyone who was hiding in there, getting the fuck out.

That's when all hell breaks loose.

Blake reloads, hitting the apartments again. A few others take inspiration from him and hurl grenades into the building windows. Glass shatters. Gunfire rents the night air.

As men run from the explosions, firing randomly at us, we manage to pick them off. But I have yet to see the face I'm searching for. Brendan better fucking be here.

Everyone's seen a photo of him and knows what he looks like. They've also been ordered to leave him for me.

Like an army of ants, we swarm the place until we're in and around every single building. At some point the tide turns and instead of fighting against us, the enemy drops their weapons and surrenders. Others flee.

Since I have no use for traitors or cowards, we gun them all down.

Wolfe and I cover each other as we search the attic of the main house. We've swept through every floor, all the way to the top. I'm beginning to worry that Brendan spent the night elsewhere. If that's true, then we won't finish this tonight. We'll have to start again. This isn't done until he's dead.

Broken, discarded furniture and stacks of dusty boxes have turned the wide open space into a maze. It's the perfect hiding place for a rat.

We weave our way through, guns at the ready, senses straining to catch the slightest movement or sound.

We've reached the back wall, when we're forced to turn back. Dead end.

There's no one here. Disappointment washes over me like a cold shower.

That's when I see it, the subtle shift of a shadow behind an old couch near the windows. Catching Wolfe's eye, I nod toward the furniture. He gives one sharp nod.

Together, we approach. Floorboards creek beneath our boots.

We're just about on the shadow when it stands up. It takes me two seconds to evaluate the scene in front of me. Brendan. Device in his hand. Reckless insanity shining in his eyes.

"Stop! Don't shoot!" Brendan frantically glances back and forth at us. "I've wired this place with explosives. If my thumb leaves this button, it's all over. We all die."

Frustration burns through my veins. Cowardly little shit. We're at a standstill.

No one moves. Wolfe and I keep our guns trained on Brendan, whose hands shake as he holds it toward us.

"You've lost," I tell Brendan. "You're through."

"Fuck you! I knew I should have put a bullet in your head before dropping you into the river."

"Deactivate that trigger," I command.

He glares at me. "As soon as I do that, you'll shoot me."

He's right. There's no version of the future where he's leaving this room alive. Which is a truth Brendan seems to read in my expression. His eyes narrow.

"At least I get to take you down with me." He lifts his thumb.

Time seems to switch into slow motion as Wolfe and I flat out run toward the attic windows. We're on the fourth floor, but I'll take the odds of surviving that fall over being blown to pieces.

Shielding my face with my arms, I break through the thin glass. My momentum launches me out the window.

Then I'm falling.

CHAPTER 62

Ravenna

I haven't slept a wink. How could I? The longer Cian's away, the more raw and sharp-edged my nerves become. If he's not back at the first sign of dawn, I'm going to emotionally implode. Not even the company of my cousins has been able to keep me grounded. Probably because they're as worried as I am and we're all swimming in fear.

Just as the first rays of dawn light the horizon, the door bangs open. Sophia, Arianna, Gin, and I rush into the main room.

I'm dizzy with relief.

There they are, all four of our husbands, plus Wolfe. They're alive, but look worse for wear. Cian and Wolfe are covered in filth, I can't tell if it's dirt or soot or a mix of both. Stranger still, small branches of pine needles stick out from their body armor.

"What happened to you two?" My hands busy themselves searching for any significant damage on Cian's body. They turn black, but I find no signs of blood or injury. Unlike Dimitri, who has a nasty cut on his forehead, and Roman with a bandage around his upper arm. Blake seems to be unscathed.

"Brendan blew up the house. We had to exit out of the attic window or get roasted. Luckily, we jumped right into a tree." His chuckle morphs into a groan. "Those branches broke our fall, but I still feel like I've been run over by a semi-truck."

"Same." Wolfe and Cian plop down on the beige sofa, completely soiling it.

"You're both insane," I murmur, relieved but exhausted. "You could have died from that jump."

Wolfe shrugs. "We had a twenty or so percent chance of surviving without that tree. Zero chance if we stayed inside."

"Yeah. Luck of the Irish." Cian snags my hand and pulls me down to sit beside him. "It's over, *broc meala.* He's dead." His lips brush against mine. I deepen our kiss, not caring that he's covered in ash.

The Manor's medical team arrives, and they sort through everyone's injuries quickly and methodically. Cian's given permission to shower. Miraculously, he didn't break anything, but those bruises are going to take a while to heal.

I give him a few minutes alone in the shower, but have every intention of joining him when Wolfe claims the chair across from mine.

He scrutinizes me for a long moment, the scowl he normally wears firmly in place. We've never gotten along, so I mentally prepare myself for whatever acrid comment he's about to utter.

"Why are you staring at me?" I clip.

"Did you really dive into the Harlem River after him?"

Hesitantly, I nod, unsure where he's going with this line of questioning.

"I see. Turns out I was wrong about you, sorceress." His gaze sweeps over me. "You're an enchantress all right, but one of the good ones. Only a truly incredible woman would jump into those waters to save her lover."

I stare back at Wolfe as silence stretches between us. Was that a compliment? Praise even?

"Thank you for not getting him killed last night." I offer my own version of gratitude.

Wolfe grins. I believe it's the first time I've ever seen that expression on his face. "Well, I'm going to head out. I aim to sleep like a rock after that night. Stay safe, sorceress."

I watch him leave, sensing a shift in the energy between us. Wolfe's acceptance and appreciation means a lot to me. For the first time among the Irish, I don't feel like a complete outsider.

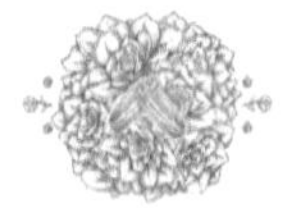

"Everyone's gone home," I tell Cian as I step into the shower with him. "We're alone."

"Thank fuck because I don't want to stay away from you for a moment longer, but I also wasn't keen on the idea of them hearing you scream." Grabbing my ass, he lifts me up and I wrap my legs around his waist.

"You're planning to make me scream?" I tease him.

"I am." He buries his face in the crook of my neck. "But first you should know I've made a decision."

"Okay."

"I'm going to continue to see that shrink—for not only my sake, but yours and our child's. I want to be the best father I can be to them. As well as the husband you deserve."

"You're already everything I want, Cian." My heart swells with so much love and tenderness.

"That's because you're a saint. No one else would have stuck with me or put up with my shit."

"You're mine, *Irlandese*, and I'm yours. That means forever and always no matter what life throws at us."

"I believe you." He claims my mouth in a toe curling kiss.

I reach between us and stroke his hard cock until his control snaps. He thrusts into me, pure awe in his eyes as he buries himself deep.

I moan, my head falling back to rest on the shower tile.

Steaming water sprays us as we make love. It washes away all of our *sorrys.* Our pain, and regrets, go with them down the drain, leaving behind an empty space for our new beginning. Everything has changed for us.

Cian's haunted past is good and buried.

I have the man I fell in love with back—he's whole again. Present.

We're starting a family. In a few months we'll be first-time parents, and our universe will shift yet again.

CHAPTER 63

Cian

The new year's right around the corner. This holiday season was the happiest and busiest one yet. Ravenna and I finished the nursery that had been sitting vacant for years. We opted to keep our baby's gender a mystery, so we went with a green and white color scheme. The little O'Rourke growing in her belly will grow up in a soothing, calm, nature-inspired space—at least that's what the interior designer said about our choices. I'm just glad the space will be ready and waiting for when our little one arrives.

This was also the first year that we spent extended time with Ravenna's cousins and their husbands. Our raid on the compound really broke the ice between us all, and being around them is like hanging out with family.

It's still a foreign, slightly uncomfortable concept to me, but I'm working on it. I even sent my own cousins, the Banes, holiday cards this year. Sappy as fuck, but I'll be a father relatively soon, and I think that kind of shit comes with the territory.

I'd like to think that I'll be a strong, protective, wise type of parent, but every time I remember Ravenna's pregnant, my heart melts. I go all gooey inside. She's barely showing and I spend every chance I get on my knees softly murmuring stories to her stomach.

Let's face it, I'm going to end up being one of those indulgent, doting fathers. I'll probably spoil the fuck out of our kids.

Who wants a piggyback ride? *Ah, fuck.*

On the flip side of things, Maximo was good for his word. He had his hands full concealing information, and paying off not only the NYPD, but also every news outlet to let the compounds destruction fly under the radar. Now, the rumors going around span from an alien crash landing, to a military exercise that got out of hand. Needless to say, we've been lying low.

Ravenna figured things out with her boss to work part-time until she goes on maternity leave. She's undecided about returning to work at some point after the baby's born, or embracing life as a stay-at-home mom. Either way, I'll support her decision.

Devlin's mysterious murder remains unsolved. A workplace tragedy.

I'm about to wrap up in my home office for the night when someone knocks on my door. "Enter."

Brion, Ravenna's new driver, steps into the room. He's younger, though not as young as Kody and Finn had been. God rest their souls.

"What is it?" I ask a very anxious looking Brion.

"Sir, I thought you should know that Mrs. O'Rourke had a secret rendezvous this evening," he speaks in a low voice. "She insisted that I stay in the car, even threatened me if I came after her. She was gone for twenty minutes in some shady apartment building in Brooklyn."

"Is that so?" I straighten up my desk.

"Yes, sir, I thought you should know."

I level him with a glare. "Is that how you do your job? Snitch on your boss?"

He blanches. "You're my boss, sir."

"You're Ravenna's driver, which means *she* is your boss. If she tells you to stay in the car, you'd better stay in the damn car." I cross my arms. "Her business is her own. Don't you dare go blabbing about it to others, and yes, that includes me. If I need to know something, I'll fucking ask. Is that clear?"

"Y-yes, sir. Sorry, sir." He ducks out of my office like the devil himself is after him with a fiery poker. But he won't be confused about where his loyalties lie from now on—with Ravenna.

If I want to know what my wife's been up to, I'll ask her myself. If she wants to share the details of her day with me, then she will.

I, myself, have been guilty of sneaking around these past few weeks. Also in Brooklyn. Coincidence?

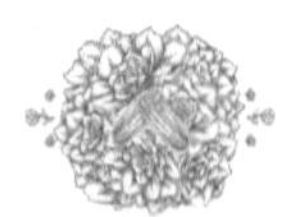

January third marks our four year wedding anniversary. Ravenna's late getting home from work, after running errands for her boss, which has given me plenty of time to fuss over her surprise. I'm oddly nervous for tonight.

"Cian? Are you home?" Ravenna calls from the foyer.

I lumber along the hall to greet her with a kiss. "You look beautiful."

"I look like I've been running around all day—which I have. I'm sorry I'm late." She sounds frazzled.

"Is your boss running you ragged? Do I need to have words with her?"

She slaps her hand on my chest. "Calm yourself. Don't you dare come anywhere near that office. I've had enough excitement in that place to last ten life times."

I pull her into me, nuzzling her neck. "I'm only trying to take care of you, *broc meala*. We don't need you overworked, ever, but especially when you've got a bun in the oven."

"I'm fine. Don't worry about me."

"I'll never *not* worry about you."

She huffs a laugh. "I know. I'm assuming we have plans tonight. I'll go upstairs and change."

"No need. We're not going out."

"We're not?"

"No. I have something else in mind to celebrate our anniversary." I pull a silk blindfold from my pocket. "Turn around."

"*Cian*. We usually do this after dinner, not before. I'm starving."

"The sooner you do as you're told, the sooner we'll eat." I stare down at her.

"In that case..." She spins around, and I secure the blindfold over her eyes.

"Good girl," I purr in her ear. She rewards me with a lustful shiver. "Come."

I lead her along the hallway to the library, where the hearth fire keeps the frigid January air at bay.

For our anniversary, I had the staff move a table in here and leave our dinner on hot plates. The table's fully set, complete with candlelight and flowers. But none of that is what I want her to dwell on when she removes the blindfold.

Moving in front of her, I face Ravenna and drop to one knee. "Take it off now."

She removes the material from her eyes, and gasps as her gaze sweeps the room, then drops to meet mine. Her lips part.

I hold the small velvet box between my palms. "Ravenna." I clear my suddenly tight throat. "My love, I should have done this years ago. You have my whole heart, my devotion, and my loyalty. On this day, our anniversary, I ask you to marry me again."

Flipping the hinged box open, I reveal the gold and diamond Claddagh ring I had especially designed for her. The heart in the center is a single solid diamond, held in hands of gold. Smaller diamonds outline the crown above it.

"That's beautiful," she whispers in awe. "Yes, I'll always marry you. Every single year for the rest of our lives."

My chest swells with a mixture of possessiveness, pride, and love. I slide the plain gold band from her finger and replace it with the Claddagh ring, heart pointed toward her, to signify that she's married. That her heart belongs to me.

"You took the words right out of my mouth, *Irlandese*." She drops to her knees, taking my hands in hers.

"You have my heart, my loyalty, and my friendship—which I think is important in a marriage. I offer you this as a symbol of my devotion."

Ravenna retrieves a ring from her pocket. It's a gold band with a Claddagh design in the center. Slipping the old ring from my finger, she exchanges it for this new one, a blush on her cheeks.

She grins. "I love that we both got each other Claddagh rings for our anniversary."

Tipping her head back, I brush my lips over hers. "I love that they come from the same designer."

"What? How can you tell?"

"Because I'd recognize Old Man Torrin's work anywhere. He's the best Irish jewelry maker in the city, even though he operates out of that shady little spot in Brooklyn."

She laughs, the sound soothes my soul. "Do you mean to tell me that we've been secretly visiting the same jeweler, narrowly avoiding running into each other, these past few weeks?"

"I do. What are the odds?" Before she can answer, I spin her around and pull her back to my chest. My fingers skim down her side, and I splay them over her stomach.

Even though she's three months pregnant, I still can't believe that I'm starting a family with the love of my life. Everything I've ever wanted Ravenna has given me—and so much more. Sometimes I'm in such a state of awe that all I can do is soak it all in.

I dip my face closer to her ear. "I can't wait for your belly to grow huge with our baby, to feel the little one move and kick, and to finally meet him or her when they enter this world."

"Patience, *amore mio*. We have a long way to go before we reach the end. Pregnancy's a marathon not a sprint."

I chuckle at her analogy. "I know. Every day will bring us something new. I'm so happy to be on this journey together."

A contented sigh leaves her lips, and she places her hand over mine. "Me too."

Tilting her head back, I claim her mouth. She tastes of mint, honey, and *mine*.

Epilogue

THREE MONTHS LATER
RAVENNA

"I'm so happy that you're finally coming home, Elle. I've missed you so much." It's true. Sisters, especially twins, should never be this far away from each other for so long. Part of my soul has been living in Italy for years now, and without Elena, I don't feel complete.

"I've missed you too," she says on the phone. "But I've also discovered myself here. You know how I love reading, and now I've been writing too. I've really discovered my voice. Touring around the country with Gin last year opened my eyes to how life can be so much more. Now that *he's* gone, I feel safer in this world than I ever have."

"I'm so glad to hear all of that."

I told her all about what happened on our previous phone call, all too happy to tell her the man who kidnapped her is finally dead. He can't ever hurt her, or anyone else, again.

"What else is going on?" she asks.

I catch her up on the latest news, starting with myself. "We just found out we're having twins."

Elena gasps. "Are you serious? Congratulations!"

"Thanks. We're happy about it, but I didn't expect that news. A while ago I did some research on twins. Apparently fraternal twins can run in families because it can be genetic, but identical twins is kind of a fluke. It's random. I figured since twins don't run in our family that I'd be in the clear. Surprise!"

She laughs, and it's good to hear. "I'm not surprised. Everything in your life has been crazy. In fact, I'm surprised you're not having triplets."

"Hey, don't jinx me or I'll end up with triplets next." We giggle. "Speaking of babies, Arianna's coming along too. Our due dates are like a week apart."

Finding out my cousin is also pregnant at the beginning of the year was a surprise. For the past several years, we've had very little talk of starting families, now all of a sudden it's happening.

"Sweet. When I get home, know that I'm free for child care whenever either of you need a break. I'll be the spinster auntie for all of them."

"I'm sure you'll marry one day." I know she's had a rough time, but someone will eventually sweep Elena off her feet.

"Nope. I'm extremely happy with my life, and after everything you and our cousins have been through there's no way in hell I'm marrying anyone."

"But we all ended up with our happily ever afters."

She scoffs. "Sorry to break it to you, but those are reserved exclusively for fiction. There's no such thing in real life, at least not for long."

"Rain on my parade, why don't you," I tease her.

"Sorry. But let's be real." Her voice grows quiet. "Even though that evil man is gone, I'm still terrified of big guys. Maybe even of men in general. I just can't."

My heart goes out to her. "You know I'd never be weird about it if you preferred women."

"I wish I did." She groans. "My sex life is nonexistent because I'm afraid of men, but I'm sexually attracted to them. It's terrible."

"That is a predicament."

"I guess that's what adult toys are for," she mumbles.

"Elena!"

"What? Too much information?"

"No." I laugh. "Just unexpected coming from you. You've always been so sweet and innocent."

"Well, I'm all grown up now."

"I know. I can't wait to see you, and have you be physically here and part of the family again."

"One more week."

"I know. But that feels like an eternity."

"I need to finish packing up all my books. See you soon, then we'll get everyone together for a proper catch up session."

"It's already planned."

We say our goodbyes and hang up. I smile at nothing, alone with my thoughts and feelings. I'm thrilled to have my sister coming home. Finally, all of us girls will be reunited and building the rest of our lives together.

A minute later my phone rings. It's an unknown number, but my intuition tells me to answer, so I do.

"Hello?"

"Ravenna?"

"Who is this?"

"Maximo Pontrelli. Sophia gave me your number."

"Oh. What do you want?" Why is the new Pontrelli don calling me? I'm not really involved with the Italian mafia much these days, and given how little help he offered to Cian when he needed it most, I'm not especially interested in being courteous.

Once family, always family, but I don't consider Maximo a close relative. So he must be calling about official business, even though I don't answer to him.

He speaks in a formal, reserved tone. "I… I would like to inform you that I'll be picking Elena up from the airport when she arrives. Even though the threat against her has been neutralized, she remains under my protection until I decide otherwise."

My skin prickles with unease, and suspicion crawls through me. "What exactly are you trying to say?"

"I'm saying that as my responsibility, Elena will live under my roof until she's ready to move out. We don't know if that man acted alone or if there are others. I want to take precautions when she arrives back in New York. Until I'm sure she's safe, she will remain under my protection."

"I see." I don't. "But—"

"No *but*. She is your sister, but as don of the Pontrelli family, I have the authority to do as I see fit. I'm only telling you as a courtesy."

"Is that so?" Annoyance creeps into my tone. "She was supposed to move in with me."

"That will not be happening. At least, not right away."

"I demand to see my sister when she arrives on that jet."

"You will. I will bring her to see you. But she will not be staying with you. I hope I've made myself clear."

There's no arguing with him. He's right, he has the authority to do whatever he wants, everyone else be damned.

He continues, "I know you Pontrelli women are strong-willed, but I will not tolerate any interference to my plans. If you attempt to hide Elena away, I will come after all of you until I find her. Do you understand me?"

"I do," I say through clenched teeth. "But if you lay one finger on my sister, I'll cut it off and choke you with it."

"It would be wise not to threaten your family's don." He hangs up.

Stronzo! Why is he doing this to Elena? Is he that obsessed with his duty to protect her, or is there more going on? Elena's barely mentioned Maximo in all these years. Surely she'd tell me if something was going on between them. Wouldn't she?

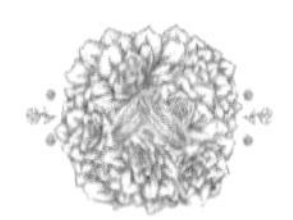

Thank you for reading *Corrupt Promises!* Please consider leaving a review, they are like tips for authors. If you enjoyed Cian and Ravenna's story, I'd really appreciate it!

Want more of this couple? Read their bonus scene here: subscribepage.io/TGsdRJ

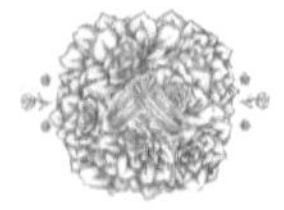

She's been under his protection for years. Now she's safe. But he's not willing to let her go. She belongs to him.

Read Maximo and Elena's story in *Brutal Proposal.*

XX,
Cassia

Newsletter Signup

For works in progress updates and new release announcements, as well as giveaways, author life snippets, and more, sign up for Cassia Quinn's newsletter: www.CassiaQuinn.com

Acknowledgments

First I want to thank you, lovely reader, for hanging in there and finishing this ridiculously long book. I knew Cian and Ravenna's story was going to be longer than the rest of the books in this series, but… wow. So thank you for seeing it through to the end!

Huge thanks to my alpha readers. Jay and Andra, you keep me from losing my mind. Thank you.

I'd also like to thank Geissa at GP Author Services for fitting me in on a tight turnaround. You're the best!

Thanks goes to my beta readers. Your feedback was invaluable and really made Cian and Ravenna's story come alive. Thank you Rida, Simge, Tracy, Rebecca, Victoria, Fatima, Angelina, Terrijana, Natheerah, Alekhya, and Niko.

Thank you to my ARC team, as well as those new to me who took a chance on an ARC. I appreciate you!

xx,

Cassia

About the Author

Cassia Quinn writes dark, angsty billionaire and mafia romance. She currently resides in the Pacific Northwest with her husband and kitty fur babies. Her favorite activity is reading on rainy days with a glass of wine.

Keep In Touch With Cassia Quinn

Website:
www.CassiaQuinn.com

Instagram:
https://www.instagram.com/cassiaquinnauthor/

TikTok:
https://www.tiktok.com/@cassiaquinnauthor

BookBub:
https://www.bookbub.com/profile/cassia-quinn

GoodReads:
https://www.goodreads.com/cassiaquinn

Also by Cassia Quinn

Twisted Arrangements

A series of interconnected standalones

Stolen Vows

Forced Union

Forever Fake

Corrupt Promises

Brutal Proposal

www.ingramcontent.com/pod-product-compliance
Lightning Source LLC
Chambersburg PA
CBHW021725190726
48289CB00008B/2697
* 9 7 8 1 9 5 0 8 7 9 8 8 5 *